WHEN TIME IS A RIVER

BY

Susan Clayton-Goldner

Tirgearr Publishing

Published by Tirgearr Publishing
Ireland
www.tirgearrpublishing.com

ISBN 978-1-910234-48-8

A CIP catalogue record for this book is
available from the British Library.

10 9 8 7 6 5 4 3 2 1

DEDICATION

For my amazing granddaughter, Elisabeth Moore. I was babysitting for two-year-old you at Lithia Park when the seed for this novel was planted.

ACKNOWLEDGEMENTS

I am indebted to so many people for this and all of my novels. Gratitude goes out to my husband, Andreas, and my children, David and Bonnie. To my critique group in Portland for both their support and their input. To the four women with whom I've written, laughed, cried and drank wine with for 20 years— Martha Miller, Marjorie Reynolds, Jane Sutherland, and Susan Domingos. To Jude and Tim Bunner who read and critiqued this manuscript in various stages. A special thanks to Susan Kelly for all the help she provided, not only in the writing, but in the marketing of my books. And as always, a big thank you to my mentor and friend, James N. Frey—who was there, providing input, from the very first scene. Thank you to Tirgearr Publishing for taking a chance on this enthusiastic, but basically unknown, writer. Finally, a special thanks to Nichole Ferrari Hamm for my author photo.

"A river cuts through rock,
Not because of its power,
But its persistence."

Jim Watkins

CHAPTER ONE

April, 1999

In the Ashland Outpatient Surgery Center, eighteen-year-old Brandy Michaelson picked at the taped gauze on her cheek. She fidgeted on the edge of the exam table, awaiting the results of her latest surgery. Her palms were sweaty. A successful surgery meant everything to Brandy. No matter how many career opportunities life brought to her, being an actress would always rise to the top. She glanced around the room. Its walls had been recently painted. Yellow. The color of hope.

Sighing, she watched her dad, a professor of English Literature at Southern Oregon University, read a student essay. She'd been disappointed so many times before. But this time would be different. "I had a dream last night," she said. "And my face was perfect."

He readjusted the crease on his trousers, that neatness he wore like a uniform. "Don't get your hopes up too high, honey. Life seldom succumbs to our timetable. This type of surgery can take years." He returned his attention to the same page of the essay he'd been staring at for fifteen minutes. How did he do it—year after year, the same freshman essays on Faulkner's symbolism in *Light In August*?

She studied her dad's jaw, chiseled with such precise angles that it must have obeyed some law of geometry. A jaw that was as stoic and rigid as his personality. If only her mother were still alive. She wouldn't have her nose stuck in a frickin' essay. She'd know how fast Brandy's heart thumped—how excited and frightened she felt at the same time. Her mother would stand beside Brandy and hold her hand.

Careful to hide it from her dad, she slipped a small, silver-framed photo from the pocket of her carpenter pants and held it in her palm. In the photograph, a tall slender woman stood forever frozen at the edge of the Pacific, waves cresting behind her back. She wore a sleeveless, yellow sundress and her hair hung to her shoulders in dark, spiral curls. Brandy wondered if as she grew older she'd look more like her mother. Wondered if she should have her hair permed into corkscrew curls.

In the photo, her mother's head was flung back and her whole body seemed to be laughing. It wasn't the kind of smile someone pasted on for a photograph. It was something deeper—something as pure as joy.

She'd died from ovarian cancer when Brandy was almost four—far too young for memories. At least that's what her dad claimed. But she often remembered small things. Romping in a backyard garden. Lilac soap. And bath oil that smelled like cinnamon and eucalyptus. The songs her mother tossed into the morning air like ribbons. Yet, despite Brandy's frequent efforts to see her again, the fuzzy videotape of movement, scents, and sounds never added up to a whole woman. She needed to know more. Especially now that she'd gotten the role of a mother in the senior class play.

When Doctor Sorenson—a tall, square-jawed man in his early forties—entered the examining room, Brandy tucked the photo back into her pocket. Sorenson wore a bright blue lab coat and his matching blue eyes had mastered the sincere look—like every other plastic surgeon who'd ever examined her face.

She smiled to herself, wondered if acting was a mandatory course in medical school. "You're looking wickedly fine, Doctor S. Why not ditch the scalpel and become an actor?"

"If I had your kind of talent, I might do just that. Speaking of acting, did you land that part in the senior class play?"

She nodded. "Tickets go on sale tomorrow."

He shook her father's hand. "How are things at the university?

Any security repercussions after that fiasco in Columbine?"

"Not yet," her father said. "But I suspect there will be."

Doctor Sorenson shook his head sadly. "Makes me glad I don't have kids." He sat at his desk, opened the drawer, and pulled out a makeover certificate from the Hair E'tage Salon. He handed it to Brandy. "A gift," he said with a flash of his bleached white perfect teeth. "Nails. Makeup. Hair. The whole kit and caboodle."

She sucked it up and gave him her best, on-stage smile. "A little putty and paint," she said. "That should give me the edge for opening night."

"My wife and I saw you in *West Side Story* last winter. With that voice, you don't need an edge."

"Before she died, my mom and I used to sing together."

"During intermission, when I told my wife you were one of my patients, she said, 'When that girl sings, the angels do cartwheels'."

Brandy smiled for real this time, then pulled her hair to one side and clipped it with a barrette so he could undo the gauze to examine her cheek and the reconstructed lobe of her left ear. Inside her head, she'd rehearsed this scene a hundred times.

With her dad standing behind him, Doctor Sorenson removed the gauze and tape, cupped her chin, and turned her face into the light. His fingers felt cool against her skin and his hand smelled like antiseptic soap and a hint of British Sterling cologne.

She braced her palms on either side of the examining table and held her breath.

"The revisions look good," Sorenson said, as if her face was a rewritten term paper.

Brandy's hands shook as she grabbed the mirror and leaned in close. The patch of grafted skin on her cheek was mottled as parchment paper and bright red. Surgery had improved the scars, but the corner of her left eye sagged. And her mouth pulled upward on that side in a freaky little half smile. One three-inch long scar, the size of a small garden worm, inched up her left temple and into her hairline.

Her dad took a step back.

She swallowed and turned away from the mirror, determined not to cry.

Doctor Sorenson smiled as he put a clean bandage on her cheek. "Wear that for another couple days. And then I guess it's time I let you go off and win that Oscar."

"I'll race right out and do that," she whispered.

Her dad moved closer and tried to take her hand. "It's too early to judge. You have to wait for—"

She jerked away. "Yeah, right. I'll wait a few weeks and then I can audition for a remake of Frankenstein or a Freddie Krueger sequel."

Her dad shot her a look that said, *cut the sarcasm*, then waited the space of three breaths before he looked at Doctor Sorenson. "What's the next step?"

She swung her legs too hard and thumped the table with the heels of her boots. "Don't even go there. I'm not letting anyone cut my face. Not ever again."

Doctor Sorenson stopped smiling. The fake sincerity sparkles disappeared from his eyes. "I know you expected more but—"

"I expected to get my face back." Brandy's voice had raised an octave. She looked toward the window and twisted her hair around her index finger.

Sorenson hesitated. "Believe me. The skin tone will even out. Your cheek will look much better in a few weeks. You form—"

"Keloids," she said, then turned to face him again. "Don't you think I know that? But you claimed you could—" She stopped and sucked in a breath. She should have known better—should have realized Sorenson was a dip-shit liar. "If this is the result you expected, why did you feed me that whacked-out beauty crap?" She glared at him.

"That's enough, Brandy," her father snapped.

Sorenson asked him to wait in the reception area and give them a few moments alone.

Her dad frowned, then turned and picked up the essay. "There must be someone who specializes in keloids."

Doctor S waited for her dad to repack his briefcase and

leave, then pushed the door closed. He clamped his big hand on her shoulder like they were best buddies. "Your dad just wants everything to be perfect for you."

"I'm going to be an actress, for God's sake," she said. "What the hell does he think I want?"

Doctor Sorenson took his hand off her shoulder.

Brandy had never said a cuss word in front of a doctor before. It felt good, but also bad. She knew he liked her, believed in her acting and had probably done his best. It was all so confusing. "My face looks like a tragedy mask."

"Listen to me," Sorenson said. "That slight distortion will disappear when the swelling does. Massage—"

She lowered her voice, tried to sound calmer. "Please don't give me the massage and vitamin E lecture. I tried it before." She unclipped the barrette, pulled her hair over her left cheek and secured it in place with her lime-green cowboy hat. She slipped off the exam table. "In case you haven't noticed, that crap doesn't work."

He stood still, looked at her, then hung his head and remained silent.

Brandy recognized that posture—that wish to crawl into yourself and vanish from someone's stare. "I'm sorry," she said. "I know you tried hard to help me." She waited for him to look at her, then she smiled.

He smiled back, but his eyes were still dull. "There are other things we can try, Brandy."

"Coach Pritchard reserves three rows of front and center seats for cast members' family and friends. I can get two for you and your wife, if you want."

A hint of sparkle returned to his eyes. "That would be great."

She gave him a quick wave and opened the exam room door. "See you around, Doctor S."

* * *

Brandy slipped into the front seat of her father's car and burst into tears.

He pulled a tissue from the box he kept in the console and

handed it to her. "I'm sorry, honey. Ashland's a small town. Sorenson doesn't know everything. There's a plastic surgeon in Portland who—"

"Didn't you hear me? I'm not having any more frickin' surgery." There, she'd said it. She waited for her father to freak out.

Instead, he stared through the windshield, his long fingers wrapped around the steering wheel, but he made no effort to turn the key.

She cried herself out, blew her nose, then grabbed another tissue and wiped her face.

"Brandy," he said hesitantly, then turned to look at her again.

He looked suddenly old. His once thick shock of dark hair had thinned. After marrying Christine, he'd started combing the strands carefully across the back of his head to hide his bald spot.

"You don't have to say it again," she said, her gaze lingering on his hair. "Internal beauty is the only beauty that matters." She echoed his trifling words, but didn't believe one of them.

"We can try one of the ones in Beverly Hills," he said. "They operate on actresses all the time."

Brandy shot him a look, but said nothing.

"I never took you for a quitter."

She turned away from him and stared over the parking lot into a line of maple trees, their spring limbs budding red against the pale sky. A part of her wanted to keep trying. Another part wanted to accept the fact that no miracle was going to erase her scars. "Don't treat me like I'm stupid. That reverse psychology crap isn't going to work."

She was no quitter. For years, while other kids played video games, went roller skating or hung out in the park, Brandy studied classic films and plastered the walls of her room with photos of singers, actors, and actresses who'd excelled despite their lack of perfection. Old actors like Humphrey Bogart and Spencer Tracy. Later there was Phillip Seymour Hoffman. Kathy Bates was no beauty, but had won an Oscar for her role in *Misery*.

He put his hand on her forearm. "Scars show you where

you've been." He softened his voice. "But, honey, unless you let them, they don't have to predict where you're going."

Brandy said nothing. What was the point? Her father would only spit out another of his bullshit philosophical platitudes.

"If I don't make it as an actress, I have my singing and songwriting to fall back on." Brandy had started singing lessons when she was four. Kathleen Sizemore, who'd been her nanny for more than a decade, told stories about the way Brandy had held a hairbrush up to her mouth, a pretend microphone, and skipped from room to room singing at the top of her lungs.

"I have no doubt you'll be successful at whatever you decide. You're smart, have an incredible voice, and you play a mean guitar." He left out his usual spiel about law school or medicine as a career.

Since she had longed to be someone else for years, imagining herself into a new role came easy. But not this time—this role was different. Big surprise—what did she know about being a mother?

"Let's get some ice cream," he said. "It'll make you feel better."

"In case you haven't noticed, Dad, I'm not two years old any more. And stop feeling guilty about my accident. It's nobody's fault. Little kids move fast. I see that with Emily. And sometimes they get hurt."

No matter how many times her dad told her differently, she still remembered being with her mother that night—both at the mall and in the hospital emergency room. She realized this was the opportunity she'd been waiting for. He felt sorry for her now. Maybe he'd open up. "Did you even read the script I gave you?"

He looked away. "I've had final essays to grade."

"You weren't always like this," she said, remembering the way it used to be when Kathleen was her live-in nanny and the three of them had talked about her roles at dinner. A time when what she did seemed important to him. "You changed after you married Christine and had Emily."

He looked as sad as a little boy who'd just watched his pet bunny get hit by a car. "A father can only do so much."

She said nothing. Tears welled again, but she bottled them for later.

He cleared his throat. "Why don't you tell me about your new role?"

This was her chance to show him why she needed to know things about her mother more than ever now. "My character, Isabella, has arranged to adopt a newborn, but when the baby arrives, he's deformed, brain-damaged, and not expected to live. Isabella's husband wants to back out. But she can't because, no matter what, she's his mother."

"That sounds pretty dark for a high school play."

"It's supposed to be poignant. And you can help me make it that way."

"I don't see how," he said.

"Tell me how Mom felt about me, especially right after the accident?"

"Christ, Brandy. Not again. How many times are you going to ask me about her?" He'd taken off his suit jacket and rolled up the sleeves of his pale blue shirt. The hair on his forearms was abundant and curled. Curled as tightly as his memories of her mother. "What exactly do you want?"

"I'll tell you three things I want. To know everything about my mom. To be an actress. And to be beautiful." She paused. "Without the benefit of any more surgery."

"Beautiful things are dangerous," he said.

"My mother was beautiful, wasn't she?"

He lowered his gaze as if remembering. "Yes," he finally said. "She was indeed." There was a hint of wistfulness in his voice.

She looked out the window. And without realizing how it happened, she found something she needed for the play. Longing. Her character longed for a baby. Isabella's yearning was a living thing, something that haunted her every day. Something Brandy understood. "Sometimes I have trouble believing Mom ever existed. Just tell me how she felt about being my mother."

"Honey, I don't know what it feels like to be a mother. You should talk to Christine."

"Yeah right," Brandy said. "Christine is four years older than me. She has so much experience—the spoiled little homecoming queen mutated into a wife and mother." Through the fabric of her carpenter pants, Brandy traced the edges of the silver frame. "Besides, my step mommy is no expert on mothering."

He clamped his hands tighter around the steering wheel and his knuckles whitened. "Okay, so she's young, but Christine is learning. Her youth doesn't preclude her talking with you."

Brandy shook her head. "I need to know about *my* mom."

"I've told you what I can remember."

"She's half of who I am. Doesn't that give me the right to know everything?"

"Everything?" He gave her a hangdog look, turned the key and started the car. "Believe me, Brandy," he whispered. "No one can know everything about someone else."

She sensed her dad's frustration, knew how much he wished he could shake her, hoping all the mother-longing would fall out and disappear. But it wouldn't. It never could.

He backed out of the parking lot. "Listen to me. I've done the best I could for you. She died. I can't change that."

"I know you keep saying you didn't keep anything of hers. But you must have something—a journal or an old yearbook from high school."

He let out another long sigh. Irritation flickered in his eyes. "I kept that photo you carry around in your pocket."

The blood rushed to her cheeks.

They turned onto Main Street. "When someone dies," he said, a slight quiver in his voice, "you have to let them go and find a way to keep living. How do you think Christine would feel if I kept my first wife's things?"

"If you ask me," Brandy said. "It's pretty immature to be jealous of a dead woman."

"Christine is trying to be a good mother. She didn't have much of a role model. And she wants to be…" He paused, searched for the right word. "Your friend."

As if he'd turned up the heater, her grafted cheek burned. "The only thing Christine wants from me is help with Emily. I'm sure she's waiting for us to get home so I'll take Emily to the park."

"Why are you always so negative about her?"

His question hung in the air between them.

Good actresses were always aware of a character's motivation. Her father probably thought she was jealous of Christine's beauty. And she was, a little. But mostly she resented Christine for taking Kathleen away. "I have my reasons."

"Maybe it's time I heard them."

She hesitated, remembered his demand that she be nice to her stepmother, and then decided she was in no mood to hide the truth. "Because from the day you introduced us, it's been all about Christine and what she wants. Kathleen loved you. And she loved me like a real mother. You can bet Christine didn't give one thought to Kathleen or my feelings when she screwed her freshman English professor and ended up pregnant."

His eyes widened. "That's not fair," he snapped.

Heat rushed up the back of her neck. She wanted to lash out, to punish someone. "Neither are all your embarrassing lectures about safe sex. You're such a hypocrite. How safe or ethical was it for you to have sex with one of your eighteen-year-old students? Why didn't *you* wear a condom?"

He actually jerked back, as if he'd been slapped. He pulled the car into the first available parking place and turned to her. "That's none of your business," he said, fists clenched.

She took a deep breath. "If you didn't want to hear the truth, you shouldn't have asked for it."

He stared at her for a long moment. "You want to know something about your mother? Some truth I've never told you before?" His words came out with the force of whips cracking.

Brandy remained silent, afraid to say anything that might make him stop.

"Your mother never wanted children." He started the car and pulled back onto Main Street.

"That's not true," Brandy said. "She was a great mother. Perfect. I remember her singing to me. And chasing me through a flower garden." She closed her eyes, saw them again—those blossoms the size of dinner plates.

They were almost home when she turned to him. "Do you think I'm ever going to look like her?"

She'd nearly given up on a response when he finally spoke. "You're nothing like her," he whispered. "Nothing."

CHAPTER TWO

*I*sat on a concrete bench exactly twenty yards from the Lithia Park playground and waited for Emily. For thirty-two days, I'd studied her movements, followed her and Brandy, the teenager Emily called Band-Aid, trying to determine exactly how and when to execute my plan.

As the sun made its low circuit across a crisp and cloudless sky, I felt grateful to be free again. To be in this place where the air smelled like earth and pine bark.

I opened my leather attaché case and removed my binoculars and *The Sibley Guide to Birds.* I set the book in a visible spot beside me on the bench, picked up my binoculars, and scanned the clumps of rhododendron bushes where Emily liked to hide. She wasn't there. Shifting the binoculars to the playground, I searched the line of children at the slides, the sandbox and finally found Emily on the merry-go-round.

Brandy ran in circles and sang as she pushed the laughing child. *"The wheels on the bus go round and round…"* Every time I saw her in the park, she was singing. Sometimes she came alone, brought a guitar and sat by the creek.

Small clouds of dust rose with the beat of her boots on the worn ring of dirt around the merry-go-round. Her long, dark and curly hair was tamed on the top and sides by a hot pink cowboy hat and her skirt flowed behind her like a multi-colored banner as she ran. A half dozen silver bracelets made music when she moved her arm. She looked like a gypsy turned cowgirl.

I focused on her bandaged cheek, flinched and looked away. More than anything, I hated imperfection.

When she skidded to a stop and the dust settled, the merry-go-round slowed and my gaze riveted on Emily. As always, she clutched her worn Pooh bear in her lap. I adjusted the lens on my binoculars until Emily appeared close enough to count the grass clippings on the back of her neck. I imagined the toddler turning somersaults on the newly mown lawn—the legs of her red corduroy pants rising up over the plump soft flesh on her calves. I tried to steady my breathing. Alive with secrets and desires, I no longer cared what the dark-suited doctors said. They never understood my needs or my dreams. Why should I swallow their pills to escape them?

Emily rested her chin on the merry-go-round's safety bar. With her legs dangling over the side, she looked like an illustration in the storybook, **Snow White***. A tiny, flawless princess—so brightly lit from the inside that I imagined sunshine, rather than blood, filled her perfect veins. When the spinning finally stopped, she stood and jumped.*

"Be careful," I whispered as I set the binoculars aside.

Emily's hair flew up, then fell back over her forehead—sunlight rippling through the red highlights in her dark curls. In midair she flashed a smile, then landed on her feet, giggling over her shoulder as Brandy chased her around the playground.

A flutter of panic rose in my throat. Brandy was so vigilant. But even careful people make mistakes.

Emily's laughter soared through the air and the two of them passed so close to me I could have reached out and touched Emily. Then the toddler turned and ran back toward the merry-go-round. As she passed by the bench where I sat, she paused and waved at me.

Happiness swelled my chest. The dream of having this particular little girl pulsed through my veins like a mind-altering drug. It aroused every nerve in my body until even my fingertips throbbed with expectation.

Brandy scooped Emily up in her arms.

She was so pure and innocent. All I needed to do was gain her trust and the rest would be easy.

I pulled the necklace from my pants pocket and smiled as I studied the garnet heart set between two diamonds.

Little girls love pretty things.

* * *

The following afternoon, Brandy sat on the edge of her bed, stewing. Her dad had lied to her again. What kind of father tells his daughter her mother hadn't wanted children? She should run away and never come back. Her father would be forced to pay attention then. Maybe he'd even feel guilty or sad.

But where would she go? She could go to Kathleen's house, but she'd just call Brandy's father to let him know she was safe and probably insist she go home and work things out. If she left Ashland, she'd let her drama coach and the other actors down. She'd promised Coach Pritchard she'd write a song for the final scene.

She stared at her guitar, the coveted Gibson Classic—a guilt gift from her dad on the day he'd married Christine. The room still smelled of paint from Brandy's redecorating efforts. She opened the window and glanced around the flower garden room.

On the wallpaper, bright purple geraniums and dahlias the size of silver dollars tangled around the picket fence posts. Flowers that brought back a vivid memory of her mother. The only memory she'd ever have, if her father had anything to do with it.

Oscar, the overweight black cat with four white boots they'd adopted nine years ago, curled on Brandy's pillows, as if waiting for her to sing. She petted him, comforted by both his loyalty and the silky softness of his fur. Brandy had auditioned dozens of country western and folk songs in front of Oscar.

Picking up her guitar, she ran her hands over the vintage woods—Sitka spruce, Indian rosewood, the curly maple neck. She glanced up at the photo of Bette Midler she'd taped on her mirror for inspiration. Like Brandy, Midler had been born with a voice. But it was also the acting that got her an Academy Award nomination for *The Rose*.

Barbara Streisand's nose hadn't kept her from directing and playing the romantic lead in Prince of Tides. And when she was younger, she'd acted alongside Robert Redford, the big hottie of the seventies, in *The Way We Were*.

Both Midler's and Streisand's recognition had come from

hard work, not perfect faces.

Hope returned. She didn't have to let the scars define her—she'd show all of them. Brandy would nail her part in *A Slender Slice of Time*. She'd been practicing in front of her mirror for weeks and would continue to practice until she became Isabella, baby Isaac's mother. Brandy would be an actress and a damn good one. After strumming a few chords, she looked up at the photo of Bette Midler again and improvised a chorus of, *You Are The Wind Beneath My Wings*.

Brandy wondered if that song could work for the play's final scene—if Coach Pritchard would let her off the hook in case she couldn't write a new song.

Emily danced into the bedroom, dragging Pooh bear by his foot and revving her lips like an airplane.

"Not now, Em. I'm practicing."

"No you not," Emily said. "You play guitar."

"Technically that's true, but I'm preparing to practice. So, leave me alone."

"Pease," Emily chimed, her blue eyes wide. She couldn't pronounce the letter L and Brandy thought it was too cute to correct. "One ride, Band-Aid." Emily held up her index finger. Band-Aid had been Emily's first word. They didn't know if it was a mispronunciation of Brandy's name or a reference to the bandages that had so often covered her cheek.

She forced herself to be stern. "I told you I'm busy. Now get out of my room."

Emily dropped her bear, put her hands on her hips and grinned, exposing small white teeth as straight and even as a string of pearls.

Brandy set down her guitar and guided Emily out the door. "Now leave me alone." She closed the door and returned to her perch on the bed.

"No, Band-Aid. Yet me in," Emily yelled at the top of her voice, then started wailing about her precious Pooh bear.

She grabbed the bear, thrust open the door, and threw him into the hallway.

Emily picked him up and snuggled him against her chest. Her bottom lip stuck out. "My Pooh bear," she said. "Mine."

Maybe if Brandy gave Emily one ride, she'd quit pestering.

Christine called out from the kitchen. "Damn it, Brandy. Stop torturing your sister."

Brandy closed her door and locked it.

A few moments later, a tiny hand peeked from under the crack at the door's bottom. Emily was lying on her stomach in the hallway. Oscar jumped off the bed, ran over to the door, and started batting Emily's fingers with his paw.

Emily giggled, a soft musical sound, like a wooden wind chime.

Brandy carefully placed her guitar back into its case, unlocked the door and opened it.

Emily scrambled to her feet, her grin wide.

"Okay," Brandy said. "You win. But just one ride." Though she often believed Emily was a nuisance, Brandy secretly liked it that Em preferred her to Christine or their father. And her chest swelled with more pride than jealousy when someone commented on the toddler's resemblance to Brandy. Emily was flawless, and watching her grow gave Brandy another chance to be beautiful.

She was about to lift Emily onto her shoulders for a wild piggyback ride through the house when, just above the ribbed neck of the child's shirt, something shiny caught the slanted light from the open blinds. "Have you been in my jewelry box again?" Brandy pulled out the pendant—a garnet heart, set between two large, and real-looking, diamonds.

Emily tugged away and stuffed the pendant back inside her T-shirt. "Mine. Don't tell Mommy."

Last week, Emily had broken the tiara Christine had encased in bubble wrap and saved from her crowning in high school. Brandy had never seen her stepmother so pissed. She'd smacked Emily hard on the butt and locked her in her room for over an hour. "Did you take it from Mommy?"

Emily lifted her arms. "Me ride now."

"Not until you answer my questions."

"Play Pooh bear."

"Did you take it from Mommy and Daddy's room?"

"I yike jelly beans."

"I know you do. Did Melissa or one of the other kids bring the necklace to preschool for sharing time?"

Emily tilted her head, but said nothing.

Grabbing Emily by the shoulders, Brandy said, "This is serious. Tell me where you got that necklace."

The toddler struggled out of Brandy's grasp, then backed away, her eyes filled with tears.

Brandy lowered her voice. "Who loves you, Em?"

Giggling, Emily lifted her arms. "Band-Aid yoves me to the stars and back a million times."

"So, you don't have to be scared, do you? I'd never hurt you. Just tell me where you got it."

"My big friend shared."

A silent alarm went off inside Brandy. "Your teacher? Did Ms. Frazer give it to you?"

Emily shook her head.

"What's your big friend's name?"

Emily hurled herself face down on Brandy's mattress.

Brandy sat on the edge of the bed and lifted Emily onto her lap. "You can trust me. We're sisters, aren't we?"

Emily nodded. "Don't tell Mommy."

"I won't if you answer my questions. Is your big friend a lady or a man?"

Emily pushed her index finger against Brandy's lips. "A yady and a man."

"Did one of them give you the bird feet you took to show and tell?" Ms. Frazer had pulled Brandy aside when she'd picked up Emily after school yesterday. "When I suggested the children bring in something from nature," Ms. Frazer said. "This wasn't exactly what I had in mind." The feet had been severed, tied with a bow and slipped into a Ziploc bag. After questioning Emily, Brandy had shown them to Christine. She'd tossed the bag into the garbage can and scrubbed Emily's hands with disinfectant wash, but hadn't seemed concerned.

Now, Emily nodded. "Birdy feet. For good yuck."

Brandy thought about Kent, the boy with Down syndrome, who liked to play with Emily in the park. Kent carried a rabbit's foot in his pocket. He'd probably found the bird feet and given them to Em. "What do you do with your big friends?"

"Play games with big boy."

Brandy's spine stiffened a little. "What kind of games?"

"Pooh bear and Tigger."

"Do your big friends ever hurt you?" She held her breath.

Emily wiggled off Brandy's lap, then stood in front of her and grinned. "No, silly goofy, they yove Emily."

Brandy breathed. There's a logical explanation, she thought—a piece of jewelry one of the nursery school kids brought in for show-and-tell. Maybe Emily traded her peanut butter cookie for it. But just to be sure, Brandy would check with the school on Monday. "Where did you meet your big friends?"

"By the ducks," Emily said, alluding to the pond in nearby Lithia Park. "My big friends. You not see them." She polished the tip of one rainbow-colored sneaker with the back of her purple sock.

The tightness in Brandy's muscles relaxed. The big friends were imaginary. But make-believe friends can't give away real necklaces. Emily had probably found the necklace in the park. Brandy clipped a loose strand of Emily's hair into her purple, butterfly barrette. But even if she did find the necklace, she couldn't have hooked the clasp. "Who helped you put it on?"

"Jodie," Emily said, grabbing Pooh by the leg then clutching him against her chest. Jodie was a teacher's aide at Emily's preschool.

Brandy knelt on the floor beside the bed and patted the back of her neck. "Climb aboard."

With Emily riding her shoulders, Brandy charged across the hallway, down the three steps that sunk into their living room with its high-beamed and angled ceiling. At the far end of the room, a river-rock fireplace rose. Brandy could still see the faint outline left by her mother's portrait. Kathleen had never opposed it hanging over the mantel. But as soon as Christine moved in, she replaced it with her high school graduation shot—a portrait too small to fill the empty space.

In the bookcases on either side of the fireplace, Christine had inserted her stupid little collection of Precious Moments figurines where Kathleen had once stored the leather-bound plays of Shakespeare, Eugene O'Neill, Arthur Miller, and Tennessee Williams. Kathleen, who'd majored in theater arts at Sarah Lawrence, had kept an entire shelf of acting books that Brandy never tired of browsing. It had been Kathleen who'd convinced Brandy's father to enroll her in Tom Thumb Players where she discovered the way acting could erase scars. Every time Brandy stepped into a part, even a small one, she rediscovered that truth. Under the makeup and multicolored spotlights, transformed into someone else, Brandy's scars disappeared.

Now, thanks to Christine, Brandy lived every day with the ghosts of both her mother and Kathleen.

Brandy bounced up the other set of steps, through the dining area and into the kitchen. "My pilot has been cleared for takeoff. Any last-minute instructions?"

Her twenty-two-year-old stepmother stood in front of the laundry closet, looking both bored and resentful. Christine wore a red-and-white-checked shirt that hung just above the waistband of her denim capris. A rubber band secured her shoulder-length hair, the deep autumn red of maple leaves. She'd been perspiring from the heat of the dryer and her usually flawless makeup had disappeared, exposing the hated freckles across her nose and cheeks.

Brandy smiled.

Christine snapped a pair of Brandy's father's slacks, as if hoping the wrinkles would disappear without an iron. Her psychology textbook lay open on top of the dryer. "Could you give Emily a bath for me tonight? I'm so tired. And I have to study for my final."

"Sorry," Brandy said. "The play opens in two weeks—I need

to practice."

Christine wiped her hands on her shirttail, then inspected a chipped nail. "Damn," she said. "It's only Friday." She had a weekly manicure on Tuesday mornings, one of the days Emily went to preschool, and Brandy knew this broken nail would drive her stepmother nuts.

"Can't Mr. Wonderful bathe her tonight?"

"Your father is picking up some visiting poet at the airport. I guess I can study after she goes to bed."

Brandy lifted Emily from her shoulders and set her on the floor in front of the washing machine. She wanted to remind Christine that Emily was her kid, not Brandy's. But her dad had set down the rules like Moses chiseling out the Ten Commandments. *Thou shalt be nice to thy stepmother.*

"This role means a lot to me," Brandy said.

When their eyes met again, Christine's were teary. "All my friends are graduating, going to parties and celebrating." She absently folded one of Emily's T-shirts. "And I'm an old married woman taking night classes so I can graduate by the time I'm forty. Not to mention trying to raise a kid. You had a nanny. I don't understand why your father won't…" She waved her hand in the air, completing the sentence with a flutter of fingers.

Brandy stared at the toes of her boots. She and Christine never had real or meaningful conversations. What was going on here? "None of that is my fault," Brandy said. "Didn't you and your mother have the—" She paused and made quote marks in the air, "Contraception talk?"

Christine stopped folding clothes and looked hard at Brandy. "I never said it was your fault. Don't you think I know you hate me being your stepmother?"

"One of the many embarrassments of having a dad who chases—" Afraid she'd gone too far and broken her father's commandment, Brandy stopped.

Christine laughed. "I wore the running shoes. Your father never even heard the starter gun go off." Her laughter died. "Half the freshman girls were in love with Professor Michaelson—

the tragic figure who'd lost his beautiful, young wife and never remarried."

Brandy took a step back. "Not Dad. No way," she said, finding it hard to imagine freshmen girls, only a year older than her, attracted to her father.

"At first it was a harmless flirtation—a kind of competition to get noticed. Or some arrogant belief I could give him his life with your mother back." She smiled, her face softening, but said nothing more.

In the silence, Brandy heard the regret.

"I can tell you one thing for sure," Christine finally said. "Thinking you want a baby and being a mother are two different things."

Brandy stared at her, stunned. What was happening? Her stepmother had never shared anything this honest before.

Christine picked up Emily and headed for the bathroom. As she turned down the hallway, Emily kicked at her mother and cried out. "Me want Band-Aid."

CHAPTER THREE

Brandy stood in front of her wicker-framed mirror, raised her shoulders, and let them drop. Three times she took a deep breath then slowly released it to center herself. Closing her eyes, she tested her memory of Isabella's lines. "I will send prayers into the night sky with your name on them, Isaac," she whispered, then opened her eyes and tried again, watching the expression on her face in the mirror—trying to duplicate the look of both disappointment and longing she'd seen on Christine's face.

Visualizing the hospital bassinet, Brandy imagined herself as Isabella saying goodbye to her dying baby. Drawing emotion from the depth of her love for Emily, Brandy's voice filled with the unimaginable pain of such a terrible loss. She thought about the character Jenny—the birth mother who gave baby Isaac up for adoption. Jenny was young and must have felt as trapped as Christine did by the pregnancy. What if her stepmother had given Emily away? Or what if her baby sister had been born with a death sentence hanging over her head? Brandy choked up. Her tears spilled over.

When she sensed another presence in her room, she turned around.

Christine stood just inside the doorway. When she noticed Brandy's tears, a look of sympathy spread over her way-too-perfect face.

Brandy wiped her cheeks on her sleeve. "I'm just playing a part. I'm rehearsing. A good actress can cry anytime she wants."

Christine cocked her head as if she weren't convinced.

"What's up?" Brandy asked. "Did you win the frickin' lottery?"

"No," Christine said. "But apparently Emily did." Her stepmother lifted her right hand. The garnet and diamond pendant swung on her index finger like a hypnotist's medallion. "Do you know anything about it?"

Emily ran down the hallway and plunged her naked body into Christine, pounding on the front of her mother's thighs with balled fists. "Mine. Give it me, Mommy."

Christine tossed the necklace to Brandy.

Brandy caught it. "Sure," she said. "It's Emily's new necklace."

"Don't you think diamonds are livin' a little large for a two-and-a-half-year-old?"

"I doubt they're real," Brandy said.

Emily kicked Christine in the shin.

Christine grabbed her by the arm. "Damn it, I'm going to count to five." Her voice wobbled as if struggling for control. "And if you don't—" Before she'd finished her threat, Emily wrenched away and took off running.

Christine chased after her.

With a mixture of amusement and concern, Brandy watched as Christine picked up the writhing toddler.

"No," Emily screamed, kicking at her mother's stomach. "You not boss of me."

Brandy muffled a laugh as a red-faced Christine dropped her daughter onto the floor, but kept holding her by the arm. "We'll see about that." She whacked Emily's behind.

Emily wailed.

Brandy's amusement turned to fear as a handprint reddened on Emily's backside.

"Where did you get the necklace?" Christine asked again.

When Emily didn't respond, Christine whacked her again. "Dammit, Emily. Tell me who gave you the necklace."

Emily was crying far too hard to respond, but Christine smacked her again.

Leaping forward, Brandy grabbed Christine's wrist. "Auditioning for mother of the year?"

Christine looked stricken.

Brandy let go of Christine's wrist and stepped away.

Returning her attention to Emily, Christine said, "Sometimes you make me so mad, I could just—" She clamped one hand over her mouth as if to stop herself from saying something she'd regret.

The toddler slipped away from her mother's grasp, threw herself on her back and kicked the wall with her bare feet, her wails loud enough to be heard on the next block.

Christine jerked Emily up, grabbed her by the shoulders and shook her a little. "That necklace belongs to someone who wants it back. Tell Mommy where you got it. Right now."

Emily froze. Only her eyes moved.

Again, Brandy thought about how enraged her stepmother had become when Emily broke the tiara. "Leave her alone," Brandy said. "I gave it to her."

A look passed over Christine's face that said she didn't quite believe what she'd heard. She released Emily. "Why didn't you say so?"

"A few bucks at a garage sale. Keep the little monkey out of my junk for a change." The lies came out of her mouth before she'd had time to think them through. What if a really bad person had given Emily the necklace? But how likely was that? Her preschool was a safe place, with a fenced and locked play yard. At Lithia Park, she almost never let Emily out of sight for more than a minute or two. She must have found it by the duck pond. The Shakespeare Festival had opened and the park was swimming with tourists.

With her thumb in her mouth, Emily huddled with her Pooh bear in the corner of Brandy's room.

Christine's face was so red it looked as if she'd just run a marathon. "Look," she said. "Your father told me about your conversation in the car and I agree with you. It's not right. He should tell you about your mother."

Brandy was too stunned to speak.

"I really want us to be friends." Christine moved toward Brandy, arms outstretched, ready to hug.

Instinctively, Brandy stepped back. Was Christine crazy?

Christine didn't miss a beat. "Come on, Emily," she said, her voice calm now. "You're stinky and you need a bath."

Staring at the red raised handprints on Emily's backside, Brandy thought about Jenny in the play and the decision she'd made to give baby Isaac away. Maybe Christine had made the more difficult choice. Maybe her stepmother wasn't such a selfish bitch after all.

"How about I give Em a bubble bath?" Brandy said.

Emily clapped.

* * *

I changed into my best suit, a crisp white shirt I left open at the neck and the black shoes I'd carefully polished. I wanted to look professional, like someone trustworthy—a person of value. I checked the full-length mirror and nodded my approval.

Except for the rain that tapped its transparent fingers on the roof, my car was as silent as a shadow. As I backed out of my gravel drive and onto the country road, I tightened my grip on the wheel. I kept my gaze fastened to the wet road ahead. I made a quick stop at a children's clothing store in Talent and bought a frilly dress, ruffled panties, and patent leather shoes for Emily.

Just moments later, the sky rumbled with thunder. The treetops shimmered in an echoing crack of light that split the gray sky like a jagged seam. Even the clouds were singing a dangerous song.

In the parking lot, I turned off the ignition. I sat for a moment, hoping the rain would stop. Finally, I opened my black umbrella and ran across the rain-drenched asphalt. I stood under the portico, rang the front bell and waited. Conversations with men in dark suits were the moments I dreaded most.

A thin, small-featured man, a little shorter than I am, opened the door. He had warm brown eyes and wore a navy blue suit, his sand-colored hair fine and downy as a baby's. He looked as if he'd been hand-picked for his job, non-threatening—the kind of man a distraught and grieving family would trust with their loved one.

My hands shook. As I stepped into the foyer, I was nearly overcome by the odd mingling of smells. Sadness and chrysanthemums. Embalming fluid and regrets.

He took my umbrella and dropped it into the brass container near the sign-in podium. "Welcome to Hillside Mortuary," he said, his voice as deep and soft as his eyes. "My name is Walter Hammond. You don't need to be nervous. We're here to help."

"I've come for a small casket." A crow's wing fluttered in my voice. I cleared my throat to still it and took a deep breath. "One of those small white ones with gold-leaf trim."

"I'm so sorry," he said, leading me into a back office with a desk and two tufted Queen Anne chairs, red as blood, placed in front of it. As he talked, I wondered about the dead people, wondered if the walls were stained with the prints of their shadows. I wondered if he was the man who clipped their fingernails, combed their hair, and painted their faces, but knew I mustn't ask.

Behind a set of closed doors, the organ music, **Jesu, Joy of Man's Desiring**, lapped against the walls like a gentle wave.

He helped me into one of the chairs. "The loss of a child is always the most difficult. But you've come to the right place. We can make all the arrangements for you."

I sat still, knowing I must speak before the music washed away my words. "That won't be necessary," I said, precisely the way I'd practiced. "I'd like to take the casket with me today."

His eyes creased to slits. "Have you…uh…chosen a final resting place?"

"Yes. In the woods behind my home."

He looked away. "That's not only…" The man paused as if searching for the right words. "I'm sure that would be a lovely resting place, and I can understand your desire to have your loved one close to you. Unfortunately, there are legal issues involved. I'd be happy to make all the arrangements for you. We have some lovely shaded, hillside sites."

I panicked. I hadn't anticipated this.

No matter how hard I tried to maintain order, no matter how vigilantly I guarded against mistakes, there was always some blemish—some imperfection lurking out of sight. Waiting to catch me off guard.

I heard the voice in my head. **Remember what we practiced**.

26

I struggled to silence it.

The man eyed me, a trace of suspicion in his gaze. I wondered if he, too, had heard the voice.

"It's all right," he said, his words as smooth as a child's hand. "Grief does terrible things to us. Just take your time."

When I finally spoke, my tone sounded too flat. "I'm afraid you've misunderstood. The casket is for my poodle. She's a standard one, about as big as a three-year-old child."

I imagined Emily then, all dressed up and sleeping peacefully in her satin-lined bed.

He glanced at me with an uneasy smile, then blinked. "There's a lovely pet cemetery just outside Medford. I can have the coffin delivered to them. They can make all the arrangements."

He thought I hadn't done my research. But I'd show him. "I know it's not illegal for you to sell me a casket. I can pay in cash. How much do you need?" I opened my wallet and took out a wad of hundred-dollar bills.

His eyes sparkled as he looked at them. "We have cloth-covered children's caskets that start at three hundred. One of them would be perfect for your beloved poodle. Let me show you what I have in stock," he said, then led me down a stairway to the basement showroom.

I smiled to myself. "That would be perfect," I said. Even I knew cloth burned much faster than wood.

* * *

On Saturday morning, Brandy bounced out of bed, happy to the center of her bones. Stone Rodgers, the guy in drama club she'd most like to call her boyfriend, was meeting her in Lithia Park. The place would be crazy crowded today. If anything like last year, The Teddy Bear's Picnic—this year's theme for the annual Children's Health Fair—would bring in hundreds of kids and their parents. It started at 10a.m. and ran until 4p.m. Maybe she and Stone could find a quiet spot in the Japanese Garden.

It wasn't exactly a date. She'd never had a real date before, but this meeting with Stone was the closest she'd ever come to having one. Stone had the male lead in the senior class play; baby Isaac's adoptive father. They planned to act out the first two scenes for

Kathleen. And Stone was bringing a picnic lunch.

When Mr. Pritchard announced he'd cast Brandy as Isabella, Stone had taken her hand. He looked at her with those ocean-green eyes. She wanted to dive into them and swim around for awhile. Stone's eyes held laughter inside them, even when he was dead serious. He raised her hand to his lips, kissed it, then held it between the two of his like he'd never let go. Her. Brandy *Scarface* Michaelson. She couldn't imagine that the best actor in the school wanted to spend time with her. Before she noticed it happening, her eyes had filled with tears—strange the way a person could hold your hand and open your heart at the same time.

She had her morning all planned out. She'd grab some breakfast, take a long bubble bath, wash her hair and carefully apply makeup over her scars. Sorenson had been right. In less than two weeks, her skin tone had grown more even, and now that the swelling had disappeared, her left eye no longer drooped. Her new white jeans were already pressed and she'd polished her cordovan dress boots. Maybe she'd wear the teal cowboy hat. Her friend, Carla, said it made Brandy's eyes look even bluer.

At the breakfast bar, Christine, still in her nightgown, slumped over a cup of coffee. The kitchen smelled like burnt toast. Emily sat in her highchair smashing Cheerios into sliced bananas with her sticky fingers.

Brandy pulled out another stool and sat between her stepmother and Emily. "Another fight with Mr. Wonderful?"

Christine shook her head. "Tanya just called. She can't babysit for me today. Her sister's water broke. Tanya is her labor coach." Christine and Tanya had been best friends since high school. Tanya lost a baby to SIDS last summer. The only time she smiled now was when she babysat Emily.

Oh brother. Christine was about to ask her to babysit again. Let her stepmother beg as much as she wanted—no way Brandy would change her plans with Stone.

"My mother will never forgive me if I don't show up for her fiftieth birthday luncheon. I've got to find a sitter for Emily and fast."

"What about Dad?"

"He's proctoring SAT exams all day. He left an hour ago."

"Dress Emily up and take her with you. Your mom would probably love to show her off."

Christine sighed. "Emily wasn't invited. They don't call them the terrible twos for nothing. My mother wouldn't want to be embarrassed in front of her country club friends."

Brandy crossed her arms in front of her waist. "I'd like to help, but I have something important to do." When Stone called last night, Brandy had squeezed the telephone receiver hard, unable to say a word for fear she'd say something stupid. Unlike the other boys, Stone, who'd entered Ashland High School as a junior, didn't seem to notice her scars—saw beyond her face to the inside. She told her stepmother about their plans.

"Stone," Christine said. "Very cool name."

"It's short for Stonewall. His father is one of those Civil War nuts who goes to reenactments and stuff."

"Way to go, girl," Christine said, as if trying to morph from a mother back into a teenager. "But, please, can you think of anyone I can call?"

Slapping the highchair's tray with her open hands, Emily said, "More Cheerios, pease."

Brandy picked up the box and poured a small mound onto the tray. "Nice manners."

Emily grinned.

"Who loves you?" Brandy tweaked Emily's nose between her thumb and forefinger.

"Band-Aid," she shouted.

Brandy wiped some banana from Emily's chin with a napkin and then turned back to Christine. "Did you try Carla or Margaret?"

"I tried everyone." Christine shook her head. "I don't even know why I care so much."

"I do," Brandy whispered. "She's your mother."

"I'd like to help you with that role in your play if I can," Christine said.

Sure. Her stepmother probably had some parenting book she'd never gotten around to reading. Brandy gathered up her defenses. What Christine really wanted was for Brandy to give in and offer to babysit Emily. "I take care of Emily so much that people in the park think she's my kid. Like I'd be stupid enough to—" She stopped.

Christine's smile faded. "Emily is crazy about you."

"Whatever."

"How about I pay you like fifty dollars?"

Fifty dollars would be enough to buy the giant Pooh bear in the toy store window for Emily's third birthday. "It's embarrassing," Brandy said. "I try to tell them she's my sister. They don't believe me. One woman shook her finger and told me never to deny my own kid—that it's not the fifties, and there's no shame in being a teenage mother."

Christine swallowed and looked away. "I don't know what to do. I'm desperate."

She'd gotten her hair cut yesterday and bought a white linen suit that wasn't really her style because she wanted her mother's approval. If Brandy had a mother and it was her fiftieth birthday, she'd do anything to be there. She felt herself weaken. "I wish I didn't have plans, but—"

"I don't expect you to change your plans with Stone," Christine said. "I remember what it's like to be young." She looked at the floor where Emily had dropped two banana slices and at least a dozen Cheerios.

Brandy stood. "Don't slash your wrists yet. Give me a minute." She'd call Stone and see if it would be okay if they met later in the afternoon. She headed into her bedroom for a more private phone.

When she returned a few moments later, Christine had her head in her hands. "Stone and I are meeting at 3:30. Will that give you enough time?"

Christine leaped up, her whole face beaming. She threw her arms around Brandy. "I'll make a dinner picnic for the two of you. I can pick up some cheese and French bread in Jacksonville."

Brandy pulled out a barstool and sat. "Now; how can you help me better understand my character?"

"I've been thinking about this a lot," Christine said, sitting on the stool across from Brandy. "And I've come up with two things. The first is for me to fill you in on everything your father has told me."

Brandy froze. "You mean he tells *you* things about *my* mother that he won't tell me?"

"It's only natural. I'm his wife."

"Yeah, right. It's perfectly natural for a man to marry a girl young enough to be his kid and then make *her* his frickin' confidant."

"I know it hasn't been easy. And I also know how much you wanted him to marry Kathleen."

Once again surprised by her stepmother's insight, Brandy remained silent.

"It's okay," Christine said. "It's not like I don't understand. Kathleen could have been a real mother to you." She paused. "Look, I know I'm young, but I'm on your side about this."

"Did he ever tell you about the night of my accident?"

Emily pounded on the tray of her highchair. "Want down, now," she said. "Pease."

Christine wiped Emily's hands and face with a washcloth and released her from the highchair. "Go play in your bedroom for a little while, okay?"

When Emily took off running, Christine returned her attention to Brandy. "Your father took you to the mall in Palo Alto and didn't strap you into the stroller. Your shoe was untied when you climbed out—"

"Does that story make sense to you?" Brandy asked. "You know how he hates to shop and he's far too compulsive to ever leave a kid unattended."

"Ordinarily I'd agree, but he had a huge fight with your mother and was pretty distraught."

"Fight about what?"

Christine shook her head. "Just getting him to admit the

perfect couple had argued was like pulling his molars out with a pair of needle-nosed tweezers."

"So where was my mother?"

Christine hesitated. "I'm not sure I should tell you this."

"It's not like I'm going to rat you out to my father."

"Your mother was passed out on the sofa. She had developed a…well…a drinking problem."

Brandy's throat tightened and she couldn't speak. She wondered why her dad hadn't told her the same, ridiculous story. "Is that what *he* says?"

"Your father wouldn't lie."

"If she stayed home, clueless, and in some kind of drunken stupor, how did she get to the hospital?"

"She wasn't there."

"I saw her."

Christine fixed her gaze on a point above the kitchen stove. "You were three years old. I wouldn't be surprised if you—"

"I didn't make it up." Brandy remembered her mother's face as shock twisted into grief, the piercing scream when she saw her daughter's face.

"It must have been awful for her," Christine said, her voice low and sympathetic. "I've tried to imagine how I'd feel if I—"

"If you what?"

Christine didn't respond.

"My mother didn't do anything to me," Brandy said, with a patience she didn't feel. "How could she when everyone claims she wasn't even there?"

Christine straightened herself on the stool. "That's the point, isn't it?"

The accusation, like a sudden slap, heated Brandy's cheeks. "If she felt awful, it was probably because *he* made her feel guilty. Made her think it wouldn't have happened if she'd been the one watching me." Brandy shook her head. "You know how lame he can be."

"No," Christine said. "That's not what I meant. You were with your father that night because he was afraid to leave you alone with your mother. He was doing something she should have done. But she couldn't take care of you. Or wouldn't."

Brandy stared at Christine as the full impact of her stepmother's words settled. Had her dad been telling the truth about her mother not wanting her? She touched the scar on her cheek. "Looks like my father didn't do such a great job either."

"That's not fair," Christine said.

"Yeah, well how fair is it that you're passing judgment on a woman you never even met?"

"Sometimes I wish I had. Maybe it would help me understand things about Daniel."

Join the club. Her father wasn't an easy person to understand. "You said there were two things. What's the other one?"

Christine's face brightened. "Your parents' wedding album has photos in the back of you and your mother horsing around together before your accident. You're about Emily's age."

"No way," Brandy said. "Dad has their wedding album? And actual pictures of me with my mom?"

Christine nodded.

"He'll frickin' kill you if he finds out you showed me."

"I don't intend to tell him. And you have to promise to look at it and then give it right back to me so I can return it before he finds out."

"Doesn't that feel like a betrayal of Mr. Wonderful? I thought you guys talked about everything."

Christine shrugged.

"Wait a minute," Brandy said, starting to laugh at the absurdity of what her dad had done. "What kind of a geek shows his girlfriend pictures of his wedding?"

Christine laughed, too. "We weren't even dating yet." Her stepmother's blue eyes sparkled as if the moment rekindled itself in front of them. "I felt privileged. Like I got to see inside him. It was like a fairytale—Daniel so young and handsome. They were obviously in love. I saw something special in the two of them. Something I…"

This might be exactly what Brandy needed to better

understand her character. "So, where is it?"

"Locked in the bottom file drawer in his office at the university, but I know where he hides the key. I'll pick it up after the birthday party and be home by 3:30 at the latest."

"All right," Brandy said, trying to contain her excitement and not jump up and down like a little kid.

Christine stared at Brandy's hands, then picked them up, held them inside her own. "You should put some cream on those." She smiled, leapt up and grabbed the bottle of lotion she kept by the sink. "You never know, Stone may want to hold them." She squirted some lotion onto Brandy's palm and massaged it into her skin.

Touched by her stepmother's concern, Brandy looked down at her long fingers full of calluses. In her excitement over the photos, she'd nearly forgotten her plans. "He plays the guitar, too."

The phone rang. Christine let go of Brandy and hurried into the hallway to pick it up. "That must be your father now," she said, her voice a silver thread still connected to the young man in the wedding album.

CHAPTER FOUR

While Emily napped, Brandy paced the family room, determined to finish writing her song. Coach Pritchard counted on her to incorporate it into her character's farewell scene with her baby. For as long as she could remember, Brandy had dreamed about songs. When she got a title, she scribbled it down on whatever was handy—the margin of a novel, the journal she kept on her nightstand, a paper towel or lunch bag. Later, with guitar in hand, she'd start singing that title over and over until the song began to form.

Singing from deep within wasn't so much about the range of notes she could hit or how long she could sustain them. It was more about honesty—about sharing the truth of the music and words, whether a song she wrote or one that touched her so deeply that she could sing it as if it were her own.

But it wasn't happening this time. Over and over, she sang the play's title, *A Slender Slice of Time*. When she finally felt the new line starting to resonate inside her head, she took her guitar out of its case, sat on the edge of the coffee table and swung it over her knees. She hummed the melody that had haunted her, and then sang the three lines she felt good about.

A child is born and she learns to sing,
She sets her heart on elusive things,
But fate steps in and dreams come crashing down.

Brandy skimmed her hair back from her face and thought about time. About the way everything changes. She hummed

35

again. Two more lines came.

Her illusions gone, a truth reclaimed,
Nothing ever stays the same.

Emily cried out.

Brandy set her guitar on the sofa and hurried into her sister's room, hoping to get her back to sleep while still inspired to write.

Early afternoon sunlight streamed through the pink gingham curtains and it took Brandy's eyes a moment to adjust to the brightness. Her dad had recently taken one of the spindled sides away from Emily's white, Jenny Lind crib, turning it into a youth bed. The room smelled like urine.

Emily stood, wobbling in the middle of her mattress, holding Pooh bear by his arm. Her hair was damp and matted against her cheeks and forehead. She wore a white T-shirt and a pair of wet cotton training pants that drooped to her knees. "You yook pretty," Emily said.

"And you woke up way too early. It's not even two o'clock."

"I wetted."

"I can see that. Don't worry. It happens to me sometimes, too."

Emily cocked her head, then reached out and touched one of the pearl buttons on Brandy's shirt. "No it doesn't. You a big girl."

"We'll change your pants and then you can finish your nap."

"No more nap. Feed duckies now."

Brandy didn't want to get all sweaty from chasing Emily. "Not today. I don't feel so good," she said, realizing it was true. She had stomach cramps.

Her period was as regular as a metronome, and not due for two more days. She was probably nervous at the prospect of being with Stone.

Kathleen had obligations in the afternoon and had been unable to reschedule their acting session. But when Brandy told Stone he'd said, "You're the one I wanted to see." She'd been afraid to breathe for fear she'd imagined his words, the sweet tentative sound of his voice.

Now, Emily jumped up and down, doing her bouncing Tigger impersonation. "Pease. Pease. Pease."

"Not today, Em. The park will be crowded with lots of kids on the playground and feeding the ducks. You can sleep with Pooh bear and his friends from the Hundred Acre Wood."

Emily put her hands on her hips. "I wake now, Band-Aid. Where my necklace?"

"You lost it. We already looked everywhere."

Emily's eyes welled. "Tigger find my necklace." She was alluding to her favorite Winnie the Pooh bedtime story, *Tigger, Finder of Lost Things.*

"He tried yesterday, remember? You lost it so good that even Tigger can't find it."

A big tear rolled down Emily's cheek.

"Don't cry. Your birthday will be here pretty soon," Brandy said. "Maybe you'll get a new necklace. Or something really special." Again, Brandy thought about the giant Pooh bear in the toy store window.

Brandy slipped off Emily's wet training pants, tossed them on the floor, then snatched a pair of dry pants from the drawer and put them on her sister. She grabbed a beach towel from the linen closet and spread it over the wet sheet. "Now go back to sleep." She gathered the stuffed animals and placed them on the bed.

"No," Emily said. "Want park now."

"I don't care what you want. This is what I frickin' want. Go back to sleep. Now."

Brandy walked out of the room, slamming the door harder than she'd intended. What a brat Emily could be. None of Brandy's friends had toddlers for siblings. None of them understood.

Emily appeared in the hallway. "Band-Aid, no mad at me. I wake up now. Pease go park."

Brandy knew her sister wouldn't go back to sleep, nor would she play quietly in her room. She'd keep pestering about the park. The time would pass faster there. Maybe she'd take Emily around to some of the health fair booths, let her listen to her heartbeat with a stethoscope.

She grabbed a pair of jeans and a T-shirt from Emily's dresser. "Okay. You win. But I'm not getting all dusty pushing you on the merry-go-round." She left a note on the kitchen counter for Christine asking her to pick up Emily at the park.

After changing Emily's bed, Brandy packed the diaper bag with snacks, a change of clothes for Emily and a wet, soapy washcloth she'd tucked into a Ziploc bag so it wouldn't dry out. On her way through the kitchen she grabbed the bag of stale bread and crusts. Not feeling up to a piggyback ride, she slipped Emily into her jacket and loaded her into the stroller, tucked the diaper bag into the mesh basket behind the seat and started toward the park. When they reached Granite Street, she heard the amplified sound of singers performing *The Teddy Bears' Picnic*. It was a song she'd sung many times to baby Emily.

Now, Brandy sang along. After a minute, she stopped singing, thought about the words and wondered for the first time if that song had ever frightened Emily.

* * *

On a warm day like this one, the air around the Plaza smelled of cinnamon and fresh baked bread. Brandy's steps had a bounce in them as she pushed the stroller along the banks of Ashland Creek where shops and restaurants in a variety of architectural styles nestled with their brick, stucco and clapboard sides touching, as if in tribute to the spirit of diversity for which the residents were well known. It was always fascinating to Brandy the way Ashland Creek flowed into the larger Bear Creek, then joined the Rogue River in its timeless journey to the sea

"Wanna see big Pooh bear," Emily said.

As usual, Brandy stopped the stroller in front of Pivorotto's Pavilion, an old-fashioned toy store strategically set on the Plaza. It was just across the street from the police station and less than a block from Lithia Park playground. Two half-moon front windows in the brick facade displayed everything from toy robots with flashing red and green lights on their chests to the life-sized Raggedy Ann and Andy dolls that now occupied the spot where big Pooh bear had once lounged—his back against a honey tree.

"Where big Pooh?" Emily asked.

Brandy preferred the classic, naked Pooh, but Emily loved the store bear, its yellow T-shirt and the fat bumblebee perched on its nose.

Someone must have bought him. A wave of disappointment washed over Brandy—so much for saving to surprise Em on her birthday.

"Bumblebee sting big Pooh?" Emily asked. "He go doctor?"

"No, it's a friendly bumblebee," Brandy said. "Maybe Pooh bear is taking a nap."

"Go fast," Emily said.

"Not today. I don't want to get sweaty."

"Pease." Her plump little cheeks turned red.

"I said, no." Brandy's voice sounded sharp.

Emily stuck out her bottom lip. "I say pease."

Brandy stooped down in front of the stroller. "I'm not upset with you, Em. I just want to stay clean because I'm meeting somebody special in the park today."

Emily grinned. "Me meet too."

Brandy pushed the stroller into Lithia Park where an Elizabethan Theatre rose from the hillside above the lower duck pond. With eleven new productions every year, it was the perfect place for a would-be actress. But sometimes, when her worst fears won out, it hurt Brandy to live so close to the dream she might never realize. She shook her head hard to get rid of the thought, and then sang an R. Kelly song softly to herself. *I Believe I Can Fly…*"

Nestled on the northern slope of the Siskiyou Ridge, Ashland had the quaint charm of an English village set down in southern Oregon. Every warm afternoon its playground came alive—a den of children's voices, their squeals and laughter rising into the spring-green foothills.

They fed their fleet of Mallards on the pond and wove their way through the crowded park toward the playground, Emily pushing her own stroller. Booths were set up in all the surrounding grassy areas, places where children could get weighed and measured, fingerprinted, and photographed. Hospital personnel wearing teddy, panda, and polar bear costumes offered immunizations. Even some of the children were dressed like bears.

On the lawn, where the Easter egg hunt was usually held, Smokey the Bear handed out balloons and showed a video about forest fires and how children should never play with matches.

A quartet of man-sized bears sang *Teddy Bears' Picnic* to a captive audience of toddlers sitting in a semicircle on the grass.

Near the first set of swings, Brandy felt the flow of menstrual blood. Damn. Just what she needed—today of all days.

Emily tried to run back toward Smokey.

Brandy grabbed her arm. "You need to wait a minute." She checked her watch. It was 3:15. Stone would be here soon. She'd had cramps all morning and should have suspected. She dug in her purse for a tampon and found one, then scooped up an unhappy Emily and set her back into the stroller.

"No," Emily protested, kicking her feet and banging her balled fists against the tray. "See bears. Want balloon."

"You can see them in a minute," Brandy said. "I have to go to the restroom first."

Kent, the boy with Down syndrome who loved to play games with Emily, stopped digging in the sand to watch. He was about ten years old and always wore a pair of white gloves, like the ones women and girls wore to church in the fifties. "Emily play with me," he said. He held a small bear with a T-shirt bearing the Children's Health Fair logo—a cluster of teddy bears on a blanket having a picnic. He looked up at Brandy and smiled.

Brandy smiled back. She'd spent months getting the shy boy to look at her, let alone ask a question. She considered leaving Emily with Kent and looked around for his babysitter. She found her sitting on a bench talking to a boy. Emily would be content to play in the sand with Kent. Brandy would only be gone a few minutes.

Inside her head, she heard Kathleen's warning. *You can never be too careful. He's older and bigger than Emily.*

Emily tried to climb out of the stroller.

Brandy forced her back into the seat and fastened the safety belt. "We'll get you a little bear, too," she said. "But you have to wait a minute." She pushed the stroller into the restroom, holding the heavy door open with her foot. She tried to pull the stroller into the stall, but space was tight. She couldn't close the door and she worried the blood might frighten Emily. Brandy pushed the stroller back out of the stall and then reached into the diaper bag for the wet, soapy washcloth she'd brought in case Emily got dirty. She grabbed a box of animal crackers. "You sit right here. And don't undo that seatbelt. I mean it."

Emily gave Brandy a mischievous look.

Brandy opened the box and handed Emily the crackers.

As she bent to tie her sister's shoelaces, Emily lifted Pooh bear from his perch beside her in the stroller and poked him in Brandy's face.

"Aren't you going to share your cookies with Pooh?"

Emily smiled. "He tired. Pooh bear need nap."

Brandy laughed. "Everyone needs a nap, except you." She tucked the bear beside the diaper bag in the mesh basket beneath the stroller. "He's sleeping now."

She moved the stroller as close to the toilet stall as possible, the back wheels visible under the metal wall, then pressed the wheel locks into place. "You wait right here," Brandy said. "I promise we'll go to the swings in just a minute, okay? Or you can play Pooh bear with Kent in the sandbox." She tweaked Emily's nose. "Who loves you, Em?"

Emily pointed at Brandy and nodded, happily munching on a giraffe cracker. A rash of crumbs dotted the corners of Emily's mouth. She held out a hippopotamus.

"No thanks. But what a good girl you are for sharing."

Brandy stepped into the stall, closed and latched the door. Someone had scraped the words *Rhonda loves Phillip forever*, exposing the metal beneath the beige paint. She shook her head and thought about Stone's laughing eyes. Thought about kissing him. Thought about forever. Brandy had never even come close to knowing what it was like to be in love. But when Stone had touched her skin, she'd felt it in her stomach and held perfectly still, as if a butterfly had landed on her hand.

Now, she sat on the commode and took off her boots, then slipped out of her jeans. There were the usual traffic sounds of kids laughing and chasing each other in and out of the bathroom.

Emily squealed, her voice rising as if she'd just witnessed a miracle. "Bumblebee no sting big Pooh. He no nap."

Brandy wondered if the toy store could order another giant Pooh bear in time for Emily's birthday. "I'll get your Pooh for you in a minute. Be patient. Does that giraffe taste good?" She jabbered to Emily as she inserted the tampon, then tried to remove the stains from her panties and jeans with the washcloth. "Pretty soon, I'll swing you and Pooh bear high in the sky. You like that, don't you?"

She knew Emily had a mouth full of crackers and didn't expect a response, but she kept talking anyway. "You're such a good girl. Emily Michaelson is the best sister in the whole world."

"I want a balloon, too," a little girl said. "Please. A red one."

Brandy leaned over and checked for the wheels of Emily's stroller. When she saw them, she continued scrubbing, but the stains were stubborn. She needed an ice cube. A sink of cold water. A quarter cup of bleach. What she had was a wet, soapy washcloth. Finally, the blood on her white jeans faded, changed to rust, then nearly disappeared. The panties; impossible. Damn.

Brandy took them off, balled them up and crammed them into a Ziploc bag she hid in the bottom of her purse. She stepped back into the jeans. After Stone arrived and Christine picked up Emily, Brandy would find an excuse to run home, grab a pad just to be safe, a pair of clean panties and change her jeans. "It's all good, Em. I won't be long now. Just another minute or two. Be patient."

Brandy zipped and buttoned her jeans, bent over in every direction to see if the staining was visible, then sat back on the commode, pulled on her boots, unlatched the door and stepped out of the stall.

The stroller stood in the exact spot where she'd parked it. But the strap was unbuckled and Emily was gone. "You little monkey. I told you not to unhook that safety belt. Are you hiding from me?" Brandy placed her hands on her hips, more amused than irritated. She'd seen the mischievous look on Emily's face—she should have known her sister would hide. "One, two, three. Where can I find Emily?"

Brandy listened for the usual giggle. Heard nothing.

Her gaze darted around the room. Two sinks. A row of stalls. Where could an almost three-year-old hide? She canvassed the room from floor to ceiling. A scattering of brown leaves clung to the skylights, filtering the sunlight and casting shadows on the floor. She listened, but heard only the incessant hum of an exhaust fan. "Where is that Emily girl?"

Brandy squatted to peer under the stalls. An empty Milky Way wrapper littered the tile of one. Wet pieces of tissue paper clung to the toilet base in another. A pair of white tennis shoes, not Emily's, dangled above the floor in the center stall.

Certain Emily watched—her blue eyes round and expectant—Brandy made a dramatic show of her search. She thrust open the door of each empty stall, expecting to find Emily crouched on one of the toilet seats with her hands spread over her face. When she didn't find her, Brandy shoved the restroom's rubber trashcan aside, grunting as she pushed. "Is there a little monkey back here?"

No Emily.

She grabbed Pooh bear from the mesh basket beneath the stroller and ran outside. "Emily. Emily," she called, over and over, as she rushed around the small, block building that housed the park restrooms. "I give up. Pooh says you win. Come on out." Her voice had a strange squeak.

Still no Emily.

A faint stream of fear trickled into her chest. She let out a long breath. "Okay," she said. "She's got to be here somewhere."

Lithia Park was a safe place—a gathering spot for the small community of Ashland. At one time or another its residents, from babies through the elderly, congregated on the stone benches and watched the trees recast themselves for another season. Swans and ducks floated year round, even when the bare branches of the cherry and dogwood trees frosted over and shone like stars.

Thinking Emily may have wanted to share her crackers with the ducks, Brandy raced to the pond. A flock of early tourists photographed the azaleas and rhododendrons that were spilling over with great clusters of pink and purple blossoms. It was so beautiful. Nothing bad could happen to Emily here. "Have any of you seen a little girl? About this tall with dark curly hair." She held her open palm about four inches above her knee.

None of the tourists remembered seeing her, but there were so many kids in the park, Emily could be anywhere.

Brandy ran back to the playground. Children crammed themselves into every nook and corner. Again and again she cried, "Emily. Emily," the panic rising in her voice with each unanswered call. She looked over at the empty spot near the merry-go-round where Kent had been digging. He was gone. And the quartet of bears had stopped their singing.

Two other little boys with plastic shovels lifted their heads and looked at Brandy for an instant, then returned to their sand castle.

One swing dangled empty.

Another pumped high, the long legs of a girl with dark hair, way too big for Emily.

Brandy studied each bobbing head as the merry-go-round twirled, shades of red, blonde, and brown hair shining in the sunlight.

Back inside the restroom, she tapped on the occupied door. "I'm sorry to bother you," she said. "Did you see a little girl in the stroller when you came in?"

A girl answered, "Nope. Just the stroller."

Please God, Brandy prayed. Where could she be?

There must be a logical explanation. Maybe Christine got home early from the birthday luncheon. Maybe she read the note Brandy had written and came to the park. Maybe she'd carried Emily out of the restroom.

No. Christine wouldn't have left without the stroller. She'd know Brandy would be worried. Surely Christine would have tapped on the restroom door, told Brandy she was taking Emily home.

Brandy raced back outside. Barely within her peripheral vision, she spotted a mound of dark curls spinning inside the hamster wheel, the bright red jacket. Her insides went soft at the center. *Thank you. Thank you. I'll never let her out of my sight again.* She ran forward and grabbed the wheel to stop it. "Emily," she said, tears rising. "You scared me."

A brown-eyed boy looked up at her. "Go fast," he said.

As if the boy could magically transform into Emily, Brandy stood for another instant staring at the wheel.

And then it hit her. What if Emily had gone back to the pond to share her crackers with the ducks, stepped too close to the edge and fallen into the water?

CHAPTER FIVE

A river of fear surged inside Brandy. She gulped in some air, then charged down the asphalt path where she spotted Stone heading toward her.

He loped rather than walked, as if everything ahead waited for him to catch up. He wore a white, renaissance shirt with tight cuffs, billowy sleeves and tiny pleats in the front. It was tucked neatly into a pair of sharply creased black jeans. When he spotted Brandy, he tipped his Elizabethan tall hat, with a purple band around the brim, in a long sweeping motion. As he bowed from the waist, his dark hair flopped over his forehead. "It's me lovely leading lady," he said, in a perfect British accent. He flashed a smile the size of Oregon. And for an instant, he looked like she imagined Heathcliff in *Wuthering Heights.*

"Have you seen my sister, Emily?" she asked. "She was wearing a red jacket."

"No." He blinked those bright eyes, the green color of sea glass—eyes so clear they could never hide anything. "Have you lost her?"

"I was in the bathroom." Her breath came in gasps. "I told her to wait in the stroller, I gave her a box of animal crackers. I saw the wheels. The stroller didn't move the whole time." Brandy choked on her words.

Stone touched her arm. "Try not to panic. Little kids live to hide from grownups. What's she got on? I'll help you look."

Brandy relaxed a little. Stone was probably right. "Blue pants and a red corduroy jacket."

Together, they raced to the duck pond. Breathing heavily,

Brandy sucked in the damp smell of soil and new grass as she scanned the pond. On the moss green surface of the water, a mother duck and six babies swam in an orderly file along the pond's edge, but no sign of Emily.

In a nearby grassy area, someone had set up a table with balloons tied to the corners. It held brightly wrapped gifts and a birthday cake. Brandy's gaze swept along the line of children waiting for a turn at pin the bow tie on the teddy bear. No Emily.

"I'm going to call 911," Brandy said.

Stone slipped his hand into hers, their fingers laced together for an instant. His skin felt dry against her palm as she let his hand go and looked up at him.

"Take a few deep breaths and try to chill," he said. "If we keep searching, we'll find her in a minute or two."

"I'm scared. Emily likes to hide, but she never did anything like this before." Brandy's voice trembled. "What if she didn't hide? What if someone took her?"

"Okay. You call 911. I'll check along the creek."

An image of Emily tumbling over rocks rose as Brandy brushed by Stone and didn't stop running until she stood inside the phone booth on the Plaza. She gritted her teeth. Her hand shook so hard she couldn't push the buttons on the telephone. Barely able to breathe, she bit her lip, leaned her elbow against the shelf to steady her hand and dialed.

Though she knew it was impossible, her body bent toward the phone as if she could pour herself into the receiver and drift inside the Ashland Police Station where, like a magic genie, she'd find Emily perched on an officer's desk, wearing his hat and eating an ice cream cone. And for an instant, Brandy imagined Emily's face smeared with chocolate.

When the operator answered, Brandy couldn't get the words out. "I…I…my sister…I think someone—"

"Slow down," the operator said. "What's your name?"

"Brandy. Brandy Michaelson."

"Okay, Brandy. Where exactly are you?"

"Lithia Park. No. I mean…I ran to a phone booth to call…I

left the park. Oh my God…I left…what if she comes back and can't find me…there are so many kids in the park today. What if—"

"Take a deep breath."

Brandy did.

"That's good," the operator said. "Now take another one."

Again, Brandy obeyed.

"Listen carefully," the operator said. "Do I need to send an ambulance? Is anyone hurt?"

"No. I don't know," Brandy said. "I don't think so."

"Tell me what happened."

"My sister…my little sister…I think someone took her from her stroller in the bathroom. The strap was belted around her." Brandy heard an echo of her own voice like someone in a tunnel. She told the operator her sister's name and age. "She likes to hide…but I already looked everywhere."

"Okay," the operator said. "Describe Emily for me."

"She has long hair. Curly. It's dark brown, but it looks kind of red in the sunlight."

"Eye color?"

Brandy fought for breath. "Blue. Dark blue."

"You're doing great. Now, what did she have on?"

"A…a…T-shirt…some blue pants." Brandy gripped the receiver and pounded her forehead against the Plexiglas. "She has new sneakers. They're rainbow-colored with glow-in-the-dark pink laces."

"That's real good, Brandy," the operator said. "But can you be more specific about the pants and T-shirt? Color? Any design?"

Brandy knew the pants were blue. But what about the T-shirt. How could she not remember? She'd just dressed Emily.

"Take your time," the operator said.

Clamping her eyes shut, Brandy re-envisioned the scene in her little sister's bedroom. Emily waking up from her nap, the wet pants. The sleep creases in her red cheeks. Tears clinging to her eyelashes. How impatient and mean Brandy had been to her—the way she'd slammed the bedroom door.

As if teetering on top of a waterfall at that pent-up instant before it all cascaded over the ledge, Brandy lurched forward, nearly dropping the phone.

The scene focused. Her own hand pulling the pants and shirt from the second drawer. "Blue denim pants with an elastic waistband. The kind you can pull down quickly. She's almost potty-trained, but she has accidents sometimes."

"You're doing good. Anything else?"

"A yellow sunflower T-shirt and a bright red, corduroy jacket." As she talked into the telephone, Brandy's voice faded in and out and the whole scene took on that slippery sensation of a dream.

"Does she have any distinguishing marks? Any scars? A mole or a birthmark?"

Brandy swallowed. "No. Emily is perfect."

"I'm putting this on the air," the operator said. "Broadcasting your description to alert officers on the streets and the cadets in Lithia Park. I want you to stay where you are." The operator's voice was calm and held a sure steadiness. "We'll send someone right over to talk with you."

"No," Brandy said. "I have to go back to the park. What if Emily returns to the restrooms? What if she's looking for me? What if she's scared?"

"Breathe for me again, Brandy," the operator said. "Tell me where in the park you'll be so I can have an officer meet you."

Brandy told her she'd be on the playground near the swings, then dropped the receiver into its cradle and hurried back to the park. She took deep breaths, willed herself to calm down. When another search of the areas surrounding the pond and theatres yielded nothing, she charged back to the playground. She climbed onto the play equipment, a center platform between two slides. "May I have your attention please? We need your help. We've got a lost child. A little girl."

The busy playground grew silent. Faces angled toward her like flowers to the sun. "She's almost three years old," Brandy said. "About this big." She held her hand out to indicate Emily's height. "Lots of dark curly hair. Her name is Emily." Brandy told them what Emily was wearing. *Oh God. I can't believe this is happening.*

A few mothers and nannies leapt from their benches, grabbed their charges and hurried out of the park. Others, wanting to help, took their kids by the hand and began to look behind trees, under the skirted tables of the vendors. They searched behind privacy screens set up for vaccinations, in the bushes and under the wooden fort. One member of the teddy bear quartet turned up his microphone and asked everyone to help. Another one flipped the wastepaper baskets upside down, fished through the contents with a long stick.

Stone returned. He shook his head. "No sign of her along the creek."

Emily. Emily. As if there were stereo speakers in the treetops, her name rang out everywhere.

No one answered.

* * *

Detective Winston Radhauser, known as Wind to his family and friends, was enjoying a rare Saturday off from work. He stood with his right boot on the bottom rail of the horse fence around their arena. His arms were folded over the five-foot high top rail, chin resting on his hands. He took a deep breath. The air around him filled with the smells of the cedar sawdust he'd used to bed the stalls, the grassy aroma of alfalfa bales and sweet feed laced with molasses.

His beeper went off.

He slipped it from his pocket. It was Robert Vernon, the other detective from the Ashland Police Department.

Damn. He'd put in for this day off months ago. It was his wife's birthday, for Christ sake. Vernon knew better than to page him today.

Out of nowhere, he thought about his other life in Tucson, the one with Laura and their thirteen-year-old son Lucas—the little boy who'd wanted to be a rodeo cowboy. Just over a decade ago, a drunk driver had killed his first family. He'd been working a case and hadn't been with them that night.

Radhauser decided to ignore the page—wouldn't let the job

come before his family. Not ever again. He watched his wife, Gracie, ride Mercedes—the six-year-old bay mare he'd bought for her thirty-second birthday. Gracie had grown up around horses, and once she'd completed her nursing degree in Tucson, it had been her idea to move away and buy this small ranch in Talent, Oregon—just on the outskirts of Ashland. She was right. It wouldn't have been a good idea to start their married life with the ghosts of his first family hovering over them.

They'd met while Radhauser was working on a murder case in Catalina, just miles north of Tucson. Gracie was a friend of the victim. And there was something about the way she'd looked at him, something in her smile and in the warmth of her dark eyes that made him want to know more about her life. It was the first time he'd felt the slightest stirring for a woman since his wife and son had died. Once the case was solved, he'd asked her to go on a picnic to watch the sunset at Gate's Pass in the Catalina Mountains high above Tucson. And when she'd brought a bouquet of flowers to Lucas and Laura's grave, he knew she was the one. The rest, as the old cliché goes, was history.

Now, she wore a pair of worn Levis, boots, and one of his plaid western shirts, tucked in tight at the waist. Elisabeth, their four-year-old daughter seated in the saddle in front of her mother, had insisted her mother wear the birthday hat. Gracie's mahogany hair was loose, the way he liked it best, and it flew out behind the cone-shaped paper hat with green and blue balloons printed on it.

Gracie talked to the horse in a soft voice and patted her neck. Each time Mercedes passed by him, Lizzie smiled at him and waved. Ever since he'd read her a picture book about cowgirls, Lizzie wanted to wear the same outfit—a short, denim cowgirl skirt with suede fringe, an orange gingham blouse, tiny boots, and a black cowgirl hat with a bright orange band around the crown.

His beeper sounded again.

Gracie maneuvered Mercedes to the fence. "Whoa, girl." She brought the mare to a halt in front of him. "Mercedes is well-trained. Really responsive to my leg signals."

He smiled. "In case you haven't noticed, so am I."

He looked at his daughter, at the dark, sun-streaked hair Gracie had braided into pigtails and tied with orange ribbons. She looked like her mom, with those big brown eyes he could never get enough of. "Do you have any idea how much your daddy loves you?"

She grinned and lifted her arms to the sky. "To outer space and back a thousand million times."

He turned to his wife. "And how about you, Mrs. Radhauser?"

"I know that look," Gracie said. "You got a page, didn't you?"

He nodded.

"Phone Vernon. Tell him no way."

"I've decided to ignore it."

"You won't be able to do that."

"Watch me."

She'd often told him he had an obsessive personality, especially when it came to his work. "Call him right now and get it over with."

He couldn't argue with her. She was right. "I suppose I should check in."

From the phone in his barn office, Radhauser called Vernon.

"A kid went missing in Lithia Park," Vernon said, then filled him in on the details. "I need your help."

"Have you turned that park upside down and shaken out the crumbs?"

"Officers Corbin and Murphy are on it. I'm heading over as soon as we hang up." He told Radhauser about the Children's Health Fair, and how the park was overflowing with kids and costumed workers trying to cajole toddlers into getting their fingerprints and photographs taken. How the sister had searched all the places the toddler liked to hide.

"Call search and rescue to wade the duck ponds. And see if you can round up some help from Josephine & Jackson County Sheriffs' Offices to check along the banks of Ashland Creek."

"It's running pretty swift," Vernon said. "All that snow melting in the mountains."

Radhauser cringed. "Girl or boy?"

"A little girl," Vernon said.

Radhauser imagined what it would be like to find Lizzie caught up in the roots of an old oak tree at the edge of that rock-lined creek. He shook his head hard. "I can be there in fifteen minutes."

Having lost a wife and a child, death was too real to him now. He understood it, like he never had before. And he worried about Lizzie getting sick or hurt. He knew there were no safe places, but surely this small ranch in Talent, at the southern end of the Rogue River Valley with its population of five thousand, must be as good as it got.

He grabbed his western-cut blazer from the hook in the barn and told Gracie what had happened and that he'd most likely be late. "I know I promised, but…"

Her arms tightened around Lizzie. She kept her gaze on him a beat too long, then shivered, as if trying to shake off a thought. "We'll have the birthday cake when you get home. I don't care if it's breakfast tomorrow morning. Just find her."

* * *

Brandy clutched Emily's Pooh bear to her chest as she raced around the pond and the thick nests of bushes surrounding it. Praying for a flash of a red corduroy jacket, she searched for any sign of Emily.

Two squirrels at the edge of the creek stopped feeding on a dead crow and chased each other up the trunk to the high branches of an oak tree. Their short-muscled bodies disappeared into the green until they were visible only through the commotion behind the leaves. The air smelled like decomposing pine needles and wet leaves. She could hear the sound of Ashland Creek plunging over its rocks. Emily wouldn't go near that rushing water, Brandy assured herself. Emily was too afraid of the roaring noise. *Who loves you, Em?*

Stone ran back from the Japanese Garden. He set his hat on a bench and stood by the pond brushing his damp hair back from his forehead. He was out of breath and there were big circles of perspiration under his arms. "No sign of her." He shook his head. "Did you hear anything strange while you were in the bathroom?"

"Just kids. Nothing unusual. One of them asked another one for a balloon."

"Wouldn't Emily have cried if a stranger tried to pick her up?" Stone said. "She probably got bored…I mean…climbed out of her stroller. Maybe the singing and all the bears distracted her and she wandered off."

Brandy shook her head, wanting so much to believe that was what had happened. "How far could she have gone? We've searched the park. Why haven't we found her?"

"She's got to be here someplace," he said, looking straight into her eyes.

"What if some child molester snatched her?" Brandy said.

"I have a three-year-old cousin who memorized whole books. Little kids are smarter than most people think. Is there any possibility she could find her way home?"

"I don't know," Brandy said. "What if she tried to cross the street? I've told her to look both ways a million times, but… What if she got hit by a car?" Brandy's chest felt caved in and she could barely breathe, it hurt so bad.

"Someone would have called an ambulance. We'd have heard sirens or something." He stared at her, then looked away. "Head up to your house."

Maybe he was right. What if Emily tried to walk home? Could Brandy catch up with her before anything bad happened? "I told the 911 operator I'd wait for the police."

"If they arrive before you get back, I'll tell them what happened," Stone said.

Brandy shook her head.

"Do you want me to go?"

Emily barely knew Stone. She might be afraid of him. "I'll check with the police first and then I'll go," Brandy said.

When the first officer arrived, he introduced himself as Officer Corbin from the Ashland Police Department. Brandy gave him the details of what had happened and where they'd searched. She asked if she could run home to see if Emily was there.

Corbin took down Brandy's home address. "Detective

Vernon will want to talk to the person who reported her missing. So, come right back."

Stone touched her arm. "I know you're scared, but I have a good feeling you'll find her before you get home."

Relief spilling out of her with his words, she handed him Emily's Pooh bear. "Watch this for me." She raced across the park, over the bridge, and up Nutley to Granite Street.

The relief was gone and everything felt wrong. The bright spring colors that swept by in liquid shades of green and yellow. A sweet-smelling flower garden. And the sun, too warm on her neck and shoulders. She couldn't fit it all together with the dread inside her. Running in the wrong direction, every step took her farther away from the place she'd last seen Emily.

Brandy drove her legs forward. Within moments she stood, panting, in front of their house. The garage door was open. Christine's Mazda RX7 convertible parked in its usual spot. *Please, God. Please.* She'd never ask for anything again. *Please, just let Emily be safe inside.* Their yard was hilly and thick with big-leafed maple trees. Double-winged seeds, the color of bones, dropped onto the driveway.

Brandy sprinted up the drive, through the garage, and burst into the kitchen. The magnetic click of the door echoed in the quiet room. Her stepmother peeled an onion at the sink, its brown skin rustling like paper. She still wore the white linen suit she'd worn to her mother's luncheon, but had replaced her high heels with furry bedroom slippers and pulled her hair up off her neck into a ponytail. Christine turned to Brandy. "I ran a little late, but I almost have your picnic ready," she said, nodding toward the half-filled wicker basket on the counter. "And I picked up the—"

"Is Emily here?"

When she turned to look at Brandy again, Christine's face seemed to rearrange itself. "Here? What do you mean here? She's with you."

As if Brandy had pushed a button that ejected Christine from her spot in front of the sink, her stepmother wheeled around, then shot forward. The onion dropped from her hand, bounced once on the kitchen floor before it rolled into the corner and stopped.

Christine rushed at Brandy, grabbed her by the shoulders, jiggled her back and forth, and then stared into her eyes. "Please. This isn't anything to joke about. Just tell me where Emily is."

The facts surrounding Emily's disappearance swelled inside Brandy like waves, silent and unstoppable. She tried to tell her stepmother what had happened.

Christine looked at Brandy's face and then staggered back, pulled on her ponytail until the elastic band broke and a red mass of hair fell over her shoulders. Her mouth opened.

Brandy felt her stepmother's breath rushing toward her, like the gust of air from a passing car. She tried to say something to calm Christine, but it was impossible.

Her gaze locked onto Brandy's and, in a flash, something significant passed between them—an acknowledgment of the awful possibilities that might await them.

The kitchen seemed unnaturally quiet. In the dream-like silence, Brandy heard the tick of the clock on the back of the stove and the sound of her stepmother's breathing.

All of a sudden, Christine squared her shoulders and barked orders at Brandy. "Find your father. Tell him what's happened. Tell him to meet me at the park. Turn off the oven. And lock up the house."

She grabbed her purse, then dug inside, searching for her car keys. When she didn't find them, she dumped the entire contents on the kitchen counter. A gold tube of lipstick rolled across the granite and tumbled onto the floor. Christine's whole face was red. She picked up the keys. "It will be all right," she said, more to herself than to Brandy. "Emily will come for me." Christine's voice cracked. "I'm her mother. She'll come when I call her."

CHAPTER SIX

Radhauser parked his Crown Vic on the Plaza, grabbed his crime-scene kit and his camera, and hurried toward the 93-acre park. He wasn't a religious man, but he prayed the little girl had merely wandered off and would soon be found, if she hadn't been already. He walked past the roadblocks, the flashing red and blue lights of other patrol cars, and the Saturday afternoon onlookers with their shopping bags.

Vernon had cordoned off the area, and two uniformed police officers were posted beside the Plaza entrance to question anyone who entered or left the park. Two others were canvassing the area around the pond.

Just as Radhauser requested, his partner had cordoned off the bathroom with police tape and designated it as a crime scene. Officer Murphy stood guard to stop any unauthorized person from entering.

"Any sign of the little girl?" Radhauser asked.

Corbin shook his head.

Red and blue flashing lights caught Radhauser's attention. A siren stopped screaming as a Medford police car came to a stop near the park entrance. Good—if this turned out to be a child abduction, they'd need all the help they could get.

He snapped on a pair of latex gloves, ducked under the tape, pushed open the door and entered the women's bathroom. He stood still for a few moments, waiting for the room to talk to him. He imagined the carbon and oxygen molecules shifting slightly because he'd entered, and then slowly settling back into place.

An empty stroller was parked in front of the back stall.

Radhauser photographed it from several angles, noting the still engaged wheel brakes. A half-eaten lion cracker stuck to the white plastic tray. Again, he snapped a photograph.

Though he knew he'd most likely find nothing, Radhauser checked each empty stall, snapped some more photographs, then examined the sinks and mirrors. He went through the trashcan and then inspected the floor marked with dozens of dusty footprints. Most of them looked like running shoes or sneakers, and many of them were child-sized. One larger set stood out—looked as if they'd been made by a pair of wide and smooth-soled bedroom slippers. Radhauser photographed them.

He'd have forensics take a look, but he was pretty certain they'd find nothing of value. He pulled open the door, then took off the gloves and tossed them into the trashcan. As the door closed behind him, it dawned on Radhauser that a child under three couldn't reach the handle and even if she could, there was no way she'd be strong enough to pull open that heavy door. Realization of what that meant trickled over him like ice water. How many times had he brought Lizzie to this park, believing she was safe in the sandbox, while he sat on a bench reading a book? If it hadn't been Gracie's birthday, she and Lizzie would have been here for the fair.

Somewhere in the distance, a woman frantically called out for Emily—three syllables rising and falling into the air.

Near the playground, Detective Vernon stood in front of a bench talking to a young woman. She wore a white suit and bedroom slippers. Radhauser's thoughts flashed to the odd footprints he'd seen on the restroom floor, then back to Vernon.

The young woman sat with her hands shoved between her knees, her shoulders slouched and a sick, terrified look on her face that told Radhauser she was the little girl's mother.

Vernon sat beside her and put his hand on her shoulder.

Radhauser took a deep breath. Sometimes, especially in cases like this one, it wasn't easy to find the balance between professional and sympathetic. And he knew this would be especially tough for him. This case would be different, though. This time he'd find the little girl alive.

Vernon spotted him. He stood, said something to the woman, and walked toward Radhauser. He filled Radhauser in on what he knew so far—that he'd notified search and rescue to wade the ponds and the creek. And that he'd done an initial interview with Christine Michaelson, the victim's mother. "Both the Jackson and Josephine County Sheriffs' Departments have dispatched officers to aid in the search. The stepdaughter and her boyfriend looked in all the places Emily liked to hide, and found nothing."

"Where is she now?" Radhauser asked.

Vernon told him Corbin had sent the older daughter home to see if Emily had found her way back, and to notify the victim's mother. That Christine had asked Brandy to call her father before returning to the park.

"What about the boyfriend?"

Vernon nodded toward the edge of the playground where a lanky, dark-haired teenaged boy, dressed like a disheveled Shakespearean actor, stood leaning against a tree. He held a small Winnie the Pooh bear in one hand and a funny-looking high-top hat in the other. Vernon checked his notes. "Stone Rodgers. Apparently, he'd planned to meet Brandy, the victim's half-sister, here in the park."

"Tell the vendors and people manning the booths to stay put," Radhauser said. "And be adamant about it. No one leaves until we give permission. Talk to them. Search every booth. That kid's got to be here somewhere." Maybe if he behaved as if he believed it, it would be true.

Radhauser stepped over to the boy and introduced himself.

The kid was polite, responsive, and told Radhauser he'd arrived at the park at 3:30.

"Do you meet Brandy here often?"

"I've run into her here a couple times, but this was the first time we'd planned to meet." Stone told Radhauser how they had the male and female leads in the class play and had planned to practice some of their lines.

"Where were you before you got to the park?"

"I was home, doing penance by washing my mother's car."

"Did you rob a Quick Mart?"

Stone shook his head. "Forgot to let my dog out. He decided the living room carpet was a good place to…" He stopped before finishing the sentence.

"What happened when you arrived here?"

"I saw Brandy running toward the duck pond. The whole place was teeming with kids. She told me what happened and that she wanted to call 911."

Radhauser jotted down notes, then asked the question he always asked in a missing child case. "What do you think happened to Emily?"

The kid didn't hesitate. He told Radhauser that at first he'd thought she wandered off and when they didn't find her, he thought maybe she'd headed home. His gaze cut to Emily's mother. "Now, I'm not so sure."

Radhauser questioned Stone for another few minutes and then told the boy he could go home.

"I'd like to stick around, if that's okay." Again, his gaze shifted to Christine. "Obviously Emily wasn't at home and Brandy's gonna be pretty upset. Maybe I can help her in some way."

Radhauser glanced at the victim's mother, then nodded, realizing Brandy would need all the understanding she could get. "Good idea."

Christine leapt to her feet and raced toward Stone. She snatched the stuffed bear and hugged it against her chest.

His empty hand hung in the air between them for an instant before he dropped it to his side.

"Where did you get this?"

He shook his head, as if embarrassed. "I'm sorry. Brandy asked me to hold it."

"It belongs to my baby. It belongs to Emily," Christine said. "She doesn't go anywhere without…"

When Radhauser believed Christine was out of earshot, he asked Vernon to compile a list of sex offenders and pedophiles within a twenty-mile radius of Lithia Park. Just saying the word, pedophile, stung the back of his throat. "Organize a door-to-door search of their houses. You don't need a warrant to do a risk assessment. But if anything looks suspicious, get one and rip out the wallboards if you need to."

If it turned out to be a kidnapping by a stranger, the outcome was usually the same—with any luck, the child would be released after the sexual assault or photography session. If not, the child would most likely be killed during the first forty-eight hours. "And see if you can get some other officers to canvas houses bordering the park."

Radhauser lifted his sleeve to check the time. He'd forgotten he wasn't wearing his wrist watch.

"It's 4:14," Vernon said.

Emily had been missing for forty-six minutes.

"Call for an AMBER Alert," Radhauser said. Ashland was only twenty-seven miles over the state border. "That kid could be in California by now. I'll see if I can get a photograph from her parents. Make up some flyers. We'll plaster the whole town with them. And notify the National Center for Missing and Exploited Children." He asked Vernon to phone the technician to schedule polygraphs for the victim's family members. "Set up a hotline number for tips."

Vernon wrote everything down in his notebook, then stepped back over to the bench where the missing kid's mother sat, still hugging the stuffed bear. He introduced Radhauser to Christine and then excused himself. "I'll go back to the office and take care of those matters we discussed." Vernon headed out of the park.

"What matters?" Christine asked. "What's more important than searching for my baby?"

"It's all related to the case. We're calling in backup from other counties," Radhauser said, his gaze landing on her bedroom slippers. "Were you in the park restroom earlier today?"

"I just got here. What are you getting at?"

He glanced at her feet. "I found some prints near Emily's stroller that looked as if they were made by bedroom slippers."

"It wasn't me. I wore new shoes to a luncheon for my mother's birthday. When I got home, my feet hurt, so I took them off.

But after I heard Emily was missing…I forgot I was wearing the slippers."

That sounded reasonable to Radhauser. Gracie often did the same thing.

Christine grabbed his wrist. "Promise me you'll find her."

Behind them, Ashland Creek rippled and swirled haphazardly over its rocks as if it were drunk on the waters of springtime.

"I wouldn't worry too much yet," he said. "Kids like to wander. And most of them turn up on their own."

Her blue eyes widened. She looked like a beautiful, but frightened kid—her face so pale that the reddish freckles across her nose and cheeks stood out beneath her makeup as if they'd been drawn with ink. "And what happens to the rest of them?"

A vision flashed through his mind. The Tyler Meza kidnapping—one of Radhauser's first cases as a detective. The six-year-old had been snatched from the men's restroom at a Tucson little league park. It remained the one case that haunted him most.

"What happens to the rest of them?" Christine asked again.

"We find them," Radhauser said. And they did, one way or the other.

* * *

After Brandy waited fifteen minutes for someone to locate the classroom where her father was administering the SAT, she closed up the house and ran toward the park. She raced across the parking lot, over the bridge spanning Ashland Creek, and into the playground, coming to a skidding stop in front of the park restroom. Yellow tape with black letters that said, *Crime Scene. Do Not Cross*, was strung across the entrance.

A few feet away, she spotted a man who was probably a detective or a police officer talking with Christine. He was tall and broad-shouldered, with dark hair just edging into gray at the sideburns visible beneath his tan Stetson. A hint of black beard showed on his chin. With his denim, western-cut jacket, jeans and boots, he looked more like a handsome cowboy than a police officer. He used his hands as he talked. They were calloused like an authentic rancher, not one of those wannabes who just dressed for the part. For some reason, this made Brandy trust him more.

When he moved away from Christine, Brandy hurried toward him. "Are you here to find my sister?"

"Yes," Radhauser said, showing her his badge. He had dark blue eyes that looked intense, but sincere—not fake sincere like Doctor Sorenson's. "In order to locate your sister, I need to ask you a few questions." He gestured toward a park bench.

Brandy forced her legs to move in that direction, but once she got to the bench, she remained standing.

While Radhauser took a black notebook from his inside pocket, Brandy watched another uniformed officer take her stepmother aside. They stood about twenty feet away. Her stepmother's eyes were still as she looked at the officer, like someone searching a crystal ball.

Radhauser patted the empty place on the bench.

Brandy sat beside him. She held her own hands to keep them warm.

He asked dozens of questions about her little sister and wrote down everything she said in his notebook. Had Emily walked up to strangers in the park? How well did she talk? Did she play with other children here? Had Brandy noticed anything suspicious— heard sounds of a struggle in the bathroom, like someone had put a hand over Emily's mouth?

The Children's Health Fair had been shut down. Costumed workers took off their masks and bear heads. And in the grassy areas around Brandy and Radhauser, vendors and booth workers packed up their goods. One by one, as the police officers questioned and then dismissed them, they quietly left the park.

Brandy answered every question, then told the detective about Emily's love of speed, the way they raced to the park almost every afternoon, the way she loved the merry-go-round, to go high on the swings. "I tried to warn her about strangers. Last year the kid's fair had a booth from the Missing Children's Clearing House. They showed a Barney film about not talking to strangers. They took her picture, fingerprinted her and everything."

Radhauser lifted his eyebrows. "Emily has prints on file?"

63

Brandy nodded.

"That's good." He jotted a note.

"Do you think someone took her?"

Radhauser waited until she looked at him. "It's too soon to tell, but we need to treat it like a kidnapping while we explore possibilities. Tell me what you think happened."

She told him how she'd first thought Emily was hiding someplace nearby or that she'd gone to feed animal crackers to the ducks. "But now, I think someone must have carried her out of the restroom." She shook her head. "I always told her to scream if someone she didn't know tried to pick her up. We even practiced. Em is a good screamer. But she didn't make a sound. Please, Detective Radhauser, you have to find her."

"We will. Kids wander off every day. Sometimes they curl up under a tree or a picnic table and fall asleep."

"Are they okay?"

The skin on his right cheek twitched. "Almost always."

Grief crept up her throat and tightened it. "Almost?"

The word weighed a ton.

CHAPTER SEVEN

For Winston Radhauser, facing the one person—usually a family member—who felt responsible was the most difficult part of a missing child case. It sometimes caused him to freeze and remember things he'd tried hard to forget. Things like the look on Janet Meza's face when she'd told him about working the Little League snack bar that afternoon and not realizing Tyler had disappeared until her shift had ended.

All around them, Lithia Park seemed still. Despite the muted chatter of children and the sounds of traffic moving along Winburn Way toward the Plaza, he heard his pencil whisper as it glided across his tablet. "This is important," he said to Brandy. "Was the main door into the bathroom closed?"

"It closes automatically."

Radhauser nodded. "I know. But sometimes I've seen it propped open with a garbage can."

"Not today. I remember because I had to struggle to keep the door open while I pushed the stroller inside."

"Was your sister angry with you over anything?"

She told him that Emily had wanted to swing, play in the sandbox and watch the singing bears, but that Brandy needed to go to the restroom. She relayed the precautions she'd taken and how'd she'd kept talking to Emily, checking the stroller wheels, and telling her they'd go back to the playground in a few minutes.

"Some reason you didn't take her into the stall with you?"

Her face and neck got red, and the scars she'd tried to cover with makeup stood out even more. They ran like a railroad track up her left cheek where they disappeared into the hairline just above her ear. "I tried to bring the stroller inside, but I couldn't close the door. I…you see I…I had a problem." She seemed to shrink inside her clothes.

While he waited, he wondered what had happened to her face and couldn't help thinking it was a damn shame. Radhauser was pretty good at sizing people up, and there was something special about this kid. Something deep and genuine. "Go on," he finally said.

"It wasn't supposed to…It came early…I…I started my period." She stared at the tips of her boots, and then up at Radhauser, her face even more flushed. "I didn't want Emily to be scared."

"You and your sister have a pretty big age difference," Radhauser said. "Do you ever resent having to take care of Emily?"

She flinched and leaned back against the bench. "Sometimes. But she's my little sister. Well, my half-sister. But people say she looks like me. And she does, except…well…she's perfect. I'm always careful with her. I'd never do anything to—" Her words rushed out, but then stopped abruptly, as if she realized what she'd intended to say was no longer true.

Radhauser hated to mention the scars, but needed to see how she reacted. "I know how bad you must feel about your face."

She looked away. "I'm only a few weeks post-surgery. Doctor Sorenson says it'll get better in time."

"Still. Must be hard to have a little sister who's so perfect." Sometimes he hated his job, the way he'd deliberately hurt someone to get at the truth.

"It's not her fault. Emily wasn't even born when—"

"I'm sure you care a great deal about her," he said, not convinced yet it was true. "Is there anything else you can tell me about Emily that might help us find her?"

Again, she looked at her cowboy boots. "There are hundreds of things I could say about her. She's a pretty cool little kid. But probably none of it would help you find her."

He held Brandy's gaze. "You get along with your stepmother?"

"We do okay. Considering."

He glanced at Christine, now talking with Officer Corbin, then returned his attention to Brandy. "She doesn't look much older than you are."

"Is that supposed to make me hate her?"

He glanced over at the boy in the renaissance shirt. "Do you ever take your eyes off her when she's playing here? To talk to your friend or something?"

"Stone didn't get here until after—"

"How about other days?"

"There haven't been any other days. This was our first… well…I guess it was kind of a date. Before today, if Stone happened to be in the park, we'd talk about acting sometimes. But Kathleen always watched Emily."

"Kathleen? Who's Kathleen?"

"She used to be my nanny. My mother's dead." The girl winced as if it still hurt to say those words. "Kathleen took care of me until my dad married Christine."

"What's Kathleen's last name?"

"Sizemore."

"Where does she live?"

"Kathleen would never take Emily."

"We'll talk to everyone who knows your sister. It doesn't mean we suspect them. Now tell me where Kathleen lives."

"Don't waste your time," Brandy said. "Kathleen loves Emily."

"I'll find out where she lives. And my having to do so will waste time I could spend looking for Emily."

Brandy stared at him, as if trying to assess his sincerity. "Near here," she finally said. "The yellow house on Vista, up behind the Shakespeare Theater."

"How long have you known her?"

"Since I was Emily's age. She's like a mother to me."

"Was she here today?"

Brandy stood. "What are you getting at? She's my friend. She lived in our house for years. She made me believe in myself." Brandy touched her left cheek. "Made me believe I could be an actress even with…" She paused, started over. "When I was little, she sewed a trunk full of costumes so I could play make-believe. Kathleen would never scare me like that."

"Is she here now?"

Brandy shook her head. "It's Saturday. She was going to coach Stone and me around noon, but I had to babysit Emily."

So, the kid had other plans. Maybe she'd grown tired of babysitting for her sister. But given how upset Brandy was, he couldn't believe she'd deliberately done anything to lose Emily. "Does Kathleen work?"

"She coaches acting at the Little Theater in Talent. And teaches it part time at the university."

He saw the pride on her face when she talked, and realized that Brandy loved Kathleen.

"She was in Talent this afternoon," Brandy said.

Radhauser jotted the name *Kathleen Sizemore, Vista,* and *Little Theater* in his notebook.

Brandy told him what he'd already learned from Stone, that the two of them had the leads in their senior class play, how she wanted to be an actress more than anything, and that Kathleen was a great coach. "She's the one who convinced my dad I should take acting lessons."

He needed to interview Kathleen. Maybe the former nanny had a problem with Christine. Maybe she'd had a dream of being more than just a nanny to Brandy.

"Why would you agree to babysit Emily when you had plans with Kathleen and Stone?"

She told him about Christine's babysitting dilemma—her mother's birthday.

"So, you didn't really want to be with Emily today?"

Brandy's eyes filled with tears. She quickly looked away, as though ashamed for him to see them. "No, I didn't. But that doesn't mean I was careless with her."

"I want you to think hard now. Anything, anything at all might be significant. Has Emily done or said something unusual lately? Mentioned someone you didn't know? A new friend?"

She shook her head. "It isn't fair. Playgrounds are for kids.

They're supposed to be safe."

He asked the question again.

"She's two-and-a-half. She'll turn three in July. Sometimes she invents things, like imaginary friends."

"Did you ask her about these friends?"

"She told me she met them in the park, a yady and a man." Brandy gave him a sad smile and told him Emily couldn't pronounce the letter L. "She said that they loved her." Brandy's gaze darted around, found her stepmother, then returned to Radhauser.

The kid looked physically ill, as if a pile of rocks had tumbled to the bottom of her stomach.

She leapt to her feet. "The necklace. Oh my God. If that necklace had anything to do with Emily's disappearance—"

"What necklace?"

She hesitated. "It's probably nothing." Her voice sounded choked, as though something had gotten caught in her windpipe.

He raised his eyebrows. "That's the funny thing about leads. They often seem like nothing at first."

Brandy paced in front of the bench as she told him about the garnet necklace, how she'd gone to Emily's preschool to talk with Jodie about it.

"Jodie at Rainbow's End Nursery School?" he asked.

She nodded. "Emily claimed Jodie had helped her put it on."

A slow, familiar fear rose inside him. What if the kidnapper had been stalking the school playground? "My daughter, Lizzie, goes there three days a week." He swallowed, looked away, his words falling on the ground like rocks.

"She must be four. Emily is in the Tuesday/Thursday class," Brandy said. "The younger kids."

He bit his lip as he wrote the words, *diamond and garnet heart necklace, Jodie and Rainbow's End.*

Brandy told him how she'd talked with Ms. Frazier, Emily's preschool teacher, gotten a list of parents from Emily's class, and called every one of them to see if anyone owned the necklace. No one did. "I even went to the parks and recreation lost and found to see if anyone reported it missing." She related the conversation she'd had with Emily that led her to believe her sister had imagined her big friend.

"You ever see Emily talking to anyone, besides other little children, in the park?"

"She's pretty friendly. And she plays with this bigger boy sometimes," Brandy said. "He has Down syndrome," she added softly, as if reluctant to say anything that might get the boy in trouble.

"What can you tell me about him?"

She told him the boy was ten or maybe eleven. That he wore white cotton gloves that seemed a little strange. "But Emily loves him. She wanted me to get her some gloves, too." Brandy paused and looked toward the sand pile beside the merry-go-round, as if searching for the boy. "He was always so nice to Emily," she added, her gaze returning to Radhauser.

He studied her. "Did Emily say the boy gave her the necklace?"

"No."

"Do you know his name?"

"Kent. But I don't know his last name. He's here a lot with his babysitter. I saw him when I took Emily into the restroom. But when I came out, he… Oh my God," she said. "He was gone. Maybe that's what happened. Emily wanted to play with him. Maybe she climbed out of her stroller and—"

"What's the boy look like?"

She gave him a description.

He wrote everything down, straight black hair—cut in bangs—dark brown eyes, green baseball cap, khaki-colored shorts, high-top red sneakers with tan socks, and the white gloves.

A female police officer, wearing the uniform of the Josephine County Sheriff's office, stood a few feet from the bench, as if waiting to be assigned a job. "Excuse me," he said to Brandy, wanting to ask the female officer to follow up on Kent.

Maxine McBride stood about five feet three inches tall—her frosted hair cut short as a boy's beneath her cap. And she wore a pair of gold rattlesnake earrings that curled around her lobes. He saw it as a message. Despite her size, she was tough enough to keep up with the good old boys on the force.

Radhauser filled her in on what they knew so far and asked her to interview park regulars, check the rosters for kids in Special Education classes at the local elementary and middle school levels. See if she could locate a full name and address for a boy named Kent. Radhauser gave her his card. "Get back with me as soon as you have something."

When he looked around for Brandy, he found her walking the path in front of the restroom. "What if I made a mistake about Kent?" She told him how Kathleen had warned her to be careful. "Kent saw us go into the restroom. What if he followed me inside and took Emily somewhere?"

Radhauser had serious doubts that a ten-year-old boy would kidnap Emily, but they could have wandered out of the park. "If she's with him, we'll find her."

She stopped pacing and a look of relief spread over her face that quickly turned to panic. "He won't talk to you. For months, he only talked to his babysitter and Emily. It took me forever to get him to even look at me."

"Does he talk to you now?"

Brandy nodded. "Do you think this is my fault?"

"I'm sure Kent is a nice boy." Radhauser tried to help her feel less responsible. She was only a kid. And judging from the glares her stepmother shot in Brandy's direction, she would be shouldering enough blame. "I'll need your help in interviewing Kent. If Emily is with him, they're probably safe and playing somewhere."

Brandy gave him a closed-mouthed smile. "They played with Pooh and Tigger a lot, and Emily always giggled."

"It's possible the necklace did have something to do with her disappearance," he said, coaxing her back toward the park bench. "Someone may have given it to Emily to gain her trust. Exactly when did she come home with it?"

She grimaced, then looked off into space. "About a week ago."

"Do you still have it?"

71

She shook her head and shrugged. "Emily's two-and-a-half. She loses everything. Do you think the necklace might help us find her?"

"It's a clue. Has she ever brought home any other gifts, ever mention her big friends before last week?"

Brandy looked at him. Her eyes pooled with tears again. "One day a couple weeks ago, she ran over to me with her cheeks stuffed with candy. I pried a wad of tootsie roll out of her mouth and yelled at her for picking it up off the playground. She started crying and told me she didn't pick it up. Maybe someone gave it to her." Brandy kept shaking her head as if she couldn't believe how irresponsible she'd been. "I missed all the signs, didn't I?"

It was a scene Radhauser had participated in a hundred times in his career. As a rookie, he thought his inexperience accounted for it being so damn difficult. But now, more than two decades later, he knew the truth. He hadn't become tougher or hardened to the pain. Every time he witnessed another person's grief, it cut out a piece of him.

"What exactly did Emily say about the friends who allegedly gave her the necklace?"

"That big people couldn't see them. That they didn't hurt her. Emily has a great imagination. I read in this magazine that you should encourage that in children." Blinking rapidly, Brandy looked away.

He gave her a moment, then spoke her name to call her back. "You said there was a lady and a man, right?" He made a note in his book.

"I think she included Kent," Brandy said. "And I really thought she found the necklace and that the lady friend must be imaginary."

"What did your parents say?"

She sat, twisted her hands in her lap. "I'm not sure my father knows anything about it. But Christine saw the necklace."

"Didn't she wonder where Emily got it?" He tried to keep the suspicion and judgment out of his voice.

"I…I told her I gave the necklace to Emily."

Radhauser stopped writing and looked at her, trying to understand how a smart kid, who seemed to care about her little sister, would lie about something like that. "Why?"

Brandy explained what happened that night.

"Does your stepmother spank Emily a lot?" Radhauser made a note to talk with the neighbors.

"Christine gets frustrated," Brandy said. "She's trying to go to college and be a wife. She wasn't ready to be a mother."

"Do you know where your stepmother was when Emily disappeared?" Again, he thought about Christine's bedroom slippers, the strange prints he'd found on the restroom floor.

"What are you trying to say? Christine didn't have anything to do with this. I shouldn't have lied to her about the necklace. She was home, packing a picnic for Stone and me. She wouldn't hurt—"

"Has she hurt Emily in the past?" He heard the sound of heavy breathing, like someone who'd been running. The faint smells of aftershave and sweat. And then a man's long shadow appeared on the ground beside him.

The man wore a dark suit and a maroon tie that he'd pulled loose at the knot. It hung crooked around his open collar. He was clean-shaven, tall and slender, with dark brown hair, slightly wavy on top. A man who looked as if he were in control, until Radhauser saw the terror in his eyes.

Brandy inched toward the opposite edge of the bench, her fear palpable. She glanced quickly toward Stone, then at the man Radhauser assumed was her father.

"What necklace?" the man asked. "And who hurt Emily in the past?"

Radhauser rose from the bench and stuck out his hand. "You must be Emily's father."

He shook Radhauser's hand, but his gaze never left Brandy's face. "I'm Daniel Michaelson," he said, then turned his full attention back to Brandy. "You lied to Christine about a necklace?"

She looked at her boots.

Christine broke away from the other officer and flung herself

73

into Daniel's arms. She leaned into him as if her spine had turned to powder. He took the dead weight of his wife and held her while she cried.

"Listen to me," he said. "I'll do whatever has to be done. I swear to you. Whatever it takes to bring Emily home."

Christine grabbed the front of his shirt, balling the cotton material in her fists. "Just tell me she's not dead."

Radhauser watched Daniel's throat muscles as he swallowed, then patted his wife's back as if she were a fragile thing, something he might shatter with his touch. "No. She just wandered off. They'll find her."

Radhauser had another vision of Tyler's small body crammed into the trunk of an old Studebaker. The boy had still been dressed in his baseball uniform—his team name, *The Cactus Patch*, printed in white, block letters across the front of his lime green shirt.

"Do either of you have a recent photo of Emily?" Radhauser asked.

Daniel let go of Christine, then opened his wallet, pulled out photographs of Emily from the plastic sleeves and spread them across the park bench.

Looking at the photos, Radhauser wanted to race home, pick up Lizzie, and hold her tight. "Can you tell me how tall Emily is and how much she weighs?"

Daniel shrugged and looked at Christine.

Christine said nothing.

"Emily weighs thirty-three pounds and she is thirty-five and a half inches tall," Brandy said.

Radhauser wrote down the information she'd provided and then examined each photograph, finally choosing a close-up of Emily on the swing in their backyard. He understood the importance of the first photo released to the public. It needed to be a good likeness for identification, but it also should make the child appealing, a child everyone could love. A child other people would feel connected to and want to help bring safely home. He needed a photograph that ensured thousands of eyes were looking for Emily.

In the swing photo, Emily laughed with her mouth wide open—light captured in her blue eyes. And her hair, tied back in a pink ribbon, caught the afternoon sun and blazed a trail of curls behind her. One dark strand had fallen loose, leaving a coil in the shape of a question mark on her upturned cheek.

CHAPTER EIGHT

Brandy stuffed her hands into her pockets so Officer Corbin couldn't see them shake.

"I know you've already answered these questions for Detective Radhauser," he said. "But sometimes a different phrasing…" Corbin paused, shrugged. "Something new comes out."

Brandy didn't care if she had to answer the same questions a million times, if it would help bring Emily back. Brandy repeated the entire story.

Emily was officially listed as missing. Other officers searched Lithia Park. Interviews were conducted with vendors, hospital employees, the bear quartet, park employees, and some of the mothers and older children who'd stayed to help Brandy and Stone look for Emily.

Forensics scrutinized every inch of the park restroom and dusted the stalls, sinks and stroller for fingerprints.

Six cadets in hip boots waded in the lower duck pond. Christine watched from a nearby bench. Each time one of them bent to lift something from the bottom, Brandy stopped breathing and didn't breathe again until she was sure it was a piece of debris and not Emily.

While Detective Radhauser questioned her father, Brandy ran through the park again, rechecking all the places Emily loved to play. When she found nothing, she started to cross the bridge into the Winburn parking lot. She would bang on the doors of every house facing Lithia Park. Someone must have seen something.

Her father caught up to her and grabbed her arm. "Don't go wandering off. We need to talk about that necklace."

She curled up on another bench, wrapped her arms around her knees. It didn't matter that she'd kept her eyes on the stroller wheels. It didn't matter that she believed she'd protected her little sister from something that might frighten her. Emily had still disappeared.

* * *

The park search yielded nothing.

Emily had been missing for nearly two hours.

Brandy was stunned to realize how unchanged this day remained for so many people. Men and women milled around waiting for the afternoon plays to begin, waiting for *King Lear* in the Angus Bowmer Theater later that night.

She closed her eyes, and when she opened them again, Stone stood in front of her. He gave her a sad smile. The sun made him squint. "The detective said I should go home now, but I want you to have this," he said, handing her a slip of paper. "It's a private line directly into my bedroom. Use it anytime you want." His gaze shifted to Christine and Brandy's dad. "You're gonna need a friend." His eyes went soft. "I want it to be me." He put his hand on her shoulder and squeezed. "Just call me, even if it's the middle of the night." He looked her straight in the eyes. Warm energy passed between them. It was as if he could see through her, all the way to her soul—see how scared and responsible she felt.

She looked away, still feeling the pressure of his hand, the heat of his stare as he waited for a response. But she couldn't look at him again for fear she'd burst into grateful tears. She tucked the paper into her shirt pocket, nodded to thank him, then watched as he stepped away so slowly it looked like he walked under water.

Once Stone was out of sight, Brandy stood and headed toward Detective Radhauser. "Make a list of everyone Emily trusts. Include phone numbers," Radhauser said to her father. "Babysitters, teachers, neighbors, friends, relatives."

Radhauser paused and turned to Brandy. "In case I need to talk to your boyfriend again, make sure his phone number is on the list, too."

"What boyfriend?" her dad said. "Don't tell me you were

fooling around with some boy when you were supposed to be watching Emily."

"He's not my boyfriend," she said, her defenses raised like a shield.

Her stepmother had circles under her eyes and crying lines that ran down both sides of her face, marking her cheeks like scars. "You had plans with Stone. You didn't want to take care of her. I practically forced you."

Brandy's mouth filled with the truth. "I love Emily as much as you do. Maybe even…" The remainder of what Brandy wanted to say disappeared. Emily was gone and that left nothing. Absolutely nothing she could say.

Radhauser's gaze shifted from Christine to Brandy and then to her father. "I'll also need a list of possible enemies. You teach at the university, right?"

Her dad's attention snapped back to Radhauser. "Yes. English Lit."

"Any disgruntled students? Parents? Kids who failed their midterms and came in to piss and moan about it?"

"Always," her dad said. "But I can't imagine…"

Detective Radhauser handed him a card with the police station phone number. "I think you folks should go home. Just in case we get a call."

Her dad reached for Christine's hand. "They didn't find anything in the pond. That's good news."

Her face grew whiter. She turned to Radhauser. "Are you saying you don't think she's in the park?"

"It's too early to tell. We're organizing more searchers. But once it gets dark, we'll need to call them off and regroup at daylight. Detective Vernon and I will follow up on any leads. You folks stay close to the phone."

Christine stuck her fist in front of her mouth as if she was trying not to vomit. "A ransom call?"

"We should be prepared for the possibility," Radhauser said. "If a call comes in before we get set up, phone us immediately, no matter what they tell you about no police."

Christine stiffened, her eyes flashed. "What if they want a million dollars?" She stumbled toward her husband. "Where will we get that kind of money? What if they've already gotten on an airplane? What if Emily…" She paused, dazed and tottering like a drunk poised at the edge of a cliff. "Oh God, what if they—"

Brandy's father turned, grabbed Christine's shoulders and looked directly into her eyes. "We'll raise the money. Even if we have to sell everything. We'll do it to get Emily back."

"It's too early to assume the worst," Radhauser said. "I think it's more likely she wandered out of the park. Or maybe was lifted out of the stroller by someone she trusted. Go home and make those lists."

Brandy didn't want to go home with her dad and Christine. She dreaded confronting Emily's empty bedroom and facing her father with the lie she'd told about the necklace.

* * *

In the garage, Brandy walked behind her dad as he helped Christine out of her car and supported her under one arm, leading her around Emily's tricycle. An image of Emily pedaling down the sidewalk in front of their house assaulted Brandy. She hurried ahead, opened the door into the kitchen, and stood aside as her dad and Christine passed.

"Just lie down for a few minutes," he said, steering Christine toward their bedroom. "I'll call if we hear anything."

"Are you fucking crazy?" Christine stepped into the hallway. "It'll be dark soon. My baby is out there. And you expect me to take a nap?" Suddenly, she stopped. She bent to pick up a stuffed animal, Tigger, then broke away from Brandy's dad and plunged into Emily's room. She slammed the door, as hard and unforgiving as a slap, then clicked the lock.

Her dad tapped on the door. "Please, Christine. Don't do this to yourself."

She didn't respond.

He took their address book from the desk in the kitchen and sat at the table to compile the list of names and phone numbers for Detective Radhauser.

Brandy sat on the carpeted step down into their sunken living room and waited for what she knew would come. She felt a desperation inside that stretched out for miles with no relief in sight.

She stared at the empty space where her mother's portrait used to hang, while Oscar weaved his furry body around her feet. When he scampered onto her lap, she stroked the cat until it purred and her hands felt warm again, then held him against her chest.

A few moments later, she heard her father push his chair away from the kitchen table. He stepped into the living room and stood in front of the step where Brandy sat, his hands clamped in front of his body. "What were you thinking when you told Christine you bought that necklace at a garage sale?"

She covered her face with her hands. They smelled like the soapy washcloth she'd used in the park restroom and the sweaty acrid scent of her fear.

She lifted her head and tried to explain the way it had all happened with the necklace, how angry Christine had become with Emily, and how Brandy only wanted to protect her little sister.

As she talked, her dad paced around the living room.

"I'm sorry, Dad. But I thought she found it."

"Damn it," he said, his face contorted and red. "Did you tell the police about this?"

"Of course. Do you think I'm stupid?"

"Strangers don't give necklaces to little kids unless they've got a reason. Did you think, just once, that Emily might be in danger?"

Brandy shook her head, her voice stuck inside her throat. Growing up around Lithia Park, she'd never believed, even for an instant, that anything bad could happen there. Maybe she was like those high school kids in Colorado. They didn't think anything bad could happen at their school either.

"Just tell me you weren't so busy fooling around with that boy you forgot all about Emily."

She couldn't respond. A terrible squeezing beneath her breastbone made it hard to breathe. "Stone wasn't even in the park when it happened."

Her father studied her face and nodded over and over, as if trying to decide what to say. "You were always so good with..." He stopped.

Brandy pulled her knees up and wrapped her arms around them. Her whole body felt limp. "I love Emily," she whispered.

Her dad walked across the room and stopped in front of her again. There was sweat on his temples and a tuft of damp hair hanging low on his forehead. He put his hands on her shoulders. "I want you to think really hard," he said, a crazed light in his eyes. "Did you see or hear anything unusual in the bathroom?"

"I have been thinking hard. I heard some kids. Normal bathroom sounds."

Brandy stumbled to her feet, took a chance and wrapped her arms around her dad. He held her against his chest, stroked her back with his open hand. "I'm sorry you have to go through this. I know you'd never let anything happen to Emily on purpose."

She felt as if she were melting into him, going back to those long, uncomplicated days when it was just the two of them working in the yard. Her daddy and the little girl he used to call Cookie pushing a yellow plastic wheelbarrow behind his lawnmower. Kathleen smiling at them from the kitchen window.

She kept waiting for him to let go, to move his hand away from her back, but he didn't. The clock seemed to stop ticking and something shifted between them. He finally pulled away. "You better change your jeans," he said, smoothing the hair around her face with his fingers. "Looks like you sat in something."

Brandy felt so many things at the same time. The irony that she'd forgotten her stained jeans—once so important she'd left Emily unattended. Despair for what her vanity had cost them, and a strange joy, tempered with grief, at the undeserved tenderness from her dad.

The doorbell rang.

Her dad leapt to answer it with Brandy only a step behind.

81

Emily's bedroom door opened, and Christine ran down the hallway to the front door.

When her dad flipped on the porch light, Detectives Radhauser and Vernon stood aside, while a tall uniformed officer carrying electronic equipment stepped into the entryway. Her dad led him to the kitchen, then returned.

Vernon lingered in the entry. His navy blue blazer and gray slacks had lost their crisp look and now appeared crumpled. He was medium height, tan and young-looking, despite his salt and pepper hair. He wore a pair of wire-rimmed glasses that made him look like a weary college professor after a trying day with his students. He followed the officer into the kitchen.

Detective Radhauser carried a clear plastic evidence bag with Emily's rainbow-colored sneakers inside, their glow-in-the-dark pink laces tied together in double-knotted bows.

Christine stared at the bag, her eyes wide, then fell back against the wall and clamped her hand over her mouth to muffle the scream. On the floor between her feet, a puddle of urine spread across the slate tile, soaking into her bedroom slippers.

Brandy pulled into herself, wanting to hide her stepmother's shame.

Her dad spoke in a low voice, barely audible. "Where did you get those?"

Radhauser stood beside the small deacon's bench in the entry. "Do the shoes belong to your daughter, Mr. Michaelson?"

Daniel looked at his wife.

Christine nodded—seemingly unaware of the puddle she'd left on the floor.

"We found them in the creek not far from the bridge into the Winburn parking lot," Radhauser said.

"Emily can't swim," Christine said. "I meant to get her lessons—"

"We don't think this is indicative of a drowning," Radhauser said. "From their position, it appeared they'd been thrown into the creek."

When Christine tried to grab the bag, her foot slipped in the urine.

Radhauser held out his arm to stop her fall.

Brandy raced into the laundry room for an old towel and used her foot to mop up the puddle.

"We need to check for prints." He shook his head. "Not likely on the wet canvas, but we'll dust it anyway. Could Emily tie a bow?"

"No," Christine said. "She's not even three."

"We're going to keep the shoe details from the press. Especially the fact of them being tied together."

"Why?" Her dad asked.

"It's what we'll use for the confessors—the people who call in and say they took Emily."

Her dad frowned. "People actually do that?"

"We've already received two," Radhauser said.

"Did you follow up? What exactly did they say?"

"They were whackos," Radhauser said. "It happens a lot."

Her dad winced, his face pale. "Does finding the shoes mean someone physically removed her from the park?"

Radhauser sighed. "Yes, sir. We do think it confirms a kidnapping."

The word kidnapping seemed to hang between them, the mere sound of it charging the air like an electrical current. One brutal word with the impact of a baseball bat.

Radhauser continued. "And the fact that your other daughter didn't hear any sounds of a struggle leads us to think Emily may have known the person who took her. Do you have those names?"

Her dad handed Radhauser the lists he'd compiled. "I can't believe any of them would hurt Emily." His gaze met Brandy's for a second, then returned to Radhauser. "Have you followed up on Kent, the boy with the gloves?"

"We're tracking down names and addresses from the special education classes," Radhauser said. "Several people at the park recognized Brandy's description. They claimed he and his babysitter get out of a gray Camry in the Winburn Way parking lot every day at three o'clock. As regular as the church bells. If we don't find a name by tonight, tomorrow, we'll be waiting."

"Tomorrow," Christine shouted. "He may have done something terrible to her by tomorrow."

Brandy tensed, remembering Kathleen's warning about the boy being bigger and stronger than Emily. "I've talked with him a lot. He's a nice boy."

"I'll need your permission to take Brandy with me when I interview Kent," Radhauser said. "Apparently he won't talk to strangers."

"Fine," her dad said. "Whatever you need. But I swear if that kid laid one—"

"Everyone we talked to in the park says he's harmless and has been coming there for years," Radhauser said. "Believe me, we won't dismiss anything without a thorough investigation. We're checking known sex offenders and pedophiles. And we've alerted the hospitals and morgues."

Christine put a hand to her mouth, then let it drop onto her chest. "You think she's dead, don't you?"

"No," Detective Radhauser said, and turned to Brandy's father. "But we need to search your house. And I'd like for both you and your wife to take a polygraph."

Her dad's gaze returned to the remains of the puddle on the floor. "Isn't it obvious Emily's not here? Why on earth would you think we kidnapped our own child?"

Christine hurried into the bedroom and shut the door.

"It's standard operating procedure whenever a child turns up missing. I once found a little boy hiding in his attic. And you never know what we might see that parents miss. After the search, we'll get started on your lists. You'd be surprised how often kidnappings turn out to be someone the parents know. Custody-related. Or some angry relative."

Her dad cleared his throat. "There are no custody issues here. Emily lives with both—" He was cut off by the phone ringing.

Radhauser grabbed his arm. "Let it ring three times before you answer. The technician isn't set up yet, but it's good to get into the habit."

Brandy pushed the towel around with her foot to clean up the rest of the puddle, then picked it up and headed toward the laundry closet. She stuffed the towel in the washing machine, then quietly closed the door.

Her dad returned with the telephone. He nodded toward Detective Radhauser. "It's for you."

Christine came out of the bedroom wearing a pair of faded denim jeans, a sweatshirt, and running shoes.

Radhauser cradled the phone between his cheek and shoulder. A clump of hair, the color of wet topsoil, fell over his forehead. "What do you mean, you can't tell?" He gestured with his hands as if whomever was on the other end of the line could see him. He had a man's hands with uneven nails and calluses on his palms. Hands that made him seem both hardworking and approachable. When he hung up the phone, he turned to Brandy's father. "They've got an unidentified at Rogue Medical Center. Brought in about fifteen minutes ago. A little girl. They found her in a gas station restroom, out near Jacksonville."

"Oh my God," Christine said as she headed for the garage.

Her dad grabbed her arm to stop her, then turned his attention back to Radhauser. "How bad is she hurt?"

"We don't know," Radhauser said. "The investigating officer can't eliminate Emily from the photo. Officer Murphy will need one of you to go with him. The other better stay here with me in case the kidnapper calls. They often hang up if they suspect the police are involved."

Brandy ran for the door. "I'll go."

"No," her dad said. "You stay with Christine. And if anyone calls and says they have Emily, agree to whatever they ask."

The man hooking up the phone equipment gestured to Radhauser. "You're all set."

"Don't worry, Mr. Michaelson," Radhauser said. "One of our officers will be with them."

As soon as Brandy's father left, Christine hurried out the front door. "I'm going back to the park. I need to look one more time."

"We have police officers patrolling the park and canvassing

the nearby houses," Radhauser said.

Christine ignored him and took off running down the street.

Brandy turned to Radhauser. "Is it okay if I make a couple quick phone calls?" She needed to talk with Kathleen, needed to hear her voice.

Radhauser nodded.

"Then I'll make some flyers on my computer."

"Great idea." He phoned the police station. Within minutes they had a number, 800-TOEMILY, and a promise that an officer would drop off an Ashland-area map they could photocopy for the volunteers.

While Radhauser and Vernon searched the house, Brandy called Kathleen, but there was no answer. She probably hadn't returned from the theater in Talent. Brandy hung up, phoned Lois, her father's secretary, Coach Pritchard, and her high-school principal to ask them to help solicit volunteers. Then she went into her bedroom to scan Emily's picture into her computer.

The wedding album Christine had promised sat on Brandy's bed. She stared at it, then picked it up, opened the bottom drawer of her dresser, and tucked it inside. She closed the drawer. She didn't deserve this gift. And she sure didn't want to get her stepmother in trouble with her father.

All the 'what ifs' swirled around in Brandy's mind. What if she'd refused to babysit? What if she'd told Emily no when she'd begged to go to the park and feed the ducks? What if she hadn't started her period? If only she could begin the day over and make different choices. But time was a river and there was no way to stop it or go back.

She shook her head. This wasn't the place for what ifs or self-pity. She scanned Emily's photo, added the information Radhauser had written down for her, then made some follow-up phone calls. In less than an hour, with the help of her drama coach and Lois, Brandy had lined up over fifty student and teacher volunteers to comb the streets tomorrow, knock on doors, and tack up flyers.

CHAPTER NINE

While the flyers slipped from her printer into the collection tray, Brandy hurried into Emily's room to hunt for the necklace. Detective Vernon had completed his search of the toddler's room while Officer Corbin and Detective Radhauser looked through the rest of the house. Vernon had found nothing, but he didn't know Emily the way Brandy did. The necklace was an important clue and she had to find it.

She flipped on the bedroom light.

Christine had organized Emily's toys, lined the top of her dresser with her favorite stuffed animals, all the characters from the *Winnie The Pooh* books. Brandy looked away. But there was no escape. She stared at the tiny bed they'd changed before going to the park, and then started to pull out the dresser drawers. Her hand stopped in midair as she tried to swallow the memory, the sound of Emily's voice inside her head. Emily had insisted on changing the pillowcase herself. "I do," she'd said. "I do."

"Please," Brandy whispered into the silent little room. "Let her grow up to be a bride."

It took Brandy a moment to calm herself and refocus on her mission. One drawer at a time, she removed the clothing Vernon had scattered about from Emily's dresser, shook each item to make sure the necklace wasn't hidden inside the fabric, then organized the contents—training pants, tights, socks, T-shirts, long pants and shorts. When the drawer was completely empty, she carefully repacked it.

She ripped the sheet and pillowcase off Emily's bed, shook out the pillow and then removed the mattress to search beneath.

That necklace had to be here somewhere.

She crawled across the floor, using her fingertips to comb through the carpet, hoping to find the necklace chain caught in the long fibers. She found two buttons and some pink plastic beads the size of small marbles Emily had gotten for making necklaces. Brandy should have spent more time with Emily, should have taught her how to connect the beads.

She searched behind every piece of furniture. She took the books and toys from the built-in bookcases, but found nothing. Finally, she tackled the wooden toy box Vernon had dumped in front of Emily's closet. One by one, she picked up each toy, shook it, and then placed it back into the toy box. She found all the pieces to the Fisher-Price barn, the fence and the silo. She put the little animals inside the barn where they belonged.

When there was nothing left but puzzle pieces and blocks, she carefully replaced the shapes into the wooden puzzles, put the stray Lincoln logs back into their cylinder, and gathered the colorful bristle blocks and dropped them into the baskets on the floor beside the toy chest.

It had to be here somewhere. Brandy remembered taking it off Emily and setting it on the dresser, but the following morning, Emily raced into Brandy's bedroom. "I yost it," she'd said. "I yost my necklace." Again, Brandy pulled out the dresser and checked behind it. Nothing.

She closed her eyes. *Think like Emily. Where would Emily have put the necklace?* Someplace safe. A place where she put her treasures. *Of course*, Brandy thought—the little pink purse Emily had gotten for Christmas. She carried it with her whenever they went on a treasure hunt and filled it with pebbles and wildflowers, a leaf fallen from a maple tree.

The purse hung from one of the three pegs her father had attached at a height Emily could reach—right beside her purple rain jacket and matching polka dot umbrella.

Brandy lurched across the room. She opened the purse and released the smell of pine and something metallic. Turning it upside down, she emptied the contents—two flat stones, a few pennies, and half a dozen tiny pinecones. Then she remembered the pocket on the left side of the purse with its nearly invisible zipper. Emily called it her secret hiding place.

Brandy unzipped it and plunged her fingers into the pocket. The necklace wasn't there. She sat on the floor, closed her eyes again, and tried to remember the last time she'd seen Emily with the necklace. Little by little, the memory returned. Emily had been playing on the floor with her Matchbox cars. She'd tucked the necklace into her pink Mustang convertible and launched it across the room where it had banged into the wall beneath the window.

It was a long shot, but worth a chance. Brandy lifted the grate covering the heater vent, and there it was nestled on an aluminum ledge. She took a hanger from Emily's closet, fashioned it into hook and fished out the necklace.

She ran through the house, looking for Radhauser, and found him in her father's study. "I've got it." She dropped the pendant into Detective Radhauser's open hand. "It's a clue, right?"

He held the necklace up to the light.

"Do you think whoever gave her that necklace is responsible for her disappearance?" Brandy asked.

"Maybe," he said, dropping the necklace into a small evidence bag that he slipped into the inside pocket of his blazer. "To tell you the truth, I hope so."

Brandy cringed. "Why?"

"It beats some of the alternatives."

"You mean like pedophilia or child pornography?"

Radhauser held her gaze. "I know how scared you must be. That necklace may be nothing more than an innocent gift. Or something Emily found in the park. But if it is connected to her disappearance, it might be a good sign. Where did you find it?"

She told him.

"That was clever thinking," he said.

Brandy looked at the floor, then told Radhauser how Emily believed her big friends loved her.

"That's what I mean," Radhauser said. "Of all the kid

snatchers, give me one that loves them any day."

Brandy wanted so much to believe him, but remembered a man she'd seen on the news—a man who had claimed to love the little girls he'd forced into sexual acts.

* * *

After Radhauser left with the necklace, Brandy sat at the kitchen table across from Officer Corbin and waited for her dad to call. She tucked her hands, palms together, between her knees. All at once, her legs started hopping up and down as if they had little motors inside them. She flattened her heels in a futile attempt to stop the shaking.

"This could have happened to anyone," Corbin said.

Her eyes filled. She turned away.

Christine burst into the kitchen, out of breath and gulping for air. She leaned against the refrigerator and sucked in a few more breaths. "The park is mostly deserted. But there are reporters everywhere. They practically chased me into the house." She stared at the quiet phone. "Has anyone called?"

Corbin shook his head.

"I need to do something," she said. "What can I do?"

Corbin reminded her that they'd initiated an AMBER alert and notified the Oregon Missing Children's Clearinghouse.

"What about the FBI?" Christine said.

"They are aware of what's happened and are watching the case. The best thing you can do is remain calm in case we get a call."

Christine grabbed the sippy cup from the tray on Emily's highchair and held it so tight the knuckles on her right hand turned pale. "Yeah, right. Calm."

The clock on the stove ticked as regular as a heartbeat. Six thirty-three. But the seconds seemed like hours. And the minutes dawdled as if each one held an entire day. "I'll make another pot of coffee," Brandy said.

When she reached into the cabinet for the filters, Brandy saw the bag of red jellybeans they kept on the top shelf so Emily wouldn't make herself sick by eating all of them at once.

She closed the cabinet and stood with her palms against the door, her face resting on her hands. They'd been so careful about something as small and harmless as a bag of jellybeans.

The doorbell rang. All three of them ran for it.

The shorthaired police officer with the Rattlesnake earrings stood on the porch. "I've made calls to the elementary and middle schools about Kent. They're tracking down the lists. I checked out the Little Theater," she told Corbin. "Get word to Radhauser that today's rehearsal was canceled." The officer stepped into the entryway.

Corbin turned to Christine. "Do you have any reason to believe Kathleen Sizemore could be involved?"

"No way," Brandy said. "Kathleen loves Emily. Whenever I was at the park with her, Kathleen never let Emily out of her sight."

The female officer locked gazes with Corbin, then jotted a note on her clipboard.

Christine leaned forward, a bright patch of color in each pale cheek. "Involved? What a perfect word. Kathleen knew my husband for years. They lived together in this house." Christine stopped talking and gazed blankly at Brandy. "He never even bothered to tell me until after I got pregnant," she added, her words painfully slow, as if this memory had been dragged from her and added to the misery of Emily's disappearance.

"You make it sound like Kathleen is some kind of home-wrecker. Of course she lived here." Brandy tried to keep her voice steady. "She was my nanny and our housekeeper."

"Grow up." Christine's mouth tightened. "Kathleen hates me. And I'm tired of protecting you."

"Protecting me from what?" Brandy asked, both transfixed and horrified by Christine's bitterness. Her stepmother was hysterical, but it still frightened Brandy to see her like this. "I want to know what you think you're protecting me from."

"Never mind," Christine said, her gaze intent on her stepdaughter. "But if you'd protected Emily, she'd be sitting in that highchair right now eating pasta for dinner."

"That's enough." Brandy said sharply. "And if you'd stayed home from your luncheon, or taken Emily with you, she wouldn't have been at the park. Blaming me or anyone else, is a waste of time and it won't bring us any closer to finding her."

Christine stared at Brandy, her face softening. "You're right," she whispered, then turned and walked away.

"I don't care what kind of fairytale she's concocted," Brandy said. "Kathleen would never take Emily."

The female officer stepped further into the entryway and shut the front door. "Inform Radhauser I also talked to the boyfriend's mother. His story checks out. He was home, helping her wash the car, until about 3:15. That wouldn't give him enough time to get to the park until after Emily disappeared."

"He's not my boyfriend," Brandy said for what felt like the hundredth time, but no one appeared to be listening. She sat on the bench in the entryway, willing herself to focus her thoughts and actions on finding Emily.

The phone rang.

Both Christine and Brandy raced into the kitchen.

Christine lunged to snatch it up before the first ring had completed its trill.

Corbin held up his hand to stop her. "Don't forget to let it ring three times," he said, slipping on the earphones. "If it's someone claiming to have Emily, try to keep them on the line so I can get a location. Ask questions or say you don't understand. It will give us time to listen for inflections and background noise. And ask for proof of life. Ask to talk to Emily."

Panic caught in Christine's eyes and unfolded across her face. "Do you think Emily is dead?"

"No," he said. "But we always ask to talk to the kidnapped individual."

Christine answered, her voice shaking so hard that Brandy had to look away. "Hello. Who is it?"

Christine listened. "No," she screamed. "I'm not interested in a home security system. Not now. Not ever. Don't you see it's too late?" She slammed the receiver down.

When the phone sounded again, Christine was in the living room.

Brandy's heart made an extra beat. After three rings, she picked up. "Michaelson residence, Br—"

"It's not Emily," her dad said. "I'm outside the emergency room. The little girl's parents are here now."

Brandy's knees nearly buckled in relief. Somehow it seemed important to know that this child, who might have been Emily, would recover. "Is she going to be all right? Is she hurt badly? What happened to her?"

"Apparently the family had six kids in a van and when the mother took them all in to use the restroom, she left one behind. I don't how that can happen, but it looks like it did."

Christine must have overheard part of the conversation. She raced toward the garage. "Oh my God. Tell him I'm on my way. Tell Emily Mommy will be right there."

Realizing her stepmother assumed the child was Emily, Brandy handed the receiver to Officer Corbin. She chased after Christine, grabbing her around the waist and pulling her away from the car. "It isn't Emily."

Christine jerked forward, then turned around, her face mottled with color as bright as welts. She looked at Brandy with an odd expression, one Brandy wasn't sure how to interpret. "This is my fault. I should have taken her with me. I should have been a better mother."

Brandy had never seen Christine so scared before, and she wanted to be patient with her. "Don't blame yourself. It was an accident," she said, avoiding Christine's eyes.

"It might not have made any difference," Christine whispered. "But I wish you'd told me the truth about the necklace."

Brandy stiffened. "Me, too. But I didn't want you to hit her again."

Christine looked stricken. "I ask you to watch her too much."

"But usually I don't mind. I…I…"

While Christine rolled Emily's tricycle to the far side of the garage, Brandy headed toward the door leading into the kitchen.

Beside the concrete steps, a pair of Emily's yellow rain boots sat on the floor, one small boot tipped over on its side.

Brandy couldn't move.

"Brandy," Officer Corbin said. "Your dad wants to talk to you again."

Corbin handed Brandy the phone, then stepped away.

"Are you still there, Dad?"

"Yes. Is Christine all right?"

"She thought the little girl at the gas station was Emily."

"Radhauser wants to broadcast Emily's picture on the news," her dad said. "He thinks the publicity might help. That someone may have seen her. I'm not sure Christine can handle it, but he thinks she should make a statement. Apparently, mothers make a bigger impact."

Brandy stared at the window over the sink. Outside, the daylight gradually faded. Emily was afraid of the dark, and had a Pooh bear nightlight in her room.

"I know it's asking a lot, but I need you to stay strong," her father said.

"Almost three and a half hours have passed, Dad. I'm really scared."

He was quiet. "I am, too," he finally said.

When she hung up, Corbin paged Detective Radhauser. A minute later, the detective phoned back. Corbin relayed the new information Officer McBride had provided.

Brandy updated Christine on the news broadcast. She would have liked to talk to her stepmother about a lot of other things. Feelings she had about Emily. Regrets about her resentment toward her stepmother and not ever telling Christine how much she loved Emily. But she remained silent—knowing she'd already told her stepmother the worst of all possible things.

CHAPTER TEN

Clutching the flyers, Brandy listened to her cowboy boots strike the pavement as she ran. The beat seemed way too slow. She intended to trace the path she and Emily usually took home from the playground, and talk to everyone who lived in a house either backing up to or facing Lithia Park.

She forced herself to run faster, and didn't stop until she reached the park. The area around the playground and restroom was still cordoned off, and uniformed officers searched, picking debris off the ground and moving bushes aside with long sticks.

Brandy leaned against an oak tree to catch her breath, then crossed the bridge over Ashland Creek, looking for any signs of her little sister. Other than patrol cars, there were only a dozen or so vehicles parked in the Winburn lot, but Brandy looked inside each one. She hammered on the trunks with her fists, just in case someone had left one open and Emily had crawled inside and fell asleep. After all, she'd gotten up early from her nap. Brandy imagined Emily curled into a corner behind a spare tire with her thumb in her mouth.

When Brandy found no one in the cars, she ran across the parking lot, took Winburn to Granite, past the Perozzi Fountain and the Japanese Garden, with its lacy-leafed maples, to the row of restored Victorian and Craftsman houses that faced the park. She'd ring every doorbell. Emily couldn't have gotten far. Maybe someone saw her and invited her inside. The muscles in Brandy's neck relaxed a little as she pictured Emily eating oatmeal cookies with a dishtowel tied around her neck like a bib.

But then her mind shifted to other, darker, scenarios. Emily's mouth taped shut. Her small arm belted to an iron pipe. Brandy cringed and forced herself to think about a positive outcome. Lots of retired people lived in Ashland. And they noticed things, especially when they faced a busy park. Maybe someone sitting in their living room, or on the front porch, or working in their backyard had looked up and seen Emily go by.

Brandy took a deep breath, let it out slowly, then climbed the brick steps to the first porch. It was a Craftsman bungalow, painted gray with burgundy trim. She rang the bell. The sun was just beginning to set and Brandy longed to move the clock back so that it was rising instead. She shuddered, thought of herself as Emily, trying to find her way home in the growing dark. She rang again. No one answered.

During the next four house visits, Brandy timed herself. Each stop took about ten minutes, the first three spent pounding on the door and then trying to explain that she wasn't selling anything. At the fourth house, a young man with black hair sticking up in spikes all over his head opened the door, glanced at her then shut it in her face. The sudden thwack of the door slamming enraged Brandy and she hammered on it with her fists.

He opened the door, chin raised in a subtle challenge. "I'm not deaf." His thick eyebrows rose at the same speed as his voice, as his gaze settled on the stack of flyers in her hands. "What is it you're taking orders for?"

Brandy straightened her shoulders and looked him in the face. She knew how to play a convincing role, to turn words into a living, breathing story. A story someone would listen to. "I'm not selling anything. I know I'm bothering you. And I'm usually polite and would have gone away when you shut the door." She gave him a wide-eyed, sincere look. "But this is a real emergency."

"I'll give you one minute," he said.

"My little sister is in danger. She's not even three years old. When she giggles, it makes everyone in the room want to laugh, too. She doesn't go anywhere without her Pooh bear. Someone may have kidnapped Emily from Lithia Park. The bear was left in her stroller. I know she's sad and crying now and she might be hurt. Please, I have to find her." Her eyes welled. There were tears in her voice, too. "Just look at her picture." She showed him the photograph.

"I already told the police I didn't see her," he said after looking at the photo. "I'm sorry."

Brandy thanked him and hurried on to the next house. The door had a brass knocker mounted just below two small windows. She used it, the sound hollow and urgent.

An old man answered. He wore a grey cardigan with a mustard stain on the front. "I'm sorry," he said. "I always used to order whatever any kid was selling. I bought donuts and Girl Scout cookies, those candy bars the Little League teams used to sell." He paused and shrugged. "But I live with my daughter now. And I'm on social security and a special diet." His eyes were watery and pale blue, but there was a kindness in them. He started to close the door.

"I'm not selling anything." She gave him her spiel. "My little sister is about as tall as a yardstick. Her name is Emily." Brandy handed him a flyer with Em's photo.

"I'm sorry. My daughter already talked to a detective. Your sister's a cute little girl, but I wasn't anywhere near the park today." He shook his head. "All those kids. They give me a headache." A small dog, some kind of poodle mix, barked and jumped on the old man's legs. He reached down to pet it.

"Emily is brave but she's afraid of the dark," Brandy said. "And someone might be hurting her right now. Please, just think for a minute. Did you see anything outside your window? A little girl with brown curly hair? Maybe she seemed lost. Or maybe you saw someone carrying a child who looked scared." Brandy gulped in some air.

He shook his head. "I didn't see anything. I was in my backyard most of the day. But you might check with Mrs. Wyatt. Three doors up. Ever since her husband died, she never leaves her house. That woman stays glued to her front window with a pair of binoculars like one of them surveillance cops."

"If you remember anything. Anything at all, please call the

number on the flyer."

"Don't ring her doorbell," he cautioned, speaking louder now as if she'd suddenly grown deaf. "She'll hide. And she won't answer. But tell ya what. Suppose I call her and say you're coming. If she wants to talk to you, she'll leave the front door open."

Brandy thanked him and hurried down the steps to the sidewalk. She ran past the next two houses. She'd go back once she'd talked to Mrs. Wyatt.

In the house next door to Mrs. Wyatt's, someone played the piano—tenuous, one note at a time, as if searching for a tune. Maybe he was a composer. Ashland was filled with artists, actors and musicians. Artists were kind people. Surely no one who made art would hurt a little girl like Emily.

When Brandy stepped onto Mrs. Wyatt's porch, a woman edged the drapes aside and peered out.

Brandy attempted a smile.

The curtains closed.

She heard the heavy sound of footsteps as Mrs. Wyatt crossed the room.

The door opened.

Brandy took an instinctive step back. Mrs. Wyatt was the fattest woman Brandy had ever seen.

"You must be the girl with the missing sister. Mr. Collins phoned and said you'd be coming."

Mrs. Wyatt had thick gray curls and wore a pair of khaki pants and a short-sleeved, black shirt big enough to fit a rhinoceros. Her arms were fleshy and thick as tree trunks.

She grabbed a flyer from Brandy and studied Emily's photo. "Come inside," she said, then lumbered over to a sagging blue plaid sofa, pausing twice to catch her breath.

Brandy fought her revulsion and followed. The dimly lit living room smelled like mothballs, garbage, and fish sticks. The room had the musty, oppressed feeling of a house that never opened its windows.

Mrs. Wyatt's belly hung down between her legs when she sat, facing a television that was turned to some cop show, but muted.

Brandy glanced around. The room looked like one of those places that package and ship things. UPS, FedEx boxes and bubble wrap were strewn everywhere. Piles of receipts littered the coffee and end tables. Newspapers stacked up in the corners.

"I don't drive anymore," she said, as if reading Brandy's thoughts. "I order what I need." She shrugged and swept the room with her gaze. "And a lot of things I don't." She offered an apologetic smile.

Through an archway into the kitchen, Brandy saw containers from Pizza Hut and Kentucky Fried Chicken. Brown Chinese food boxes with little wire handles. And delivery bags from Greenleaf and other restaurants on the Plaza were lined up on the kitchen counters.

Trying to keep the shock off her face, Brandy gave Mrs. Wyatt her spiel about Emily and waited, eager to get back outside into the fresh air. "Did you see anything?"

Mrs. Wyatt clutched the hem of her shirt. Her hands were plump and dimpled, her fingernails perfectly manicured and painted hot pink. "I watch people coming and going from the park all day." Her gaze traveled to the windowsill where a pair of binoculars sat, lenses down, on the ledge. "No one would believe the things I witness."

Brandy felt sorry for her. "Did you see anything out of the ordinary this afternoon between 3:15 and 3:30?"

"I don't know. I saw a lot of things. What happened to your cheek?"

Brandy couldn't waste time being evasive. "An escalator accident when I was three. Did you see my little sister by herself or…" She swallowed. "Or with someone?"

"I'm sorry about your face. Did you fall?"

"Tripped over my shoelaces." Brandy's gaze found the binoculars again. "Were you watching the park today?"

"Plastic surgery works wonders. I saw this program—"

"I've had more than a dozen surgeries. The police say our best bet at finding my sister alive is during the first twenty-four hours. Please, Mrs. Wyatt, I'm begging you. Did you watch through your binoculars today?"

"I don't have much to do anymore," she said, lowering her gaze. "So, I watch people."

Such a sad life. "That's great. I was hoping to find someone like you who keeps a lookout for innocent little kids like my baby sister. So, please, Mrs. Wyatt, what did you see today?"

"It was an unusual day," the fat woman said. "So much activity. I love music. And there were so many little children. All those bear costumes."

"I know," Brandy said. "Just look at Emily's photo again."

Mrs. Wyatt studied the picture of Emily on the swing for another long moment and then shook her head.

"Close your eyes," Brandy said. "Sometimes that helps me remember things."

When Mrs. Wyatt nodded, her four separate chins folded in on each other like a Chinese fan. "It was probably nothing."

"You never know when something might be important. Did you see her? Was she alone? Or did someone…"

Mrs. Wyatt opened her eyes. And for the first time, Brandy noticed they were thick-lashed, beautiful and dark, the iris nearly as black as the pupil. "I can't be sure."

"But you do remember something, I can tell."

Mrs. Wyatt said nothing.

Brandy's hands shook and she couldn't keep the flyers from trembling. She had to find a common ground, something that would make Mrs. Wyatt trust her enough to tell her what she'd seen. "I've been blaming myself for what happened to Emily. You see, she's my half-sister and sometimes I'm jealous because she's so perfect. Everyone talks about how beautiful she'll be when she grows up. And I have these scars that make people turn away from me. Like I'm some kind of freak."

The woman's fleshy face filled with sympathy. She knew what it was like to be seen as a freak. "You're like a willow branch, so slender and beautiful. Don't let the scars take your life away." Her voice was wistful and she kept nodding, as if she understood and felt everything Brandy had ever endured.

"I did see a person," Mrs. Wyatt finally said. "A man, I think, in a Pooh bear costume. He put a little girl into a car seat and drove off. What struck me as strange is he didn't take off the bear head. And it was pretty awkward for him getting into the front seat. He still had it on when they drove out of the lot. The girl had dark hair, but I can't be sure she was your sister. And he could have been one of the workers. It could have been his own child."

Brandy tried to keep her voice calm. "Could you see what the little girl was wearing? Did she have on a jacket?"

"I don't know," Mrs. Wyatt said. "Maybe something red."

Brandy had to refrain from leaping into the air. "Like a red corduroy jacket?"

"I can't be sure. But I think so."

"What kind of car?"

"I don't know. Maybe a station wagon or one of those minivans. A grey or blue/grey color. I'm not good with makes and models."

"Do you know what time this occurred?"

Mrs. Wyatt shook her head.

Brandy glanced across the room at the television set. "What were you doing? Were you watching a program?"

"I think it was around 3:30 or so. Oprah was about half over. It was during the commercial break." She attempted to get off the sofa, but failed and had to rock several times before she stood. "I'm sorry I can't be of more help."

Brandy tried to contain her excitement. This was an important lead. "But you did help. Would you be willing to tell the police what you told me?"

"No." Mrs. Wyatt made her way toward the door. "The police don't like me. I've called them before. They never believe anything I say."

"Why not?" Brandy asked.

She shrugged her massive shoulders. "Who knows? But I won't talk to them. Not ever again. Besides, I didn't really see anything that would hold up in court. Lots of little girls have brown hair."

"I don't care about court," Brandy said. "This is my little sister's life."

About halfway to the front door, Mrs. Wyatt paused and caught her breath. "You could stay for a while if you like. I have some fresh cookies I had delivered from the bakery. You must be hungry."

Brandy needed to talk to Radhauser. "Thank you. Maybe some other time."

"Did I tell you about my brother's son? The way he got lost on a camping trip."

Quickly placing both hands over one of Mrs. Wyatt's, Brandy said, "I'll come back after we find Emily. You can tell me anything you want." Brandy vowed she'd take out the trash, wash the dishes and do whatever she could to help this woman. Mrs. Wyatt said she loved music. Maybe Brandy would bring her guitar and play some songs. She'd force herself not to think about the smell inside the house or all the empty food cartons.

Brandy opened the front door. "Thanks for talking to me," she said, realizing how much it had cost this woman to let anyone inside.

CHAPTER ELEVEN

Brandy raced up her own street to the driveway, hoping Radhauser was still there. Reporters from the local television and radio stations who'd been loitering on the periphery of their house now swarmed around the porch, pencils and pads at the ready. It was dark now and the yard lit up like a stage set.

She pushed her way through the crowd to get to Radhauser who was talking to the videographer. Brandy tugged on the sleeve of his denim jacket. "I just talked to a woman who—"

"Not now," he said without looking at her. "We're about to go live on Channel 12."

A blonde woman wearing skinny denim jeans, high heels, and a teal blue jacket, finger combed her hair, then turned to Christine. "Are you ready?"

"Please," Brandy said to Radhauser. "It's important."

He raised his finger to silence her. "This won't take long."

She backed away, stood over to one side, and watched a photographer angle a camera at Christine. When the flash went off, her stepmother grimaced and turned her head away.

With video cameras running, Christine stood on the front steps, her eyes red from crying, and made a tearful and heartfelt plea for the safe return of her daughter. She announced the family was offering a $5,000 reward for information leading to her return. "Emily is just a little girl. She's spunky and full of mischief and life. She loves her Pooh bear, her big sister, Brandy, and Bing cherry ice cream cones. Her daddy and I miss her so much, and she needs to come home to her family." As if she'd exhausted all her reserve to stay calm, Christine's voice wavered, rose and fell before it dropped to a whisper. "All we want is Emily's safe return."

Brandy's stepmother had changed so much in the past few hours that she no longer looked anything like the sassy redhead who'd left to attend her mother's birthday luncheon. Above them, helicopters hovered, casting their strobes onto the ground like spotlights. With the thump-thump of the rotor blades, Brandy's shoulders relaxed a little. If Emily were out there alone, surely those helicopters would find her.

Her father hurried over and stood beside Christine. He draped one arm around her waist to help hold her up.

Radhauser took the microphone and introduced himself. "At this time, we've issued an AMBER Alert," he said to the reporters. "And a hotline has been…"

Brandy, too excited to listen, bounced up and down on the balls of her feet and reviewed the things she wanted to say to Radhauser. *Hurry up*, she kept thinking as he held up the photo of Emily, relating the height, weight and description she'd given him. He slowly recited the hotline phone number. And then, as if to be sure, he said it again.

As soon as he put the microphone back into the news commentator's hand, Brandy rushed to Radhauser again. "I think I uncovered an important clue."

The blonde commentator straightened the collar of her blouse and flashed her brilliant, toothy smile. "There's a subdued atmosphere here in the mountainside town of Ashland, Oregon, as neighboring communities join forces in the search for…"

Radhauser pulled Brandy away from the crowd of reporters. "Be careful what you say. You'll have those news hounds chasing you everywhere."

She quickly told him what she'd learned from Mrs. Wyatt. "It makes sense. Emily wouldn't be afraid of someone dressed up as Pooh." She tried to keep her voice calm, to sound like a professional. "Mrs. Wyatt was pretty sure the little girl wore a red jacket."

He gave her a look that was a mixture of pity and warning. "Look. The police have already interviewed residents on Granite.

And we've had a lot of contact with this Wyatt woman. She's called in dozens of suspicious things she allegedly saw in the park."

"What kind of things?"

He stared at her, as if considering how much to say. "Kids on rollerblades she called aliens. A young couple making out in the back seat. She phoned it in as a rape and murder in the Winburn lot."

Brandy squeezed her fists shut as if she could crush his words. "I think she's telling the truth this time."

"I'll talk to her."

"No," she said.

One of the reporters shot a worried glance at her, then quickly looked away.

She lowered her voice. "Don't do that. Mrs. Wyatt begged me not to tell the police."

"I'm not surprised," Radhauser said.

The spotlights that made the yard seem as bright as a sunny afternoon went out, and it took a moment for her eyes to adjust to the darkness.

"It's not because she's lying." Brandy's voice sounded squeaky and a little too high. "She's just embarrassed about her weight." She thought about Mrs. Wyatt stuck in her garbage-filled house, curled up in her own loneliness.

Radhauser said nothing.

"I don't care what you think," Brandy said. "We should check with the costume shops. See if anyone rented a Pooh."

A local newsman carried a tripod and video camera across the front yard to his van.

Radhauser dropped a hand onto her shoulder. "You're thinking like a detective, kid. And that's good. Believe me, I don't take any leads lightly. We'll contact every costume shop within a fifty-mile radius of Ashland." He hurried off to the patrol car he'd parked in their driveway.

Brandy watched him drive away, then trudged around the side of the house where she could be alone. She tried to keep her mind from skipping ahead to scenes she didn't want to imagine.

The sun had set, casting streaks of purple and orange low in the sky. She sat on the grass with her back against the oak tree outside her bedroom window. When she wrapped her arms around her knees, her limbs felt numb as if they'd fallen asleep. She didn't care what Detective Radhauser thought. She'd developed a rapport with Mrs. Wyatt and there was no way she'd lie about what she'd seen.

* * *

Radhauser needed to find out the extent of Kathleen Sizemore's relationship with Daniel Michaelson. How she felt about Christine. And where she was this afternoon when Emily disappeared.

As he drove toward Kathleen's house, Radhauser couldn't get the image of Christine and Daniel Michaelson as they stood in front of the news cameras out of his mind. The life had gone out of them. They were two people as absent from themselves and each other as the little daughter they were so frantic to find.

Radhauser imagined what he and Gracie would look like, standing in front of a wall of reporters, if Lizzie had gone missing. He wished he felt more positive about the hotline, but experience had taught him most of the calls were useless, lonely people in search of attention—or just plain nut jobs like Mrs. Wyatt. But he couldn't take any chances. Perpetrators sometimes called—seeking the thrill of taunting the police.

It was dark when Radhauser parked the patrol car in front of Kathleen Sizemore's house on Vista. What he assumed to be her teal blue Taurus was in the driveway.

He jogged up a set of concrete steps to a pathway lined with solar lights tucked in among yellow, red and purple flowers. Gracie would be able to identify them all. Radhauser recognized only the daffodils. The beds had been recently mulched and smelled of pine bark.

The house, one of the garage-less Craftsman bungalows built in the fifties and so popular in Ashland, was set on a hill and painted a soft shade of yellow with dark blue trim. While he was taken in by the neatness of the little house and everything that it said about the woman who lived here, he thought about the old saying, *hell hath no fury like a woman scorned.* And he remembered Millie, a waitress in Tucson who'd murdered her ex-lover's current girlfriend—not because he'd left Millie for this other woman, but because the new woman had hurt Millie's man in a pretty horrific way.

He double-checked the numbers beside the door with the address Daniel had provided, and then rang the bell.

Light flooded over the porch. Someone peeked out between the lace-curtain panels that covered the door's window.

Radhauser waited.

A small woman, wearing a gray-flowered dress with a peach-colored sweater draped over her shoulders, answered. She had walnut brown hair, streaked with silver she hadn't tried to hide with hair coloring. A woman secure in herself—one without pretense. Her eyes were kind and the rich brown color of dark chocolate.

He took off his Stetson. "Are you Kathleen Sizemore?"

She nodded.

He removed his badge from his jacket pocket and introduced himself.

Her eyes widened as she took a step back. Her gaze wandered over his jacket, his jeans, and then landed on his boots. "Are you sure you're a police officer?" She spoke to him through the screen door.

"Detectives are rarely in uniform. I'm here to ask some questions about Emily Michaelson."

Her brow furrowed. "It's terrible. I saw Christine on the news. I've been trying to call Brandy. Is she all right?"

"She's a strong kid. And she's trying hard to help."

Kathleen scrutinized him for another moment, as if trying to determine if he was safe enough to invite inside. "Why aren't you out looking for Emily?"

"I am. It's why I'm here."

Her mouth stayed open, as if the full implication of what he'd said dawned on her. "I can assure you Emily is not with me."

"I didn't think she would be. I'm talking to everyone who

knew Emily."

She opened the storm door.

He stepped inside.

"I left tea water boiling on the stove. Would you mind talking in the kitchen?"

Though Kathleen was probably not any older than Radhauser, he felt as if he were entering his Boston-raised grandmother's house. Maybe the best way to get Kathleen to open up was to have tea with her.

Her hands were so white he half expected them to leave a floury print on her skirt as she wiped them. A woodsy smell seemed to linger on her clothes, as if she'd just taken them from a cedar-lined closet.

As she led him through her house, he took in the details, trying to get a feel for the person who lived here. The living room was furnished with an overstuffed sofa and chairs upholstered in a blue and yellow flowered fabric. Above the sofa hung at least twenty needlepoint pictures, expertly done, framed in dark wood and artfully arranged. His mother and grandmother had done needlepoint. Some of Kathleen's looked like antiques. Even if she'd purchased them, they told him she was an old-fashioned woman who took pride in her home and in the traditions of her female ancestors. The kind of woman who'd be scandalized by her lover's affair with his student.

They passed through what was meant to be the dining room, but Kathleen used it to house her piano, an old mahogany upright that hosted an assortment of framed photographs, most of which he recognized as Brandy. In all of them, she'd turned her scarred cheek away from the camera.

In the kitchen, he took a seat at a round oak table that looked out on a small backyard. He set his Stetson on it, crown down.

She gave him a look that said she didn't approve of hats on the kitchen table and nodded toward an extra chair.

He'd go ahead and humor her, if it would help put her at ease. He picked up the Stetson and placed it on the seat cushion.

"Would you care to join me?"

When he nodded, she handed him a saucer and bone china teacup. Her hand trembled slightly as she placed a matching plate of oatmeal cookies on the table in front of him. What was she hiding?

After pouring him a cup and covering the teapot with a quilted cozy, Kathleen took the seat across from him. "Are you sure Brandy's okay? I know she must be terrified and I'm worried sick about her."

"You'd be proud of her."

"I always have been. Now what is it you want from me?"

"The answers to some routine questions." It was a canned reply and Kathleen was astute enough to know it, but too well-mannered to say anything.

Her gaze found his, and for the span of several heartbeats their eyes held.

She looked away.

He could tell by her expression she knew he wasn't being entirely straightforward. "Do you own a garnet heart necklace set between two diamond-looking stones?"

"No," she said. "I didn't give that necklace to Emily."

"Brandy told you about it."

She nodded.

"Did it seem suspicious to you?"

"I know for a fact Brandy called every parent in Emily's preschool class, because she did it from my phone. No matter what Christine might be saying, Brandy is a responsible young woman, Detective Radhauser."

He said nothing, suspecting he'd get more information from Kathleen if he listened and took a soft-spoken approach. He nodded to encourage her to keep talking.

"I'm sure Brandy thinks this is her fault," Kathleen said, a flash of irritation in her eyes. "No doubt Christine's doing. I can tell you one thing for certain—Brandy is always careful with Emily."

"She seems like a responsible kid," he said, careful to keep judgment out of his voice. "But this time she left the stroller unattended."

Kathleen grimaced. "She's a teenager, and if you ask me, Christine expects far too much."

"Brandy says she often meets you in the park and that you never take your eyes off Emily."

"She reminds me a little bit of Brandy when I first met her."

Radhauser's radar went off. Maybe Kathleen wanted another chance to be a mother. But if so, what had she done with Emily?

"Have you noticed anything out of the ordinary when you meet Brandy in the park? Someone paying too much attention to Emily? Someone who appeared to be watching her?"

She told him about Kent and the way she'd warned Brandy to be vigilant. "I'm sure I overreacted the last time. It was this past Tuesday. April 20th, the same day those two boys went on that killing spree out in Colorado. Everyone was talking about it. Such a horrible tragedy." Kathleen paused and shook her head. "I told Brandy no one suspected those boys at Columbine were planning a mass murder either."

"Did she make Emily stop playing with him?"

"No, but she did talk with him."

"Do you know his last name?"

"I'm sorry. I don't."

"Are you sure?"

"Look, Detective Radhauser. If I could do something to help find Emily, don't you think I would? For Brandy's sake, if nothing else."

She had a point. Kathleen didn't strike him as the kind of woman who'd deliberately hurt someone she obviously loved. "Does Brandy take care of Emily often?"

"What do you think?"

"I'm asking the questions. How often does Brandy take care of her sister?"

"Nearly every afternoon on school days. And most of the day on Saturday."

He heard the resentment in her voice. "You don't like Christine Michaelson much, do you?"

She stared at him hard. "It's a complex situation."

He met her gaze, kept his steady. "Unravel it for me."

"Have you ever heard that crass saying? 'The more you stir excrement, the more it smells.' That's part of my past I prefer not to visit."

He smiled at what it must have taken for her to repeat those words. "I guess that saying is true, ma'am, but this is a kidnapping investigation."

"I didn't kidnap Emily, so I don't see why you need to probe into my private life."

He smiled. "You make me sound like a proctologist. Until she's found, everyone who had any connection to Emily is a suspect."

She sucked her bottom lip under her top row of teeth while she tried to find the words. And when she began to talk, she closed her eyes as if unable to witness herself saying them. "Daniel Michaelson hired me to take care of his little girl. She was three-and-a-half, scarred inside and out. I loved her from the moment I saw her, peeking at me from behind her dad's pant legs. After a few years, Daniel and I fell in love, too, and planned to marry."

She told him what he already knew—that she'd been Brandy's nanny since she and her father had moved to Ashland. She'd gotten Brandy involved in acting, and had encouraged her singing because Kathleen had understood it was a way for Brandy to grieve her mother; that the three of them had become a family.

Kathleen paused and shook her head, a look of profound sadness on her face. "Then one day Daniel came home and told me about Christine. He cried. Apologized. Asked for forgiveness." She paused, met his gaze, and lifted her eyebrows. "The usual clichés and platitudes. As pathetic as it sounds, I probably would have forgiven him. But he told me Christine planned to have the baby and he intended to marry her. Brandy was just fourteen. When I moved out, she stood on the front porch crying and begging me to take her with me."

Fourteen. Just one year older than his son, Lucas, had been when he died in the car accident—a vulnerable age, caught between the child and the adult they'd one day become. "I appreciate your being so candid," he said. Judging from the tears welling in the corners of her eyes, it hadn't been easy.

"I found out later Christine had a boyfriend. If you ask me, that baby could—" She took an audible breath. "I'm sorry. I'm not usually one for gossip."

Interesting. Wouldn't be the first time an old boyfriend showed up looking for his kid. "And you know about this boyfriend how?"

"I work part-time at the university. I saw them together on campus. It was no secret. Everyone in Liberal Arts was talking about it."

"What precisely were they talking about?"

She pursed her lips, hesitating. "I've already said too much."

"This is a kidnapping, Ms. Sizemore. A child's life is at stake."

"I wasn't there. But apparently he confronted Christine in the Student Union, in front of faculty and students."

"Confronted her about what?"

She picked up her linen napkin and wiped her mouth. "About the paternity of Christine's baby."

"You wouldn't happen to know this alleged boyfriend's name, would you?"

She lowered her gaze and directed her answer at the tabletop. "I don't remember."

Radhauser knew she was lying. "I think you do."

"Are you a psychic as well as a proctologist?"

"I interview enough people to know when someone is avoiding the truth."

She closed her eyes, nodded as if trying to pull a name from her memory. "Glenard," she said with her emphasis on the last syllable. "It's Gaelic. Glenard Dewar, like the scotch. He was a student at Southern Oregon University, just like Christine. He'd be a senior now."

Radhauser made a note of this new information. "Do you mind if I have a look around your house?"

"Whatever for? You can't possibly think I had anything to do with that child's disappearance."

"Where were you between 3 and 3:30 this afternoon?"

She sat back in her chair and shook her head. "Are you this… this rude with everyone?" She pressed her fingertips against her temples as if checking for an irregular pulse.

"I'm doing my job. I don't know anything about you. But some people would say you had motive to hurt Christine."

Kathleen picked up her teacup and carried it to the sink. The cup rattled against its saucer.

"You have a pretty good reason to hate her."

She turned to face him, blinked twice. "There's a price to hating. And I'm not willing to pay it. As for where I was at three o'clock today, a pipe broke at the Little Theater in Talent and our rehearsal was cancelled. So, I took advantage and went to Costco in Medford. Where do you think I got those oatmeal cookies you've been scarfing down?"

Heat rose on the back of his neck. He hadn't eaten since lunch. "Did you see anyone you knew there?"

"Not that I recall." She held her hands out in front of her. "Are you going to handcuff me and read me my rights, Detective Radhauser?"

"A little girl is missing. And her life may be in danger. I have to check out everything and fast. The first twenty-four hours are crucial."

"Go ahead. Look anywhere you want. Then maybe you'll start searching in a place Emily might actually be."

He checked the guest room that doubled as a sewing room, the bathroom, and Kathleen's bedroom. He opened closets and looked under the beds. Before he returned to the kitchen, he pulled down the ladder that led to the attic, jerked the long string that turned on the light, and climbed the stairs, Kathleen only a few steps behind him.

She stood with her back pressed against a supporting roof beam while Radhauser searched the attic.

Elaborate costumes hung from the rafters. He recognized Tin Man and Lion from *The Wizard of Oz*. Elizabethan costumes and fancy sequined gowns sparkled in the light from the single bulb. The attic smelled like mothballs.

On the off chance that Mrs. Wyatt was telling the truth this time, he needed to question Kathleen about the costumes.

"Did you make these?" he asked.

"Running a small theater and giving acting lessons doesn't pay the bills. I make a little extra money now and then sewing costumes for local theater groups."

"Were you asked to make any costumes for the Children's Health Fair?"

She shook her head.

"Have you ever made a bear costume?"

She cocked her head and stared at him. "Not so far. But I suppose I could if you need one."

CHAPTER TWELVE

Radhauser found the apartment building five blocks from the university, parked in a gravel lot, trudged up the three flights of stairs, and stopped on the landing of a small complex outside Apartment 3-B. He looked down into the beer-can littered courtyard and then rang the bell.

A tall, broad-shouldered young man answered. He had dark reddish-blond hair that hung over his collar—and deep-set eyes the color of new leaves. His eyebrows, even redder than his hair, had a funny arch to them that gave him a look of perpetual astonishment. He wore charcoal gray flannel pajama bottoms with zebras printed on them and a black and white striped rugby shirt. His feet were bare.

"Are you Glenard Dewar?"

The kid smiled, showing big white teeth that took over his whole face. "Depends on who wants to know. You're not with the FBI or IRS, are you?"

Radhauser showed his badge. "I have a few questions I need to ask you." He tucked his badge back into his jacket pocket and took off his Stetson.

Glenard didn't appear to be fazed by a visit from the police. He opened the door and gestured for Radhauser to enter. The apartment smelled like cigarette smoke and something deep-fried. "What's this all about?"

"Christine Michaelson," Radhauser said.

"Has something happened to Christine? Is she all right?" he asked, genuine concern on his face.

"She's okay." Radhauser did a quick scan of the scene.

115

The apartment was a studio, typical student fare, with a small, cluttered kitchen in one corner, a twin bed that doubled as a sofa near the sliding glass door that led to a four-by-eight foot patio, and a small wooden table with four chairs. Two tall bookcases were crammed full of paperback novels like *Moby Dick, The Scarlet Letter*, and *For Whom the Bell Tolls*. Row after row of textbooks, from Intro to Philosophy to the complete works of Camus and Nietzsche. It looked as if he'd kept every textbook he'd had during his four years at SOU—a fact that told Radhauser Glenard wasn't paying his own way through college.

A bag of partially unpacked groceries from the Ashland Co-op sat on the square table.

Radhauser tried to keep himself from being judgmental. This could have been his son's apartment, he thought, as he tried to imagine Lucas as a college senior—living alone—maybe in a studio like this one near the University of Arizona campus in Tucson.

Glenard paced across the kitchen, his hands jammed into his pockets. "If Christine is okay, then what's this really about? Is she in some kind of trouble?"

Radhauser pulled out one of the chairs, sat and took out his notebook. "Christine's two-and-a-half-year-old daughter was kidnapped this afternoon."

"Oh no. That's terrible." He pushed the groceries aside, pulled out the other chair and sat. He shot Radhauser a questioning look. "Believe me, I'm real sorry Christine is going through something like this with her kid. But why are you wasting time talking to me about it?"

"I understand, Glenard, that you used to date Ms. McCabe."

"If you don't mind, I prefer to be called Glen."

"Did you date Christine McCabe?"

"All through high school. And most of freshman year at SOU."

"So, she was your girlfriend?"

The lines on his face softened. "It depends on who you ask."

"I'm asking you."

"I thought she was."

"What does that mean?"

Glen settled his gaze on Radhauser, then drew it away—a movement Radhauser usually associated with guilt. But, if what Kathleen had told him was true, maybe it hurt this kid to talk about what really happened with Christine.

Radhauser suspected Christine had locked some major pain inside Glenard Dewar. And he wondered how far this jilted lover would go to pay her back.

"It means I didn't know she was banging old man Michaelson."

Radhauser had to give the guy credit for his honesty. "I'll bet that hurt."

Glen shrugged. "I'm over it." His voice went soft and his hangdog expression conveyed something different than his words.

In a flash, Radhauser thought about the night he'd tried to propose to Gracie. He'd stumbled over the words, desperate to say something unique to the two of them. But after what had happened to Laura and Lucas, Radhauser no longer believed in forever. Gracie had turned to him and smiled.

"I guess we're always a little bit in love with the first one," Radhauser said with a silent apology to Gracie for stealing her words.

Glen said nothing.

Radhauser tried again. "I'll bet it also pissed you off."

Glen's face reddened. "I wanted to kill the asshole."

"Christine or Michaelson?"

Glen leaned forward, as if intent on defending his position. "Who wouldn't have been pissed? Christine had picked out a wedding dress. And chosen her bridesmaids. We'd been planning it since tenth grade. In high school, we were voted senior couple most likely to get married."

Radhauser made another note, then looked Glen straight in the eyes. "Do you spend much time in Lithia Park?"

"I've been there a few times. Who hasn't? And I dated Christine, but I didn't kidnap her kid, if that's what you're getting at? Why would I?" He balled up the paper bag that had held his groceries and tossed it into the metal trashcan. When it hit the bottom, it made a low note that lingered in the silence.

"Maybe because you thought Emily was your daughter." Radhauser studied Glen's face for a sign, but the kid merely slumped further down in his chair.

Radhauser continued to push, hoping Glen would break out with something that might lead him to Emily. "Maybe you thought it was about time you got some visitation rights. Or maybe because she and the professor screwed you over and you wanted to get even."

Glen's face tensed. "Shit, man. Are you crazy?" He gestured with his arm, sweeping it around the apartment. "Does this look like a place to raise a kid?"

"How about your parents, Glen? They have any grandchildren?"

He straightened himself in the chair. "Yeah, matter of fact they do. My brother in Michigan has two little boys—five and seven."

"So, a little girl would round things off nicely."

Glen just stared at Radhauser, brow furrowing. "My parents love Oregon, but they moved to Michigan before Christine and I broke up so they could be closer to their grandkids. And besides, Christine swore the kid wasn't mine."

"Did you believe her?"

Glen's gaze sought the small, dusty window above the kitchen sink. "I…I don't know. I figured she'd have red hair if she were mine."

"How do you know she doesn't?"

"I saw her at the park with Christine."

"Did you talk to them?"

"No. I hightailed it out of there as fast as I could."

"I'm a father," Radhauser said. "And it's hard for me to believe you could walk away from a child who could be your daughter, without finding out for sure."

"I wanted Christine to get a DNA test to be positive, but she refused." He paused and shrugged. "I'm not all that into kids. The way I figure, I dodged a bullet."

"So, you were having sexual relations with Ms. McCabe in the fall of nineteen ninety-five? Say late October, early November."

"Look, I got an organic chemistry final tomorrow and I really need to get studying." He stood.

Radhauser remained seated. "And I've got a missing girl, maybe your daughter, and I need to find her. Now sit back down and answer my question."

Glen sat. "Yeah, Christine screwed around with both of us at the same time. But when I said the baby might be mine, she claimed our sex was too planned. Like I lacked spontaneity or something." He laughed without smiling and shook his head. "But she was right. We always used condoms."

"Condoms can fail. Were you in the park this afternoon between 3 and 3:45p.m.?"

"No."

"Where were you?"

"I went to a matinee at the Varsity Theater on Main Street."

"What time did it start?"

"Around 2p.m. I was there until after six."

"Did anyone go with you?"

He shook his head.

"What did you see?"

"After the Academy Award presentations, the theater brought back *Saving Private Ryan* and *Life is Beautiful*. I saw them both."

"Did you run into anyone you know there?"

Again, Glen shook his head. "It was dark, man."

Radhauser made another note. The Varsity Theater was only a few blocks from Lithia Park. "I need to take a look around, open up your closets, the kitchen cabinets, and check the bathroom." He gestured with his arm, sweeping it around the apartment. He wasn't about to leave any lead unchecked. "Is that okay?"

"Do I have a choice?" Glen said.

"Yes, but if you say no, I'll get a warrant."

Radhauser stood, stepped across the room and opened the door to the small bathroom, checked behind the shower curtain and in the linen closet. He found nothing there or anywhere else in the apartment, the storage locker assigned to Glen's unit, or the Volkswagen Beetle he kept parked in the gravel lot.

"I'll need contact information for your parents in Michigan."

"They don't know anything about that kid."

"I'll be discreet," Radhauser said. "Just give me the number. And don't plan on a spring break in Ft. Lauderdale. Or anywhere outside of Ashland."

Once inside his car, Radhauser made a note to check the Josephine and Jackson County Assessors offices to see if the senior Glenard Dewar, who loved Oregon, still owned property here.

* * *

It was 8:15p.m. when Radhauser got the call from McBride. "The boy's name is Kenton Jenkins, but everyone calls him Kent. He lives with his mother, Justine Jenkins, in a green Victorian on the corner of Pioneer and Vista." She gave him an address. "According to his teacher, he has a sweet disposition and the mind of a four-year-old. Apparently, he's shy around strangers."

Radhauser drove back to the Michaelson home to pick up Brandy for the interview. Nearly five crucial hours had passed since Emily's disappearance. He parked on a side street to avoid the reporters, and came in through the kitchen door.

McBride sat at the table, manning the phones and jotting notes onto interview forms.

"Where's Corbin?"

"He's warding off starvation," she said. "Did you have any luck with the pawn shops or lost and founds?"

He shook his head. "No one claimed to have seen the necklace before."

Radhauser found Brandy in the living room, frantically writing in a spiral notebook. She was desperate to help. And if Kent wouldn't speak to strangers, he hoped she'd get more information out of him than he could. He cleared his throat in an attempt not to startle her.

She looked up at him. "I'm making a list of the things we know so far. Did you check out that lead Mrs. Wyatt gave me?"

120

"We're compiling a list of costume rental shops. Most of them are closed now. But I'll have someone on it first thing in the morning. Right now, I need you to go with me to question Kent Jenkins. Find out if he saw anyone with Emily in the park this afternoon."

"Is it okay with my dad?"

"I cleared it with him."

She shot him a grateful look, then leaped off the sofa and practically ran to his car.

Five minutes later, he pulled into the driveway of the green Victorian, with the wraparound porch, on North Pioneer. It was dark, but there were spotlights on both sides of the house and others pointed up at the tops of the birch trees in the front yard.

Radhauser parked behind the gray Camry. He doubted Kent was involved, but maybe he saw something that could help. He rang the doorbell, Brandy at his side.

A plumpish woman opened the door. She wore baggy jeans, a man's T-shirt, and a pair of gardening gloves. She pushed her horn-rimmed glasses to the top of her clipped gray hair and stared at him. Her steel-colored eyes remained steady, but on guard.

"Are you Justine Jenkins?" Radhauser asked.

She nodded, wiped the front of her jeans with a gloved hand and smiled. "I was on the back porch planting the window boxes. There never seems to be enough daylight to get everything done."

"I'm Detective Radhauser from the Ashland Police Department." He showed her his badge. "I'd like to talk with you about your son."

Her smile faded instantly, the steel in her eyes darkened. "What's going on? Has Kent done something wrong?"

"You don't need to be concerned," Radhauser said, trying to put her at ease. "We don't think your son has done anything wrong. But a little girl disappeared from the park restroom this afternoon. Apparently, she and Kent liked to play together."

Radhauser introduced Brandy.

Mrs. Jenkins looked at Brandy, her head cocked. "Do I know you?"

121

"We've seen each other at the park," Brandy said. "I sometimes push both Kent and my little sister, Emily, on the swings."

"That's right," she said. "Kent really loves your little sister."

"May we come inside?" Radhauser asked, taking off his Stetson.

She moved aside so they could step into the house. It smelled like chocolate—something recently baked. She nodded toward an L-shaped sofa with fat green cushions, lining the back wall. Brandy and Radhauser sat.

Mrs. Jenkins removed her gloves, releasing their warm earth smell. She set the gloves on a small table and slipped her glasses off the top of her head and put them back on, then stood with her arm resting on the leather recliner across from the sofa.

"I heard about it on the radio." Mrs. Jenkins turned back to Brandy. "It must be awful for you and your parents, but Kent couldn't be involved. He's a good boy. He doesn't know he's big. He likes to play with stuffed animals like the little kids."

Radhauser slipped the necklace from his inside pocket and showed it to Justine. "Does this belong to you?"

"No. Do I look like I'd own something like that?"

It was the answer he'd expected. "I'd like Brandy to speak with your son. He knows her and may be less intimidated and more likely to talk to her than to me."

"Please," Brandy said. "You have to help us. I know Kent is a nice boy and my little sister likes him a lot."

Mrs. Jenkins started to pace, but kept talking as if she hadn't heard Brandy's plea. "Besides, I drop him off with his babysitter and pick him up every day. We left the park early this afternoon because Kent had a dentist appointment. After that we visited his grandma in Medford. You can check it out. He's been with me the whole time. Do you think he's been lugging around a toddler in his backpack?" She clutched her hands.

"We can do this here, or I can arrange for someone to talk with him at the police station."

"He's in the kitchen." She glanced at her watch. "I try to have him in bed by nine o'clock. I don't like to interrupt his routine."

Radhauser stood and stepped forward. "We won't take long."

Mrs. Jenkins led them into a bright yellow kitchen with black and white checkerboard tiles on the floor. Kent sat on a barstool with a half-full glass of milk and a plate with two chocolate chip cookies in front of him. He wore his white gloves and a pair of Superman pajamas—his stuffed Pooh bear seated on the next stool.

When Brandy touched his shoulder, he turned and grinned up at her.

"Hi," she said. "Do you remember me?" Just as Radhauser had instructed, she kept her voice low and non-threatening.

Kent nodded. "From the park. Emily's big sister."

Brandy smiled and showed him one of the flyers with Emily's photo on it.

He pointed a stubby, gloved finger at the picture. "Emily fly up high. She my friend."

Again, Brandy smiled at him.

He sucked his bottom lip. "My total name is Kenton Robertson Jenkins. But my mom calls me Kent. Superman's name was Clark Kent." He smiled. "I want to be a superhero, too."

"Emily likes playing with you a lot. And so, I'm hoping you can help me with something."

"Sure. You can be Lois Lane. I'll call you from the phone booth. I'm a good helper." He glanced at his mother, who stood in the kitchen doorway. "Just ask my mom."

"Did you see Emily today at the park?"

He nodded. "Sh…sh…sure. With Pooh bear."

Radhauser stood in the doorway next to Mrs. Jenkins. When Brandy shot a look toward him, he nodded. The kid was doing a good job.

"He stutters when he gets nervous," Mrs. Jenkins said.

Brandy lifted Kent's Pooh bear from the barstool beside him and sat. "Emily loves her Pooh bear."

Kent took the bear from Brandy and held a cookie to its embroidered mouth. "Me, too."

"I want you to think hard," Brandy said. "Was Emily in her

123

stroller when you saw her with Pooh bear today?"

He closed his eyes and scrunched up his face as if thinking. When he finally opened them, he grinned and shook his head. "N…N…No."

"Was I with her?"

Still shaking his head, he said no again. "A real Pooh carried her. He had balloons and wore gloves like mine." Kent held up his gloved hands, flapping them around nervously.

Brandy and Radhauser locked gazes.

He'd better pay Mrs. Wyatt a visit.

"Where did they go?" Brandy asked.

The boy shrugged. "Prob…probably P…P…Pooh Corner. Emily had a yellow balloon. It was pretty." He smiled and clapped his hands.

Great. Radhauser imagined the headline. *Kidnapped toddler found carrying a yellow balloon at Pooh Corner.* If only it could be true. If only they'd find Emily safe, and happy. He'd follow up and interview every person who'd rented a bear costume. But that would take time and manpower. Radhauser didn't have much of either.

Brandy gently took the boy's shoulders and looked him straight in the eyes. "Are you sure a for-real Pooh bear carried Emily?"

Kent nodded his head three times.

"It wasn't Teddy Bear, Smokey Bear or Panda?" Brandy said.

"No," he insisted. "It was a real Pooh bear. With a yellow shirt."

"Was Pooh bear big, like a grown-up?"

"Yep."

"Was Emily crying?"

He shook his head. "She was happy."

Again, Brandy shot Radhauser a look. He looked away, but not before he saw the hope in her eyes. Maybe Mrs. Wyatt really was telling the truth this time. Dressing up would be pretty clever of a kidnapper. Perfect for a health fair full of kids and bear costumes. A place where no one would be suspicious of a costumed pervert carrying a laughing toddler.

"Kent makes up stories about his stuffed animals all the time. He thinks they're real," Mrs. Jenkins said to Radhauser. "He has a great imagination."

"Before we go, I'd like to take a look at Kent's bedroom," Radhauser said.

"What for?"

"Because he was one of the last people to see Emily in the park."

"Do you think he has her hidden under his bed?"

Radhauser said nothing.

"Look as much as you want. You won't find anything."

While Kent finished eating his cookies, Mrs. Jenkins led them upstairs, down a hallway, and into a small, but neat bedroom with a twin bed, an ancient mahogany dresser, and bright yellow and green plastic cubes stacked four feet high and crammed with children's books, toys, and stuffed bears. The walls were covered with framed Winnie the Pooh prints. "Why does your son wear those white gloves?" Radhauser asked.

"When he was little, he tried to pick up a flaming log because he thought it was pretty." Her gaze landed on Brandy's cheek.

Brandy didn't turn away. "An escalator accident. But from what I understand, burns are more painful and leave the worst kind of scars."

Mrs. Jenkins winced. "Kent wears gloves because he thinks his scarred hands are the reason people stare at him."

Radhauser didn't know what to say.

"My Kent wouldn't hurt a flea," Mrs. Jenkins said.

Radhauser scanned the boy's bedroom. When he spotted the empty box of animal crackers in the wastebasket, he nodded to Brandy.

She covered her mouth with her hand and ran toward the wastebasket.

He pulled her back. "Do you keep these animal crackers on hand for him?"

"No," Mrs. Jenkins said. "I don't like him eating a lot of

preservatives. I don't have any idea where he got those."

"Do you mind if I take this empty box?"

She gave him a puzzled look. "No. Go ahead."

He slipped on a pair of latex gloves, lifted the box from the garbage and placed it inside an evidence bag.

"What's going on?" Mrs. Jenkins voice sounded higher, panicky.

Brandy looked as if all the air had left her chest. "I gave Emily a box of animal crackers like those. Just minutes before she disappeared. Is it okay if I ask Kent where he got them?"

"Oh my God." Kent's mother lifted her glasses and rubbed her eyes before she regained her control. "It doesn't mean anything. I told him never to ask for food. But people feel sorry for him. They give him things all the time."

Brandy touched Mrs. Jenkins' arms. "I don't believe Kent would do anything to hurt Emily. She probably gave them to him. We've been teaching her to share."

"Go ahead," Mrs. Jenkins said. "Ask him."

Brandy took the stairs, two at a time.

CHAPTER THIRTEEN

Back home, Brandy lingered in the hallway just outside Emily's bedroom, realizing how terrible their lives would be if they didn't find Emily alive. Brandy thought about what Kent had said when she'd asked him about the cookies. "I wanted to go with Emily. Big Pooh bear said no. But he gave me cookies."

Mrs. Wyatt had claimed to see a costumed person loading a little girl into a car seat around 3:30. If that person was the kidnapper, it was probably a good sign he'd used a car seat to keep Emily safe. For the first time since Emily disappeared, Brandy had some real hope that Emily wouldn't be harmed. Anyone who'd dress in a bear costume to entertain kids and give Kent cookies so he wouldn't be sad, was probably kind. She was grasping at straws. No kind person would take Emily in the first place.

Sleep. Brandy was so tired she could barely stand. But her mind was obsessed by two repeating questions: Had she seen anyone in the park wearing a Pooh costume? Had her subconscious registered the yellow T-shirt like the one on the bear in the toyshop window?

She paced the hallway for a few moments, wondering what to do next. Maybe the police had missed something in the park. Some clue connected to Emily that only Brandy would understand. Maybe retracing her steps would help her remember. She needed to go back, but her father would never allow it. She'd have to wait until he thought she was asleep.

The door to Emily's room stood ajar, and she pushed it open and turned on the light. Christine had spread a quilt over the comforter that covered the mattress. It was made from four appliquéd blocks that spelled out the word *love*. Small bears with butterflies on their noses wrapped themselves around each colorful letter. One of Christine's college friends had made the blanket for Emily's baby shower but, before today, Christine had thought it too beautiful to use. She'd packed it away in the top of Emily's closet.

Brandy turned toward the sound of Christine's bedroom door opening. Her stepmother leaned against the doorframe, staring into space. When she broke her trance, she turned and made eye contact with Brandy for an instant that had the impact of cymbals crashing.

"Where's Dad?" Brandy asked.

"He's at the police station getting a lie detector test."

"Is it okay if I take a shower?" Brandy smelled the scent of her own sweat. "I feel so dirty."

"Since when do you need my permission?"

"I didn't want to disappear in case you need someone to answer the door or the phone."

Her stepmother's eyes glazed over again. "Officer Corbin and I can handle the phone."

"I can shower later if that will make it easier."

Christine's whole face darkened. "Easier?" She lurched forward, bumped into the wall, then headed to the kitchen. Had she been drinking? She smelled of cigarettes and Brandy was pretty sure Christine had started smoking again.

Brandy locked herself in the bathroom. She closed her eyes. When the silence settled around her, she slumped on the closed toilet seat. She thought about Kent again, his claim that a big Pooh bear carried Emily. Maybe his mother was right. Maybe it was all a story Kent had made up. But that didn't make sense. He had the box of animal crackers. That couldn't be a coincidence. His story matched perfectly with what Mrs. Wyatt had said. Brandy needed to talk with Mrs. Wyatt again, see if she could learn anything more. Did the bear costume have a yellow shirt? Other than the big stuffed animal in the toy store window, Brandy had never seen a Pooh bear wearing a yellow shirt. The Disney version was red.

And the traditional Pooh wore no shirt.

Moving lights shone through the bathroom window, the headlights of a neighbor's car. The room brightened, then slid back into darkness.

She turned on the light. On the hook behind the door, Emily's nightgown hung, soft and pink as cotton candy.

Brandy hurried to the shower and pulled back the curtain to a tub piled with Emily's boats and rubber ducks, the set of dolphins Brandy had given her for Christmas.

She quickly picked them up and set them in the sink, then turned the shower to full blast. She stripped off her clothes and tossed them into the hamper. Adjusting the temperature so that it ran as hot as she could tolerate, she stepped into the tub, pulled the shower curtain closed, and stood under the steaming spray, hoping the needles of water would stab every cell of her body. She wanted them to work their way into her bones and keep her alert to search for Emily. She couldn't give in to the sadness. She had to stay strong.

When her legs began to shake, Brandy sat down in the bottom of the tub and let the water pound the top of her head. She was tempted to stay there, but knew she didn't have time for self-pity. She'd made a mistake, and now she had to fix it.

She stood, lathered her hair with Emily's apple-scented baby shampoo for good luck, then rinsed. The water cascaded, warm and soapy, over her skin. She closed her eyes and held the smell of her little sister for as long as she could stand, then flipped off the shower. *Please, God, let Emily be okay.*

Drenched and shuddering, she wrapped a towel around herself, another around her hair, then slipped quietly back into Emily's room. Brandy picked up Pooh bear from the line of stuffed animals Christine had arranged on Emily's dresser. Once inside her own bedroom, Brandy crammed the stuffed animal into her backpack. One thing was certain, whenever they found Emily, her little sister would want to see her friend.

Brandy pulled on a pair of blue jeans and a T-shirt. She ran a brush through her hair and then crept down the hallway and stood outside the door of her parents' bedroom, hoping to hear her father's voice. Once he'd returned, she could say goodnight and then execute her plan. She heard nothing except the television. "The Ashland Police Department is asking for your help in the kidnapping case of two-and-a-half-year-old Emily Michaelson. Emily disappeared from the restroom near the playground at Lithia…"

Brandy stepped into the room.

Christine sat on the foot of the bed, her face in her hands, rocking back and forth.

A blow up of Emily's picture, the one her dad had given the police, filled the entire television screen.

Brandy stepped closer, reached out and touched Christine's shoulder. She gave a start, as if she'd been burned, and Brandy quickly withdrew her hand.

Minutes passed. The news went on to another story—an update on the living victims of the Columbine shootings.

"I feel so numb and dizzy." Christine's voice was uneven, a breakable thing. "Like I'm not inside myself anymore. Drunk or something." She talked as if she were thinking out loud. "When I first found out I was pregnant with Emily, I considered an abortion. I wasn't blind to the fact your dad wanted to marry Kathleen."

Brandy knew Christine regretted her earlier accusations. "It doesn't matter now. Nothing matters except finding Emily."

Almost as if she hadn't heard Brandy, her stepmother began again. "I wanted to finish college. Glen and I wanted to join the Peace Corps. I wanted to be a teacher." Christine kept twisting her hands as if trying to warm them. "So many things I wanted for my life." With a look of horror on her face, she turned to Brandy. "I was so selfish I couldn't see beyond myself. God wouldn't punish me now, would He? He wouldn't let an innocent child…"

Brandy sat down beside her stepmother and reached out to comfort her. This time Christine folded into Brandy's embrace. "Can I get you something?" Brandy asked. "A soda or a glass of water?"

Christine drew back, then sniffed the air. "You used Emily's shampoo." She had circles under her eyes and dark lines of mascara on her face.

Brandy didn't know how to explain, to tell her stepmother that she wanted nothing more than to stay inside Emily's room, pressed into the lingering scents of her baby powder and shampoo. But Brandy wouldn't allow herself that luxury. She had to keep searching. She had to find her little sister.

Brandy stood and stepped away from the bed.

Her dad walked in with an Ashland map in his hand. He stared at them. "What's going on here?"

"Your daughter is trying to explain why she used Emily's shampoo."

Brandy's face got hot. She glanced up at her dad, trying to come up with some defense.

"Think about it, Christine," he said. "This is hurting her every bit as much as it is you and me. In case you haven't noticed, Emily prefers Brandy to either of us." His eyes were deep and dark-rimmed, wounded as if saying this actually hurt him. "Maybe she's trying to feel close to her sister." He sighed. "Search and Rescue has stopped for the night. They'll start again at sunrise. Have there been any developments here?"

Brandy told him how she found the necklace and had given it to the police. That Detective Radhauser claimed Emily's insistence that her big friend loved her might be a good sign. And about what Kent had said about the big Pooh bear he'd seen carrying Emily. Knowing her dad would be upset with her for banging on doors alone, she left out the part about Mrs. Wyatt.

"Does Radhauser believe the boy's story?"

"I don't know," Brandy said, then told him what Kent's mother had said about him believing his stuffed animals were real. "But Detective Radhauser checks out everything." She slipped the map from her father's hand. "I'll scan this and make some copies for the volunteer teams."

She was headed for her bedroom when the phone rang. Brandy froze in the doorway.

Her dad ran past her into the kitchen.

Brandy and Christine followed.

As Officer Corbin had instructed, her dad waited for the third ring, held the receiver against his ear, said "hello" and "yes" twice, then handed the phone to Christine. "It's your mother. She saw it on the news."

Christine took the phone, closed her eyes and listened before she spoke. "Emily wasn't in the restroom by herself, *Mother*." Her voice was taut, vibrating like a wire about to snap.

Brandy pleated the bottom of her T-shirt with her thumb and forefinger. Whatever thin cord Christine had wrapped around her restraint broke. "I know…I know, Mother…I should have…" Christine held the receiver as if it were a lifeline and gulped in air. "I should have called you. I should have told you what happened so you didn't have to hear it on the news. I should…I should…I should…" She screamed the phrase over and over. "I should have been a better mother."

Her dad rushed toward Christine, wrapped his arm around her shoulder to steady her, and took the phone. "I know you're upset, Mrs. McCabe. We all are. But we need to keep the phone lines open. We'll call you as soon as we know anything," he said, then hung up.

Christine cocked her head, as if realizing something for the first time. "I should have never given my mother so much power over me," she whispered. "I should have brought Emily with me. So what, if she fussed or spilled her milk. So what, if my mother's friends thought she should be completely toilet trained by now. They all would have lived through it."

Her dad led Christine through the kitchen. Halfway across the room, she stopped and abruptly twisted around, as if someone were following her. "They'll come here first if they find something, right?"

"In a flash," Officer Corbin said. "Don't worry."

In the silence that followed, the grandfather clock in the entry ticked, its pendulum swinging back and forth. A steady flow of time. Each tick seemed to take them further away from Emily.

Christine opened the cabinet, grabbed the brass pendulum and stopped the clock. It was 9:45p.m. "I can't stand it," she said in a quiet and hoarse voice. "All that God-awful noise." She frowned and rubbed her hands down the sides of her jeans as if trying to clean them.

* * *

Radhauser pounded on Mrs. Wyatt's door. "It's Detective Radhauser. I need to talk with you." The light seeping between the cracks in the front draperies darkened.

She was inside. As far as he knew, she never left her house.

He tried again. "I know you're in there and it's important that I talk to you." Silence. He walked around the outside of the house, looking for evidence of life, but found only darkness and more silence.

Returning to the front door, he knocked again. "One way or the other, I'm going to talk with you. Don't make me get a search warrant. It will waste valuable time." He waited a moment. Again, there was only silence.

He'd give it one more try. "Mrs. Wyatt. I know how you hate to go anywhere, but I will bring you down to the police station for questioning, if you don't open this door. Now."

The door opened.

He stepped inside. "I understand you saw someone in a bear costume loading a little girl into a car seat."

"I saw nothing," she said, wrapping her fat hands around her bare shoulders. She wore a yellow flowered nightgown, big enough to tent a Boy Scout troop.

He kept his gaze on her eyes. "That's not what you told Brandy Michaelson."

She backed up a step. "The girl was upset. I just wanted to help. To make her feel better."

"Are you saying you lied to her?"

"I could tell she blamed herself. She's a nice girl and she has those scars on her face. I'm sure people stare and talk behind her back. I…I just wanted to help."

"Lying in a kidnapping investigation doesn't help anyone," he

133

said with a patience he didn't feel.

"Why should I talk to you? You never believe anything I say."

"Wasting my time could cost that toddler her life."

"Then get out there and look for her. She's not here with me."

"Look, I know we've had our misunderstandings," he said, trying to keep himself from shaking her hard. "But if you know something, I need to hear it. Now."

"What's the point? You're just like everyone else. You ridicule me. Think I'm a fat, stupid, and lonely woman."

Radhauser was taken aback by this truth. "I'm sorry. I hope you'll give me another chance."

She stepped back and allowed him to move farther into the room. "I saw what I saw. But it was the Children's Health Fair. There were bears everywhere."

CHAPTER FOURTEEN

It was 10p.m. when Radhauser showed the doorman his badge, then took the elevator to the fifth floor. He rang the bell at Irene McCabe's condominium in the rolling foothills above Ashland.

"It's too late for visitors," a female voice said. "Check back with me tomorrow."

"It's Detective Radhauser," he said, holding his badge up to the peephole. "I'm here to talk with you about your granddaughter's disappearance."

A deadbolt turned. She opened the door wearing a long velvet robe, the color of Merlot wine. "Have you found her?"

Radhauser took off his Stetson and stepped inside. "I'm afraid not."

She let out a long sigh. Irene was tall, like her daughter, and had the same auburn hair. She led him across an entryway tiled with white marble to the living room. Her feet were bare and her toenails polished in the same wine color.

His cowboy boots sunk into the plush carpet. The whole place was spotless, and except for a few shocking splashes of bright red and black, it was decorated in all white. A white couch, white carpets, white appliances, tile and cabinets in the kitchen. Not the kind of place where a grandmother decorated cookies with her granddaughter.

Mrs. McCabe nodded toward the sofa.

Radhauser sat. He set his hat on the glass-topped coffee table with its shining chrome legs. A CD of classical music, one of Mozart's violin concertos, played softly in the background. "Mrs. McCabe. I'm sorry to—"

"I divorced that cheating Irish asshole and his name years ago. Please, call me Irene. Or just plain Rene," she said, putting her emphasis on the last syllable. "All my friends do." A smile broke across her face. She poured herself a glass of red wine from the open bottle on the coffee table.

He declined her offer to join her.

Lights from nearby Ashland sparkled through the plate glass wall of windows. On either side of the fireplace, white bookshelves rose to the ceiling. Even from the sofa, Radhauser saw the hardcovers were alphabetized by their authors' last names. "You have a beautiful place here," he said, noticing there were no photos of Christine or Emily.

"I'm sure you're not here for the home tour. What can I do for you?"

He pulled his notebook from his jacket pocket, jotted down the date and time and that he was interviewing Irene McCabe, the victim's grandmother. "I understand that Christine was at your birthday luncheon earlier today."

"That's right." She lifted her wine glass. "Happy birthday to me."

"Was there some reason you didn't want Emily there?"

"If I'd wanted children around, I would have celebrated with Happy Meals beneath the golden arches."

Radhauser said nothing.

She cleared her throat, dropped her gaze to the floor, then shook her head. "Look, I love my granddaughter, but I'd prefer she not attend my functions until she learns how to behave."

Everything was wrong with the picture she drew for him. Most grandmothers would have been pacing in front of the windows, shoulders hunched—a sick and terrified look on their faces. Irene should have had the television on a local station, the radio onto another. She should be eager for news about her granddaughter—unless she already knew Emily's whereabouts. He asked the question he asked everyone. "What do you think happened to Emily?"

She stared at him without blinking. "I can only hope some

patient person found her wandering around and is fixing her a healthy meal, while trying to find out her name and where she lives."

Not likely, Radhauser thought, given how much news coverage her disappearance had already generated. "Has your granddaughter wandered off before?"

"I assure you I'm the last person my daughter would tell if something like that happened. Maybe Emily ran away in search of some boundary-setting parents. From what I've read, kids want them."

"Where was the birthday luncheon held?"

"At the Mark Anthony on Main."

She confirmed what he already knew from Christine. That historic hotel was only a couple blocks from the park.

"Did Christine stay for the entire party?"

She cocked her head slightly, and gave him a long, appraising look. "Why is that important? You can't think she had anything to do with Emily's disappearance."

"Just answer the question, please, ma'am."

"You watch too much television," she said.

"Sometimes *Law & Order* gets it right. It's protocol to check out everyone the child interacts with. More times than not, child kidnappings are custody-related. And we think, based on the fact that Emily didn't call out when she was abducted, that she knew the person who took her."

"If you're thinking that person was her mother, I can assure you you're on the wrong path. Christine got to the luncheon around 12:30 and she left when I did at 2:45p.m."

"That's pretty exact," he said.

"The dining room had a big clock over the doorway. I noticed it as we were leaving."

He wrote down the times and circled 2:45. That gave either of them plenty of opportunity to grab Emily at 3:15. But he'd already searched the Michaelson house. Where could Christine have taken her and been back home preparing a picnic when Brandy arrived around 3:45?

"How often do you see your granddaughter?"

"Emily is an unruly child. And my daughter, who is little more than a child herself, has no idea how to control her."

The room fell silent. Something was missing inside this woman. Radhauser's own mother died years ago, but Gracie's mom loved being around Lizzie. And Lizzie believed her nana painted the constellations and pasted all the planets in the sky.

"How about her grandfather? Does he have a relationship with Emily?"

She shook her head. "I managed to walk my daughter down the aisle when she married Daniel, but I had to drink half a bottle of wine before I could make my feet move."

Radhauser took that as a no. "Why were you so opposed to their marriage?"

She laughed. "Isn't it obvious? Marrying a man old enough to be her father. Textbook behavior for a girl who grows up without one. My daughter's a spoiled and beautiful fool, Detective Radhauser." She looked at him, her eyes darkening. "I suppose you, like most people, think that's my fault."

"I don't know. Is it?"

"Maybe. I wanted the best for her. Wanted her to have every opportunity I didn't. But I sure as hell didn't expect her to fall in love with her freshman literature professor. She actually told me she knew she loved him after he showed her his wedding album to his first wife. Can you imagine?" She paused and looked at him, as if expecting him to respond.

He said nothing.

"Christine believed she'd have all the magic Daniel had the first time around." She shook her head and gave him a sad smile. "Like that happens more than once in a lifetime. If that's what she needed, Christine had a better chance with Glenard. Not that he's any prize."

"What do you know about the Dewar family?"

"Glenard Senior made his money in computers, down in the Bay Area. They retired to Oregon around the time their son entered high school, but moved to Michigan after he graduated.

Why are you asking all this? You can't think they had anything to do with Emily's disappearance."

"I check out everyone with even a remote connection to Emily."

Her gaze shot over to him, then moved swiftly away. "Christine claimed she and Glen had broken up, long before she got pregnant."

"Claimed?"

She shrugged, but Radhauser saw the answer in her eyes before she said it. "Christine is a lot like her father."

"In what way?"

She smiled. "Let's just say fidelity isn't either of their strong suits."

Radhauser was taken aback, but tried not to show it. "I imagine you were pretty unhappy your daughter dropped out of school to have Emily."

"I won't lie to you. And maybe this will make me sound heartless."

Radhauser smiled to himself.

"But I wanted her to have an abortion. You may be one of those pro-lifers, but I had dreams for my daughter, Detective Radhauser. And it didn't include being a teenage mother. I wanted her to finish college and maybe even go on for a master's degree. Rest assured, I never dreamed of her married to a man more than twice her age. But that doesn't mean I had anything to do with Emily's kidnapping. What in the world would I do with *that* child?"

The only answer Radhauser could come up with was she'd dispose of *that* child, maybe get her wish for her daughter after all. "Where did you go after the luncheon?"

She touched her fingertips to her temples, then flicked them outwards as if this whole conversation scrambled her brain. "Like I've already told you, the last thing I'd ever want is custody of that child."

Radhauser repeated his question, fighting the urge to grab her by the shoulders and slap that I-can't-be-bothered-with-a-grandchild attitude off her face.

"I came directly home and have been here ever since. Check with the doorman. I walk right by him to get to the parking garage."

"I will," Radhauser said.

She stood, a clear signal she wanted him to leave.

"Do you mind if I look around?"

"Suit yourself, but you won't find anything."

She followed him as he checked the hallway bathroom—opened the shower door and linen closet, then moved onto the master bedroom and checked under the bed, the bath and closets as well. He found no trace of Emily, not even a toy she might have left behind. Again, he thought about Gracie's mom, the way she kept a box of Lizzie's favorites in her family room, an assortment of children's books on her bookcase and coffee table.

When he tried to open the door to the second bedroom, it was locked.

"There's nothing of interest in that room," Irene said. "Just some furniture I'm saving."

"I need you to open the door."

A frown creased her forehead as if she'd lost her place in the script. Then she recovered, took a deep breath and said, "Do you have a warrant?"

"No, but I can get one."

She studied him, as if to determine whether or not he was serious, then took a small Allen wrench from above the doorframe and stuck it into the lock.

The door opened.

The room was painted sage green and furnished like a princess bedroom. A pink canopy twin bed was angled into the corner. The bed sported a big fluffy comforter and five sage green throw pillows with pink letters spelling out *Emily*. A small rocking chair held one of those expensive German teddy bears, a perfect sage bow tied around its neck. The room was large enough to hold a matching dresser, mirror, and small desk. A bookcase with books that looked as if they'd never been opened, toys that had never been touched by a child's hand. And on the desk, an eight-by-ten glossy photograph of an infant he assumed was Emily. It took a moment for it to sink in. Maybe Irene had dreamed things would be different.

"When did you decorate this room?"

"Before Emily was born."

"Why would you do that if you didn't want a grandchild?" Radhauser quietly shut the door and turned to face Irene.

She looked as if she'd aged five years in the last few minutes, her eyes and cheeks sunken. She quickly turned away from him, but not before he saw the tears. "Emily's not coming home, is she?"

Maybe it wasn't so much that there was something missing inside Irene, but that she'd buried it too deep to find.

Don't go soft in the head, he told himself. *Suspects lie all the time.* And maybe she lied about the room. If she'd decorated it before Emily was born, why didn't it have a crib or a cradle? This room was designed for a three-year-old, not an infant. Maybe Emily was stashed away somewhere with a friend, or Irene's sister or brother. Maybe Irene planned to retrieve her after the investigation died down.

"It's too soon to think the worst," he said. "But rest assured, I won't quit until I find her." He'd assign an officer to watch Irene McCabe, see if she made any house calls or purchased anything a three-year-old might need.

He took his Stetson from the coffee table. "I have a couple more questions before I leave. Do you have any siblings?"

"No."

"Do you own any other property in Oregon?"

"What are you getting at?"

"Answer the question, please."

"No. I own no other property in Oregon or anywhere else."

"Are your parents still alive?"

"My father died of a heart attack when I was in high school. My mother's in an assisted care facility in Medford. She has dementia, wears diapers, and uses a walker. I think she'd attract

141

attention if she tried to kidnap her great-granddaughter."

"How about your ex-husband? Where does Mr. McCabe live?"

"In Medford. He and his new wife own McCabe's Furniture Warehouse. Don't waste your time with him. He didn't even want his own kid."

"Men change," he said. "Maybe he wanted to see his granddaughter."

She walked him to the door and opened it. "That would sure shoot your theory that Emily knew her abductor, wouldn't it?"

CHAPTER FIFTEEN

Brandy closed her bedroom door and paced. She didn't care what her father said; she had to go back to the park and search one more time. She pulled on a hooded sweatshirt and was tying her shoes when she heard the knock. Her dad stepped into the room and looked at her, his brow furrowing. "Where do you think you're going?"

The lie crept up her throat. "Nowhere."

He studied her for another moment. "Just because you helped Radhauser with an interview doesn't make you a member of the police department. Let the detectives do their job."

Brandy said nothing.

He took a step closer. "It's after ten o'clock. Don't make us add you to our list of worries." He told her he needed the Ashland maps she'd printed. He and Christine planned to divide up the streets for the volunteers to canvas.

Brandy took the stack from her dresser and handed them to him. "I made fifty. I can print more if you need them."

Her dad looked as if he carried rocks on both shoulders. "I unplugged the phones, except for the kitchen. Officer Corbin will be here all night. I'll let you know if we hear anything." He started to leave.

"Dad."

He turned around.

"Do you...I wondered if..." She couldn't find the courage or words to tell him she needed reassurance—needed to be sure he still loved her.

"You wondered what?"

She swallowed. "Do you want me to help highlight the streets?"

He looked at the stack of maps, smiled sadly, then shook his head. "Christine and I have it under control. Get some rest." He handed her a pink and white capsule. "The doctor prescribed these for Christine. It will help you sleep."

"That's not what I need," she whispered.

He set the pill on her nightstand. And though he turned and walked away, the pain in his face wavered in front of her like a mirage.

She heard the door close and then nothing, just hollowness as deep and empty as the long night ahead of them. Absently, she picked up the fake Oscar she'd won for her role as the wicked witch in *The Wizard of Oz*.

Standing in front of her dresser, she considered the face in the mirror as if it belonged to someone else. She ran her hand over the uneven surface of her cheek. The scars were pale and shiny. Without pores or fine hairs, they had no character—revealed nothing. For an actress a face matters, but she'd been vain and stupid to think it mattered so much.

She backed away from the mirror until her shoulders hit the wall on the opposite side of the room. If they didn't find Emily, nothing would matter. The scars. Her songwriting. The trophies. The stupid dream of being an actress. She hurled the ridiculous trophy much harder than she'd intended. It hit the mirror—the sound as loud as lightning splitting a nearby tree. Glass shattered and flew.

Her father thrust the door open. A horrified, then frightened look passed over his face. His shoulders seemed even more sunken. He said nothing.

Brandy stood in the exact spot where she'd thrown the trophy and stared at the shattered glass. She couldn't stop shaking. She tried to steady herself.

"Listen to me, Brandy—"

"I'm sorry, Dad. I didn't mean—"

He held up his hand, as if he had to say it now or he'd never be able to say it. "This isn't the time for craziness. In the end, life scars every one of us. It gets us again and again." His voice grew thin, like a rope unraveling. "Now clean this mess up before Emily—" He looked at her as if unable to believe what he'd just said, then covered his face with his hands and left the room.

Brandy listened to the sounds of his footsteps in the tiled hallway as he walked away. Above her dresser, jagged pieces of glass still hung from the wicker frame. She picked up the big shards and put them into her trashcan, then grabbed the vacuum from the hall closet. When she finished, she closed her door and turned off the light.

Moonlight filtered through her mini blinds in thin silver bars across the wall. She sat on the edge of her bed, formulating a plan.

She tucked her pillows under her comforter to look like a sleeping body, hooked her backpack over her shoulder, and climbed out her window. Nothing would ever be right again until she found her sister.

On the road in front of their house, a patrol car inched toward their driveway. Its headlights spread out in two yellow bands over the black asphalt. The driver wore a Stetson. Radhauser.

She pulled up the hood of her sweatshirt and ducked behind a tree until the car passed, hoping he hadn't seen her, then she took off running toward the park. Though late, several houses on Pine and Granite still had lights burning inside. And she was glad there were people awake, people who might see and hear a small child call out in the night. One of the houses belonged to Mrs. Wyatt.

Brandy raced up the steps and rang the doorbell.

No one answered.

She knocked hard. "Mrs. Wyatt," she yelled. "It's me, Brandy. You talked to me earlier about my little sister."

When she heard nothing, she stepped over to the window. The curtains were parted ever so slightly, and she saw Mrs. Wyatt sitting on the sofa in a yellow-flowered nightgown.

Brandy returned to the door and pounded. Again and again, she banged on the door, jiggled the doorknob. Her hands throbbed. Her left index fingernail tore away. Her insides knotted like a fist. "Please, Mrs. Wyatt. It's really, really important." Brandy bit off the remainder of her nail, then stuck her injured finger in her mouth, sucked on it and tasted blood.

The porch light came on before the door opened. Mrs. Wyatt stood in front of the storm door. Her massive body blocked any view into the living room. She panted to catch her breath, then spoke to Brandy through the storm door. "I trusted you. You're nothing but a snitch. You sent that awful police detective here." Her dark eyes narrowed.

"I begged him not to bother you, but I had to tell him what you'd seen in the parking lot."

"Maybe I didn't see anything. Maybe I was wrong."

"No," Brandy said. "You were right."

"What are you doing out this late?"

"I have to talk to you again. May I come inside?"

"Can't this wait until tomorrow?"

"No," Brandy said. "My sister could be dead by tomorrow." The fist clutching her insides tightened its grip.

Mrs. Wyatt looked down at her flowered nightgown. "I'm not dressed for company."

"Just keep talking to me through the door, then. Please."

Brandy asked about the person in the bear costume Mrs. Wyatt had seen loading a little girl into a car seat. "Are you sure it was a Winnie the Pooh costume?"

"I don't know. It could have been."

"Think, please. This is really important. Was the costume a butterscotch color? Did it include a T-shirt?"

Mrs. Wyatt remained quiet.

"A little boy claimed he saw my sister in the park. He knows Emily and they often play together. He said a big Pooh bear was carrying her."

Mrs. Wyatt shook her head, but remained silent.

A lump grew in Brandy's throat. She tried to clear it. "Don't you see? His story matches what you told me. You might be the one who saves my sister's life. Please, close your eyes. It helped you to remember before."

The woman clamped her eyes shut and her long dark lashes curled up over the lids. Brandy took deep breaths while she waited.

Mrs. Wyatt opened her eyes. "I definitely saw red. The little girl's shirt or jacket. The bear. I don't know. I can't be sure. I saw the costume again, when the man tried to get into the front seat without taking the bear head off. Wait a minute." She squinted her eyes as if thinking. "Maybe a T-shirt. Yes. And I'm pretty sure it was yellow."

That's it, Brandy thought. Someone wore a costume that matched the bear in the toy store window. Emily's bear. "Thank you. Thank you." Brandy headed down the porch steps, then turned back and threw Mrs. Wyatt a kiss. "I love you," she said, and then hurried for the payphone near the park entrance to call Detective Radhauser. On the way, she practiced what she'd say, how she'd make him believe Mrs. Wyatt was telling the truth this time.

There was a full moon and a peppering of stars lit the sky. Her flashlight cut a narrow beam on the spongy path through the Japanese Garden. She slowed down. There were three sets of luminous eyes peering from behind a conifer tree. She stopped. Deer.

Ashland Creek tumbled over its boulders. Brandy breathed in the smell of pond algae and wet earth. Heard the soft rustlings of a swan's wing. The park sounds were all amplified by the quiet, but as intimate and safe as her own room. At least she'd thought so. Until today. She took off running and didn't stop again until she stood in front of the payphone.

It had been a little over nine hours since she'd called the police station to report Emily's absence. *Please, God. Make Radhauser believe me.*

Brandy dialed. A female answered. "May I please speak to Detective Radhauser?"

"Detective Radhauser isn't here right now, but I can get a message to him."

He must have been headed home when Brandy spotted him.

147

She needed to talk with him herself. She had to convince him that Mrs. Wyatt told the truth. "Can you give me his home number?" she asked, explaining that she was Emily's sister and it was really important.

"I'm sorry, we don't give out home numbers. And you won't find him there anyway. I'd bet my eyeteeth he's still out looking for your sister. Tell me the nature of your call and I'll relay the message to him."

"Never mind." Brandy hung up without leaving a message. She walked toward the park restrooms. And though she knew it was irrational to think Emily might still be there, Brandy lifted the crime scene tape and slipped underneath it. When she tried the door, it was locked. Fingerprint powder rubbed off onto her hands. She tried to wipe it on her jeans.

Brandy didn't know what to do. The worst thing she could ever imagine had happened. But she had a solid clue now. Maybe she'd remember seeing a bear walking away, the back of its yellow T-shirt. Or perhaps she'd find something else. Surely if she looked long and hard enough, she'd find something that would confirm the Pooh bear story—something that would lead her to Emily.

She stood, propped against the rough cinderblock wall. She wasn't cold, but her teeth chattered.

Brandy retraced the steps she'd taken with Emily, the way she'd held the door open with her foot and pushed Emily's stroller inside. She stopped every few seconds, closed her eyes and tried to remember what she'd seen. But there'd been so many people in the park today. So many children and adults dressed in bear costumes.

Though she knew the police had already searched, Brandy walked slowly around the restrooms, shining her flashlight along the footings, looking for anything that might provide a clue to who took Emily and why.

Finding nothing, she roamed around the empty playground, looking for something only she might recognize. Her flashlight punched a bright hole in the darkness. In order to get to the parking lot, the kidnapper would have taken Emily over the bridge. She always begged Brandy to hold her up to see the water. Had the man in the Pooh bear costume carried her over this bridge?

Brandy raced to the center of the bridge and shined her flashlight into the creek—slowly moving it across the boulders, then leaned over the rail to flash the light beneath the bridge. She held her breath. When she saw nothing, she breathed, then walked along the banks, shining the beam from one deserted side to the other. Heavy dew shone from the cobwebs in the trees. Every few moments, she called out Emily's name, tried to imagine what else might have lured her little sister away from the park.

There'd been that adorable Spaniel puppy chasing after a red ball. What would Emily do? Maybe she followed him—a little girl innocently chasing a puppy. She imagined her giggling as she ran. Brandy closed her eyes and could hear the musical sound. Emily was okay. She had to be. But if she'd chased after the puppy, wouldn't someone have seen her and brought her back?

Again, Brandy retraced the steps they'd taken that afternoon. She tried to sift through each tiny detail, trying to find something, anything that might lead them to her little sister.

She got down on her knees and crawled into the thick nests of rose and rhododendron bushes where Emily liked to hide. Branches scraped the sides of her face. Her hair caught in brambles. She pulled it away. The ground smelled like bark, decaying leaves, and wet soil. As she moved farther into the undergrowth, the space opened up, as if someone had trimmed the lower branches. Her hands felt something soft, slippery and padded like a sleeping bag.

She shined the flashlight.

A man's face, lined, dirty, and stubbled with gray whiskers, leered up at her. "Get out," he said, putting his hands over his eyes to shut out the light. "This here's my private bedroom." He smelled like body odor and alcohol.

The scream rose in her throat, a knot of fear so hard and tangled she thought she might choke. Brandy crawled backwards. "I'm sorry. I'm looking for my little sister. She's almost three."

"Well she ain't here. And I'm trying to get some sleep. So get the hell out."

She scrambled from beneath the rhododendrons. Small

stones and bark bit into her hands as she moved.

When she cleared the bushes, she tried to stand. Her legs trembled and the palms of her hands stung, but she forced herself to get as far away from him as possible. She kept looking over her shoulder. After a few moments, when she still saw no one, she walked around the pond three more times, shining her flashlight into every dark nook. When she grew too tired to think any more, she stared up at the theatre on the hillside where one of this year's plays, King Lear's tragedy, had just ended. She heard the sound of applause and a few minutes later, a buzz of conversation, an occasional burst of laughter as the audience stumbled out into the brick courtyard.

Brandy pulled Emily's Pooh bear from her backpack and hugged him against her chest. She sat on a bench outside the restrooms where there was moonlight and the pulse of crickets. She looked down at the muddy knees of her jeans, her scraped and bloody palms.

After the theater closed and the attendees returned to their homes or hotels, stillness as quiet and eerie as an empty church settled over everything.

When she heard footsteps, Brandy's throat seized. She wondered if the man in the sleeping bag intended to hurt her.

In the dim light, she spotted the cowboy hat. Radhauser stepped from behind the restrooms. He carried a big flashlight, shining it against the concrete footings as he walked around the cinder block building. He pushed a candy wrapper aside with his foot, and inspected the shrubs on either side of the walkway with his flashlight. He picked up a twig in his right hand and snapped it into small pieces, dropping them, one by one, onto the asphalt path.

She remained on the bench, still clutching the Pooh bear. "Are you following me? Or just an insomniac?"

"Yes to both questions."

"I talked to Mrs. Wyatt again."

"I know. I asked you to leave the investigating to the police." There was a trace of irritation in his voice.

Brandy said nothing.

"Do I need to get a restraining order?"

"I'm only trying to help."

"I suppose Mrs. Wyatt has consulted her psychic and knows exactly where Emily is."

"She said the bear in the costume was wearing a yellow T-shirt."

"That's interesting," Radhauser said. "She denied seeing anything when I asked."

"She doesn't trust you."

Brandy described the bear in the toy store window. "Emily would trust someone who looked like her friend at the toyshop."

"I've got officers checking it out," he said. "And I've assigned someone to talk to the fair coordinator, get the names of every costumed worker."

"I think Mrs. Wyatt is telling the truth."

"We can't waste any more time with a known quack. Do your parents know you're here?"

When she didn't respond, he shone his flashlight over the muddy knees of her jeans, her damaged palms. "You shouldn't be here at night. It's not safe."

"I did something really stupid tonight." She hung her head.

"I know. Marvin is pretty territorial when it comes to his bedroom."

"You saw me?"

"I was following you, remember?"

"Emily likes to play hide and seek in those bushes. Do you think he—?"

"Marvin is loud, but harmless. Otherwise, I'd never allow you to disturb his sleep."

"You can't know that. What if he took Emily?"

"It's my job to know. Marvin sleeps here. He goes somewhere else during the day." Radhauser sat beside her and set his flashlight on the ground. "Want to talk about that stupid thing you did? How it might have played out if Marvin wasn't harmless and I wasn't here?"

151

"I was talking about something else." She told him about the broken mirror. "As if my dad doesn't have enough to worry about, I had to go all psycho."

"We all do crazy and irrational things when we're stressed. Come on, Brandy, I'll take you home."

"But what if Emily is out here in the dark? You just said it isn't safe. What if she's cold and scared? And she can't find me."

"I don't think she is. I'm no fingerprint expert, and I won't know for certain until Monday, but I'm pretty sure Emily's prints are on the animal cracker package Kent claims Emily gave him."

"That means he really did see her after I took her into the bathroom."

"The hotline is getting calls now. We'll have a solid lead soon. Someone had to see something."

"Kent saw her being carried out of the park. By someone in a Pooh costume. Mrs. Wyatt saw the same thing in the parking lot. The timing is a match."

Radhauser shook his head. "Kent's mother told us he makes up stories about stuffed animals all the time. He thinks they are real. And Mrs. Wyatt has basically recanted her story. Chances are, if she saw anything, it was someone putting his own child in his car seat."

"You shouldn't have talked to her. She made me promise I wouldn't tell you."

For a few moments neither of them said anything.

"I believe her," Brandy said. "She had details. Like the color of Emily's jacket. And the yellow T-shirt."

"She could have gotten the jacket information from the news broadcast."

"What about the yellow T-shirt?"

"How much did you prompt her?"

"I'm not stupid," Brandy said. She told him how she'd asked if the bear might be wearing a shirt and that Mrs. Wyatt had closed her eyes and remembered it was yellow.

"If anyone rented a Pooh bear costume, we'll find him."

"What if my little sister is roaming around somewhere?"

"She couldn't go far on her own without shoes. Besides, I've got police cars cruising up and down the streets. And others who spent the entire afternoon knocking on doors and showing Emily's picture. By Monday, that picture will be on the front page of the *Medford Tribune*, the *Grants Pass Courier*, and the *Ashland Daily Tidings*."

"Monday is a long way off."

"I know. I've faxed it to Portland. With any luck, it will appear in their Sunday paper, too."

"What time is it?"

"Time you went home."

She wanted to tell him how strange everything seemed at home. How she moved through the house afraid to sit down. Just staring at things she'd seen every day for most of her life. Only now it seemed like she was a visitor in that house and everything belonged to someone else. "What time is it really?"

He lifted the cuff of his jacket.

She pointed her flashlight at his wrist.

He hastily pulled down his sleeve, but not before Brandy read the blue name tattooed in a white circle of skin protected from the sun by his watch.

She shone the light on his face.

"I was supposed to have today off," he said. "It's my wife's birthday. I never wear a watch on my days off." He gently pushed her flashlight away from his eyes.

She turned it off. "Who's Tyler?"

He rubbed the sides of his face as if they hurt. "Does your dad know you're here?"

"Is Tyler your son?"

He puffed out his cheeks, then slowly released the air. "No. Come on, I'll see you home. I'll even be a gent and walk you up to your window."

She didn't move. The night was so quiet she could hear sounds from the pond, a Mallard dipping into the water, the croak of a nearby frog.

"Come on," he said again, reaching out a hand to help her up.

She stood and they walked side by side across the bridge. When Brandy saw his patrol car parked in the Winburn lot, she told him to go ahead, she'd be fine. But Radhauser kept walking toward her house.

"I know you want to help," he said. "And you can do something important for me. Find a quiet place. Close your eyes and try to remember every single moment from the time you headed to the restroom, until you called 911. Write it down, minute by minute. Everything that happened. Then keep adding details as you remember them. I don't care how small or insignificant they seem. Think about sounds and smells. People you saw there. Write it all down."

"Was Tyler kidnapped?"

He cleared his throat, tapped his fingers against his pant leg. "Yes."

She swallowed. "Why do you have his name on your arm?"

He came to an abrupt stop.

"Is Tyler dead?" she asked. In the moonlight, Brandy could almost see the thoughts in his mind as he looked for a way around her question.

"He was six years old and went missing from a Little League Park in Tucson where I used to live and work." His gaze shifted off Brandy's and looked at nothing. "I screwed up. It shouldn't have come down the way it did."

They walked along, the silence ticking between them. When the tears rose, she didn't attempt to wipe them away—merely let them roll down her cheeks and drop into the neck of her hoody.

At the edge of their front yard, he handed her a card printed with both his office and home phone numbers. "I want you to have this. Call me if you remember anything important. Or if you just need to talk. I mean it. And I don't care what time it is, either. If I'm in my office, I'll tell the front desk to give you access."

He put his arm around her shoulder and gave her a quick, reassuring squeeze, the kind her dad used to give her before she performed on stage. "Emily is lucky to have a sister like you."

CHAPTER SIXTEEN

Brandy pulled her old corkboard from the back of her closet and set it on her desk. She counted out fifteen three-by-five index cards and numbered them—one for each of the fifteen minutes between the time she'd started toward the restroom and the time she'd run into Stone at 3:30 and then called 911.

She'd do exactly what Radhauser suggested. She'd keep replaying that time, minute by minute, over and over, until she remembered something new. She used pushpins to tack the cards onto the corkboard. One by one, she took them down, closed her eyes and tried to recreate the scenes. She wrote out the details.

On the first card, she remembered the look on Emily's face when Brandy told her not to unhook her safety belt. A look that said it was exactly what the toddler would do. She put a red star beside it—a reminder to tell Radhauser.

By card three, she remembered how she'd bent to tie Em's shoelaces, but then Emily had distracted Brandy by pushing her little Pooh bear into her face and telling her he needed a nap. Brandy had forgotten to tie Emily's shoes. This could be important. The rainbow sneakers were untied. Someone tied them in double knots and tossed them into the creek? Why? Another red star. She made more notes to tell Radhauser.

On card five, she wrote about the way she'd sat on the commode and took off her boots and jeans. How Emily had squealed, "Bumblebee no sting big Pooh. He no nap." *Holy shit*, Brandy thought. Emily had sounded excited. Maybe she hadn't been talking about her own Pooh. Maybe she meant the one in the toyshop window. The one Emily called big Pooh. Did that

155

mean someone brought the big stuffed animal to the restroom? It must have been sold on Thursday or Friday, because she and Emily had seen it Wednesday afternoon. Had someone bought that bear to entice Emily? Or was it a coincidence? Maybe what Kent saw wasn't entirely make-believe. Maybe he really did see a big Pooh wearing a yellow T-shirt, and imagined it carrying Emily. Another red star. Another note for Radhauser.

There'd been a little girl in the restroom, not Emily, asking for a balloon. "I want a balloon, too," she'd said. "Please. A red one." Who was she asking? Emily didn't have any balloons. Was there an adult in the bathroom handing out balloons? Another child? Had that person given a yellow one to Emily? Something else to mention to Radhauser.

For two hours, she studied the cards as if her brain had no off switch. She closed her eyes and tried to recreate every second of those fifteen minutes. Tried to remember what she'd seen when she stepped out of the restroom.

Over and over, she asked herself the same questions, trying to find a way to connect the dots. *Think. Think.* A birthday party going on. Balloons tied to the corners of a long table. Children laughing and standing in line. Had they hired a clown to hand out balloons and twist them into the shapes of animals? Had the big Pooh bear been a gift for another little girl's birthday?

When the index cards started to blur together, Brandy flopped, fully clothed, onto her bed. She'd swallowed the pill her father had given her earlier, but didn't sleep. Instead, she thought about all the words she might never have a chance to say to Emily. Words that now seemed too sad to ever come out.

She picked up her guitar and strummed some soft chords in G major. Before she knew what happened, she played music and sang words she must have stowed away in the back of her mind. Within minutes, the song for Emily coursed through Brandy, like some swollen river after the spring snows thawed.

I've heard love can conquer anything,
Be a fortress in the storm.

156

It can lift you to the mountaintop,
And hold you safe and warm.

She wrote three more stanzas, then called Stone on the private number he'd given her and sang it to him.

He was quiet, and when he spoke his voice sounded gentle and almost breakable. "I don't know what to say. Wasn't it Chagall who said that art must be an expression of love or it's nothing?"

Brandy told him how the song had arrived in her head, fully formed as if her mind had been working on it without her knowledge.

"Coach Pritchard and the drama team want to put together a candlelight vigil. We can hold it in Lithia Park. He said it will raise community awareness. The more people we can get looking for Emily, the greater the chances of finding her. Would you be willing to sing that song?"

"I don't know if I could without breaking down."

"You sang it to me."

"That's different."

"I'll work out an accompaniment," Stone said. "You've already done the hard part. Creativity takes real courage. Singing is only a performance. Please. We have plenty of people to take care of the details. All you have to do is show up and sing to me."

For a long moment, neither of them spoke.

"I'll try," she finally said. It couldn't hurt to get other people looking for Em.

* * *

After canvassing the park one more time, Radhauser got into his patrol car and backed out of the lot off Winburn. He mentally crossed Brandy Michaelson off his list of suspects. He'd cancel her polygraph. He knew it deep in his gut. Aside from a moment that some might call carelessness, that kid didn't have anything to do with Emily's disappearance.

One of the hardest things about a kidnapping investigation— with a child's life in danger—was knowing when to call it a night. Radhauser needed sleep, but didn't know how to stop being a detective. As he drove toward his ranch, he couldn't escape the feeling he'd turned his back on Emily Michaelson.

His thoughts leaped to Brandy. He knew exactly how she felt. He'd been too busy and self-important to listen to his wife and go with her and Lucas the night of the accident. Too busy to even remember the last words he'd exchanged with them. He wanted to be able to sleep without his first wife and son entering his dreams. Time. It was a river that kept moving. There was no way to stop it and no way to go back and change the moments he regretted.

It was after 2a.m. when he pulled into his driveway. The night was cool, lit by a full moon, and littered with stars. He hit the remote for the garage door, parked, and turned off the ignition. In the mudroom between the garage and the kitchen, he sat on the bench and pulled off his boots. He tiptoed through the kitchen, where Gracie's birthday cake sat untouched on the counter. Sometimes he hated his job.

On his way down the hall to their bedroom, he stopped in front of Lizzy's door and inched it open. The nightlight cast a warm glow on the room they'd redecorated for her fourth birthday, just two weeks before.

Gracie had painted the room a soft pink and added a border of pink and teal dragonflies. They'd bought a twin trundle bed—planning ahead for the nights Lizzie would have sleepovers with a friend. He kneeled beside her bed, fingered the quilted bedspread Gracie's mom had made, and watched his daughter sleep.

She wore a lavender nightgown with a ruffle at the bottom. It was bunched up around her thighs. She was on her back, sprawled sideways across the bed, her mouth open and moist. Her thumb must have slid out at the moment she drifted into sleep and landed still cocked next to her cheek.

Someone else's daughter was missing, but his Lizzie lay safe in her own bed.

He pressed his lips to her cheek and she curled into his arms without waking, so willing to surrender into love.

After a few moments, he laid her back down in the center of the bed and covered her with her quilt. He picked up her stuffed bunny that had tumbled onto the floor and tucked it beside her. "Sweet dreams, darlin' girl," he whispered.

Despite his need for sleep, it was difficult to leave her room tonight. But volunteers were gathering at dawn to canvass Lithia Park again, along with the surrounding neighborhoods. He closed his eyes and said a prayer for his daughter.

Again, his thoughts returned to Emily.

"Why did you take her?" he whispered. He knew from experience that once he understood the why, he could likely figure out who.

His eyes were still closed when he felt the pressure of a hand on his shoulder.

In her long, white nightgown, Gracie looked almost ethereal in the moonlight. Without saying a word, she took his hand and led him into their bedroom, then climbed back into bed. He undressed and lay down beside her. "I'm sorry about the birthday cake."

"Shhh," she said. "We'll have it with coffee for breakfast."

He didn't tell her that he'd be gone long before she and Lizzie had breakfast.

"I saw the mother on the news," she said. "Are you any closer to finding her little girl?"

"No. Not one solid lead. And I've got an eighteen-year-old half-sister who believes it's all her fault."

"Poor kid." When Gracie stroked the side of his face, he wished he'd taken a few minutes to shave. She tucked her head into his shoulder. Her neck still carried a hint of the rose-scented soap she always used.

He'd been lost after Laura and Lucas died, and Gracie had brought something solid and alive back into his life.

But he had no real talent for words and had never found a way to say the many things he felt. "You know how much I love you and Lizzie, don't you?"

She ran her hand over his cheek. "After I turned off the news, I sat on the floor beside Lizzie's bed and watched her sleep for over an hour. They'd have to institutionalize me if anything like that happened to her."

He stroked her hair and wished it were some other night. "We won't ever let that happen." Even as he uttered the reassurance, he feared it might not be true. Time was a traitor. You planned and waited for the good things. But bad things happened fast. And he knew, better than most, they could happen to anyone.

For a few moments, they lay holding hands and listening to the restless flutter of the bedroom curtains in the early morning air. Then Gracie rolled over on her side and the steady sound of her breathing descended into the rhythm of sleep.

Caring too much was a dicey thing for a detective. The work required objectivity and a clear head. He needed to be concerned enough not to appear callous or cynical, but able to walk away and make the difficult decisions when necessary. He knew he wasn't doing a good job with the walking away part. A detective who allowed his emotions to get tied up in a case was the worst kind of fool.

Though he tried for over an hour, Radhauser couldn't sleep. He slipped out of bed, tiptoed into the kitchen and made a pot of coffee. He sat at the table, meticulously reviewed his interviews and notes again, hoping to find something he'd missed—anything that might lead him to Emily.

* * *

Brandy jerked awake in her own bed. She lay, paralyzed in the dark, until her fear found a name.

Emily.

Both feet touched the floor. She was still wearing the same muddy-kneed jeans, T-shirt and hoody she'd worn the night before. She bolted through the darkened hallway.

Her dad had closed the door to Emily's bedroom as if that barrier could make them stop feeling the life that no longer went on inside that room. It didn't work. The closed door was like a bruise you could run your fingertips over and feel the pain. The walled-off section of their home made Brandy's eyes fill with tears just passing by on her way to the bathroom.

She hurried into the kitchen. Officer Corbin was gone. In the dim light from the nightlight above the stove, she saw her dad was asleep at the oak table, his head dropped onto his crossed arms. His shoulders rose and sank, his breath ruffling the paper napkin beneath his coffee cup in steady waves.

The sun slipped from behind a cloud and caught in the window. Its bright heat warmed the air so gradually she was barely aware of it. She checked the clock on the stove. Six-thirty. Emily had been missing for fifteen hours. Brandy turned away. The maps, with the streets each volunteer was to canvass highlighted in orange, were stacked on the counter next to the flyers. She grabbed both stacks and headed for the park.

* * *

Detective Radhauser was one of the first to arrive in the Winburn parking lot. His job would include instructing the volunteers on evidence-gathering procedures. He made a quick sweep of the area around the playground, hoping to see something that might shed new light on Emily's disappearance. At just after 7a.m., the sky opened up and rain came down in silver sheets that fell over the Ashland hills, soaking down through the tree canopies. It drummed on the tin roof of the restroom at Lithia Park and pocked Ashland Creek and the pond where the ducks and swans floated.

Damn. Rain was the last thing they needed. He hurried through the downpour to the volunteer staging area set up in the community center across the street from the park. He spotted Brandy and a woman he assumed, because Brandy had told him she'd planned to arrive early, to be Daniel Michaelson's secretary, Lois. It was a wooden building, with one huge room that smelled like pinecones. Folding chairs had been set up in long rows.

Standing behind a row of tables at the back of the room facing the chairs, Brandy collated packets—maps, a spiral notebook with a pen tied to it, a stack of *Help Us Find Emily* posters, a roll of tape, a spool of yellow ribbon, and a loaded staple gun. Lois handed them out to the volunteers as they took their seats.

Brandy stopped working and hurried over to him. She told him the new things she'd remembered. About the excitement in

Emily's voice when she'd said, "Bumblebee no sting big Pooh. He no nap." The way Emily loved that big Pooh in the toy store window, and how she wouldn't have mistaken it for just any bear costume because of the yellow T-shirt and the big bumblebee on his nose. She reminded him of what both Kent and Mrs. Wyatt had told her.

"Good," he said, impressed by her critical thinking. He remembered the curious prints he'd photographed on the floor of the restroom. Could the kidnapper have carried a big stuffed animal meant to entice Emily? Not very likely. Besides, Kent claimed a big bear was carrying Emily. More like the prints came from someone dressed in a bear costume. He pulled out his notebook, jotted a reminder to interview the toy store owner. He needed the name of the individual who bought the giant Pooh bear. Maybe they'd turned it into a costume.

"The bulletin board is a great idea," he said. "Keep looking at it—going over and over in your mind what happened. You may remember other things. And calls are coming in from people who were in the park yesterday. We'll have a solid lead soon."

"We already have one," Brandy insisted. "And I plan to talk with her again."

"You'll do nothing of the sort. This is my last warning and I mean it. Leave the interviewing to the police."

She looked away.

He understood how bad she felt and how much she wanted to help, but he couldn't let her sabotage his investigation.

"Mrs. Wyatt opened up to me," she said. "Not you. And what about Kent? You were the one who asked me to interview him."

She had him there. "That was a special situation. He trusted you. And you did a good job. Probably better than I could have done."

Brandy smiled, then returned to compiling packets.

Radhauser watched her for a moment before turning his attention to the room. All the available chairs were now filled with volunteers. He gave a brief orientation and some instructions on interviewing, making sure each resident looked closely at Emily's photo. He gave them a list of the proper questions to ask during their neighborhood canvasses, and described Emily and the outfit she'd been wearing. And though he doubted they'd find much, he hyped them up about the importance of their mission, how they might uncover the one piece of information that could lead the police to Emily.

"Don't touch any evidence," he said. "Leave it exactly the way you find it. Report anything suspicious to your team leader. Pieces of fabric or clothing you may see in the bushes, places where the ground appears to be disturbed. I don't care how unimportant it may seem. I want to know about it."

Moments later, volunteers from Josephine and Jackson County Search and Rescue, along with neighbors, Eagle Scout troops, students and teachers from both Ashland High School and Southern Oregon University fanned out in all directions. They moved through the rain, slowly, deliberately, the way he'd described to them in his orientation. Some searched the park and the wooded areas surrounding it on foot. Many of the search and rescue teams went on horseback. Student volunteers tied yellow ribbons to telephone poles along Main Street and used staple guns to tack up the flyers bearing Emily's photograph.

When he was confident the searchers understood their mission, Radhauser returned to the police station.

Vernon met him at the door. "Glenard Dewar, Senior, owns a cabin at Emigrant Lake."

The lake was only five miles southeast of Ashland. "Go check it out," Radhauser said. "Take Murphy with you. Walk the land around the cabin and look for anything suspicious. It's a long shot, but you never know."

Around 10a.m., Radhauser oriented a fresh group of volunteers. Some posted fliers in store windows and replaced those on trees and telephone poles the rain had destroyed. Others formed lines to sweep across fields and meadows, and head down dirt pathways to search woods. He instructed them to look behind bushes, in ditches, barns, abandoned cars, and old refrigerators, everything that was in their path.

A few moments later, the canine unit arrived. The tracking dogs sniffed Emily's sneakers and one of her shirts Brandy had taken from the bathroom hamper. For a while they just ran around in circles, and he'd nearly given up when one of them leapt across the stone and wood-planked bridge over Ashland Creek. He stopped in the middle and sniffed the rock wall, then looked at his trainer.

"The kidnapper stopped here," the trainer said.

Radhauser thought about the sneakers, the way they were tied in double knots. A picture formed in his mind. The kidnapper had perched Emily on the rock wall and taken off her shoes. But why take the time to tie a double knot? He remembered what Brandy had told him about Emily's shoes being untied. Was the kidnapper sending a message to her parents?

The dog raced forward.

Radhauser and the dog's trainer followed. The dog ran down the bank of Ashland Creek, stopped and looked at his trainer again, then turned and headed back up the bank and toward the south end of the Winburn parking lot. He circled one of the parking spaces for a few moments before he gave up.

"He's lost the scent," the trainer said.

"Could it be that this is where the abductor's car was parked?" Radhauser asked.

"It's likely," the canine officer said.

Radhauser thought about Mrs. Wyatt and what she'd said to Brandy about a costumed adult putting a little girl into a car in the Winburn lot. Maybe it was time he got a warrant and paid her another visit.

CHAPTER SEVENTEEN

It took Mrs. Wyatt a few minutes to get to the door. She opened it a small crack. "This is harassment," she said when she saw Radhauser standing on her porch. "Why can't you people leave me alone?" Her breathing was heavy. Behind her, the television blared out a talk show.

"I assure you I don't want to be here," Radhauser said. "But a little girl is missing and I can't stop looking until I find her."

"I already told you I didn't see anything. And I sure as hell don't have that little girl."

"You told the victim's sister that you did see something."

Mrs. Wyatt looked at him hard. "That girl was extremely kind."

"Listen to me," he said, fighting to keep his voice calm. "I know some of your reports haven't panned out, but—"

"You didn't have to make me feel like I'm one of those crazy crank callers you see on television." Her dark eyes blazed.

He tried to imagine what she felt, the embarrassment of her weight, and the humiliation of having been caught seeking attention. "You're right. But I did investigate every lead you gave me."

"You never thanked me or showed one iota of appreciation for how I watch out for people. My late husband founded our neighborhood watch."

"I'm sure he was a good man, but I need you to tell me about the car you saw in the Winburn parking lot. About the person in costume."

"I already told that girl what I saw."

"I need you to tell me. That girl won't be bothering you again."

"She was nice to me." The door opened. Mrs. Wyatt filled most of it. "Unlike you, she was no bother."

"Please, Mrs. Wyatt, just tell me what you saw."

She smiled and took a step back. "Has my careful surveillance actually provided you with a lead?" A trickle of sweat rolled down her jaw and into the neck of her ugly flowered dress.

Though she'd never given him anything but a headache, he nodded and then told her about the dog stopping near the south end of the Winburn lot after sniffing Emily's sneakers. "Did you see a small child wearing a red jacket being put into a car seat by someone in a bear costume?"

"I did, indeed."

"Are you positive it wasn't someone carrying a life-sized stuffed animal and a little girl? Could that person have put the stuffed animal into the front seat?"

She thought about that. "I don't think so. I mean…I noticed he didn't take the bear head off before driving away. But I did see a little girl in a red jacket. And a stuffed animal couldn't have put her in the car seat."

Though she'd probably seen an attendee of the fair put his or her own child into the safety seat, Radhauser couldn't take any chances. "You may have witnessed something important this time. Could you be specific about the car and the exact spot it was parked?"

"Will I get my name in the paper?"

"There's a good chance. That is if your information leads us to the missing child."

"Is there a reward?"

"The family is offering a $5,000 reward."

She moved out of the doorway.

He stepped inside.

On the television, Geraldo Rivera introduced his guests, three men who liked to wear lace panties. The audience clapped. Radhauser shook his head.

"I'll let you look through my binoculars," Mrs. Wyatt said. "I can identify the exact spot where the getaway car was stashed."

* * *

When Brandy spotted Stone, she avoided him. Embarrassed by her late night phone call, she headed out of the park.

He caught up with her. "Did you bring me a copy of the song?"

She slipped the melody and lyrics out of her backpack and handed them to him.

"It was amazing," he said. "Really moving."

She looked away and kept walking.

"We can team up," Stone said. "I mean, it might be easier for you to be with someone you know."

She stopped near a clump of madrone trees. Reddish bark hung like flypaper from their trunks and littered the ground in jagged circles. "Nothing is easy. I see Emily everywhere. I can't even shut my eyes because she's inside my head, too."

He took her in his arms, burrowed his face in her hair. "It smells like rain," he said. His lips brushed against her forehead.

Brandy wanted someone to blame so she wouldn't have to carry the burden on her own. She pulled away from him.

As if reading her mind, he said, "No one blames you." He reached up and touched her face, brushing his thumb slowly across her scarred cheek. His eyes were so green.

Brandy felt woozy and leaned against a tree to keep herself upright. Everything was changing—falling apart, one molecule at a time. She wanted to both disappear and to thrust herself into his arms. "She tries to hide it, but Christine blames me. Why wouldn't she? It wasn't exactly responsible of me to leave Emily alone in the stroller."

"You were only three feet away." He looked at her. "You're not the only one in the hot seat. When Detective Radhauser came to my house last night, my mother freaked out. I figured I'd be grounded for the rest of my life." He stopped and kicked a piece of madrone bark into the air, following its launch before returning his attention to Brandy. "You don't think I had anything to do with her disappearance, do you?"

"Of course not."

"Then why are you acting like you do?"

"Christine and my father have already taken lie detector tests. I'm pretty sure I'll be next."

"Why would anyone suspect you? You're the one who reported it."

"Because more than half the kids hurt or abducted are taken by the same person who reports them missing." She buried her hands under her armpits and slumped back against the madrone.

He winced and pressed his hands against his temples. "It wasn't your fault," he said again. "And it wasn't mine either."

She didn't trust herself to look at him. "I know that. But I made such a mess of everything." She struggled to find a way to explain herself, to make him understand.

Stone tried to put his arms around her again.

She pushed him away. "I'm sorry. It's just that if I hadn't been so preoccupied with impressing you, I—"

"Wait a minute. Let's get something straight. You don't have to do anything to impress me." He lowered his gaze. "I already am." He stopped to let his words sink in. "And I've seen you with Emily enough to know you love her and would never intentionally do anything to harm her."

Brandy had an irrational desire to laugh. "Everyone says they know how much I love her. But the truth is—"

He pressed a finger to her lips. "Don't. Coach Pritchard called. It's all set. Tonight at 8p.m. They've got a minister coming. And the kids in Emily's preschool are doing a song."

Brandy swallowed, overwhelmed by this show of support and love for Emily.

"I know," Stone said. "It's awesome, right?"

She nodded, still unable to speak.

"Don't forget your guitar. And come early so we can practice together." He paused and smiled. "I've got a great feeling this vigil will help bring Emily home."

"I don't know. I'm not sure I can do it."

"You have to keep believing the police will find her. Detective Radhauser is smart. He probably has all kinds of leads he's following up on right now."

Brandy wanted so much to believe him. She told him what Kent had said, how Mrs. Wyatt's story seemed to confirm his story, and what Emily had said in the bathroom. Brandy was certain of one thing, no matter what Radhauser said, she needed to talk to whoever bought the big stuffed animal.

* * *

After interviewing the coordinator for the Children's Health Fair and getting the names of everyone who'd participated, Radhauser wrote Emily Michaelson's name on a file folder, and scribbled a few new pages of notes about the last eighteen hours, including Vernon's trip to Emigrant Lake where he'd found the Dewars' cabin locked up tight. He'd seen no evidence of any disturbances in the ground around it, but the property was heavily wooded and the recent rain may have masked something. Officer Murphy was assigned to watch the place all day to see if anyone showed up.

Vernon had spoken to the property management company that maintained the grounds and learned Dewar Senior and his wife spent about a month every summer in the cabin, that occasionally their son had a party there, but for most of the year it remained vacant.

But Radhauser wasn't ready to eliminate Glenard Dewar, Jr. as a suspect. Not until he'd talked with Christine about her polygraph results. As he studied his notes, the cop part of him was intrigued by the puzzle, needed to know how and why this child had been taken. The father part of him shuddered, horrified by how quickly a little girl could disappear.

He used the abbreviated words he'd jotted in his pocket-sized notebook to document the interviews he'd conducted so far, including frequent visitors to the park and the neighbors on both sides of the Michaelson's hillside home.

As he put down his pen, Christine barged into his office, the receptionist manning the front desk a few steps behind. "I'm sorry...I tried—"

"It's okay, Shirley."

Christine's face was flushed and devoid of any makeup—her auburn hair still damp from the morning downpour. She slumped into a chair in front of his desk. "Why are you wasting time questioning me? I've told you everything I know. Why aren't you out looking for my baby?"

He closed the file and turned it face down so she didn't have to see her daughter's name. Outside his window, the sun shone, but the pearl-colored sky was still smeared with the remains of the storm.

"I understand how you feel. We've got dozens of personnel from two counties out looking for Emily. But as the lead investigator, I have certain procedures I'm required to follow. I called you in to discuss your polygraph. I'll be recording this interview." He turned on his tape recorder, stated the date and time, his own name, and the fact that he was conducting a post-polygraph interview with Christine Michaelson, mother of two-and-a-half-year-old Emily Michaelson.

"It was horrible," Christine said. "All I could think about was my baby and why wasn't that man out looking for her instead of asking me a bunch of stupid questions. He kept telling me to relax. But I couldn't relax."

"No one can relax," Radhauser said. "But they read your baseline. It doesn't matter how nervous you are."

"You didn't need to put me through all those embarrassing questions."

"Your neighbor claimed she heard Emily crying Friday night. That you screamed, 'You make me so mad I could just...' She reported hearing a door slam." He paused and stared at her. "That's a threat. You were so mad you could just do what, Mrs. Michaelson?"

Before she had time to answer, a new thought entered his mind. What if someone who wanted to protect Emily had taken her, not someone intending to exploit, abuse or ransom the child? He made a mental note to pursue.

"I wanted Emily to settle down and tell the truth about the

necklace. I was exasperated and scared. Brandy's window was open. You know how sound carries at night." Her bottom lip trembled. "My neighbor needs a course in mind your own business."

Radhauser knew she wanted sympathy and he tried to conjure up some. Maybe everyone had a moment when life derailed. Despite the way Christine behaved, she'd just lost her little girl. He'd seen dozens of different reactions to grief. But, he reminded himself, no matter how it manifested, grief didn't necessarily mean innocence. He remembered the Diane Downs case, how she'd accused a bushy-haired stranger of flagging down her car and shooting her two kids on a back road in Springfield, Oregon. Diane had shot her own children because her married boyfriend didn't want kids. Over 400 kids are killed by their parents each year. Three out of five of them are under five years old.

Christine looked like a kid herself, with her fresh face and freckled nose. The way she played with the ends of her hair. Her denim jeans added to the illusion—the blue sweatshirt that made her eyes turn to topaz.

"So, you were concerned about the necklace?"

"Of course," she said. "Until my responsible stepdaughter told me she bought it at a garage sale." She watched him, as if waiting for his reaction.

The sympathy he'd conjured up disappeared. Brandy had explained the reasons for her lie. They seemed legitimate to him, given Christine's anger toward Emily. "I searched previous incident reports and discovered that another one of your neighbors called Child Protective Services on January 14th. Do you know anything about that?"

Christine's face reddened. She pushed back against her chair as if the act of distancing herself from him would make his question go away. For a long moment, she looked at him, but remained silent. Not even a shake of her head. It was one of those times when silence had a voice of its own.

"Do you have kids, Detective Radhauser?"

"I'm the one asking the questions."

"It was a mistake," she insisted. "A false alarm."

"CPS is a busy agency. They were concerned enough to send someone out to investigate on January 30th."

Radhauser wanted to observe her reaction.

She was silent for a moment. "It's a simple matter of human endurance. If you had children, you'd understand."

"Two-year-olds can be challenging. But these days, most parents don't hit or threaten their toddlers. How did Emily break her wrist?"

Christine gave a short nervous laugh. "She fell off her swing and landed on her wrist. Just because CPS investigated a bogus incident, doesn't mean I'd hurt Emily. I smacked her on the butt with my open hand a couple times. And I yell a lot. That's all. I swear to you. If I get her back, I'll take parenting lessons and learn other ways to discipline." Christine straightened herself in the chair and gave him a look that could wilt spinach. "I can't hide the way I feel. Brandy's the one who took acting lessons."

He wished he were the kind of cop who could smack a suspect across the face. "When was the last time you saw Glen Dewar?"

For the first time since the interview began, she looked down. His question had touched a raw spot she didn't want him to see. Glen's name hung in the air, and then she looked up and glared at him. Her eyes seemed to darken. "He's got nothing to do with this."

Radhauser understood her embarrassment, but the polygraph had indicated a level of deception when she'd been asked about her marriage to Daniel and their daughter's paternity. "Probably nothing, but Dewar claims you were in a relationship with him when you got pregnant with Emily."

"You had no reason to talk to Glen."

"This is my investigation. And you may rest assured I will talk to everyone I suspect might be involved. Could Glen think Emily is his daughter?"

"Glen and I always used protection."

"Protection can fail."

She folded her arms across her chest and rubbed her shoulders as if she'd gotten cold. "All right. I worried at first, but once I saw Emily she looked just like Daniel and Brandy." Christine swallowed. "Besides, Glen would have no interest in Emily—even if he thought she was his daughter. He's headed to graduate school. Peace Corps. We…I mean…he had plans. I…" She paused, shrugged. "No use in thinking about that now."

"What happened to your plans?"

"Falling in love with Daniel happened to mine." Her voice sounded distant. "I'm the first person to admit I didn't mean to get pregnant."

"I suspect you got pregnant on purpose because you wanted to marry Daniel Michaelson."

Again, Christine glared at him. "You've been talking to Kathleen Sizemore. That woman doesn't know anything about me."

"You knew about protection and, by your own admission, you used it with Glen."

Tears pooled in the corners of her eyes.

Radhauser swallowed and handed her a box of tissues. Sometimes he really hated his job.

"No matter what I did, Glen could never hate me enough to take Emily. We'd been together like forever."

"What if you're wrong? He must have been pretty upset by your betrayal—reason enough to hurt you or Professor Michaelson."

She hung her head. "Glen was hurt that I cheated on him, okay. But he didn't want children. Not then. Maybe not ever."

"Men grow up. They change their minds."

"Why are you treating me like a suspect? I'm a victim. I had nothing to do with my baby's disappearance. And neither did Glen."

"I've told you this before. When a child goes missing, more often than not, the reason is close to home."

Christine lifted her head and looked at him, her eyes still watery. "I'm sorry for all the mistakes I made. I want another chance. Just find my daughter, Detective Radhauser. Please."

There were things about Christine that appeared suspicious, but Brandy had run home minutes after Emily disappeared and found Christine packing a picnic. She wouldn't have had time to dispose of Emily and get home that quickly. Officers had searched the house and both cars. Christine may be a liar and a lousy mother, but she didn't kidnap Emily unless she had help. "Can you think of anyone who might want Emily? Someone who shows a lot of interest in her. A jealous friend. A relative who wanted a baby. Someone who had a child die recently. Or—"

"Tanya," she said. "Her baby died last summer from SIDS."

"What's her last name?"

"Buchanan. She lives on Orchid Street. Up by the university. I don't think she'd hurt Emily. She loves her. But…"

"But what?"

"I don't know. She's always on my case. Maybe she's jealous that Emily lived and Samantha didn't. Oh my God." She stood. "I have to go talk to her."

"Sit down."

She did.

"Interviewing Ms. Buchanan is my job." Radhauser added Tanya's name and address to the people he still needed to interview. "When you make that list of names, include anyone who might want to hurt you or your husband."

"Daniel already made a list."

"Make your own. I understand there may be some overlap." Radhauser glanced at his watch. "I've kept you long enough. You should go home now."

Christine stood. "I'm sorry. I know you're doing your job. But please, even if you think I'm a lousy mother, you have to find her."

"We are doing everything in our power to bring Emily home." He walked her to the station door, opened it, and stood watching as a group of a half dozen or more reporters blocked Christine's path.

A young man in khakis and a flannel shirt thrust a microphone in front of her face. "Have there been any new developments, Mrs. Michaelson?"

She said nothing.

A female reporter, high heels clicking on the pavement, nudged her way to Christine's right side. "Has the kidnapper made contact?"

A second man maneuvered to her left. "Were you given a polygraph? Do the police consider you a suspect?"

She busted through them, splitting the group in half as adeptly as a linebacker. And then she kept walking, head up, her hands deep in the pockets of her jeans.

Radhauser returned to his desk. He leaned back in his chair with his eyes shut, trying to conjure up an image of Emily that might evoke a sense of whether she was dead or alive. Behind his eyelids, he saw only darkness.

* * *

A brass bell jingled when Brandy opened the door to Pivorotto's Toy Pavilion. She hurried down the aisle of wooden shelves housing colorful boxes of sailing ships, planes, and model cars, her heart drumming inside its cage. This could be the lead they needed to find her sister. She ran past the menagerie of stuffed giraffes, hippos, dragons, and alligators, to the counter where a two-foot high monkey that played cymbals and marched when you wound him up stood beside the cash register. The store smelled like peppermint candy and the vinyl skin of new dolls—like those long-ago Christmases with Kathleen and her father.

Mr. Pivorotto glanced up at her from behind the counter where he frowned at a stack of invoices. He was a little man, not much taller than Brandy, and wore a silky red shirt, a black polka dot bow tie, and a tan leather blazer old enough to belong to one of the Beatles. He had a dark mustache so thin that it could have been drawn with the eyeliner Christine never let Brandy borrow. The moustache curled up on the ends into fat little apostrophes. His hair had started to thin on top, even more than her dad's. At least he didn't try to comb it over his bald spot. His dark eyes twinkled. He looked exactly like a man who should own a toyshop.

"I'm sorry about the Pooh," he said. "I would have called to see if you wanted me to order another one, but I didn't know your last name."

A long model train, with a steam engine and a bright green caboose loaded with Beanie Babies, circled the store on a shelf near the high ceiling. Every ten minutes or so it let out a long, low whistle and a puff of steam rose from the smokestack.

She waited for the whistle to stop, then told him her last name.

"I could have one here in two weeks. Will that be in time for the little one's birthday?" Despite his small body, he had a big, booming voice that filled all the space in the empty store.

"My sister was kidnapped yesterday in Lithia Park."

"Good Lord," he said, his voice suddenly smaller. "That little girl on the news. She's your sister?"

Brandy nodded.

He glanced toward the flyers she clutched in her hands. "I'm sorry about your sister. But surely you can't expect me to post those here. I can't draw attention to a kid taken so close to my toy store."

Brandy took a step back. She couldn't believe it. This was the first opposition to the flyers she'd encountered. She thrust three flyers in front of his face. "Do you want me to tell the police you won't cooperate with a kidnapping investigation?"

He kept his hands at his sides. "Look. I'm really sorry about your sister, but I'm terribly busy right now."

"I'm helping out the police," she lied. "Detective Radhauser asked me to conduct some of the interviews because I know my little sister better than anyone."

"That's interesting. Detective Radhauser was waiting at the door when I opened this morning." He jerked the flyers from her hand and set them on the counter. "Now go investigate somewhere else. I'm up to my neck in bills right now."

"Do you have a record of who purchased the big Pooh?" She told him how she and Emily had passed the store window yesterday afternoon. That Emily noticed the bear was gone. Brandy repeated what Emily had said in the restroom just minutes before she disappeared. "It's my fault she's missing. I should have watched her more closely."

His face softened a little. "Just like I told the detective, it doesn't matter, I'm afraid it was a cash sale."

"It was a woman who bought it, right?" Brandy said, remembering the woman she'd seen in the park organizing the games for a child's birthday party.

He said nothing.

"And she bought it for her little girl's birthday. It was yesterday, right?" Brandy tried to bring the line of children at the pin-the-bowtie on the teddy bear game into focus. "Or maybe it was a little boy."

"I can't tell you that. You're not a police officer and it's private information." Mr. Pivorotto swallowed.

Brandy took a deep breath and let it out slowly. "If I bought toys for my kid in your store, I'd like you a lot better if I thought you'd help someone in need. Please, Mr. Pivorotto. The police think my theory is farfetched. But I know how Emily reacts to things. I know what she'd say if she saw—" her words were little more than croaks, but she forced them out"—that giant Pooh bear she loves so much."

He raised his right eyebrow and stared at her.

"I know you agree with the police," she said.

"I didn't say that."

"Your eyebrow did."

"Look. The police are right. Your theory is farfetched. But I don't have time for this right now. If that damn Walmart rolls back its prices one more time, the life will be sucked out of my store. I have to hold on to the few loyal customers I have. And some people expect privacy, especially when the police are involved."

She took another deep breath. "Why would lose a customer just because you tried to help?"

"There are certain ethics involved in running a business."

She could read the righteous conviction on his face. It was a cheap trick, but actresses used it all the time. Brandy imagined the worst-case scenario—that Emily was dead. But it wasn't necessary to pretend. Her tears were real. "I'm one of your loyal customers, and so are my parents. And I'm not trying to be difficult," she said,

177

looking him straight in the eyes. "But what's more important? Your ethics or my little sister's life?" A single tear rolled down her cheek.

He chuckled. "This is Ashland, missy. I get actresses in here every day." He took a crisp white handkerchief from his inside jacket pocket and offered it to her. "Here—wipe your crocodile tears."

She didn't take it. "You think I'm just a stupid girl," she said, steam building, more tears flowing. "But my high school has tons of kids who shoplift as an extracurricular activity. And I'll tell you something else, mister toyshop mannequin, those kids are nicer than you are." She paused, suck in a ragged breath. "Many of them are out looking for my sister right now. Wonder what they'll do when I tell them you won't help."

"Are you threatening me?"

"I took a class in motivational speaking."

His face was so red he looked as if he might explode. "I should call the police and have you arrested for harassment."

"Do whatever you have to, Mr. Pivorotto. I'm desperate. What would you do if it were your little sister?" She turned to leave.

He touched her shoulder.

She turned back to him.

He sighed and remained quiet for a moment. "I already told Detective Radhauser this, but the customer who bought the Pooh has come into the store before and always paid cash. I don't know her name. But just last evening, she bought a Pooh storybook, *Tigger, Finder of Lost Things*. You know, the one where Tigger finds Pooh's honey pot."

"Emily loves that book," Brandy said.

"She was a quiet, but well-dressed lady, looked like a professional of some kind, who said she was buying the bear for her daughter's third birthday."

"Thank you. Thank you. Thank you." Maybe this was the lead they needed. "Did she mention her name? Or her little girl's name?"

"No. But I carried the bear out to her car."

"What kind of car?"

"What do you intend to do with this information?"

"I'll give it to Detective Radhauser."

"He already has it."

"Okay, then, I'll tell my friends how hard you tried to help. Whoever bought that bear may have been in the park restroom when my little sister went missing. Don't you think your professional-looking customer would be proud if she was one who led us to Emily?"

His bushy eyebrows shot up. "You think she witnessed the kidnapping?"

"Yes," Brandy said. "I do."

He kept nodding as if reassuring himself it was okay to talk. "It was a dark gray Volvo station wagon with a child's safety seat in the back. I'm not sure of the year. Pretty new, though."

Brandy thought about Mrs. Wyatt and smiled, barely able to contain her happiness. Mrs. Wyatt said she saw a gray or blue-gray station wagon or minivan, and a man wearing a bear costume put a child into a car seat. But it could have been a woman. This had to mean something. "Did you notice anything about the license plate?"

He shrugged. "Why would I? Nothing suspicious about her."

Maybe it was a coincidence. Gray cars were pretty common. "Please. Just think about it. You never know what else you might remember." She glanced at the wall behind the cash register and spotted the camera attached to the bottom of the shelf where the train ran. "Is that a surveillance camera?"

"We were burglarized two years ago. Maybe some of your nicer-than-me high school friends."

"So, you could have her on tape?"

"There's a chance I do. But you'll have to check with the police. Your detective friend confiscated it this morning."

CHAPTER EIGHTEEN

The Sunday morning headline announced the kidnapping above a half-page colored photograph of Emily Michaelson on her backyard swing. Detective Radhauser read the article, then folded the newspaper and placed it on the credenza behind his desk. His meeting with Christine's friend, Tanya Buchanan, had led to another dead end. She'd been at the Ashland Hospital all day on Saturday. Hospital personnel confirmed her alibi. He needed a solid lead. He'd asked Vernon to stop whatever he was doing and compile a list of Volvo station wagon owners registered in Jackson and surrounding counties, and call every damn one of them.

Frustrated, he spread out the notes from the interviews he'd conducted so far, along with the phone tips that had been called into the hotline, organizing them into stacks. The ones obviously made by nutcases in one pile—reports of aliens, of Elvis or Santa Claus carrying a small child in the park, a professed psychic who'd had a dream about Emily. If it weren't such a pathetic waste of time, it'd be laughable.

He'd picked up the telephone, about to return the first call, when Brandy raced into his office, red-faced and out of breath.

"I didn't know there was a triathlon in Ashland."

"What did it show? Did you get a good look? Have you put out a description?" She stopped and sucked in a breath. "The person who bought the bear." She told him about her interview with Mr. Pivorotto. "She could know something that could help us find Emily."

Not again. How many times did he have to tell her to stop interfering with his case? He hated to be so hard on the kid, given what she must be facing at home, but carrying out her own investigation could put her in danger. "Stop mucking around in my case."

If she heard, she paid no attention. "A woman bought it for her kid's third birthday. I told you what Emily said. I know her. And she saw that exact bear. The birthday kid was too small to carry a bear that big. That means his mother had to be in the bathroom. Even if she wasn't the one who snatched Emily, she must have seen someone lift Emily from her stroller."

He thought about the odd footprints he'd photographed in the restroom. No question this kid was smart. If one of his officers had delivered this information, he would probably compliment them on the work. He hated to do it, but he had to get Brandy to let up—if for nothing else, for her own protection. "Don't you have a term paper to write or something?"

She lowered her gaze, told him how she and Emily had been eyeing the bear for months, how Brandy hoped to buy it for Em. "Don't you get it? This matches Mrs. Wyatt's story."

He told her Detective Vernon was following up on the Volvo and that he'd let her parents know if they found anything. "I mean it, Brandy, if you don't stay out of this, I'll have you locked up for interfering with a police investigation." Radhauser felt the heat climbing up the back of his neck.

She squared her shoulders and glared at him. "Everyone is threatening to arrest me. Don't I have any rights? This is my sister, Detective Radhauser. I'm the one responsible for whatever is happening to her right now." She stopped, sucked in another breath. "Use your imagination and try not to barf."

He could hear the tears forming in her voice and tossed his handkerchief across the desk.

"Could I at least see the tape? Maybe I'll recognize her from the park."

Radhauser dropped the tape into the player. Static. He backed it up, played it again. The tape was blank.

When he looked at Brandy, he saw the desperation in her eyes. He felt like hugging her and telling her what a great sister

181

she was to Emily. Instead, he tried to harden his features, put far more bravado in his words than he felt. "Now get out of here. I've got work to do."

* * *

While door-to-door canvassing Ashland neighborhoods, Brandy had an idea. Although not listed in the phone book as a costume-maker, Kathleen often sewed for local theater groups. Maybe she knew others who did the same thing—people the police wouldn't know about and couldn't investigate.

Besides, she longed to talk with Kathleen. Someone who wouldn't respond with that slow, sad shake of the head she'd come to expect. Another door closing as layer after layer of hope disappeared.

The sun centered itself in a cloudless sky as she climbed the concrete steps. A purple-leafed plum tree next to the landing formed a canopy against the sun. The rain had washed everything clean and the sawdust around the trees had turned apricot. All around her, the air smelled like spring and the pine mulch Kathleen always used in her flowerbeds.

She rang the bell and waited.

Kathleen opened the door. "Oh, honey. I've been worried to death."

"I'm sorry I didn't return your calls," Brandy said. "The police want us to keep the phone lines open and I've been trying so hard to find Emily."

Kathleen took Brandy's hand and pulled her inside. "I know how difficult this must be for all of you. I'm so sorry, honey." Kathleen cupped her hand gently around the back of Brandy's head.

The tenderness undid Brandy, and she stumbled into Kathleen's arms and all the tears she'd held back wet the soft flesh of Kathleen's neck.

"It's okay, honey," Kathleen said. "Let it out."

When the sobbing subsided, Brandy breathed in Kathleen's scent, as clean and fresh as sheets left to dry in the sun—a scent that made Brandy want to stay close to Kathleen forever. Finally,

Brandy drew away. "I have an idea," she said, and told Kathleen about her interviews with Mrs. Wyatt and her suspicions about the giant Pooh bear in the toy store window. She asked Kathleen to make a list of independent costume makers.

"I'm happy to give you the ones I know, but it will take a little time to get the addresses."

"We don't have much time."

"Are you taking care of yourself, honey? Have you had anything to eat?"

"Not since lunch with Emily yesterday."

"I'm making you a sandwich." Kathleen took Brandy's hand and led her into the kitchen. The radio was tuned to a classical music station. All of a sudden, the music stopped. *"We interrupt your usual broadcast for this breaking development in the Emily Michaelson kidnapping case. Medford police have found a child in a dumpster behind Fred Meyers, assumed to be two-and-a-half-year-old Emily. Ashland police and Emily's parents are…"*

Kathleen flipped off the radio.

"Why'd you do that?" Brandy raced over to the radio and turned it back on, but it was only music. "No," Brandy said, her voice so strangled she could barely understand her own words. "It's not her. It can't be her."

Kathleen made a low sound in her throat and began to say something, then changed her mind. She handed Brandy a tissue.

"I have to call home," Brandy said.

Kathleen walked Brandy to the kitchen table and kept a firm hand on her shoulder while she dialed.

A strange voice answered. "Michaelson residence."

Everything stopped. An instant of utter stillness, like the kind that happened in sleep. Brandy didn't recognize the voice. A family member was supposed to answer in case the kidnapper called. "What's wrong? Why are you answering our phone?"

"It's Officer Corbin," he said. "Your parents just left with Detective Radhauser. They're following up on a lead. I didn't want to leave the phone unattended."

Brandy's thoughts whirled and her legs started shaking again.

"Has there been any news?"

"Where are you?"

"I'm at Kathleen Sizemore's house."

"Good," he said, asking her for the number. "Stay put until I call back."

"No. This is my sister. I want to know now."

"It's been on the news," he said, as if he needed to give himself permission to answer her question. "Police found a child in a—" He stopped, started again. "In Medford. Your father and Christine are headed over to make an identification."

"I know about the dumpster. Is it Emily?"

"We don't know yet."

"What do you mean, you don't know? Have someone ask her. Emily can talk. She can tell you who she is."

He said nothing. And in the terrible silence, fear swelled inside her, crept along her spine and spread out into her veins. "Oh my God. She's dead, isn't she?" Kathleen grabbed the phone. "Call us when you know something definitive." She hung up and took Brandy by the elbow. "Let's get some air," she said, in the take-charge tone of a schoolteacher. She led Brandy out the back door into a yard enclosed with a hedge of mock orange, lush emerald leaves fragrant with tiny white stars. Kathleen stopped in front of a wooden bench at the edge of her rose garden and gently nudged Brandy onto the seat.

From a neighbor's yard, the high tinkling sounds of children, of laughter, tumbled over Brandy, clung to the goose bumps on her arms. She turned her ear in the direction of the sound.

Kathleen knelt in front of the bench. Her eyes, round and large, searched Brandy's face. "Why don't we wait until we hear back from the police officer before we assume the worst?"

"They found a dead body, didn't they?" Brandy's voice sounded about an octave lower than usual. *Dead*, the word sunk in and repeated itself. *Dead.* Her little sister was dead. She couldn't imagine what would happen to their lives without Emily. She tried to stand, but her legs shook too hard and she dropped back onto the bench.

Kathleen placed her hand on Brandy's knee and left it there. "They didn't give out much information over the radio. I think we should wait and see."

Emily in a dumpster with sticky coke cans and empty wine bottles.

Brandy clamped her eyes shut. She needed the darkness to block out even the remote possibility of something so horrible happening to Emily. But the sun's light remained. And behind her closed eyelids, strands of red strung across the black. Emily had to be all right. She couldn't be dead. With Brandy's intense awareness of her little sister, she would have known, felt it in some deep place, if something violent had happened.

Brandy's eyes shot open. "I have to keep looking." She leapt to her feet. "Did you make that list of independent costume makers?"

"Honey, you just asked me. I'll do it as soon as I can."

"I need it to be fast."

"Try to stay calm, sweetheart."

"I am. But I can't just sit here. I need to find my sister. She's been missing for almost twenty-four hours."

"The police officer said he'd call back. If you're out looking, how will I get a message to you?"

Maybe Kathleen was right. Medford was only ten minutes away. How long could it take for them to see the child in the dumpster was not Emily? Brandy couldn't sit still and she began to pace across the yard.

"I'll make you a sandwich. Will you be all right until I get back?"

Kathleen climbed the back steps slowly, turned twice to check on Brandy, then disappeared into the house.

Brandy continued to pace. Beyond the hedge, in the limbs of a neighbor's oak, the sun burned yellow. There was something so peaceful about Kathleen's backyard, with its lush blooming plants and birdfeeders—so much life. A robin dug for a worm in the bed of cosmos and zinnias, then flew to its nest in the eaves.

She watched the momma bird, thinking about what Christine

must be going through right now. Brandy remembered the time she'd found a robin in her bedroom. It must have flown in when Kathleen cleaned the windows. And when they shut the house up before going away for the weekend, it got trapped.

When they returned, two days later, the robin was still alive and sitting on the window ledge. Brandy had opened the window and it flew out and directly to the nest in the oak tree only a few feet away from her window. She'd been ten at the time and felt sorry for the dead babies.

Now, watching what Emily's disappearance had done to Christine, Brandy understood that the real suffering had been for the momma bird, watching helplessly while her babies died.

Kathleen emerged onto her flagstone patio, carrying a tray of hot tea and sandwiches. She set it on a glass-top table, then beckoned to Brandy.

Brandy pulled out a green metal chair, gone to rust at the bolts that held it together. She stared at the back door. "Will we hear the phone?"

Kathleen nodded toward a set of bells for the phone above the doorway. "Don't worry. We'll hear it."

Before Brandy could lift the teacup to her mouth, the phone pealed, loud as a siren in the still yard.

Brandy flinched. Her gaze met Kathleen's and held for a terrified instant. Knocking her chair over in the rush, Brandy took the steps two at a time, then plunged through the kitchen door. "Hello?"

"Is this Brandy?"

"Yes," she said, her voice strangled.

"Your father just called," Officer Corbin said. "The child in Medford was not Emily."

* * *

Brandy and her dad moved around each other in the kitchen with polite concern. The child in the dumpster turned out to be a little girl missing from northern California. People could be so vicious. Someone had kept that little girl a whole year before killing her.

Unable to sit, Brandy started the washing machine, loaded

the dishwasher with coffee cups and water glasses, and wiped the granite counters with a damp sponge. When her dad swept the Cheerios and cookie crumbs from beneath Emily's highchair into a dustpan and headed for the plastic trashcan beneath the sink, Brandy cringed. "Don't do that." She wanted to keep everything Emily had touched the way it was until her baby sister came home.

Her father looked at her, then dumped the dustpan's contents back onto the floor beneath Emily's highchair. One Cheerio rolled to a stop beside the highchair's front leg.

With her back against the pantry cabinets, she stared at the Cheerio as if it held some key to the future. The silence of Emily being gone rang in Brandy's ears. A three-foot high silence that seemed to scream out: *please, you have to find me.*

When her dad put on a fresh pot of coffee, he phoned the police station for the hundredth time, then joined Brandy at the kitchen table. They reviewed the day's events.

The doorbell rang.

"Not again," he said. "I can't face another round of pity hiding behind a batch of chocolate chip cookies."

Each time the bell rang, her father had answered the door, politely thanked the givers, then crammed the perishables into the already-packed refrigerator. The baked goods were stacked, untouched, on the kitchen counters.

Eager to do something helpful, Brandy stood. "I'll get this one," she said, hurrying toward their entryway.

She opened the door.

Detective Radhauser stepped inside. "Is your father home?"

As Brandy ushered him toward the kitchen, Christine appeared in the hallway. "Have you found my baby?"

When he shook his head, her stepmother turned without a word and headed back to her bedroom.

Brandy led Radhauser into the kitchen, offered him a cup of coffee.

He took it, pulled out a chair, and joined Brandy's father at the table. "The prints on the animal cracker box match Emily's."

"Where is he?"

"We let the boy go home. He didn't have anything to do with Emily's disappearance."

Her dad leapt to his feet. "Maybe not, but he has to know something. You're just being soft on him because he's not right in the head."

"The boy's story checks out," Radhauser said. "We've had our share of cranks and cons, but we got a call on the 800 number. A young woman who works as a nanny said she saw someone in a Winnie the Pooh costume carrying a giggling little girl who loosely fit Emily's description. The caller thought they were playing a game. Five minutes later, we got another call. Same story. Except this one thought someone had hired the Pooh bear for a birthday party. She said the child carried a yellow balloon."

"Yellow is Emily's favorite color," Brandy said. What would Emily do if someone posing as Pooh bear had entered the women's restroom? Brandy didn't need to think about the answer. Emily would have lifted her arms to be picked up. Kent and Mrs. Wyatt had been right.

Her dad clamped his hands together, then pushed them back out until his knuckles cracked. "How can you be sure it was Emily and not some other little girl?"

"We can't be one hundred percent certain, but it adds credibility to what Kent told us."

"But the boy has Down syndrome."

"That doesn't mean he can't see," Radhauser said. "And we now have two other accounts to support his story."

"Three," Brandy said. "Don't forget Mrs. Wyatt."

Her father looked at her. "Who is Mrs. Wyatt, and why do you know about her when I don't?"

Brandy held her breath, uncertain of what to say.

"Your daughter talked to her on one of the neighborhood canvasses," Radhauser said. "She has a long history with Ashland Police and is not the most reliable witness." He told Brandy's father how Mrs. Wyatt claimed to have seen a person wearing a bear costume load a little girl into a vehicle parked in the Winburn lot.

"I think she's telling the truth this time," Brandy said.

"It's beginning to look that way," Radhauser agreed.

Her dad paced across the kitchen. "Jesus Christ. What kind of a person would do something like this?"

The muscles in Brandy's neck stiffened. Emily would think someone wearing a costume that looked just like the one in the toyshop window was the real thing. She'd be excited and she'd say, "Bumblebee no sting big Pooh. He no nap."

"A smart one," Radhauser said. "Someone who knew Emily wouldn't be afraid of Pooh."

"Shit," her dad said. "Where do we go from here?"

"I interviewed both callers and they were credible. Vernon is working the list of known sex offenders. We've got officers visiting all the costume shops and talking with the costumed healthcare workers from the Children's Health Fair. We're going to find her."

Brandy braced herself. But it didn't keep the image from forming. Emily empty-eyed and exploited by some pervert with a video camera and an email list of pedophiles with credit cards. She looked at Radhauser and he looked at her.

"We scented the canine unit with Emily's sneakers." Radhauser let out a long puff of air. He told them about the way the hound had stopped in the middle of the bridge where they now believed the perp had taken off Emily's shoes, and then circled a parking place in the Winburn lot.

Her father's eyes looked puffy and rimmed in red. "What kind of a weirdo would do something like that? It doesn't make any sense. Why would someone in a big hurry stop in a busy park to remove her shoes?"

Radhauser stiffened. "I hope to find that out, Mr. Michaelson."

"So, you're telling me someone dressed up like Winnie the Pooh carried Emily across the playground. Stopped in the middle of the bridge to take off her shoes. Took the time to tie the laces together in double knots, and then tossed them into the creek. Why?"

"I don't know," Radhauser said. "But it sure looks that way."

Brandy's father tapped his index finger on the table. "I don't believe this. Some freak, wearing a costume, with..." He paused.

"With a damn shoe fetish, has Emily."

Radhauser sat back, raised his eyebrows, but said nothing.

A gust of wind from the open window ruffled the edge of the finger painting Emily had stuck onto the refrigerator door. Above the painting, five magnetic letters floated in a plastic, child-like script. Multicolored and insistent, they spelled *Emily*.

"Jesus," her dad said. "It's been an entire day since she was taken. She could have been put on a plane and be halfway around the world by now." He laced the fingers of his hands together as if he were going to pray.

Brandy turned and gripped the counter, her hands wet and icy. She leaned over the sink, trying to purge all the muddled things inside her. But in the back of her mind, a plan began to form.

CHAPTER NINETEEN

If a missing child wasn't found in the first forty-eight hours, they probably never would be. Emily Michaelson had been missing for nearly twenty-six. Radhauser glanced at his watch. He needed a solid suspect. Now. What the hell was taking Vernon so long?

Detective Vernon tapped on Radhauser's office door, then stepped inside. "I got Stefan Wysocki in the interrogation room. He's our man." Vernon's face was red, the way it got when he was excited. He'd taken off his blazer and there were circles of perspiration under his arms. He held up an evidence bag holding a 6-inch high stuffed bear. It wore a blue T-shirt with the words Children's Health Fair and the logo of the local hospital printed across the back. A plastic stethoscope hung around the bear's neck. "We found this in his bedroom. I checked with the fair's coordinator. They only handed them out to kids under six."

Radhauser's muscles went loose in relief. "Nice work," he said, feeling hopeful for the first time since Emily disappeared. "It's about time we caught a break." He tucked the bear into his briefcase to pull out when they needed it.

Vernon jerked over a chair and sat in front of the desk. He looked both frazzled and exhausted—probably hadn't gotten any more sleep last night than Radhauser had.

"This is what I know about the scumbag," Vernon said. "He's got no sheet. But he lives alone in that expensive high rise near Mountainside Elementary. Tenth floor. Overlooking the playground. We found binoculars on his bedside table."

The headache that had dogged Radhauser all morning ratcheted up a notch as he imagined the small playground behind

Lizzie's preschool. Little girls on swings, their skirts lifting in the wind. Little girls clambering around on the monkey bars and seesaws. He clamped his eyes shut, hoping the images would go away. "Do you ever wonder why we keep doing this job?"

"Every day," Vernon said.

As a detective, Radhauser had seen almost everything, but nothing repulsed him quite as much as the twisted mind that allowed a grown man to take an innocent little girl and use her for his pleasure. If anyone ever laid a hand on Lizzie—

Vernon opened Wysocki's laptop and downloaded a file. He slipped the computer across the desktop to Radhauser. It was filled with photographs of little girls in bathing suits. Little girls in party dresses with ruffles and patent leather shoes. Toddlers wearing sailor suits and Easter bonnets.

"He had an entire bedroom full of kiddie lingerie, child-sized sequined evening gowns. Even boxes of tiny high heels in every color. It was fucking creepy. But it was the teddy bear that convinced me."

They spent a few moments discussing strategy, then Radhauser stood, slapped a hand on Vernon's back. "Let's get this over with. Try not to scare him into silence." Radhauser worried about Vernon. This case was getting to him and it showed.

By the time they stepped into the interrogation room, the two west-facing windows were already steamed up. It was a small, olive green room, about eight feet by eight feet. It held only a square wooden table with circular stains from coffee cups and coke cans, a tape recorder and four mismatched wooden chairs.

Stefan Wysocki stood in the center of the room, his right hand slipped casually into the pocket of his slacks like a fashion model. He was a good-looking man—slender, but broad in the chest and shoulders. "How may I be of help, detectives?"

Despite his handsome features, his body looked like it had been made from parts taken from other bodies—his arms too short for his long legs, his head a little too big for his slender neck. His dark hair was neatly styled as if he was ready to broadcast the weather on national television. He wore a starched white shirt open at the neck, and a tan linen jacket with brass buttons. He looked like a man who never passed a mirror without casting a lingering glance into it.

Radhauser pulled out a chair and motioned to Wysocki. "Thank you for coming in."

Wysocki sat, adjusted the creases on his pants, and then folded his long-fingered hands in front of the recorder that rested on the table. His nails were neatly filed and had a pink sheen.

Radhauser cringed, pictured Wysocki painting Emily's fingernails and then his own.

"Ever since I heard it on the news," Wysocki said, "I've been worried sick about that little girl. But I'm meeting a client at four." He had the soft, melodious voice of a man who could convince any little girl to help him look for a lost kitten. A man who knew how to get what he wanted.

"I understand you're in an interesting line of work, Mr. Wysocki," Radhauser said. "Would you tell us a little bit about it?"

"Pageant attire for girls in sizes 2-T to 6X. Three-toddler is my most popular line. I guess you could say I consult on wardrobe issues. And I put together photographic portfolios for contestants." Wysocki shrugged. "It pays the bills."

Vernon walked to the corner of the room and backed into it, watching Wysocki intently as if trying to get a sense of what went on in his brain.

Wysocki looked over at Vernon and flashed him a big smile, a wink, and a pinkie wave. The cocky son of a bitch.

"Don't wink at me, you…"

Radhauser shot Vernon a look and set his briefcase on the floor. He pulled out the chair across from the suspect, then turned on the tape recorder. He stated the date, time, and location, and that Detectives Radhauser and Vernon were interviewing Stefan Wysocki, a person of interest in the Emily Michaelson case.

Wysocki listened, then glared at Vernon. "Person of interest? You can't possibly think I had anything to do with that little girl's disappearance."

"Well, gee whiz," Vernon said. "Could it be because you're

always hanging around the park, taking photos of little girls?"

"Did you check the ice cream shop?" Wysocki jeered. "I hear the last missing kid was found napping under a table there."

Beneath the bravado, Radhauser heard a hint of fear.

"You've got no probable cause. Do I need to call my lawyer?"

"You're certainly entitled to do that," Radhauser said. "But we're not arresting you. We just have a few questions. And you were nice enough to come in."

Vernon moved closer. He softened his voice. "Like how do you explain the kiddie porn on your computer?"

"There's nothing pornographic about those pictures. And lots of people like little girls. Why do you think those kid beauty pageants are so popular?"

A line of sweat broke just under Radhauser's hairline and trailed slowly down the back of his neck. The little girls in Wysocki's online photo album were around Emily's age—between three and four years old. "My daughter is interested in competing," Radhauser lied, hoping to lower Wysocki's guard, make him less defensive. "Maybe you can show me and my wife some of your outfits."

"It would be my pleasure. I've got the best selection in the valley. Some of them are..." He paused, shrugged. "Sweetly provocative. Just perfect for pageants."

Provocative. The word echoed inside Radhauser's brain, his thoughts coming rough and relentless. What kind of person found a three-year-old girl provocative? He sucked in a breath. "Do you spend much time in the Lithia Park playground?"

"That park has an incredible variety of bird species. It's beautiful and inspirational. My true calling is poetry. And I'm published, I might add." He lifted his chin.

Vernon laughed, then pulled out the other chair and sat next to Radhauser. "Would that be in the National Association of Perverts Anthology?"

"Go ahead and make your stupid jokes. You have no idea how hard it is to get poetry published. I've placed a few of my photographs, too."

"Congratulations," Radhauser said. "Were you in the park yesterday?"

"Half of Ashland was there."

"I know. I've spoken with a lot of them. But were you there?"

"I'm trying to remember."

"You're a little young for Alzheimer's. Besides, I have signed statements from two witnesses, former clients of yours. Both of them saw you near the park playground yesterday, taking photographs. It was about the time Emily Michaelson went missing."

Wysocki shifted in his chair, lifted the cuff of his shirt and checked his watch. "People lie all the time. Besides, that little girl was snatched from the women's restroom."

Vernon stared at him for a long moment. "Listen, you little faggot. With a fucking wig on, you'd be able to use the women's restroom. I heard rumors you enjoy dressing like a woman."

Wysocki jerked back in his chair as if he'd been slapped. "I most certainly do not." His pale cheeks reddened. "Why are you harassing me?"

"Do you carry costumes as part of your fashion line?" Radhauser asked.

Wysocki nodded. "Child pageants often include interpretive dance or acting as part of the talent segment."

"Do you have access to bear costumes?"

"Why, Detective Radhauser, do you need one?" There was a mocking tone to his voice.

Radhauser wanted nothing more than to slap that wise-ass attitude off Wysocki's face, but he wasn't the kind of detective who resorted to violence.

"I suppose I could order a bear costume if one of my clients wanted one."

Radhauser felt the heat rising on the back of his neck. "Have you ever worn a bear costume, Mr. Wysocki?"

Wysocki jumped to his feet. "The cops searched my apartment. They didn't find any evidence to support that claim." He puffed out his chest. "I told you my line is for toddlers and preschool girls. You may have noticed I'm a bit larger than a size 6X."

"Sit down," Radhauser said, his head throbbing. "Tell me why you were in the park yesterday."

Wysocki sat. "It was a beautiful day. The fair, the music, all the kids running around. I snapped a few photos on my way to an early dinner. No law against that, is there?"

"Where did you eat?"

"Angela's Grill. It was too early for the dinner menu so I sat outside by the creek and had a glass of wine. Pinot Gris."

"Can anyone verify that?" Radhauser asked.

"The place was packed, what with the fair and all. Now, I need to get going." Wysocki pushed his chair back from the table. "This client is important. Poets don't make much money. And I'd like to pay my rent and keep eating."

"We're not done with you yet," Vernon said.

"If you have some legitimate reason for keeping me here, detectives, I'd like to hear it."

Vernon slapped his hand on the table.

Wysocki flinched.

"You tell me exactly what you did to Emily Michaelson and where we can find her," Vernon said.

"I never saw that little girl. I did nothing. I got no idea where you can find her. But I'm calling my attorney. Now." He flapped his hands in front of his face.

Good, Radhauser thought. The cocky son of a bitch was getting nervous. Radhauser pushed his chair away from the table, stood, and brought Wysocki the phone. Vernon was pushing too hard. Radhauser needed the freedom to question Wysocki without the silencing presence of his lawyer. "It's 3:15. Your attorney would need at least an hour to get here. Why don't we go ahead and wrap this up so you can keep that appointment?"

Wysocki placed the phone back into its cradle. He nodded and a strand of hair slid over his forehead. He raked it back with fingers that seemed to tremble. "No matter what either of you think, I'm innocent of this."

From his briefcase, Radhauser pulled the evidence bag with

the teddy bear inside. "Would you like to tell me where you got this?"

Wysocki's brow furrowed, the line of his jaw rigid. "At the Children's Health Fair. Isn't it obvious?"

"Was Emily with you?" Vernon asked.

"I already told you I was alone."

"They only gave these bears to children under six," Radhauser said.

"I found it on a bench near the playground. I planned to give it to my nephew."

"Did you see anyone wearing a Winnie the Pooh costume carrying a little girl?" Radhauser asked.

"The park was filled with people in bear costumes. Lots of them were carrying kids."

"Emily had on a red jacket and a pair of rainbow-colored sneakers. She was holding a yellow balloon."

Wysocki shook his head. "There were so many."

His face contorted, Vernon stood and paced. He pulled a small pair of thick, cotton panties from his pants pocket—the same kind Lizzie wore when they were potty training her.

Radhauser was pissed. Vernon hadn't mentioned this piece of evidence. It wasn't bagged, hadn't been through the regular chain of evidence. What was going on here?

Setting the panties on the table, Vernon grabbed Wysocki's arm. "Did you find these on a bench, too?"

Wysocki stared at them and then his gaze shifted between Radhauser and Vernon, disbelief frozen on his face. He picked up the phone and called his lawyer, but he was out of the office and wasn't expected back until morning.

"See how they're stained yellow," Vernon said. "You scared Emily so much she pissed herself." His voice lilted a little, the way voices sometimes do when they lie. He sat down again.

A shiver passed through Radhauser. Vernon knew how he felt about coercing a suspect with planted evidence. He'd deliberately withheld his plan.

"I...I...I...never saw those before. I...I...don't know

anything about them. This is entrapment." Wysocki kept shaking his head. His brow was soaked in sweat. His voice cracked, and he looked so scared that Radhauser almost felt pity for him.

Grabbing Wysocki by the shoulders, Vernon shook him hard. "The tooth fairy must have planted them under your pillow. Now tell us where Emily is."

Wysocki twisted away from Vernon. "Are you deaf? I swear I don't know where that little girl is or how those got in m…m… my bed."

His hopes sinking, Radhauser studied him.

The room went silent except for the fluorescent light hissing above them.

Wysocki looked at Radhauser. His face had loosened, turned soft with fear. "About the underpants," he said. "I can only think of one, pretty farfetched, possibility. My sister spends the night sometimes. Her husband's a real jerk when he's drinking. I give her and her son my bed and sleep out on the sofa."

Leaning across the table until his nose was just inches from the suspect's, Vernon stared into Wysocki's eyes. "Do you like to play dress up with little boys, too, Stefan?"

Wysocki squirmed under his gaze. "Oh, God, no."

"Does your sister trust you alone with her kid?" Vernon asked.

Wysocki's face twisted as if the question had caused him pain. "Of course she does. I'm his uncle. She knows I'd never hurt Flynn. Besides, I change my sheets every Saturday evening. I…I…would have found those pants yesterday if they were there."

As much as Radhauser hated to admit it, Wysocki was telling the truth. He was a strange man, with an unusual profession, but he didn't kidnap Emily. He'd been at the job long enough to develop a radar about truth and lies.

Radhauser was about to let Wysocki go when Vernon slid a naked photo of a little girl onto the table. It was one of the photos they'd confiscated from a known pedophile. The child was standing in a bathtub, her back to the camera, looking over her shoulder at the camera, a sultry look on her face.

Wysocki glanced at it, then quickly looked away.

"Do you find this sweetly provocative, Mr. Wysocki?" Vernon asked.

Wysocki's gaze returned to and lingered on the photo. He stared at Radhauser for a second before his gaze darted back again.

For the next thirty seconds, Vernon said nothing. "Stand up, Stefan," he finally demanded. "Now."

When Wysocki hesitated, Vernon grabbed him by his arm and pulled him to his feet.

Wysocki tried to cover the front of his trousers with his hands, but Vernon jerked them away.

The suspect was obviously erect. His entire face flushed and a pulse beat in one of the veins at his temple. "I know you think I'm some kind of scum because of my line of work." There was an edge of hysteria sliding into his voice. He sat back down, put his face in his hands. He seemed to curl into himself and when he lifted his head, there were tears in his eyes.

"Just looking at a naked three-year-old gave you a hard-on," Vernon said. "What are we supposed to think?"

"Okay. Okay. I find little girls' b…b…bodies beautiful. The way they hold a hint of the woman they'll one day become. I want to be near them. Hear them laugh. But I'm not some kind of p…p…pervert. And I swear to you I've never, not one time in my whole life, acted on my feelings."

Radhauser pushed his chair away from the table and stood. Wysocki was most likely a sexual deviant. But they couldn't hold the man for getting an erection. "You're free to go, Mr. Wysocki. And I'm sorry for the inconvenience. But there is something you can help me with."

Maybe they could salvage something from this interview.

Relief washed over Wysocki's face. He stood and shot a glance toward Vernon, then looked back at Radhauser. "You treated me with respect and I'll help you in any way I can, Detective Radhauser. As long as I don't have to talk to that asshole again."

Vernon slammed out of the room.

Radhauser escorted Wysocki to the door. "I'd like to take a look at the photos you snapped in the park yesterday."

"No problem. I'll bring them by later." Wysocki slipped a business card from his inside coat pocket and handed it to Radhauser. "Give me a call and we'll set up an appointment for you and the missus."

As soon as the door closed, Radhauser ripped the card into pieces and tossed them into the garbage can.

CHAPTER TWENTY

After the interrogation, on a strong hunch he hoped wasn't true, Radhauser sat alone in his office. The throbbing in his head had become something else, something worse and incessant. He grabbed the aspirin bottle from his desk drawer and swallowed three. Vernon had an impeccable record and Radhauser admired him, the way he gave everything to the job. But with no other choice he could live with, Radhauser called Vernon into his office, shut the door and waited for him to sit. "What where you hoping to accomplish in there?"

Vernon said nothing. He stared out the window and wouldn't meet Radhauser's gaze.

"Where did you really find those pants?"

"In that pervert's bed."

"Are you sure about that?"

He met Radhauser's stare. "Absolutely. Check with Officer Sullivan. He was searching the bedroom with me."

Radhauser saw it, the brief side stepping of Vernon's eyes that meant deception.

Vernon opened his mouth, and then closed it.

"If that's true, why didn't you put those underpants through the regular chain of evidence?"

"There wasn't time. Send them to the lab. You'll find Emily Michaelson's DNA. Ashland doesn't need that scumbag. Maybe he hasn't acted on his lust. But someday he will." Vernon paused and looked at Radhauser hard. "You've got a little girl. And I got a two-year-old granddaughter." Vernon's jaw tightened.

"You've never lied to me before. We talked about our strategy.

You should have told me about the pants then.'"

Vernon's face changed and in it, Radhauser saw an admission of guilt. For a long moment, Vernon stared at his shoes. "Everything in my gut told me he'd confess."

"Next time, try using your brain," Radhauser said. The air between them could blow up if someone lit a match.

"Don't you think it was worth a try?"

"No, I don't. And even if Wysocki turned out to be guilty, you know planted evidence would result in a mistrial."

"I'm only five years from retirement. I didn't enter the pants in the evidence log. No one has to know. Please don't cost me my pension."

Radhauser couldn't respond. He leaned back in his chair. It made a terrible sound, like the squawking of a crow. He liked working with Vernon. And there were some decisions even good cops made that crossed the line between right and wrong because the line was blurred by emotion. In a case like this, when a little girl's life was at stake, there was often no time to weigh the circumstances or think about consequences. What Vernon did, lie to a suspect during an interrogation, wasn't against the law.

"I knew you'd be pissed," Vernon said. "But I was certain he was the one. If he'd confessed, where I got the underpants wouldn't have mattered."

"Where did you get them?"

"I found them on the floor in Emily's room yesterday."

"I'm taking you off active in the Michaelson case."

Vernon didn't say a word. He turned on his heels and left the room, slamming the door behind him.

Radhauser dropped his head into his hands. Time was running out. They had nothing except three reports of a person in a bear costume carrying a little girl who loosely fit Emily's description— one of them from a known wacko. A single costume in a park filled with unidentifiable adults dressed up like bears and carrying little kids.

* * *

Guitar case in hand, Brandy stepped out of her bedroom and

headed for the kitchen where Detective Radhauser had relieved Officer Corbin of telephone duty. She planned to go the park to meet Stone at 4:30p.m.

Her father and Christine were outside with reporters, recording another plea for Emily's safe return. The kitchen smelled like oranges. She glanced at the untouched basket of fruit on the counter one of the neighbors had delivered yesterday.

Radhauser nodded toward the guitar case. "You headed for Nashville?"

"Some day. Right now, I'm helping the drama club set up for the prayer vigil. And having a practice session with Stone. He's going to accompany me when I sing tonight. Tell me the truth. Do you think this vigil is a good idea?"

"Anything that increases public awareness is good. The more people we have looking, the better chance—"

The phone rang.

Radhauser looked at her. "I need you to answer that."

A rock dropped to the bottom of Brandy's stomach. What if it was the person who had Emily? "I can't," she said, trying not to show her fear. "I'll be late for the setup."

The phone trilled again.

"A kidnapper will hang up if he thinks the police are involved. It's always better if a family member answers."

"Can't you pretend you're my dad?"

"It's not worth the chance—the possibility it's someone who knows your dad's voice."

It was probably Christine's mother. Her father had told Mrs. McCabe not to call so often, that they needed to keep the lines open, but she hadn't listened.

When the third ring completed, Radhauser signaled for Brandy to pick it up.

"Michaelson residence. Brandy speaking."

"Listen carefully," a mechanical-sounding voice said. "I have the little girl. I want you to meet me at Rogue Valley Mall." The voice was strangely flat as if the person behind it read something out loud in their sleep—labored and way too slow.

Brandy shook so hard she had to hold the receiver with both hands. She kept nodding, as if the person on the other end watched her, but Brandy couldn't think of a single thing to say.

Radhauser stretched out his arm, cupped his hand palm-side up and wiggled his fingertips. A motion that meant keep them talking.

"Is she all right? Is Emily safe? Is she eating vegetables?"

"Yes," the voice said. "We're happy to be together again. Even the crows have silenced their voices."

Brandy was confused. What did he mean they were happy to be together again? Was the kidnapper someone who knew Emily? Brandy tried to hand the phone to Radhauser.

He shook his head, gave her a stern look and then scribbled a note. *Ask if you can speak with Emily.*

Brandy did.

"Not now. She's napping."

"Please. Give her back. Don't hurt her. We love her so much. And we miss her." She heard the rising panic in her own voice.

Radhauser shook his head, flicked his hand up and down, a gesture meant to calm, then held up a piece of scrap paper.

She read it out loud. "What do you want us to do?" The question hung in the air.

The garage door opened. Christine and Brandy's father stepped into the kitchen.

Radhauser quickly shook his head, put his finger to his lips to keep them silent.

They both stopped, as frozen as a couple in the wax museum—a look of panic on Christine's face. Brandy's father's hands knotted.

"Oh," the voice said. "Go to the far end and wait on the bench outside the upper entrance to JC Penney's. A family reunion. Even you, the one little Emily calls Band-Aid. But no police." The voice dragged on so slowly it seemed like five minutes before it paused.

Brandy opened her mouth to ask if Emily had been crying for her Pooh bear, but afraid of saying the wrong thing, she said nothing. The silence lengthened.

Radhauser's dark blue eyes widened as he frantically wrote another note. *Ask if you should bring anything.*

Her words returned and she asked the question.

"Yes, of course. Bring ten thousand dollars. Leave it under the bench at 5:45p.m. sharp. Walk to Mervyns. Emily will be in a stroller parked in the baby department." One moment, Brandy thought it was a male voice, the next it sounded female.

"Will someone be watching her? It's dangerous there," she said, remembering the way the escalator rose just behind the shelves of diaper bags and footed sleepers. "She knows how to unbuckle the belt. What if Emily climbs out of the stroller?"

Brandy's answer was a dial tone. "They hung up."

Christine lurched across the room and grabbed Brandy by the shoulders. "What did he say? Does he have Emily? Is he giving her back?"

Brandy clutched the receiver, too stunned to reply.

Her father removed Christine's hands from Brandy's shoulders. "For Christ sake, give her a moment," he said, then placed the phone back into its cradle.

"Are you insane? She knows where Emily is." Christine grabbed Brandy by the shoulders again and shook her hard. "Was it a man or a woman?"

Still unable to speak, Brandy shrugged.

"You should have listened harder."

Radhauser gave two thumbs up. "We traced it. Rogue Valley Mall."

The fact that the kidnapper phoned from the mall must be a good sign, Brandy thought. A sign they were telling the truth about holding Emily there. When her voice returned, Brandy twisted away from Christine and turned to Radhauser. "Why would the kidnapper say they were happy to be together again, that even the crows were silent?" Before Radhauser could respond, Brandy remembered the crow's feet Emily had brought to school for show and tell. She told him.

Her father looked at her, horrified. "Emily brought something like that to school and you didn't tell anyone?"

She stared at his hand, resting on Christine's arm. Brandy didn't want to get her stepmother in trouble, so she hung her head and said nothing.

"Brandy showed them to me," Christine said. "I threw them away and washed Emily's hands with disinfectant. I thought they were something she'd picked up in the park."

Her father stared at Christine as if he couldn't believe what she'd said. He inched away from her. "Emily is a baby. We're supposed to protect her."

Radhauser held up his hand like a traffic cop. He looked tired, but excited. Stubble darkened his cheeks and chin. "You need to focus. We just received a ransom call." He told her parents what had transpired in the phone conversation, leaving out the part about no cops.

Brandy closed her eyes. *Emily will be okay. Okay. Okay. Okay.* The word bounced around inside her head until it lost its shape and meaning. But she kept thinking it anyway, believing, hoping, praying that if she thought it hard enough it would be true.

"There is always the possibility the call was a prank," Radhauser said.

"Hardly anyone knows this, but Emily often calls me Band-Aid."

"Good. I'll mobilize the officers."

"But the kidnapper said no police." Brandy's voice was unnaturally high.

Christine's gaze shot to Radhauser and hardened. "Why didn't you tell us that? We're going alone. Just the three of us. Like the kidnapper said."

"Statistically, the survival rate is much higher if police are involved."

Daniel took Christine's hand. "I know you're scared. But we should do what the police say. They're the experts."

"How can you be so calm?" she snapped.

"I'm trying not to panic. There's a danger of panicking here." Christine said nothing.

Brandy stared at the poster on the kitchen table with Emily's photograph. *Have you seen this child?* A panic that burned like acid seeped into her. No thoughts would come, no words. She just stood there looking at the Cheerios on the floor beneath Emily's highchair.

When Christine finally spoke again, the voice that came out of her sounded different from any one Brandy had ever heard before. It was tight and loud with fear. "What if the kidnapper knows the police are there and does something terrible to Emily?"

"None of us will be in uniform or a marked car. We'll look like ordinary Sunday shoppers."

"Pull cops from out of the woodwork," her father said. "Whatever it takes to catch this bastard."

"Is the money a problem?" Radhauser asked.

"No," her father said. "But the banks are closed today."

"Don't worry," Radhauser said. "We've got stacks of money we confiscated from a drug raid last week."

CHAPTER TWENTY-ONE

In the nearby Rogue Valley Mall, Brandy examined the face of her watch again. The hands didn't appear to be moving. *5:25. 5:25. 5:25.*

Don't look at them, she told herself. *Think about something else.* She scanned the wide and well-lit corridors, peered into the strollers of a dozen safe toddlers as their mothers pushed them, moving in slow motion in and out of stores. She listened to the high, eager voices begging for cookies, an ice cream cone. Heard mothers saying no and her own voice inside theirs, the many times she'd said no to Emily. And she fought the urge to shake the parents until they gave in. She turned toward her dad. "Is it okay if Emily sleeps in my bed tonight?"

He held the shopping bag between his legs and studied the tips of his shoes. "We have to find her first," he said without looking up.

She glanced at Christine. With her head bent forward and her coppery hair a tangled mane around her shoulders, her stepmother looked like a little girl. The invisible belt around Brandy's chest tightened. She touched Christine's arm.

Christine looked up, her eyes glassy and red. "I hope I can hold it together." She puffed out her cheeks, letting the air out slowly. "Your father," she whispered. "He's so fucking composed."

Her father's eyes were suddenly wide and on fire. "I'm not fucking composed," he said, his voice rising. "I'm Emily's father and I'm damn upset. Do I need to prove it to you, Christine? Pound on my chest and scream? Or would you rather me pull my hair out by the roots?"

"Please," Brandy said. "Can't you be Ward and June Cleaver for one hour?"

A silence fell over them.

5:30. Brandy imagined Emily climbing out of the stroller and racing into her big sister's outstretched arms. No, that's not how it should go. She'd stand back and let Christine be the first one to scoop Emily up. In fifteen more minutes, they'd get Emily back. Brandy watched an ant furrow into a bright purple gumdrop that had rolled to a stop against the concrete trash container. The air around them smelled like chocolate from the Rocky Mountain candy store.

Stationed throughout the mall, police officers in street clothes stood, their watchful eyes scanning.

At exactly 5:45, her dad tucked the bag under the bench, took Christine's hand and, just as Detective Radhauser had instructed, walked the long corridor to Mervyns. Though she wanted to run, Brandy adjusted the strap on her backpack and trailed along behind them. She played her role, the seemingly disinterested teenager shopping with her parents.

Her dad and Christine were halfway down the escalator when Brandy panicked in front of the top step and stood, gawking at the moving staircase. She hadn't been on an escalator in nearly fifteen years. She always took the elevator or the stairs toward the center of the mall. In her anxiousness to find Emily, she'd forgotten.

Other shoppers walked around her. She forced herself to breathe from the bottom of her diaphragm. It was time to stop running from her fear and grow up. She had her little sister's Pooh bear in her backpack. She had to get it to Emily.

Envisioning the exact placement of her right foot, she planned her step with the appearance and descent of the next metal stair. Imagined her hands gripping the black rubber rails.

But before she could move forward into the scene she'd visualized, two girls in leather skirts hurled disgusted looks in her direction. "It won't eat you," the shorter one said before her gaze settled on Brandy's cheek. "On second thought, maybe it already did."

"At least I can blame my face on an accident. What's your excuse?"

With exaggerated steps, the two girls giggled, then stomped in front of Brandy and onto the same escalator stair without even a glance toward their feet.

Brandy considered shoving them hard, but decided it might cause a scene and frighten the kidnapper away. If Brandy took off running, she could get to the center stairs in less than two minutes, but then it would take another two for her to reach the baby department in Mervyns. Four minutes was a long time. She wanted to be there when her family was reunited. She couldn't let a couple of clueless dweebs stop her from getting to Emily.

You can do it. An escalator required a simple and basic maneuver easily mastered by little kids, preteens in leather skirts, and old people. With her sister's name ringing inside her head, Brandy plunged forward. Once on the stair, she closed her eyes and gripped the rails so tightly she couldn't distinguish their vibrations from her own trembling.

Near the bottom of the escalator, her dad turned just as Brandy opened her eyes. A look of panic crossed his face and he struggled to climb back up the steps. But blocked by a clot of descending shoppers, he stood near the last stair and waited. When she'd descended, he grabbed her arm and pulled her against his chest, then let her go. "Are you okay?"

Brandy looked over her shoulder at the escalator—unable to believe she'd come down it. "I did it."

Her father smiled, grabbed her hand, and ran towards the entrance to Mervyns. Christine was already racing up and down the aisles in the baby department, shoving shoppers out of her way. "Emily," she called. "It's Mommy." In her now frantic search for the stroller, she knocked over displays of ruffled dresses, little sailor suits with red stars on the collars. A store security guard restrained her. "You have to let me go. My baby's been kidnapped."

Shoppers stopped what they were doing and stared.

Brandy's father caught up. He explained the situation to the guard who then released his grip on Christine, turned her over to her husband, and began to search the store.

"What's the matter?" Christine said to Brandy's father. "Have I embarrassed you?" She jerked away from him and hurried over to Brandy, grabbed both of her arms. "Are you sure you got it right? Sure it was Mervyns and not Meier and Frank?" She sounded hysterical.

Her father gently pulled Christine away. "The kidnapper could be watching," he whispered to her. "You have to get control over yourself. You may have already frightened him into hiding."

"I can't get control over myself. My baby is missing."

Brandy's father turned Christine to face him. "Go ahead. Don't let me stop you. Get as hysterical as you need to. But I'm aiming for sanity here." He stared at her and then his words fired like bullets. "And don't you ever suggest I don't care about my daughters." He trembled as if he was about to explode, then slowly walked away. "I'd give my life for those girls," he whispered.

Brandy swallowed.

Christine grew still. Her face contorted. "It's not my fault," she said, her gaze landing on Brandy.

Under Christine's scrutiny, the skin around Brandy's scars began to itch. She shuddered, then shifted her gaze to the floor.

They waited until a half hour after the stores closed. No one claimed the ransom.

And Emily was still missing.

* * *

It was close to seven when Brandy's father unlocked the front door.

Christine stepped into their living room and froze. The drawers had been yanked out of the end tables, their contents dumped into a pile on the living room carpet. The sofa and chair cushions were strewn across the floor like gravestones. Books and Christine's Precious Moments collection on the shelves next to their fireplace had been scattered about. Kitchen cabinets were open, things pushed aside in the pantry. Whoever had done this had been out of control, frantically looking for something.

While Detective Radhauser searched the house for an intruder, Brandy stood in the entryway, staring at one of the bookcases as a row of dislodged encyclopedias tumbled like dominoes onto the floor.

Radhauser returned. "I sure misread this one. The old lure-the-homeowner-away trick."

Brandy tried to track the meaning of what he'd said, then shifted her gaze to her stepmother.

Christine sat on the sofa, confusion all over her face. She bit at her already bloody cuticles, then wiped at her eyes with her index fingers. She looked as if she could fall apart, like a soggy tissue paper. "What kind of a sicko would call and say they had Emily just so we'd leave our house?"

Radhauser sighed and shook his head. "It's a small force. I wanted every available…" He turned to Brandy's father. "I'm sorry."

"I insisted you bring every cop," her dad said. "The house doesn't matter. Nothing matters except finding Emily."

"There's no evidence of forced entry," Radhauser said. "Does anyone outside the immediate family have a key?"

Her dad shook his head.

"Are you sure all the doors were locked?"

"I'm compulsive about the doors, but the windows are another story." He paused and looked at Brandy. "I've considered putting a door knob on her bedroom window."

Brandy cringed. She knew they'd find it unlocked.

Christine had moved from the sofa to the steps leading into the living room. Tears gathered in the corners of her eyes.

Radhauser told them to remain in the living room. He called a team over to fingerprint. Once they left, he asked Brandy's father to search the house. "It could be a coincidence. There has been a series of break-ins in Ashland. Mostly stolen jewelry and cash."

"But the person who phoned knew that Emily calls me Band-Aid. If that person didn't have Emily, then how—" Brandy was interrupted by her dad's return. Her heart jerked against her chest as she waited.

"The screen is off on your window," her father said. "You might as well put a goddamn welcome sign next to it."

"I forgot," Brandy said.

Her father scowled at her. "I'll check the house for missing items."

"When someone wants to get inside," Radhauser said, "they find a way. A bump key. Or they break one of those panes on the kitchen door, reach in, and unlock the deadbolt."

A few moments later, her father reappeared in the living room. "Whoever it was didn't steal anything that I can see. The layer of dust on Christine's jewelry box hasn't been disturbed."

"If it bothers you so much, hire a cleaning lady," Christine said.

Her father continued as if he hadn't heard his wife. "Even though it appears they didn't steal anything, they took everything out of Emily's drawers, her closet and her toy box. They even took the pillows and comforter off her bed."

"Maybe I should take a look," Brandy said. "I know Emily's stuff better than anyone."

"Right," Christine said. "You're the one who pays attention. The one who knows how much Emily weighs and how tall she is. The one Emily clearly prefers. A regular Mary Poppins."

Brandy didn't know what to say. "I'm only trying to help."

Christine started to cry. "You're right. I'm a terrible mother."

Brandy hurried into her sister's room. Just like her father had said, everything had been pulled out of Emily's closet and drawers. Her toys were scattered around the room. And there was an odd smell in the room, something vaguely familiar, but definitely not Emily's smell of apple shampoo and baby powder.

Less than five minutes later, Brandy returned to the living room. "They took some of her stuffed animals," she said to Detective Radhauser. "All the Winnie the Pooh characters. Tigger, Kanga and Roo. Piglet and Eeyore." She didn't mention the strange smell in Emily's room or that she still had Pooh bear in her backpack. Christine would want him. And Brandy couldn't let him go.

Christine was still slumped on the steps, her face in her hands. Radhauser dropped a hand on her shoulder. "If the kidnapper did this, it's a good sign. It tells us he's concerned about your daughter's wellbeing. That she's alive. And being cared for."

Her stepmother spoke so softly that Brandy had to strain to hear. Christine's voice came as close to heartbreak as anything audible. "And it tells us he'll never give her back."

CHAPTER TWENTY-TWO

In his years as a detective, Radhauser had attended more than his share of candlelight vigils for both the living and the dead. He'd thought it was important for him to be there, believed perpetrators often wanted to witness, first hand, the fallout from what they'd done. He'd always spent his time searching faces in the crowd, trying to read something in an expression or a gesture.

But tonight, he'd asked Officer Sullivan to take charge for the few minutes Lizzie would be on stage. The Rainbow's Edge Preschool was performing the opening song. Lizzie didn't fully understand what was going on, but insisted she wanted to participate. "Emily goes to my school, Daddy, and she got lost. I want to sing so she can hear me and come home."

It was Lizzie's first on-stage performance and Radhauser wanted to watch as a father, not a detective. Still, he couldn't help looking around at the gathering crowd, examining every face, wondering if the kidnapper might be in the audience—knowing the urge to return to the scene could be strong. He spotted Sullivan and several other law enforcement officers dispersed among the throng.

The clouds had disappeared and the night sky reeled with stars. Lithia Park had that smell of wet pine and mown grass soaked in rain.

The Ashland High School Drama Club had set up a wooden stage in the grassy area near the playground. A movie screen in the background flashed life-sized photographs of Emily. Someone had brought in a piano and set up a sound system, with microphones across the stage and four giant speakers in the corners.

215

In front of the stage, Christine knelt beside a pile of gifts that kept growing, encroaching on the area where the spectators stood. Friends of the Michaelsons and total strangers dropped off bouquets of spring flowers and storybooks left open to special passages. Burning candles encased in glass. Teddy bears and stuffed lambs with little signs printed in a child's script, *We Love You, Emily.*

Yellow ribbons wrapped almost every tree in the park. And flyers with Emily's photograph clung to telephone poles and fence posts, graced nearly every window on the Plaza and Main Street. Two drama club students were posted at the park entrances, handing out votive candles and matches donated by area businesses.

A muffled scream caught Radhauser's attention and he spun around, his heart hammering. It was Christine.

Both Sullivan and Radhauser raced toward her.

She held a big Ziploc bag filled with chestnut-colored curls. The kind of ringlets mothers often clipped for a child's baby book.

"Where did you find that?" Radhauser asked.

She nodded toward the piles of flowers and stuffed animals.

Radhauser felt as if the temperature had dropped ten degrees. Did the hair belong to Emily? Why cut the child's hair? Had the kidnapper wanted to change Emily's appearance? There'd be no need to disguise a child you intended to kill. Leaving the hair at the memorial could be a sign of remorse.

He turned to Sullivan. "Get me an evidence bag. And see if you can put a rush on a DNA comparison. We have Emily's hairbrush." This was huge. If it turned out to be Emily's hair, it meant that the kidnapper had not left the area. It meant he or she was close enough to Lithia Park to leave Emily unattended. He remembered Emily had said she had two big friends. Maybe the kidnapper was working in tandem with someone else. But either way, it appeared this kidnapper had a conscience. And, with any luck, didn't plan to kill Emily.

Sullivan returned and bagged the evidence.

Radhauser scanned the crowd. No one looked suspicious.

Everyone looked suspicious.

"Try to keep this away from the press," he whispered to Sullivan and Christine.

Cameramen from three local television stations had set up their equipment to video the vigil. Reporters from newspapers in Grants Pass, Ashland, Medford, and Portland milled through the crowd, asking questions of area residents.

A young man in khakis and a dark blue turtleneck grabbed Radhauser's arm. He had a small notebook in his right hand, a pencil behind his ear. "I'm Quinton with the *Medford Tribune*. Are you the lead investigator?"

"I'm working on the case," Radhauser said. Again, he scanned the crowd.

Quinton nodded toward the memorial—still guarded by two officers. "I heard a scream. Why are the police keeping the press away?"

"We need to examine the gifts. Sometimes the kidnapper leaves a message."

"Did you find anything?" Quinton asked.

"Just a lot of love for Emily Michaelson. And you can imagine how painful this is for her mother."

Quinton cocked his head. "So, Mrs. Michaelson was the one who screamed."

"The officers will be finished in a few minutes and you can get your photograph."

"Do you have any new leads?"

Again, Radhauser scanned the crowd. "We're working on several, but divulging details to the press at this point could hinder the case. If you'll excuse me, Quinton. My four-year-old is about to perform."

At exactly 8p.m., Gracie and several other mothers herded up three and four-year-old kids and marched them, single-file, onto the stage. Each child wore dark pants, a white shirt, and held a battery-powered candle. The moon slipped behind a bank of clouds, and the light from the stars overhead seemed to thicken and gather like smoke.

When the stage lights dimmed, Gracie took his hand, but her gaze never left the stage. His fingers entwined around hers, grateful not only for her but for the daughter she'd given him. And for the way their presence in his life had eased some of his grief over Laura and Lucas.

On stage, the children clutched their candles in both hands, the flickering bulb just under their chins. Their small faces radiated in the golden light. He couldn't take his eyes off Lizzie, who noticed him watching and waved.

Ms. Frazer, the preschool teacher, stepped up to the piano. She wore black pants and a gray, cowl neck sweater. Her short auburn hair had an unexpected streak of gray, like a lightning flash through the crown of her head. He'd heard it was the mark of a feisty and temperamental woman. She played a piano introduction and the children began to sing. *This Little Light of Mine.* Their voices were as fragile as the bubbles he blew for Lizzie to chase around the backyard. And as easily snuffed out.

He tried to make the morbid thoughts go away. No one wanted to believe a person you loved could vanish forever. He tightened his grip on Gracie's hand.

When the preschoolers' song was over, Radhauser made a brief presentation to the crowd, asking for anyone's help who may have been in Lithia Park between 3 and 3:40p.m. on Saturday. He announced the hotline number, mentioned the child's birthday party held in the park, and asked that anyone who'd seen a person dressed in a Pooh bear costume please come forward and call the hotline. The number flashed across the screen beneath Emily's photo.

After he finished, he stood beside Gracie who'd lifted Lizzie onto her shoulders. Ordinarily he would have taken her, but now that he knew the kidnapper had been in the park, he wanted freedom to run at a moment's notice.

A minister from the local Methodist church gave a brief prayer, asking everyone to light their candles and bow their heads. He implored God to help bring Ashland's little girl back safely.

While hundreds of candles burned, Brandy and Stone

stepped onto the stage. They both wore black jeans and white shirts with long sleeves. Brandy's jeans were tucked into a pair of black cowboy boots. She had on a black Stetson with an ornate silver chain around the crown. Stone's was white.

She sat on a high wooden stool, bent over her guitar, tuning it with so much focus that Radhauser felt as if he should look away. But he couldn't. He thought about her scars, the way she sat sideways on the stool—the left side of her face toward the back of the stage. He thought about all the emotions of today—the fear Emily was dead in that Medford dumpster; the ransom call; and the ensuing disappointment. Coming home to find their house ransacked. Brandy's open window the point of entry. He didn't know how she conjured up so much strength.

Stone announced their song was one Brandy had written for Emily.

Brandy kept her head down while he talked. Though the scarred side of her face was nearly invisible to the audience, she reached up as if by instinct and smoothed her hair over her left cheek.

Stone beat a soft rhythm on his guitar and tapped his foot against the wooden floor. They played some chords together, then he moved the microphones closer to their faces.

Brandy lifted her head and sang. The wind carried her words.

I've heard love can conquer anything,
Be a fortress in the storm.
It can lift you to the mountaintop,
And hold you safe and warm.

Holy shit, Radhauser thought. The kid had a voice. And not just a singing-in-the-school-choir voice. Brandy Michaelson had a flat-out-grab-the-heart-and-rock-the-world kind of voice. The kind of voice that could make scars disappear. Make even the coldest heart melt a little.

When the world is dark with sorrow,

219

And you think it's yours alone,
With doubt and fear assaulting,
Only love can bring you home.

The song was somewhere between country western and
folk. As her singing soared and then came back, Brandy seemed
oblivious to everything except the sound her fingers and voice
made. She sang as if a door in her heart broke open and there was
no one in the audience except Emily and God. She was all breath
and sound—a shiver up the back of Radhauser's neck, a catch in
his throat, and a reminder of everything beautiful and easily lost.

And now our prayers for Emily,
Are lifted loud and high.
In hopes that she will find them
In the stars that light her sky.

In her clear pitch, there rang so much sadness and loneliness
that Radhauser wondered how she could continue to sing. Or
how he could continue to breathe and still listen. He had no idea
this kid was so gifted.

So, in this night of crisis, Lord,
When she's scared and all alone,
We beg you, Father, please,
Please love her safely home.

Brandy stopped singing.
A hush fell over the crowd.
Radhauser closed his eyes, trying to hold on to the incredible
feeling she'd provoked for as long as he could. With the last notes
of her song still ringing in the cool night air, it was a magical
moment—one when time literally seemed to float above them.
A moment when anything seemed possible. Even finding Emily
alive.
When he opened his eyes, his first thought was about his

son, about Lucas, and how much he'd wanted to be a rodeo cowboy. It was the dream of his boyhood. Who knew that dream would disappear? Out of nowhere, Radhauser was walloped again with the powerful grief of missing his boy. Had he lived, Lucas Radhauser would be twenty-three years old now—a grown man. But for his father, Lucas had been forever frozen as a thirteen-year-old boy.

He sighed.

The moment passed.

A man started to clap, a soft respectful sound. A woman joined in, then another until the audience went wild, roaring, stomping their feet and whistling, like in the sixties at a Beatles concert.

In the commotion, Brandy put her guitar into its case, stepped off the stage and disappeared behind it.

Radhauser hurried to the back of the stage where he found Brandy sitting on the ground, her head in her hands. He stopped in front of her, touched her shoulder, and waited for her to look up at him.

When she did, her eyes were puddled with tears.

"What you did up there was brave and beautiful."

"Maybe." Her tears spilled over. "But what good did it do? It won't bring Emily back." She stood and started to walk away, but stopped when she spotted her stepmother. Brandy looked as if a truckload of pain barreled straight toward her.

Before Radhauser could stop her, Christine grabbed Brandy and shook her back and forth. "How dare you turn this into a rock concert when my baby is missing."

"I didn't mean…I didn't know anyone would clap. I just…" Brandy stopped talking, as if she knew there was nothing she could say.

"That's enough," Radhauser said, grabbing Christine's wrist and pulling her away.

She jerked her arm free and took a step backward, her gaze tumbling over the playground, her face lifeless.

Brandy stood motionless, before she stumbled backwards.

Gracie, holding Lizzie by the hand, turned the corner and leaped into action. She led Brandy to the back edge of the stage and lowered her into a sitting position. Gracie introduced herself and then sat down beside Brandy and opened her arms. As Brandy seemed to collapse into Gracie's embrace, he'd never been more proud of his wife.

Christine balled up the hem of her T-shirt in her fists and stared at the ground.

"I know you're hurting," he said. "But Brandy had no idea people would applaud. That's not what she was looking for and I think you know it."

"I don't know what to think," she said, her voice quivering. "It's like I'm not even me any more without Emily." Her gaze shifted to Lizzie—sitting on the stage beside Brandy—then back to him. "All those people clapping. You have no idea what it feels like to lose your child."

He looked at her, then turned and walked away.

CHAPTER TWENTY-THREE

When Brandy returned home from the vigil at a little after 9p.m., Christine sat alone at the kitchen table, red-faced and surrounded by broken pieces of dishes. Brandy pulled out a chair, hoping they could talk. "Where's Dad?"

"We had a fight," Christine said. "He stormed out." Her gaze swept over the broken dinner plates on the floor. "Can you blame him?"

Her father's car was in the garage, so he couldn't have gone far.

"Ever since she disappeared," Christine continued, "I've been destroying things and I can't seem to stop myself."

In the last thirty hours, her stepmother had become a totally different person.

"It's okay," Brandy said. "I understand how you felt about the applause. I didn't expect it to happen. I sang because I hoped it would make people rally around and help us find Emily." She stood, got the whiskbroom and dustpan from beneath the sink, and cleaned up the broken dishes. After dumping them into the trashcan, she returned to the kitchen table.

Christine said nothing. She drew in a long, shaky sigh. "I'm sorry. I don't know what happened to me. It was the cheering, like they were all so happy, holding onto their kids' hands. What kind of a person would leave those sweet curls for a mother to find?"

Brandy didn't have an answer.

Christine talked as if she were in some kind of trance. "Half the time I have no idea what I'm saying, because underneath my words there's so much fear. It's Emily. Every minute. Emily."

Christine stood, laid her hand over her chest, and walked away.

The shower came on.

Brandy sat alone at the kitchen table and stared at the phone equipment the police had installed. The kidnapper had made no attempt to pick up the ransom money or deliver Emily. He wanted the stuffed animals. Did that mean he wouldn't call again?

She knew she wouldn't sleep, but she picked up her guitar case and tiptoed into her bedroom. Sitting on the bed for a few minutes, she studied the corkboard with her pathetic little 3 x 5 cards. She thought about the vigil, feeling more alone than ever. If only her mother had lived, she'd understand how hard Brandy had tried, how much she loved Emily, and how she'd done something stupid, but not because she'd wanted to hurt her little sister.

Exhausted, she fell back against her pillows and fingered the quilted surface of her flowered bedspread. She watched the moon as it rose like a face in her window. Then she remembered the photo album with pictures of her and her mother. Together.

Brandy got up, pulled out her dresser drawer and removed the box containing her parents' wedding album. Inside, she found a leather book, white as an Easter lily. In the bottom right corner the words, *Daniel and Rose Michaelson, June 10, 1978*, were embossed in gold leaf.

She pressed her face into her arm to stifle her joy. She wanted to reach out and feel the skin of her mother's thin arms, close her eyes and hear the musical sounds of laughter, of Rose Michaelson singing in the garden. Maybe now that she had the album she really could make her mother come back to life.

With each flip of the page, time ran backwards to a place when Rose Michaelson lived and Brandy didn't. A time when her mother was so in love that the mere photographs made Brandy's throat ache with a desire to touch this woman she had never really known.

The first page, the one used to record the specifics of the day, had been carefully removed. A thin, ragged strip of parchment peeked from the binding.

Brandy dawdled over it, certain her dad had taken it out.

She wondered what information it could have held that he didn't want known. The names of their bridesmaids and groomsmen. He didn't want Brandy to find any of her mother's friends. But why?

In the first shot, her mother peered into an oval mirror, her face smooth and flushed peach at the cheekbones with the extraordinary joy of her wedding day. She wore a lace slip, long and elaborate as a bride's beaded gown. Her hair tumbled around her shoulders in loose mahogany curls. Sparks spilled from her blue eyes, and they were so bright Brandy could almost see the burst of laughter that must have come after the shutter clicked.

She turned to the back of the album and the photographs of three-year-old Brandy with her mother. It was incredible how much the little girl in those photos looked like Emily—the resemblance so striking. In the photos, both Brandy's cheeks were flushed and flawless.

In four shots she sat beside her mother in the thick grass in front of a garden. They wore matching yellow sundresses. In all the photographs, her mother looked at the camera. But Brandy was turned, ever so slightly, her gaze on her mother. There were green hills in the background, all of them covered with grape vines planted in rows so straight it looked as if they'd been drawn with a ruler.

In another photo, Rose stood in a maze of green. She'd lifted Brandy into the air where the photographer caught them—staring into each other's faces. A mother's hands, slender, warm braces, that linked them to each other and to the sky that Rose must have believed would forever curve, polished and blue, around them both.

Brandy tried to visualize her mother alive, pressed her hands against her closed eyes until stars blossomed behind her lids. In that different world, the world that held her mother, Brandy wouldn't know Kathleen, Christine or Emily.

The thought opened her eyes. Unable to imagine a life without her little sister, Brandy sighed and flipped the pages back to a series of photographs by the sea. Her mother was barefoot and wore the same slip she'd worn in the mirror shot. The photographer had caught her running in the sand, hair streaming in dark waves. Her father held her hand, running by her side. He wore black tuxedo pants with bright satin stripes on the sides. He'd removed his shoes, coat, and tie. His white pleated shirt was open at the neck. Wind caught inside the fabric and ballooned out around him.

In the final shot, her mother turned a cartwheel on the sand. Like a white bird caught in flight, the photographer had captured a wildness in her mother's eyes. Yet at the same time, upside down, she looked fragile and brave. Somewhere within, Brandy felt the passion of that day as if she'd absorbed it. And it was almost too much to comprehend—this peculiar, yet distinct love affair that lifted itself off the photographs and landed so many years later inside the daughter they had not yet conceived.

Again, she studied each one as if it were an opening, a doorway leading to the other side, an unknown world where her mother waited to comfort her now.

She was halfway through her second viewing when she noticed the pendant her mother wore. A heart-shaped red stone set between two clear stones. Brandy rushed across the room to her desk, dumped the contents of her drawers onto the floor and rummaged through them until she found her old stamp collection, the magnifying glass still tucked inside the cover.

Her hand shook as she held the thick glass circle over the photograph of her mother's neck, and a heart-shaped red stone with a diamond on either side emerged. Brandy dropped the magnifying glass. Maybe she was wrong. If it were the same necklace her mother had worn at their wedding, why hadn't her dad recognized it?

And then she remembered. Her father hadn't seen it. She'd given it to Detective Radhauser while her dad and Detective Vernon had gone to the hospital to identify the little girl they'd found in Jacksonville.

Brandy's thoughts jumped from one thing to another so fast she could barely keep up with them. Was it a coincidence? Even if it were the same necklace her mother had worn in the wedding photos, how would the kidnapper have gotten it? Could her

mother have given it away before she died? Sold it? But what were
the chances it would end up in Ashland?

She pulled the photograph out of the album, slipped it
into a manila envelope, opened her window and climbed out,
carefully closing it and replacing the screen. Crouching beneath
the windows so Christine wouldn't see her, Brandy made her way
to the side door into the garage and grabbed her bicycle. Racing
down Granite toward the Plaza, she prayed she wouldn't run into
her father. She needed to bring this new information to Radhauser.

* * *

After Gracie and Lizzie left the memorial, Radhauser returned to
his office and sat at his desk in the Ashland Police Department.
He stared at the pocked tiles of the drop ceiling, then resumed
checking the lists of registrations for late-model Volvo station
wagons. He reviewed the notes Corbin and Vernon had made as
they called each owner. So far, no one admitted to purchasing
the giant Pooh bear. Of course, if that purchase had anything to
do with Emily's kidnapping, the perp would be an idiot to reveal
herself.

It was late, 10:14p.m, but he needed to follow up with the
last four Volvo owners on the lists. If one of them admitted to
buying the stuffed animal, the others could be eliminated. If no
one did, he'd have to visit each house, wasting valuable time. He
was far from certain of a connection between the purchase and
Emily's disappearance, but he had to follow up. He'd picked up
the phone and dialed three numbers when Brandy burst into the
room. He sighed, placing the receiver back into its cradle. Should
he regret his decision to give the kid unlimited access to him?

She stood beside his metal desk, tapping one cowboy boot
against the linoleum, a manila envelope and a magnifying glass in
her hand.

"Isn't it past your bedtime?" he said, though he knew she
hadn't gotten any more sleep than he had since Emily disappeared.

"You told me I could talk to you anytime. Day or night. I
wouldn't have come here if it wasn't important."

Folk music from one of the bars on the Plaza drifted in

through the open window. He softened, remembered her incredible performance at the vigil and her stepmother's reaction to it. He glanced at the magnifying glass and smiled. "You look like a cowgirl version of Sherlock Holmes."

She pulled the photograph out of the envelope and thrust it into his hands. "It's my mother."

The woman was striking, with her dark hair tumbling like silk over her pale shoulders. "She was quite beautiful." He looked up to meet her gaze. "You look a lot like her."

Radhauser could almost see the grief as it crept over her face and into her eyes.

"My dad claims I'm nothing like my mother." She looked at the floor as if composing herself. When she looked up again, the tears were gone. She cocked her head. "Check out the necklace she's wearing, my dear Watson."

Radhauser took the magnifying glass and studied the photo again. "Give me a minute," he said, stepping out of his office to retrieve the pendant from the evidence room.

When he returned, he used the magnifying glass to compare the two necklaces. The clear gems, maybe diamonds, were offset from the garnet at the same angle. It could be the necklace. Still, heart-shaped pendants were pretty common. Thousands of brides wore them every year. A coincidence? Another dead end? But he didn't believe in coincidences, not when it came to a kidnapping case. Had Daniel Michaelson given that necklace to Emily? And if so, why hadn't he said something?

He glanced up at Brandy, hating to pull the thread that would make her optimism unravel. "I'm not sure." He slipped the photograph back into its envelope and placed it in his briefcase. "Have you talked to your father about this?"

"Christine made me swear I wouldn't tell him she showed me the album." Brandy explained what transpired between them on Saturday morning when she'd agreed to change her plans with Stone and babysit Emily.

"Did your mother have any sisters? Someone she may have given the necklace to?"

228

"Unless my father lied, my mother was an only child."

"Why do you think he'd lie to you about your family?"

She shrugged. "He's always been secretive about my mother." She told him how the front pages of the album had been ripped out.

Radhauser thought about Daniel Michaelson's polygraph. It had shown a level of deceit when questioned about his former wife—not the fact that she'd died, but the timeframe. After reviewing the initial results, Radhauser had dismissed the issue as being inconsequential. Now, he wasn't so sure. He needed to interview Daniel Michaelson again. "What happened to your mother's things?"

The kid curled into herself, as if her chest had caved in. "I don't know. I was only three."

He lowered his voice. "Is your grandmother still living?"

"I know almost nothing about my grandparents, only that they moved to Italy after my mother died."

"Could it be something your father kept for you? Maybe something Emily found and then made up the story about a big friend?"

"My father didn't keep anything of my mother's."

"He kept the wedding album."

"Yeah, he kept it away from me. You have no idea how many times I begged him for anything that had belonged to my mother."

"I need to talk to your father."

"He's not home. Please, don't tell him about the photo album."

"Where is he?"

"I don't want to get Christine in trouble." She told him what her stepmother had said about their fight, her father storming out.

"Come on," he said. "I'm driving you home before I go looking for your father. You've got no business being out this late."

"What about my bicycle?"

"It'll fit in my trunk. Let's go."

CHAPTER TWENTY-FOUR

Brandy couldn't stop thinking about the photograph, the necklace her mother wore. She wondered what other secrets might be hidden in her dad's office—if there were other things that might lead them to Emily's kidnapper.

The back door opened, signaling his return—his quick steps through the kitchen and into the hallway. He paused outside her room, close enough to darken the seam of light beneath her door.

She considered calling out to him. But before she'd summoned up her courage, he walked the remainder of the hall and into the master bedroom. Brandy waited for the bedroom door to reopen, for the sound of his footsteps heading toward her room to confront her about the album. She heard nothing.

A half hour later, around 11:30p.m., she plumped her pillows under her comforter and tiptoed into the kitchen. She took her father's keys from the hook by the door. Dropping them into her pocket, she returned to her bedroom, climbed out her window and rode her bicycle to the university campus. The streets were dark and mostly empty. She was frightened for her own safety and nervous that someone might discover her in her father's office. But Emily was missing and nothing else mattered.

Once inside his office, Brandy waited as her eyes adjusted to the darkness. She pulled the flashlight from her backpack and scanned the familiar room her dad shared with Melville professor, Steven Willingham. Two desks faced each other in the room's center. Even if she'd never been there before, the one that belonged to her dad would be obvious.

Devoid of any clutter, the top held only a framed photograph of the four of them, an empty inbox, and a stack of letters he'd signed, ready for his secretary to pick up and mail.

The credenza on the sidewall behind her father's desk was unlocked. She slid one of the doors to the center. It moved soundlessly across the narrow track. Brandy dug through the stacks of manila folders, lecture notes, and textbooks, then moved to the other side.

More folders. A line of paperbacks, mostly Shakespeare plays. She wiped her sweaty palms on her jeans, and then rummaged through the four shallow trays in the center. Nothing.

She expected his desk to be locked, but the middle drawer opened, releasing all the others. Brandy studied the contents, being careful to replace everything exactly. Once again, nothing.

Only the file cabinet remained. She jerked on the metal handle. When it didn't budge, Brandy fished in her pocket for the keys. "Please, God," she prayed. "Let one of them fit."

After four tries, she found one that did. Three drawers of file folders hung on metal rods. Arranged alphabetically, the white tabs printed in her dad's neat hand. Her gaze moved quickly over the tabs. At the end of the row, she fingered a folder labeled with the letters *S&M*.

Brandy pulled out the folder, opened it, and read the first page. The ampersand on the file tab was really an R. Sophia Rose Michaelson. Brandy dropped the file. Legal papers scattered across the floor and dust motes floated up from the carpet.

As if she'd just awakened from a dream, Brandy waited until the whole thought formed. Her mother's first name had been Sophia, not Rose. When she'd asked her dad about a middle name, he'd lied, claimed Rose was name enough for any woman to live up to.

Brandy re-aimed the flashlight. A custody hearing. The word *mutilated* pulsed from the center of the page. She couldn't see anything else. With each thump of her heart, that word swelled, then receded. She shrank from it, looked around, then picked up a newspaper article carefully cut from the August 9th, 1985 edition of the *San Francisco Chronicle*.

She studied the headline, then skimmed the first paragraph. Once again, words, not sentences, caught her, held her in their grip. *Blaze. Vineyard. Arson.*

A dog yelped from somewhere far away and a damp smelling wind came through the main door as it opened, then swished closed. The barking sounds muffled into footsteps in the corridor.

Flipping off the flashlight, she scooped up the papers and knelt behind the desk, attentive and poised as a cat. Thin slices of light from the corridor shined through the closed blinds on the top half of the door.

She tightened her hold on the flashlight, held her breath and listened. Through the opaque glass on the top half of the door, she saw a man's bulky shadow. He held a ring of keys, rhythmically banging them against his right leg like a tambourine.

Grabbing her backpack, she scurried under her father's desk and pulled the chair back into place behind her.

The man unlocked the door and stepped inside.

He flipped on the light.

Brandy heard the sound of paper shuffling on the other desk. It must be Doctor Willingham.

With her eyes wide open, she clutched the folder of information about her mother and huddled against the inside wall of the desk. *Oh God*, she prayed, *don't let him see me.* It must be almost midnight. Her dad had often alluded to his office mate's workaholism, but this was ridiculous.

She saw the scuffed toes of his rubber-soled shoes, the brown polyester slacks as he walked past the desks on his way to the room's only window. He lowered the window blinds and walked out of the office, leaving the light on. The door closed automatically behind him.

The bathroom. He must be going to the bathroom.

Brandy crawled out from under the desk and inched forward. She quietly opened the door and peered into the hallway, just as the door to the men's room closed and the long corridor grew silent.

Clutching the folder against her chest, she raced down the

232

corridor and out the door—not stopping until she reached a bench outside the campus library.

Maybe that fire had nothing to do with her mother. No—they had to be connected. Why else would he have kept the articles with the custody papers?

Though the night was cool, Brandy's shirt stuck to her back and her hands felt wet and clammy. "Custody?" She said the word out loud, abruptly realizing it could mean only one thing. Her parents got divorced. Why hadn't she known?

She slumped against the bench. And in that strange, out of sync world, she lingered over the rainbow sneakers, their laces tied in double knots, the odd fact that the kidnapper had taken off Emily's shoes. Without warning, her thoughts jumped to the details of her escalator accident. She catalogued each separate detail, felt the accumulative weight of their meaning.

Needing a safe place to examine the file, she followed a young man up the library steps.

* * *

Only a few students sprawled out on the black leather sofas or sat reading at small tables by the windows. Most of the computer desks were empty. The library smelled like paper, glue, and old leather. Brandy took a seat by the window, opened the folder, and took out the newspaper articles.

Vineyard Destroyed in Sonoma Fire
Sonoma detectives suspect arson in the fire that destroyed the home and vineyard of fifty-one-year-old Victor Delorenzo and his forty-eight-year-old wife, Sylvia.

She skimmed over the details of the fire, the charred metal gasoline can found on the front porch. She searched for something, anything that connected this house to her mother. At the end of the article, she found it.

The couple owns Sophia Rose Vineyards in Napa Valley, named for their daughter, Sophia Rose Michaelson of Palo Alto…

Oh my God. Sylvia and Victor Delorenzo were her grandparents. She'd seen the wine bottles in Safeway, the purple ones with the fancy gold rose on their labels. But never, not even for a moment, did she imagine anything like this.

Damn her dad. She'd asked hundreds of questions about her mother's family. He should have told her.

Arson.

Brandy tried to imagine who could have done something so horrible, and why. She cringed, wondering how her mother had survived something this terrible. Her barrage of thoughts stopped. Her mother hadn't survived. Brandy had read articles on the relationship between cancer and stress. Her dad had kept this terrible secret. Her hands shook so hard she could barely control them. She returned to the article, skimmed it again, then moved on to the next day's edition where she found two paragraphs on page four interviewing a forensic toxicologist who confirmed police suspicions of arson.

She scanned the headlines until five words sucked the remaining air from her chest.

Daughter Suspected in Vineyard Fire.

She stood and backed away, as if eye contact or even proximity to the words would stain her mother's memory with a level of guilt that didn't belong to her. There had to be some mistake. This didn't make any sense.

All around her, bookshelves were spinning. She wiped her hands on her pant legs, then slumped against a long wooden table, hunched forward, forcing deep breaths.

Her hands shook as she picked up the article. She was afraid to answer the questions that had driven her here, but she had to find out what happened to her mother.

Palo Alto police are questioning twenty-five-year-old Sophia Rose Michaelson in connection with the August eighth fire that destroyed her family vineyard…

Her mind spun with possible explanations. Maybe her mother had been taking care of the place while her parents were out of town. Maybe she'd left a cigarette burning close to the ashtray's edge. Or cut the grass for her father and set a half-filled gasoline can on the front porch. *Oh my God, did my mother die in prison?*

She stuffed the articles back into the folder, crammed it into her backpack, and hurried out of the library.

Once outside, she ran toward the bicycle rack. All around her, through the breaking layer of clouds, moonlight fell on the Ashland hills, like tarnish on old silver.

Everything inside her demanded the truth about what happened to her mother. Maybe it shouldn't matter, but it did.

It mattered so damn much.

* * *

Long after 1a.m., with the notes she'd made from the newspaper articles held firmly in her hand, Brandy squared her shoulders, tried to still her furious breathing, then stepped into the hallway. There was a seam of light beneath her father's study door. What she had to say to him couldn't wait. She knocked.

He didn't answer.

She knocked again, harder.

"Take the hint, Christine. I'm busy."

Brandy tried the knob. It was unlocked. She opened it and stood stiffly in the doorway, her heart still thumping fast against its cage.

Her father sat behind his desk with a stack of student papers in front of him.

"This is more important than those damn essays." Her voice was thick and her whole body trembled.

He glanced up, hope on his face. "Have there been any new developments?"

She shook her head.

He motioned her inside.

She seated herself on the loveseat adjacent to his desk.

"I was proud of you tonight. That was a beautiful song you wrote for Emily."

She wished for an instant that she still wanted nothing more than to please her dad. Her resolve was disappearing fast. She didn't know how to begin, and kept fingering her notes.

He took off his reading glasses, reached for an orange from the basket he'd brought in from the kitchen, and pointed to papers in her hands with a nod. "Are you stuck on some homework assignment?"

"It's a…just stuff from newspaper articles."

"That's good. I'm glad you're keeping up with your studies. You might think about going to school tomorrow."

He must be frickin' insane. "I'm not going anywhere until we find Emily. The notes have nothing to do with school. I read some articles about a fire." With the word fire, her toes curled inside her shoes. "I know it's a bad time to bring this up, but it can't wait."

"It's okay. Though it seems like it to us, the world didn't stop because…" Like he always did, he kept his gaze on the orange, intent on peeling it in one continuous spiral. The citrus smell, tangy and sweet, spilled into the air around them.

"My articles are from the *San Francisco Chronicle*. A series they ran in the summer of 1985."

His thumbnail dug too deep and the spiral broke. One long piece dropped into an orange curl on his desk. He peeled the remainder, then separated out a section with his thumb and forefinger. His hand quivered slightly, though his face remained impassive as he ate the segment orange, then leaned back in his chair. "Is there a point to your research?"

She looked at the sheet of paper she'd so carefully folded into fourths, and considered wadding it into a ball and walking out of the room. Instead, she unfolded the sheet. "On August 8th, a vineyard and house burned in Sonoma. It belonged to Sylvia and Victor Delorenzo, my grandparents."

His eyes narrowed. "Why do I feel like I'm about to be interrogated?"

"I don't know. Is there something you've been hiding from me?"

He picked at the peel on his desk, sending out a fresh burst of strong orange scent. "No one has a perfect life." He tossed the peel into the wooden trashcan. "I gave you everything I could."

Two words hung in her chest and she held them like a fist, then let them fly. "Sophia Rose," she said, surprised by the evenness of her release. She watched his face for a reaction, a stiffening of the muscles in his neck or a flicker behind his eyelids, but there was nothing.

He pushed his chair away from the desk and crossed his study in three quick strides. Standing in the doorway, he flicked a nervous glance up and down the hallway, then closed the door.

"Last time I saw Christine, she was on the back deck. She started smoking again," Brandy said, stunned to realize her stepmother, her father's supposed confidant, didn't know any of this. "The investigators suspected arson from the beginning. Two days later, the police arrested my mother. She was arraigned and charged. That's a lot to happen to a dead woman."

The room seemed to hold its breath. Her dad didn't speak, but his blue eyes were so open Brandy believed for an instant she saw his soul.

He kept looking at her, his mouth ajar as if he'd forgotten how to make words. "Brandy, listen. Just let me explain," he said finally. "I can explain everything." He paced in front of his desk, face rigid, every muscle tight.

"My father, the great explainer. I'm beginning to understand. And I hope you'll save me some work and tell me the rest."

"What precisely are you asking?"

"Try the truth for a change. Is my mother dead, or is she still alive?"

"Your mother is dead. She died from cancer in 1988."

"You told me she died in 1984 when I was three. Where was she during those four years? Why didn't you take me to see her?"

"People are never what they seem. Everyone has secrets."

"Maybe. But keeping a mother's life a secret from her only daughter? That's frickin' over the top, even for you."

He pressed the fingertips of both hands into his temples, then sighed. "I'm sorry," he said, as if he really meant it. "Though

I'm certain it doesn't feel that way to you, Cookie, I did what I thought best."

His use of her childhood name caught her off guard.

"I also did what your mother wanted."

He sat beside her on the loveseat and took her hands.

She pulled them away.

"We did it for you. Honest to God, honey. You were just a little girl, barely more than a baby. And you'd already been through so much." He stopped and looked at her.

"I have a right to the truth," she said.

"What you discovered isn't the truth. It only looks like it."

Something inside her snapped. "Cut the crap, Dad. Did she do it, or didn't she?" Her fingernails bit into her palms. He'd clam up if she lost control. She couldn't let that happen. Not now. Not when she was so close to the truth.

He tried to speak, but his voice splintered and seemed to snag on his words. "The judge acquitted your mother."

Brandy's eyes brimmed. "She didn't do it? They found her innocent?"

Her dad hesitated.

She felt the pressure of all the words he'd rather leave unspoken. "Please."

He cleared his throat and tried again. "Rose was innocent. She loved her parents, and never would have intentionally done something to hurt them." His fingers danced nervously on the loveseat. "I know it's hard to understand, but your mother thought what she did would save them. She wanted—" His tears surfaced.

Brandy had never shared a moment with her dad as exposed and intimate as this one, never once seen him cry. When she looked at him again, reality spread through her as inevitably as ink along the threads of a linen napkin. "Oh my God. I had a crazy woman for a mother."

"Don't say that. Mental illness is a terrible thing."

Her dad held his hand suspended in midair for an instant before he reached for her arm. "I've researched this. It isn't passed down to the children. I mean it can be, but you, you're okay."

The impact of his words hit hard. "Are you saying this could happen to me? I could be like my mother? I could be crazy, too?"

He grabbed her shoulders. "Don't worry. The signs would be here by now. What you did to your mirror—it was nothing. I overreacted and I'm sorry. You were just frustrated and angry about Emily."

"Oh my God. I think I finally understand. She isn't dead. My mother's locked up in a nut house somewhere, isn't she?"

He tightened his grip on her shoulders. "No. How many times have I taken you to her grave?"

She jerked herself away. "A grave with a fake date of death on it." She closed her eyes in an attempt to regain some control. She could almost feel it, that huge echoing space. Her mother had been dead to Brandy for nearly three-quarters of her life. And yet, she still felt so sad.

"I'm caught in an impossible situation," he said. "No matter what I do, I can't make it right. I received a letter from a law firm stating she'd died in Bayview Hospital and asking what arrangements I wanted to make. I had the ashes shipped to Ashland, bought a cemetery plot, and buried them so you'd have a place to visit."

Brandy said nothing.

His eyes flashed. "Do you think this is easy for me? Think I can hide from myself? Hide from the way I felt about your mother…" His voice cracked. "You, Christine, and Emily are the most important things in the world to me now."

She turned and glared at him. "No, we're not. Hiding from the past is."

"How many times do I have to say it? I wanted to protect you. Surely you know that!" he said, so fiercely that she grew quiet.

He tried to say something more, but his voice cracked again. It took him a moment to recover. "Maybe you don't know. Maybe Emily didn't either. And that tears me apart."

Behind the image of that fire, other mysterious things lurked—a dark bulging sack of them. Brandy feared those things almost as much as she wanted to let them out. "She was schizophrenic, wasn't she?"

"Yes. And bi-polar. When we first met, she was happy and bubbly, a friend to everyone. She believed in a beautiful world and that the two of us were part of that beauty. I was captivated. And then one day, the love of my life vanished. But it doesn't mean anything about you."

Brandy licked her dry lips. "I want to know about the night of my accident. Did my mother scream when she saw the doctor stitching my face?"

"Yes."

She swallowed, but the nervous tightening inside her throat didn't go down. At last, her dad was telling the truth.

"She took you to the mall that night," he said. "I stayed home grading papers. When the call came, I met the ambulance at the emergency room. Your mother wasn't in it."

"What do you mean? You just told me—"

"She came later. She stayed at the store for a little while."

What kind of a lousy mother would finish her shopping while an ambulance carted off her bleeding three-year-old? Maybe her father had told her the truth. Maybe her mother had never wanted children.

"It's not like it sounds. She wouldn't let them restart the escalator until…" He paused, thought for a second, then continued. "The store manager told the police she knelt in front of the bottom stair with a…"

A quick glance at her dad's face caught his horror. "With a what, Dad?"

He watched her, but remained silent.

She tried again. "My mother knelt with a what? You've gone this far. You might as well tell me everything."

"Oh, Cookie, are you really sure you want to hear this?"

She nodded.

The muscles in his throat tightened as he swallowed. "A pair of tweezers. When she got to the hospital, she handed the doctor a blood-smeared envelope. Tiny pieces of your skin. Rose insisted the surgeon could…" Again, her dad stopped and stared at

Brandy. "The nurse called for a psychiatric consult. They admitted your mother that night." Her father's last sentence came out in a whisper.

As another part of her past reassembled itself, Brandy saw the scene clearly. A frantic woman, gathering the missing pieces of her child's face. A mother who had loved her daughter beyond measure.

"Your mother was inconsolable," her dad said. "She blamed herself."

"So, my accident started her mental illness?"

"No. There were other signs, but I missed them."

"Christine said she had a drinking problem."

"People often self medicate. It wasn't her fault."

"Maybe I'm really dense, but I don't get it. Why would you blame yourself all these years?"

"I thought it would be hard enough for you to grow up without her."

Brandy sat, motionless, slowly coming to terms with this new truth about her dad. "Did she ever come home from the hospital?"

"They stabilized her on medications. And she came home, but she hated the drugs. She stopped taking them."

"Why would she do that?"

"She said they made her feel as if she were sleepwalking. Your mother was dynamic and creative, a great singer—just like you." He paused, swallowed.

"Then why did you claim I was nothing like her?"

He remained silent for a few moments. "After the trial, she knew she'd probably never be released from Bayview. She begged me to divorce her, to take full custody of you and move away. She wanted us to start over in a new place where you wouldn't have to live with the stigma of what she'd done. I was—"

"If you loved her, how could you just leave her like that?"

He cocked his eyebrow. "You think I left her. You may be too young to understand this. But the people who matter the most stay inside. I can't tell you how many times I've seen your mother's face in my classroom, spotted her in the produce aisle at the Safeway. On the swing in Lithia Park."

To her surprise, Brandy felt a lump in her throat. At this moment, the past was more alive than the present. She swallowed, pushed it down.

"I tried to honor her wishes," he said.

"What about my wishes?" Her voice was soft, barely more than a whisper.

"When do you think I should have told you? When you were five? Ten? It was stupid, I see that now, but I thought if I didn't talk about her, you'd stop asking."

Brandy shook her head, unable to respond.

"Your mother wanted me to wait until you were old enough to comprehend. She wanted me to give you the wedding album for your eighteenth birthday so you'd have those pictures of the two of you together before—"

"Before I found out she set fire to my grandparents' home and vineyard?"

"Yes. We only wanted you to have a normal life."

She touched her cheek. Ordinarily, she would have reacted to his ridiculous use of the word, normal, and repeated it back to him. But she couldn't. "I've already seen the album."

He cupped his head in his hands. "I know," he said, without looking up. "Radhauser found me in the park. We went to his office, and he showed me the photo of your mother wearing the heart pendant I'd given her for our first Valentine's Day."

"Do you think it could be the necklace Emily had?"

"I can't imagine it's anything more than a coincidence. After your mother was institutionalized, most of her clothes and jewelry were sold at an estate sale and the proceeds put into a college fund for you."

She stared at him for a moment in which she saw the weight of the years on him. Maybe there was always more than one truth, different perspectives, all going on at the same time—contradicting and getting in the way of each other, but true nonetheless. She touched his arm. Her dad had always been so unknowable. But there were times when she had sensed both the terrible darkness inside him and his attempts to shield her from it.

CHAPTER TWENTY-FIVE

While her dad and Christine argued in the kitchen, Brandy curled up on her bed. It was 4a.m. Narrow bands of moonlight leaked past the edges of her closed blinds. And Sunday morning when she had awakened and looked around the familiar bedroom, realizing again that Emily was gone, seemed like a lifetime ago.

She clamped the pillow over her ears in a useless attempt to muffle their voices. Her mother had been mentally ill. Who could say it would never happen to Brandy? She'd been reading the statistics in Christine's psychology book. Maybe something abnormal waited in Brandy's DNA, some gene perched inside her brain, something that could make her set fire to someone or something she loved.

"I don't get it, Professor Michaelson," Christine shouted. "Was there some maturity test I had to pass before you could confide in me?" A fist banged on the table.

Her dad said something so softly Brandy couldn't distinguish the words.

"What she overhears is not my problem," Christine said. "You never should have lied to her. Or me. You think you're the big authority on everything. You have no idea how much I hate you right now."

Brandy heard their bedroom door slam.

Sometime after 5a.m., the loneliness became too much for Brandy. She tiptoed down the hallway and into the kitchen to discover her dad was gone. Thinking he'd finally surrendered to sleep, she turned and headed back toward her own room. Her eyes lingered on the thread of light still spilling beneath his study door.

She inched it open.

Her dad lay fully clothed on the love seat, his gaze focused on the ceiling. Tears oozed from the corners of his eyes.

Brandy stumbled back. Some strange force seemed to press her against the wall. She'd gone eighteen years without seeing her dad cry and now, in the course of hours, the unthinkable had happened twice. The sight frightened her and she didn't know what to do. After a moment, she slipped into her own room and closed the door.

The second long night without Emily had already begun its slow tilt toward morning. She tried to imagine a happy ending for all of them—conjured up images of Emily running down the hallway after her bath, her dark curls bouncing against her back, shoulder blades sticking out like wings. Of Christine finding a way to forgive Brandy for both the lie about the necklace and her carelessness in leaving Emily unattended. Forgive her father for his lies about Brandy's mother.

She returned to his study and knocked on the door.

He didn't respond.

She tried again. "Okay if I come in?"

"It's not a good time."

Brandy heard the whisper of a tissue as he pulled it out of the box. The sound of him blowing his nose, then rearranging himself. Finally, he cleared his throat.

"Please, Dad. I need to tell you something."

"Try to get some sleep, honey. Things will look better in daylight." There was no trace of conviction in his voice.

She opened the door.

He sat with his elbows on his desk, eyes puffy and red.

Brandy watched him in silence—saw the vulnerable bald spot on the top of his head he'd failed to comb over.

He took a swipe at the wetness under his eyes, so hard that it seemed like a slap. "Christine needs her rest." His gaze skated across his daughter's face and then off into the darkened hallway behind her.

Brandy swallowed and took a tentative step toward him. "Christine doesn't want you in the bedroom, does she?"

He looked at her, then shook his head. "She's focusing her fear and rage about Emily on me. Four solid years of grievances." He passed a quick finger across his tear-mottled cheekbone.

Brandy reeled, a sick, dizzy feeling in her stomach. She hung her head.

"None of this is your fault," he said. "I lied to Christine about your mother from the beginning, and now she thinks everything I tell her is a lie." He paused and thought for a second. "Let's face it. I've made a shit-load of mistakes with both of you." He was silent for a moment. "I'm not sure Christine will ever forgive me." Again, he stopped talking, but a small involuntary sound emerged from his throat.

"I lied about the necklace because Christine was spanking her, hard. Emily was sobbing. I just wanted to make it stop. I wanted to be loyal to my sister."

He gave her a sad smile. "I know that."

Brandy stepped across the study and around the desk, until she was standing beside him. "I believe your lies were about loyalty, too. You were trying to protect me and whatever good memories I had of my mother." She leaned down and into his shoulder. "You wanted to honor my mother's wishes."

He wrapped his arms around her. "I'm forty-seven years old and still stupid." He shuddered, then shook his head. "And I'll be forty-eight tomorrow."

* * *

At 7a.m. on Monday morning, Brandy sat at the kitchen table eating a bowl of cereal with her dad. Neither of them spoke. Christine appeared in the doorway, quiet as a shadow.

Brandy didn't breathe.

Christine pressed her lips together, moved into the room and stood near the table, silently staring at Brandy's father. Christine crouched beside his chair and pushed her face directly in front of his. "It's Monday morning. Emily has been missing for two days. But you're not going to let something like a simple kidnapping, a child you didn't want in the first place, keep you from your classroom, are you?"

He blinked, then drew back to absorb the pain of what she'd said. "Please, don't do this. Not now. I can assure you I won't be going anywhere until we find Emily."

When Christine moved away, he pushed his chair back from the table, but remained seated. "You haven't eaten. Let me make you some breakfast."

A hopeless feeling passed over Brandy. The air inside the kitchen seemed to change density and she could tell something was about to happen. Lowering her head, she stared into her cereal bowl and counted the raisins beneath the milky surface.

Again, her stepmother bent at the waist, thrust her face close to Brandy's dad. "Won't the world come to an end if you miss one of your precious obligations?"

He grabbed her wrist and pulled her toward him in an attempt to make her stop. "That's enough."

Christine yanked back, her fingers caught in the pocket of his shirt, ripping it away from his chest. She stood upright and planted her hands on her hipbones. "Breakfast. Yes, that would be lovely. Or why don't we do a brunch? Eggs Benedict would be nice. Oh, and don't forget the muffins." Her face twisted and her pitch escalated. "A little orange marmalade while some pervert does unspeakable things to my—"

"Stop it, I said. Stop it right now. She's my daughter, too, and I love her just as much as you do."

"You never wanted her," Christine said. "You never wanted either of us."

"I said, stop." He glanced toward Brandy, a look dark with concern.

In an attempt to halt her tears, Brandy swallowed, dropped her gaze to the soggy flakes of bran in her cereal bowl.

"That's right," Christine said. "We must protect the firstborn, the child of the beloved, but crazy, wife. Well, who protected Emily?" She lifted his white coffee mug from the table and flung it across the room.

A fragrant stream of coffee flashed through midair and landed, a sparkling brown vein, on the tile. The cup shattered against the edge of the kitchen sink, and bits of ceramic sprinkled across the floor like rock salt.

"Leave him alone," Brandy said. "He told me the truth. He's doing the best he can."

Christine ignored her, surveyed the damage, then pivoted as crisp as a drum major and marched out of the room.

Brandy wanted to run after Christine and shake her, but knew it would do no good.

Her dad kept his gaze on the tabletop. He skimmed his right hand over the oak grain, again and again, as if smoothing the wrinkles out of a linen cloth.

"Some birthday, huh, Dad?"

He didn't respond.

After a few quiet moments, he stood, jammed his hands in his pockets, then withdrew them and busied himself tidying the kitchen. He swept up bits of broken coffee mug with a whiskbroom and dustpan, then got down on his hands and knees and mopped the floor with a dishtowel, careful not to disturb the Cheerios under Emily's highchair.

While he worked, Brandy folded her paper napkin into smaller and smaller squares. "Will she be all right?" she asked softly.

He answered without looking up from his task. "She's scared half to death. I don't know what to do for her." He shook his head. "For any of us." He rose to his feet, tossed the wet, coffee-stained dishtowel into the sink, then turned his gaze on his daughter. His shirt pocket gaped open like a wound. "What Christine said is the truth. I didn't want to marry her and I didn't want another child."

Except for the ticking of the clock above the stove and the steady hum of their refrigerator, the entire room fell silent. They were caught in a hollow place where lies unraveled. Just the two of them, holding each other up with their eyes.

Brandy didn't want to be first to look away. Then she remembered the worst thing that could happen already had. She squared her shoulders, realizing there was little to fear. "You really loved my mother, didn't you?"

Her father's Adam's apple bobbed up and down for an instant before he spoke. "It's an essential misunderstanding that we're in control of anything where love's concerned. In that split second when I met Sophia Rose Delorenzo, she changed everything about me. Forever."

Brandy remained silent, afraid that if she said anything, he'd stop talking.

"Rose tried so hard to rise above it, but the illness won. She lost her family and her little girl. But worst of all, she lost herself." He lowered his head. "I'm just beginning to imagine the depth of her loneliness."

In the silence that followed, Brandy lifted the tiny wad of what remained of her napkin, then bit the edges again and again in an attempt to make something hold together.

* * *

Outside, cars lined up along their street. Reporters sat on blankets, sipped coffee and soda from Styrofoam cups as if picnicking at the Britt Festival. "Any word?" one of them asked Brandy, thrusting a camera in front of her.

She shook her head and kept walking toward the police station.

Wide yellow ribbons were tied in plump bows around the trees in their front yard, whimsical and bright as a child's birthday presents. Electric candles burned in neighborhood windows. Brandy took off running.

Sifting through the details of the day Emily disappeared had become as natural as breathing. In her mind, she parked the stroller outside the bathroom stall and knelt in front of it. She had just reached out to tie Emily's shoe when her little sister thrust Pooh bear into Brandy's face. The tiny voice rang again inside her head. "He berry tired. Pooh bear need nap."

Though her legs felt too heavy to lift, Brandy plodded forward. In spite of her movement, she had that odd floating sensation again, a perception that time had stopped, that everything had suddenly hushed and grown motionless.

She picked up speed, raced down to the Plaza and crossed the street to the police department. It was just after 8:30a.m. when she burst into Radhauser's office and closed the door behind her. He sat behind his desk, notes spread out in front of him. He had taken off his jacket and the sleeves of his western shirt were rolled up above his elbows—the same shirt he'd worn to the prayer vigil. "Did you spend the night here?"

He nodded. "I hoped we'd get a legitimate lead on the hotline."

She could tell by his hangdog look that no such lead had come in. "We need to contact Vital Records in California."

"What's with the we, Columbo? I took you off the case, remember?"

"Okay, then you need to find out if there is a death certificate for a Sophia Rose Michaelson."

"Your mother?"

"Last night, my father admitted he'd lied to me about her for years."

Radhauser angled his head, a suspicious look on his face. "Maybe this isn't about a lead. Maybe this is something else. Something old between you and your father. And I think that's where I should leave it."

She met his stare. "I tried to call them myself, but they said I had to put my request in writing and that it would take about six to eight weeks. Please. You could get the information right away."

Detective Radhauser tapped the eraser end of his pencil on his desk. "I thought your mother was dead. Are you saying he lied to you about that?"

"He lied about the date." Brandy didn't doubt her father believed her mother was dead, but he hadn't seen the body—only a box of ashes.

She told Radhauser the things she'd learned last night about her mother's mental illness and her acquittal on the arson charges, her hospital confinement. "You told me you investigate every lead. You said you never know when something might be significant.

Isn't that what you said?" Hearing the hint of impatience in her voice, she tried to stay calm. "If there is a death certificate for my mother, we—I mean you—have to call the hospital. What if my mother gave the necklace to someone—maybe another patient about to be discharged? Maybe my mother asked this friend to give me the necklace. If so, we have to find that person. She could have Emily."

Brandy reviewed all the things she'd already told him. "Everyone says Emily looks like me. I've read about schizophrenia and bi-polar disease. Sometimes the patients are delusional, especially if they stop taking their medications. What if this person with the necklace had the same illness as my mother? What if my mother showed her my photo, told her where I lived, and this other woman saw Emily in the park, and thought she was me?"

"That's a huge leap," he said.

She needed to say something to make him understand. "How high would you leap if Lizzie were missing?"

Radhauser stared out the window. "I'd turn over every rock in Ashland Creek. I'd search until the day I died."

"Good answer," Brandy said. "You know how I feel. I've gone over and over the details, just like you told me to. Please listen to me."

"I'm listening."

She told him what her father had said about the night of her escalator accident, how she'd been with her mother at the Palo Alto Mall. "I tripped over my shoelaces. I had long hair like Emily. It got stuck in the escalator teeth. The kidnapper may have tossed Emily's shoes and cut her hair to keep her safe."

His gaze softened. "Didn't your mother die from cancer?"

"That's what I've been told."

"Have you ever visited her grave?"

"Many times."

"Then why don't you believe she's dead?"

She told him about the dates on the newspaper articles.

"You say your mother was acquitted of the arson charges and put in…" He paused as if searching for the right wording. "A hospital near San Francisco."

"Bayview. Don't you see the similarities? If my mother died in that mental hospital, like my dad was told, California would have a death certificate, wouldn't they?"

"Okay," Radhauser said. "Give me a couple hours and I'll see what I can find out."

CHAPTER TWENTY-SIX

Brandy pounded on Kathleen's door.

Within seconds, it opened.

With a leaf-green scarf wrapped around her head like a turban, Kathleen looked small and frightened.

"I hope I didn't scare you." Brandy panted, out of breath. "I should have called first."

"Nonsense, dear. There is no one I'd rather see than you." She smiled sadly. "Well, there is one. Little Emily."

Brandy closed her eyes for a second, caught her breath, then met Kathleen's gaze. "I need that list of costume makers and I need to borrow your car."

"I teach a class at the university at 11."

"My only other option is to become a car thief."

"What's this about? Do you know where Emily is?"

Brandy shook her head. But the trap door that held her feelings for her little sister opened anyway. She couldn't allow herself to tumble into that emptiness. Not now. She gulped, took Kathleen's arm, and led her into the living room. "Please. I'll drive you to campus."

Kathleen backed up, but didn't take her eyes off Brandy's face. "Of course." She reached for her purse, dug inside, then handed Brandy a set of keys and a list of part-time seamstresses not listed in the telephone directory. "I can catch a cab. Keep the car. Use it whenever you need to."

Brandy told Kathleen about her suspicions.

"Maybe you should give that list to the police."

A quick glance at Kathleen's face showed her worry, as sudden as the change in air when someone opened a window.

Brandy gave her a big smile. "Radhauser is following up on another lead. It's no big deal." She shrugged. "I'm visiting some costume makers. They're good people, like you."

Kathleen didn't look so sure. "I'll cancel my class and go with you."

"No," Brandy said. "I've got this."

"You're just like your father. Stubborn as a blueberry stain."

"Detective Radhauser said we need to check out everything—you never know when something is important. Good detectives have to follow their instincts." She hugged Kathleen. "And my instincts tell me that whoever bought that Winnie the Pooh bear from the toy store, turned it into a costume and is responsible for Emily's disappearance."

The kidnapper had lured Brandy's family out of the house and tried to retrieve Emily's stuffed Pooh bear. It all came back to that clue. The person who took Emily knew how much she loved her Pooh bear. And that person had played their role so convincingly that Emily had allowed herself to be lifted out of the stroller and taken without a sound.

"Does Detective Radhauser know you're doing this?"

"Absolutely. He gave me the assignment."

* * *

Brandy glanced at her watch. It was 10:30. Emily had been missing for forty-three hours.

After the familiar burgundy and gold Shakespeare Theatre flags that lined Main Street had all paraded by her window, Brandy speeded up. The morning sun beamed through the windshield as she drove Kathleen's Taurus up Siskiyou Boulevard, past the university campus where her father hid his secrets, to a squat brick bungalow—the first costume maker on her list.

She parked in the driveway, wiped her clammy hands on her jeans, and knocked on a dark wooden door with varnish so thick she could see her blurred reflection on the surface. The air smelled like pear blossoms and marigolds from the front window boxes.

Behind the house, a chainsaw roared to life, the sound so

loud she felt the buzz of it in her teeth.

A sharp-featured, bone-thin woman with deep wrinkles in her cheeks and forehead answered the door. "Are you here about an order?" She wore round black glasses that made her look like an ancient college student. Her gray bob hung to her shoulders.

Brandy introduced herself as the sister of the little girl who'd gone missing on Saturday. "I know this will sound like an odd question, but did anyone hire you to turn a large stuffed Pooh bear into a costume?" Careful not to say too much, she explained why she believed the person wearing the costume may have seen something that could help them find Em.

"I don't make many, but the ones I do are either made from patterns my customers provide, or ones I design myself."

"Are you sure?"

The woman smiled, but it didn't lift up into her eyes. "I may be old, but my memory is good."

Brandy apologized, thanked her and moved on to the other addresses on her list, going through the same explanation. After five houses, no one had admitted to making the costume.

She was running out of options, only two more names on the list, when she pulled into a small gravel lot in front of a clapboard farmhouse just outside Talent. A wooden sign directed her away from the wide ramp to the front door and down a paved path to a side entrance. All along the pavers, azalea bushes spilled over with clusters of pink and red blossoms like the ones in Lithia Park. She wondered if the flowering bushes would always be a reminder of the day Emily disappeared.

She took a deep breath, tried to convince herself she wasn't wasting time and rang the bell. There were two 3-foot high garden gnomes perched on either side of the door. A good sign that whoever lived here might be whimsical and kind, Brandy thought.

A short, middle aged and slightly overweight man with pale skin and a fat round face the size of a basketball appeared at the door. His hair was thick and black. He had a tape measure around his neck and a mouth full of straight pins with multi-colored flowers on their ends.

Brandy took a step back. She'd expected a woman.

When he pulled the pins out of his mouth and smiled, two deep dimples indented the center of his cheeks. "Don't be embarrassed. Everyone expects a woman." His eyes were dark with a sparkle of mischief—a playful man who designed costumes and greeted his customers with gnomes. At ease now, Brandy smiled back.

"What can I do for you this morning?" His breath smelled like peppermint candy and a recent cigarette. A man who smoked, but didn't want anyone to know it.

She introduced herself and said she wanted to talk with him about a costume.

"How did you get my name?"

"Kathleen Sizemore," Brandy said. "She used to be my nanny."

He opened the door.

She stepped into a big workroom with sunlight streaming through open windows on both sides. The walls were lined with shelves housing bolts of silk, satin, tapestry and cottons. A huge table sat in the center of the room with a cutting mat marked off in inches. Hundreds of spools of thread, arranged by color, filled racks attached to the walls just beneath the windows. And there was one dressmaker's mannequin so huge it made Mrs. Wyatt look like a Barbie doll.

"Do you make a lot of costumes?" she asked.

His gaze darted to the mannequin. "I mostly sew for Momma. She's in a wheelchair now, but still likes to dress up. You should see the gown I made for her to watch the Oscars." He shrugged. "She likes to pretend she's been invited."

It was an image Brandy couldn't quite conjure up, but she now understood the reason for the front ramp. "Have you ever made a costume from a big stuffed bear?"

"Big is my specialty. I did a rush order for a woman last Thursday. She needed it in time for The Children's Health Fair on Saturday." He smiled. "Do you want me to do something similar?"

Her spine seized up for a second. A tingling sensation spread into her chest and it was hard to breathe. "Was the bear wearing a yellow T-shirt? Was there a bumblebee on its nose?" She was trying to sound light, but her voice had a little quiver in it.

"Right on both accounts."

It seemed as if the earth had stopped spinning. Brandy was too excited to say a word. She went mute and just stared at the gnome man, while inside her head one sentence kept repeating itself. *This is it—the lead we've been waiting for.*

He kept watching her, as if expecting her to go on.

Brandy tried to sound professional, like a real policewoman. "I'll need her name and address."

"If you want references, I can provide them. Even the Shakespeare Festival has called upon me when King Lear or Macbeth were plus-sized actors."

"I don't need a reference. Just the name and address of the woman who ordered the Pooh costume."

"I can't do that."

Here we go again. Just like Mr. Pivorotto at the toy store. "Can't, or won't?"

"No reputable businessperson would."

A chorus of bird voices twittered. The sound made Brandy feel sad. It didn't seem right, the way everything went on as if the world wasn't changed by Emily's kidnapping.

She told him she was Emily Michaelson's sister—the little girl who'd disappeared from the park restroom. "The police believe this woman might have seen something," Brandy said.

"The police have been asking anyone who knows anything to come forward. If she knew something, she would have called the hotline."

Not if she's got Emily. "Maybe she hasn't been listening to the news or reading the papers." She looked at him hard. "But you obviously were. Why didn't you come forward?"

His fat cheeks reddened and he looked at her for a long time without saying anything. "Because I didn't buy the stuffed bear and I wasn't in the park on Saturday."

"But you knew who did. Don't you think that information should have been reported to the police?"

256

His jaw tensed. "Maybe," he said, his voice low and edged with anger. "But not to some wise-ass kid who shows up at my door, questioning my judgment. I'd like you to leave now."

"Please, mister." She told him about the ransom call, the trip to Rogue Valley Mall with the money, and the way they'd come home to find their house ransacked, and only Emily's stuffed animals missing. "Whoever took my sister isn't planning to give her back. It's my fault. I shouldn't have left her alone in her stroller. You can help me make it right."

"My customer was a professional-looking, middle-aged woman. Not some low-life kidnapper."

Brandy told him how Emily loved the giant Pooh, what she'd said in the restroom. "We believe the woman in that costume was the last person to see Emily before she disappeared."

"What if she didn't see anything?"

"Then at least I will have tried," Brandy said. "I will have followed up on my hunch."

"If my customer finds out I gave you her name and address, she won't trust me to work for her again. This woman already has a daughter. That's why she was going to the fair."

"If she has a daughter, she'll understand what my family is going through."

He opened his mouth, then closed it and looked at his shoes.

"I'm not a bad person," Brandy said. "And I'm usually not a wise-ass. I'm just an eighteen-year-old kid who did something really stupid because I thought Lithia Park playground was safe. But it wasn't and if Emily isn't found soon, there's a good chance she won't ever be." She told him about the 48-hour statistics.

"I have a lot of sympathy for you and your family."

"Sympathy won't find my sister. If I call Detective Radhauser, he'll come, his lights and sirens blaring. Think how frightened your mother will be. He'll bring a warrant, if that's what you insist upon, and he might even arrest you for not coming forward." What was it called, that thing she'd heard on *Law & Order*? "For obstruction of justice."

His dark eyes flashed. They were piercing, searching her, and she could see the rage. "Are you threatening me?"

"No. But we're wasting valuable time. What's worse? You losing a possible customer or me losing my baby sister forever?"

His gaze darted to the mannequin. "Who would take care of Momma if they arrested me?" he whispered more to himself than to Brandy.

She tried one more time. "After Emily disappeared, hundreds of people helped us look. There was all this noise and energy." Her voice cracked and she could tell it was coming. She wouldn't cry. She tried to stop it in her throat and hold it like a fist. "Inside all that noise was the awful silence of Emily being gone."

When the sob escaped, Brandy placed her hand over her mouth and tried to hold back the tears. It was useless. Her dad was wrong. She did know what it felt like to carry someone inside you.

He stared at the floor, then back up at her, his face softening. "Hang on." He crossed the room and pulled open a file drawer.

Finally, Brandy had a name, Althea Wineheart, an address on the outskirts of Talent and directions on how to get there.

As she backed out of the parking lot, a thought arose with the sudden force of a revelation. She knew exactly what she had to do. If her hunch led to Emily's kidnapper, Brandy had to come prepared to perform a role of her own.

CHAPTER TWENTY-SEVEN

Radhauser tossed the paperclip he'd been fiddling with into the desk drawer and stood. His stomach growled from lack of food and all the coffee he'd been pouring into it. It was the place a child abduction case always got him—in the gut. He opened the window and stood with his hands on the frame, sucking in breaths and feeling the cool air on his face. What was keeping Vital Records from calling him back?

Vernon, now assigned to desk duty on this case, had found no gray Volvo registered to either a Sophia or a Rose Michaelson, or anything even close. The calls they'd made led to nothing. No one admitted buying the big stuffed Pooh bear from Pivorotto's Toy Store.

He'd had one of the clerks go through the phone book and call everyone listed in Grants Pass, Medford, and Ashland who did alterations, but found no one who'd admit they turned a stuffed animal into a costume.

Though he'd studied each one with a magnifying glass, the photos Stefan Wysocki had taken in the park that day revealed nothing that could help. The hotline had proved pretty useless. One psycho phoned in around midnight to tell them she'd spotted Emily at the Imperial Palace in Beijing—worshipping at the belly of the Buddha.

DNA on the hair would take a while, but the initial microscopic exam looked as if it could belong to Emily. He kept thinking about what Brandy had said. How her hair had caught in the escalator's teeth. Was that why the kidnapper cut Emily's hair and sent it to her family? Was it a message of some kind only

Brandy and her father would understand?

He shook his head and his thoughts moved on to Brandy's request. He stared at the phone as if he could will Vital Records to call back.

If Sophia Rose Michaelson had been arrested for arson, her face should be in the system. He called California State Police, and within minutes they faxed him a photograph.

He put the two photos side by side—the wedding photo from 1978 and her arrest photo from 1985 where her face was puffy, her hair oily and tangled. Only seven years between the two, but though he tried, Radhauser couldn't make a strong connection.

One dead end after another.

He thought about the last forty-four hours, pictured them spread out behind him like a trail. He saw every wasted second, every false lead that had sent him nowhere. Every cup of coffee he'd stopped to buy. The fast food he'd crammed down on the run. All of it measured against time—minutes and hours—until it would be too late to ever find Emily.

He pushed his forehead against the window.

The phone rang. It was California Vital Records.

When Radhauser hung up, he knew one thing for certain. He needed to talk to Daniel Michaelson. Now.

* * *

In the interrogation room, Radhauser took off his jacket and draped it over the chair, watching Daniel Michaelson as he did. "If you want me to find your daughter alive, you need to cut the shit and tell me the truth about your former wife."

Michaelson stared at Radhauser in silence, clearly disturbed by what he'd heard.

Radhauser remained convinced that something shameful lay hidden behind Michaelson's silence. He saw its guilty shape swimming in the man's blue eyes. Radhauser needed to bring Daniel's guilt to the surface. He didn't know any other way to do it than to hammer him with the details he'd accumulated.

Before he had a chance to begin, Daniel spoke. "Rose died in a mental hospital near Palo Alto, California. A place called

Bayview. It closed about a year ago."

"How did you learn about her death?"

Daniel told him he'd gotten a letter from an executor of Rose's trust, informing him of her death and asking what he wanted done with the remains.

"When did you get this so-called letter?"

"Look," Michaelson said. "I can understand why you're suspicious. I told Brandy some lies to protect her from the truth about her mother's mental illness. After we moved to Oregon, I drove down to Palo Alto a couple times a year to visit Rose. But then, one day in November 1988, I received the letter." He told Radhauser he'd made arrangements with the Ashland cemetery so Brandy would have a place to visit.

Radhauser had already verified this with the cemetery. "Do you have this trustee's name?"

"It was a woman. I may still have the letter." Michaelson leaned forward and told Radhauser how Rose had begged him to move away, to divorce her and tell Brandy she was dead. "Believe me, it was one of the most difficult things I've ever done. But under the circumstances, I thought it was the right thing."

Michaelson's face clearly held a deep and painful loss—the kind of loss Radhauser understood. He thought about the time he'd left a lariat Lucas had coveted on the boy's grave. As if he could make up for what he hadn't done. As if he could make up for letting him go.

He refocused on the case. "Well, Mr. Michaelson, I've got a news flash for you. I've talked with Vital Records in California. There is no death certificate on file for Sophia Rose Michaelson."

Daniel went white, then shook his head firmly. "That can't be possible. I...I would have known if she was still alive." He looked away, but not before Radhauser saw how much Daniel Michaelson both longed for and feared that possibility.

"Get that letter," Radhauser said. "I need to call that trustee and see if she can help me get to the bottom of this."

* * *

Brandy parked Kathleen's Taurus in front of a white bungalow

261

with peeling paint and a parade of wooden characters wearing costumes across the small yard. She wanted to rent a Tigger costume. Emily believed Tigger could find anything. Mr. Pivorotto had told Brandy the woman who bought the Pooh also purchased the book, *Tigger, Finder of Lost Things*. If Brandy was right and Althea Wineheart bought into the fantasy, this plan had a good chance of working.

Inside, a shabby, middle-aged man with a long neck and small squinty eyes that made him look like a pervert stood behind a wooden counter in what had once been the living room. He ate a jelly doughnut and drank coffee from a Styrofoam cup. Tiny pieces of granulated sugar clung to the dark hairs on the back of his hand. When his doughnut leaked onto his fingers, he licked them, making a deep gurgling sound in his throat.

An eleven-by-fourteen-inch poster of Emily was taped to his display case. Everywhere she went she saw them now, as if Emily's smile had somehow multiplied and blossomed overnight. Everyone had been so cooperative about hanging the posters. So many people wanted to find her.

Brandy shuddered, unable to tear her gaze away from Emily's face. How could anyone harm a little girl who looked like that? Even as she tried to convince herself otherwise, she knew the truth. Every year, the evening news told hundreds of stories about monsters who hurt innocent toddlers like Emily. Brandy looked into her sister's laughing blue eyes until her throat ached—until she could finally look away.

The shop walls were lined with the kind of clothing racks found in Goodwill stores. Everywhere, costumes hung from wire hangers. Above each rack, a long, unpainted shelf held a large assortment of heads—skeletons and space creatures, apes and hippos, Barney and Garfield.

The man wiped his sugary hands on his khaki pants and gazed at her cheek. "You looking for perfection—a Marilyn Monroe or maybe something more modern, say a Cindy Crawford."

"Not today," she said, wanting to get what she needed and get out. "I want to rent a tiger."

"Hmmmm." His gaze swept over her body to her jean-clad legs, then up again, landing on her breasts. "Ferocious or playful?"

"Bouncy. Like Tigger in the Winnie the Pooh stories."

"You got some costume party over at the high school?"

She nodded.

He kept staring at her, with his squinty eyes that made it seem like he was trying to see beneath her clothes. He made no effort to fill her request.

"Well," she finally said. "Will you rent it to me or not?"

He found the costume. "One size fits all adults," he said. He lifted the Tigger head from the shelf and placed it inside a cardboard box with a packet of powder. "Dust with a little of this and it'll go on easier."

She paid with the MasterCard her dad had provided for emergencies, leaned against the counter, dotted with sugar and donut crumbs, and signed her name.

He examined the credit card before his gaze shifted to the poster. "Ain't you the sister of that little kid gone missing from the park?"

In an unseen place within her, she felt an entire world spread out. A place no other person could ever reach. The home of her feelings for Emily. She closed her eyes so she could say it. "Yes. Emily Michaelson is my little sister."

His gaze found the poster again, then returned to Brandy. "It's a shame, pretty little girl like that. I hate to even think…" He paused and shook his head. "Cops came by here. Wanted to know if I rented out the Pooh."

"Did you?"

"What business is it of yours?"

"The police believe someone wearing a Pooh costume was responsible."

"I'll tell you the same thing I told the cops. I ain't rented that costume for more than a year. Thomas the Train, Barney, and Casper are my best rentals for kiddy parties this season."

In the silence that followed, Brandy felt the heat of the man's stare. "I know how you must feel," he said.

Brandy lowered her head. "Do you?" Again, she sensed his beady eyes on her, his uneasiness.

"Hope we don't have some whacko kid killer out there."

Brandy cringed.

"Seems a bit strange, don't it? You bouncing around in a Tigger suit with your little sister missing. You ain't playing some kind of sick joke on your parents, are you?"

Afraid of what she might say, Brandy tucked the credit card into the back of her wallet, gathered up the costume and stepped outside. Halfway down the walk, she turned back. As the shop door reopened, the poster fluttered in the wind, rippling Emily's features.

Behind the counter, the man clutched the telephone receiver against his ear.

She knew she should take her new information to Radhauser. But she also knew he'd never agree to her plan. Time was running out. "Ask for Detective Radhauser," Brandy said. "Tell him I'm following up on a lead. A really big one."

* * *

Radhauser studied the letter Daniel Michaelson had delivered. It certainly looked official—and Daniel had every reason to believe his ex-wife was dead. Radhauser wouldn't take any chances. Needing to confirm, he picked up the phone and placed a call to Lockhart, Dewey and Bliss—the attorneys appointed trustees for the fund Victor and Sylvia Delorenzo had set up for their daughter, Sophia Rose.

He identified himself and asked to speak to Althea Wineheart.

"I'm sorry," the receptionist said. "No one by that name works here."

"Could you check the records, see if she worked for you in 1988?"

"Hold on." She put down the receiver.

A few moments later, she returned. "No, sir. We have no record of anyone named Althea Wineheart ever working at Lockhart, Dewey and Bliss."

He asked if the firm managed the trust fund for Sophia Rose

Michaelson or Sophia Rose Delorenzo.

"The daughter of the Italian wine makers," she said. "Don't we wish?"

Radhauser thanked her for her time and hung up. Everything he thought he knew about this case flew out the window. What the hell was going on here?

He closed the Emily Michaelson file, waited a moment, then opened it again—determined to read it through. He'd go over everything for the hundredth time. He must have missed something.

And so he read the 911 operator's record of Brandy's call, the interviews he'd conducted in the park. The calls that had come in on the hotline. His interviews with Ms. Frazer at the preschool, Mrs. Wyatt, Stefan Wysocki, Kent and his mother, Glenard Dewar, and Christine's parents. The toyshop owner. The lie detector results for Christine and Daniel Michaelson. Nothing made sense. Nothing connected.

Something snapped in his head, like a puzzle piece he'd been unable to click into place. He'd learned to accept things when they came to him in this abrupt and chilling manner, because experience had taught him it was almost always right.

He picked up his phone and called Officer Corbin. "Check with the DMV, Census, and IRS. See if you can find an address for an Althea Wineheart. And while you're at it, check Sophia Rose Michaelson. Or Sophia Rose Delorenzo."

"That Wineheart name sounds familiar," Corbin said. "I think she was on my list of Volvo station wagon owners."

Radhauser opened the folder and checked the two lists Vernon had compiled to make the calling go faster. "Althea Wineheart has an Oregon driver's license and an address just outside Talent." He grabbed his Stetson. "Come on, Corbin, we're taking a ride."

CHAPTER TWENTY-EIGHT

Brandy gripped the steering wheel of Kathleen's car, following the directions she'd gotten from the costume maker—confident every saved minute brought her closer to Emily. She drove seventy miles per hour, fishtailing around sharp curves on the narrow country roads. After two miles, she turned onto an even more isolated stretch of gravel with front yards littered in weeds, old appliances, and junk cars up on blocks. Brandy hit the brake, slowed to fifty. *What if Em managed to get away from the kidnapper? What if she's been trapped in one of those stinky old refrigerators?* Brandy's chest tightened. It was hard to breathe. The Tigger costume made her hot.

She rolled down the window and sucked in a breath of air that smelled like pinecones—like the woods in Lithia Park after a rainstorm. She pressed down on the accelerator. Tiny pieces of gravel pinged off the underside of the car. The wind made the cedars and pines sway. She crossed a wooden bridge, its planks rattling under the tires.

The gravel road ended, and the car bounced on rutted tire tracks with tufts of grass growing in between. She gripped the wheel tighter. Her mouth went dry. *What is going on here? Where are the houses?* Over the next rise, the trail ended. She skidded to a dusty stop. And there it was, right in front of her. A gray Volvo station wagon with a child's car seat in the back.

Her eyes opened wide. This was it. The car Mr. Pivorotto described. The woman who drove it bought the stuffed bear, had it made into a costume, and kidnapped Emily. Brandy uttered a silent prayer of thanks. The mantra she used with her baby sister rose inside her. *Who loves you, Em?*

The dust settled. A blue metal roof of a small log house emerged above a wide-board fence. Made smaller by the vastness of the woods, the house cringed inside a dark fist of green.

Brandy sat, her limbs stiff with fear. Could she really pull this off? She'd made a big mistake by not calling Detective Radhauser. She should have told him where she was headed. She would go back, but she didn't have time. Couldn't take the chance. Maybe if she kept saying the mantra, Emily would stay safe until Brandy found her.

If Althea had met Brandy's mother in a mental hospital, there was a good chance Althea was crazy, too. Brandy had no experience dealing with a crazy person. But she was an actress. She could play any role. Again, she breathed, determined to remove the personal and take on the identity of someone else.

She slipped the packet of talc from her purse and dusted the inside of the Tigger head so it would slide on more easily. *You can do this. You can convince Althea that Tigger found Emily's Pooh and wants to return it.* It might not lead to anything, but it was worth a try. She opened the car door, got out, and stood quietly beside the vehicle for a moment.

She adjusted the head so that she could see through the eyeholes, then checked her backpack to make certain Pooh bear was inside. She re-zipped the pack and slipped the straps over her shoulders. Straightening her back, she took a deep breath and moved toward the cabin, a swing to her steps.

Brandy slid the gate bolt aside, then jerked on the handle, but the gate didn't open. She kicked at the bottom and then stood on her tiptoes. A shiny new brass bar bolted the gate closed at the center. Wood shavings littered the ground. She kicked it again. "Dammit. Open." She grabbed a stick and pried the center bolt aside. The gate opened. Somewhere, hidden in the weeds beneath it, a cricket chirped.

In the front yard, a rope dangled from a wide oak branch and a child-sized picnic table was set with two plates of soggy cookies, and tiny teacups filled with curdled chocolate milk. Mr. Pivorotto said the woman who'd bought the giant Pooh bear had a little girl. Maybe she'd taken Emily as a playmate for her daughter. Brandy relaxed a little. Emily loved tea parties. It had to be a sign Althea was taking good care of Em.

A yellow-jacket circled a plate, then landed on a gingersnap. Emily was afraid of yellow-jackets. Wind caught the gate, which made a groaning sound as it swung and slammed back into place. Brandy startled. She fought the urge to call out Emily's name.

One moment, the scene—like a vacant day care center—felt distant; one of those desert mirages she'd read about. The next moment it was all so real she expected the yard to come alive, like those animated dancing elves in Macy's Christmas display. Children stuffing cookies into their mouths as towers of ABC blocks tumbled.

Brandy tapped on the front door. Beneath her Tigger paws, her fingers were stiff as twigs.

No answer.

She tapped again.

Still no answer. Brandy turned the door handle. It didn't budge.

She hurried to the back of the cabin and searched for another way to get inside. The bottom half of the back door was wood. The top had three rows of glass panes, each one about six inches wide and nine tall. Brandy peered through one of them into the kitchen. The counters were piled with dirty dishes—a wooden highchair, small enough for a doll, was nestled up to the round wooden table.

Last summer, after a neighbor boy slammed a baseball through a pane in the French doors leading out to their patio, Brandy had helped her father replace the glass. But she needed something to pry the mullions away. She rummaged through her backpack, found a metal nail file, and tried to slip it under the wood and lift up. The file snapped in half.

Brandy pulled herself together for another try. She raced around the house, cautiously checking every window, found one on the west side that was raised about an inch. She clawed at the screen, trying to make it pop out the way she did with her bedroom window at home. Her index fingernail broke off. The screen remained intact.

She hurried to the back door, searched the ground for the broken tip of her nail file and, when she found it, she slashed the screen, lifted the window, and climbed into a small bedroom. She searched under the bed and in the closet, hurried down the hall to the bathroom. No sign of Emily, but the room had a familiar smell—like cinnamon and eucalyptus. Like the smell in Emily's room after the ransacking. Inside the Tigger paws, Brandy's hands sweated. This woman had Emily somewhere. The question was where.

She tiptoed down the hallway to a closed door. The latch clicked and the knob seemed to jump inside the cage of her fingers like a living thing. She pushed the door open and slipped inside a big living room. Kenny Loggins sang about Christopher Robin—a song from his House At Pooh Corner Album.

Brandy glanced around. A tall, slightly disheveled woman stood to the right of a massive river rock fireplace and stared out the window into the woods. She wore a pair of wrinkled linen slacks and a red blouse with a dark stain on the sleeve. In midair, her fingers moved with the notes of the child's song, as if she played an unseen piano.

Tigger, Finder of Lost Things topped a stack of children's books on the coffee table. She had a fleeting memory of Emily on her lap at bedtime, fresh from her bath, smelling of apple shampoo and baby powder. Her sweet little voice, "Read Tigger one more time, Band-Aid." Brandy's arms ached with longing to hold her sister. For the first time in nearly forty-eight hours, she dared to believe she'd again read that story to Emily. Brandy's plan had to work.

A canopied baby crib had been tucked into the room's corner. As quietly as she could, Brandy started across the room. *Hold on, Em, I won't stop until I find you.*

The woman turned, stiffened. Her dark hair was stretched straight back into a tight bun at the nape of her neck. Her red lipstick bled into the tiny wrinkles around her mouth, like Joan

Crawford in the old classic movie, *Mommy Dearest*. She raced over to the crib and stood in front of it, arms out to her sides like a crossing guard. Her cheekbones were sharp as scissor blades beneath her pale skin. "Stay away from her." There was a high pitch to her voice.

Beneath the Tigger mask, Brandy smiled. She'd been right. This woman had Emily. Her jaw relaxed. She sucked in two deep breaths and let them out slowly, squared her shoulders and took a step toward the crib.

"Get out," the woman said, holding up her hands and pushing the air as if she could shove Brandy back outside.

Brandy froze.

The woman's eyes went so big Brandy could see white all the way around the irises. She flapped her right hand in front of her face, her head jerking like a bird's. "Who are you?"

Forget the fear. Forget yourself. Forget everything except the role. Tigger in the Disney movie she'd watched fifty times with Emily. Cheerful. Flamboyant. Happy. Bouncing up and down on the balls of her feet, Brandy sang as she skipped closer. "Who am I? It's easy to see. I'm Tigger with a capital T and two little g's."

The woman took a step forward. "No, you're not."

"Of course I'm Tigger. Who else could I be?" As if hopping on a spring, Brandy jumped up and down. "The little girl missed her Pooh bear and I…" She drew out the word and pounded herself on the chest. "I…being a world-renowned sleuth…found him." Fully into her role now, she gave a sharp nod toward the crib. "You know as well as I do, madam, that little girl is crying for her Pooh bear."

The woman stuck her fingers in her ears. "You're not real. The devil sent you." She stomped her foot, her voice soaring.

Don't panic. Brandy drew a trembling paw to her Tigger mouth, then dropped it to her chest, feigning shock. "Don't be ridickerous. Tiggers are God's messengers. It's a conflict of interest to make deals with the Dark Ones." She crossed her orange-striped Tigger arms over her chest like a genie. "Don't you want to make your little girl happy?"

The woman blinked and glanced at the ground, her body swaying back and forth. "Yes. But the doctors said sometimes I see things that aren't really there."

Brandy flipped off the music. "Tigger is here and real. But I'm at a slight disadvantage because I don't know your name."

The woman laughed a deep-throated laugh that seemed to come from her belly. The muscles around her eyes crinkled. "Althea. It means healer. And the baby's sick." She touched the side of what Brandy had believed to be an empty crib and gazed, lovingly, into it. "She has a high fever."

Emily was in that crib. But why was she so quiet? She must be asleep, drugged, or really sick. There's no way she wouldn't be climbing over the crib rail at the sound of Brandy's voice.

Brandy headed toward the crib again.

"Stop. No one goes near my baby," Althea screamed, her voice harsh and threatening.

Brandy backed up. She had to be careful. Althea could go postal and Emily could be hurt. "Tigger has come all this way to deliver Emily's Pooh bear. Why are you being so rude?"

"Tepid water is what you do for fever." Althea smiled and puffed out her chest—all proud as if she'd just discovered a cure for cancer. The woman was loony tunes.

"You're a wonderful mother," Brandy said. "You take such good care of your little girl." *Please, God. Make that be true.*

"Yes," Althea said. "That's what healers do."

Brandy bounced up and down again. "Well, Tiggers have a job, too. They find lost friends and return them to children."

Althea smiled and held out her hands.

"Oh no," Brandy said, still bouncing. "I have to deliver the Pooh bear myself. It's part of the Tigger code of ethics."

Althea tried to jerk the backpack from Brandy's shoulders. "Good mothers don't break promises to their little girls."

Brandy had to calm her down, to gain Althea's trust. "Tiggers are non-violent, but amazing and compassionate creatures. Maybe I can make an exception in your case, since you promised, but I need you to answer some questions first."

271

Althea stood with her legs apart, both feet firmly on the ground. Her eyes bore into Brandy. "Black questions make the sun go away."

Brandy did another little bounce. "Tiggers don't ask black questions. Just bright yellow ones."

"I never get them right," Althea said, her voice soft now.

To Brandy's surprise, a lump grew in her throat. She swallowed, pushing it down. "Don't worry. There are no wrong answers in Tiggerland."

Althea cocked her head. "She wouldn't stop crying."

Brandy's uneasiness was growing as if she were on a dark street with footsteps behind her. Althea must have done something to silence Emily.

"It's why I've come," Brandy said, fighting to remain optimistic. "To stop your little girl from crying."

"I don't trust you," Althea said.

"Why don't we just talk for a few minutes? Just the two of us. Healer and Tigger."

"Okay, but don't go near my baby."

"Have you ever known anyone named Rose?" Brandy asked.

Althea dropped her hands to her sides, her gaze drifting toward a small, drop-leaf desk. "Rose is dead."

Brandy felt her diaphragm lift, heard her breath as it expelled. All at once the air grew smoother, easier to breathe. Her father had told the truth.

Althea hurried over to the desk. While she rummaged around in the top drawer, Brandy inched closer to the crib. Emily wasn't more than ten feet away now.

Althea turned from the desk and moved toward Brandy, then handed her a small, framed photograph—a smaller version of the photograph of Rose Michaelson holding three-year-old Brandy up in the air.

She clamped her eyes shut in a feeble attempt to keep tears from falling. Her mother had saved that photo of the two of them. Brandy had been right. Rose had shown this woman a picture that looked a lot like Emily.

Brandy took another step toward the crib.

Althea grabbed the fireplace poker. "I told you. Stay away from my baby."

Brandy backed up until her knees hit the sofa. She sat.

Althea's face was shut off from expression now, as if she were the one wearing a mask. "I used to be Rose, but they crucified me for my sins. Now I'm born again. Just like Jesus."

Stunned, Brandy was speechless. Had this crazy woman stolen the photograph and the pendant? Had she taken on Rose's identity?

Brandy sucked in a breath, pretended she played a role in a play—a part she'd memorized. Althea played another role—a quirky off-centered character. Everyone knew mentally ill people had trouble knowing what was real.

"Did you know Rose Michaelson in the hospital?"

"Oh yes," Althea said, the poker still in her hand. She sat in the rocking chair beside the crib. "But she got better and they let her leave. She tried to take her dream-stealing pills, but they bring clouds. It's hard to outrun the voices. They told me to change my name so I could be a healer." Her eyes jerked repeatedly away as she spoke.

Brandy attempted to regulate her breathing—tried not to overreact. *Revise your role. Think like a playwright.* This whacko woman believed she used to be Rose—used to be Brandy's mother.

Brandy took a chance and whipped off the Tigger head. Her hair was wet, beads of sweat rolled off her chin, and her ears felt as if they were ready to ignite.

"I know who you are," Althea said, raising the poker above her head. "You're Brandy, the scarred teenager from the park." Althea stood and lunged toward Brandy.

Brandy leapt up. "I'm not here to hurt you or your baby. You're right, I am the teenager from the park. And I'm also the little girl in the picture you just showed me. I'm Rose's daughter, Brandy."

Althea stared at Brandy for what seemed like a long time. "Oh no. That's not true. You're too old. You can't be my daughter."

Brandy couldn't find words. *Think about Emily. Only Emily.*

"I was three years old. I'm grown up now. I had surgery on my face." She spoke too fast, but couldn't slow down. She grabbed Althea's free hand and lifted it to her scarred cheek. "It was an accident," Brandy said, her voice shaky and too high. "It wasn't your fault."

"The voices said it was my fault," Althea said.

Again, Brandy swallowed back tears.

Althea stared at Brandy for a long moment, then dropped the poker. It made a loud clanging sound against the stone hearth. Before Brandy could reach her, Althea turned to the crib and gently lifted a dark-haired porcelain doll in a frilly dress, its left cheek covered with gauze and surgical tape. "This is my daughter."

Brandy couldn't move. She faltered, inched back against the wall. She'd been so certain Emily was in that crib. Brandy trembled so hard her teeth banged together as if she were freezing. *Please, God, don't let my baby sister be dead.*

Althea pointed to the bandages. "God called her up the silver staircase. I didn't mean to let her go. But she climbed out of her carriage. She got hurt really bad. Doesn't her little cheek look awful?" A tear rolled down Althea's face. "It's all right, baby. Don't be afraid. I'll take care of you this time. I'll be careful."

Brandy's heart hammered in her ears. Something curved around her brain like when she was a little kid and hung her head over the edge of her bed and saw everything upside down—that weird dizziness and lack of orientation. In spite of her need to pretend this woman into someone else, she knew the truth now. Althea was her mother—the beautiful woman turning a cartwheel in the wedding album.

Trembling, Brandy ripped open her backpack. No matter what, she wouldn't give up, wouldn't stop searching until she'd found Emily. Brandy tossed the Pooh bear onto the coffee table, hoping Althea would finish caring for her doll, then pick up the bear and lead Brandy to her little sister.

Grabbing the Tigger head, she stumbled outside and ran into the woods—ran until she had no more breath, then sat, her back against a big-leaf maple tree. Her hands fluttered in her lap as if pieces of her mother's craziness had stuck to them.

The air around her smelled like Christmas. And then Emily was behind Brandy's eyes again, running into the family room in her footed Winnie the Pooh sleeper, squealing and freaking out as she scrambled onto the new tricycle with hot pink streamers on the handlebars she'd found under the tree.

Brandy swallowed. *Who loves you, Em?* She thought about the life she'd had before Emily disappeared—before she'd found her crazy mother. In spite of Brandy's efforts to call it back, that life didn't seem to belong to her any more. She thought about her father's lies. She now understood the truth wasn't always simple. And she considered the possibility there were times when we needed someone to lie. That lies could be gifts. She understood something about her dad and the past he wanted to forget. Hanging her head, she sobbed for her baby sister—for everything they'd lost.

Brandy wiped her face on her sleeve. She had a mission and she couldn't give up now. She had every reason to believe Althea would take Pooh bear to Emily. If she wasn't still alive, why had Althea been so determined to get her hands on the bear?

Brandy drove Kathleen's car over the rise where the road turned to gravel and Althea couldn't see it, then tossed the Tigger head into the backseat and ripped off the costume. Twilight approached and the tree shadows lengthened over the road. In the quiet, she heard the soft tick of her wristwatch, the sound of time passing.

CHAPTER TWENTY-NINE

B randy found a spot where she could see both the back door to the cabin and the Volvo. She hunkered unseen in the bushes and waited for Althea to lead her to Emily. *Who loves you, Em?*

Ten minutes later, Althea emerged with Pooh bear tucked under her left arm. In her right hand, she carried what looked like a gasoline can, the kind her dad used for his lawnmower.

Brandy breathed. *Thank you, God. Thank you.* Her plan was working. Maybe Emily was still alive.

Keeping a safe distance behind Althea, Brandy stayed out of sight. Music drifted from somewhere in the woods. As Brandy darted from the protection of one tree to the next, the music grew louder. An old-fashioned hymn. *The Old Rugged Cross.* Church music. The kind played at funerals. Brandy cringed, picked up the pace.

Finally, Althea stumbled into a clearing, Brandy a few paces behind. All around them, cedars, pines and spruce trees were decorated with golden stars, moons and angels. Two saw horses stood in the center of the cleared woods. A white fabric box trimmed in gold sat on top of them. Beneath the box, a fireplace grate was filled with kindling and stacked logs. Sprays of spring flowers, daffodils, forsythia, lilac and tulips, stood on green metal legs. Candles burned in a circle around the scene.

Brandy took it all in. Her heart pounded, as if being chased from side to side by something she didn't want to imagine, but couldn't shut out. Something unthinkable. Something that wasn't supposed to be there.

It wasn't an ordinary box.

It was a coffin.

A small child's coffin.

Fear rushed into Brandy like air into a vacuum. This was a funeral pyre, like the ones she'd studied in her world religion classes. The kind used for cremation of the dead in the Hindu and Sikh religions. *What if Emily was inside that coffin? Her mother. That long-ago vineyard fire.*

* * *

When they'd passed the edge of town, Detective Radhauser and Officer Corbin raced toward Talent. They had to get there fast. Radhauser couldn't survive another child dying because of his negligence. And what if Brandy had figured this out—what if the lead she'd discovered was Althea Wineheart? What if he lost both Brandy and Emily?

For safety, he drove an unmarked patrol car, radioed in their location, the time, and his odometer reading, then turned onto an unfamiliar road that stretched out like an asphalt ribbon, black and empty.

The car phone rang. Corbin picked it up. When he hung up, he turned to Radhauser. "Althea Wineheart owns ten wooded acres. I'll call for backup."

"Tell them to hold their damn sirens," Radhauser said, thinking about Tyler Meza. The way his kidnapper had strangled the boy just as the police closed in. Radhauser should have gone in alone and kept the kidnapper from panicking. He should have ignored protocol and acted upon his first suspicions. "We could be all wrong about this. But just in case, call for a bus. Tell them to turn off the siren and the lights before approaching."

He thought about the Ziploc bag of ringlets they'd found at the prayer vigil. The accident that had scarred Brandy's face when her hair got caught in the escalator steps. The kidnapper had wanted the Michaelsons to know she'd cut Emily's hair to keep her safe. That's why she tied Emily's sneakers into double knots before tossing them into the creek at Lithia Park. All doubt left him. Althea Wineheart had Emily. But where?

* * *

Brandy watched as Althea placed the gasoline can on the ground, then stood in front of the pyre, opened the coffin lid, placed Emily's Pooh bear inside, then reclosed the lid.

Her fingernails bit into her palms as she stepped closer. She couldn't catch her breath. She wheezed, a soft choking sound. *Emily is in that coffin.*

Frantic, Brandy lunged toward Althea.

She grabbed Brandy by the shoulders. "Don't touch her. She's almost there."

"Where?" Brandy said, struggling to move closer to the coffin. "Almost where?"

Althea let go of Brandy and smiled. "To Heaven. With God. While she's still perfect."

"No," Brandy screamed as she raced across the clearing. "You can't take her away from me."

Althea grabbed her arm. "God is waiting." She tried to pull Brandy away from the coffin.

Brandy flipped around, punched Althea in the mouth with all the strength she could muster, then shoved her to the ground.

She yanked open the casket.

Althea babbled something Brandy couldn't understand.

Somehow, Brandy held back another scream and stood frozen for a second.

Emily's short hair clung to her head like a curly wet bathing cap. She wore a pink dress with puffed sleeves and rosebuds on the yoke, and a lace pinafore with satin ribbons woven through the eyelets.

A satin blanket covered her sister's legs. Piglet, Tigger, Roo, Kanga, and Eeyore nestled at the foot of the coffin, along with a prescription bottle and a jar of half-eaten applesauce. Emily's eyes didn't open.

Brandy was too late. Emily was dead. *Oh, please, God. Please, God. Please. Don't let her be dead.*

Her tiny hands were folded over her chest. A thin trail of something, probably applesauce, dribbled down her chin. Brandy lifted Emily to a sitting position. Her skin felt warm to touch. She checked the side of her neck for a pulse. It was weak. Tears of hope rose.

When she smelled gasoline and heard the crackle of wood burning, Brandy stuck the prescription bottle in her pocket, grabbed Emily, limp as a rag doll, and ran into the woods, Althea a few steps behind them.

"The dream-stealing pills," Althea screamed. "I need them. I have to go with her so she won't be afraid."

Sunset faded, and at the other side of the sky, darkness rose. Brandy ran like a blind person, pitching forward, grabbing at saplings in an attempt to keep her balance. She could smell the smoke from the fire Althea had set. As Brandy bolted down the pine-needled path, tree branches scraped across her face. She tried to convince herself Emily would be fine. Althea must have given her sleeping pills. *What if she never wakes up?*

Near the main cabin, Brandy spotted the ambulance. A long sigh of relief rushed from her lungs.

A paramedic took Emily from Brandy's arms. Someone turned on the lights, and their swirling cast surreal blue and red shadows onto the fence.

And then Radhauser stood beside her.

Officer Corbin had handcuffed Althea and was leading her toward the police car. He held his hand over her head as he helped her into the backseat. Big white clouds of smoke floated above the trees.

The paramedic found Emily's pulse, slipped an oxygen mask over her mouth and nose. "She's alive," he called out, the excitement in his voice palpable.

Brandy handed him the prescription bottle.

"It's an antipsychotic," he said. "We'll call the poison control center. They'll be ready when we get her to the hospital."

Brandy's tears rose, and there was nothing she could do to stop them from falling now. She crumbled to the ground behind the ambulance, dropped her face into her hands, and sobbed.

Corbin turned to Radhauser. "I've called the fire department."

Radhauser helped Brandy to her feet and wrapped his arms around her. She cried into his shoulder. "Althea is my mother."

When she stopped crying and backed away, he took off his Stetson and bowed. "You're a gutsy kid," he said, then helped her into the ambulance.

* * *

In the waiting area outside the emergency room, Brandy listened to the sounds of her dad and Christine running down the tiled hallway. When they hit the carpet, the thumping noise stopped, but she heard their panting as they came closer, a kind of frightened anguish in their breathlessness.

As the stainless-steel doors swung open, Brandy spotted Emily's pink sleeve, the eyelet woven with satin ribbons, reflected in the bright steel surface. When the doors closed again, she leaned back against the sofa and closed her eyes. Exhaustion clung to her like cobwebs.

Time passed. It could have been fifteen minutes or an hour.

Someone called out her name. In the instant it took for her to recognize the voice, her dad stood in front of her. Brandy leaped up, then stumbled into his arms and tried to find enough words to form a sentence.

He hugged her to his chest, rubbed his open palm against the back of her head. Her hair was sticky with sweat and matted from the tiger head. "They've taken her off the respirator," he said. "Emily is breathing on her own."

As if someone had unhooked a belt cinched way too tight, Brandy felt the air surge into her lungs and flow back out. She wanted to tell him then, to let him know how she'd been changed. But there wasn't any need, because he knew. So, she stood hugging him, not thinking about anything except Emily.

"They've pumped her stomach," he finally said. "She's being moved to pediatric intensive care."

"Intensive care?" Brandy said, fear rising again. "Do they think she's going to die?"

"No. She swallowed some pretty strong pills. We have to watch for seizures and make sure her liver is okay."

He tightened his arms around her. Beneath the thin cotton of his shirt, she heard his heart beating.

After a moment, she backed away. "What's going to happen to my...to Althea?"

"I don't know. That will be up to the District Attorney."

Brandy sat on the edge of the sofa, testing the weight of that new burden.

Her father's face looked stricken and empty of defenses. He took a step toward her. "I've made a lot of mistakes. I—"

"Don't," Brandy said, holding up a hand to stop him. She didn't know anymore if truth was something worth pursuing at all costs. She'd discovered there were many—an assortment of diverse truths going on inside different heads and hearts at the same time.

Her dad tried again. "Listen, I don't know how to say this. But I have to. What you did was brave and selfless..." Again, he hesitated. "You saved Emily's life."

When the heat rose in her cheeks, Brandy looked away. "It's okay, Dad. I've been pretty busy, and I didn't know what else to get you for your birthday." She shrugged.

He smiled, then looked at Brandy as if he were seeing her for the first time, looked at her in a way that made her want to cry. "My daughter the actress. Radhauser told me everything. How did you ever figure it out?"

"Remember all the problems I had with fractions? It was like finding the common denominator. And I couldn't have done it without Detective Radhauser. He trusted my instincts." She thought about the tattoo on his wrist. "He wanted so much to find Emily alive."

Her dad hugged her again. "I feel responsible. If only I'd..." He held Brandy by the shoulders and looked directly into her eyes. He wiped her cheeks with his fingertips. "I'm so sorry, Cookie."

"I want to see Emily," she said, already headed toward the stainless steel doors.

* * *

Christine sat in a straight-back chair beside the metal crib. She stroked a small patch of skin on Emily's calf just above the ankle, her eyes fixed on her child's face. When she saw Brandy, she leapt up.

A quiver of anxiety coursed through Brandy. She took a step back.

But Christine lunged forward, grabbed Brandy, and pulled her to her chest, hugging her hard. It was as if all the warmth and love inside Christine transferred into Brandy, and her whole body heated with her stepmother's touch.

After a moment, she held Brandy at arm's length so they could make eye contact.

Brandy saw the pressure of tears building behind Christine's eyes. She pressed her fingertips hard against the skin of her temples as if she could force the tears to stay inside. "I'll never forget what you…"

She looked into her stepmother's eyes and saw the regret—the terrible fear that had lived inside her chest since Emily disappeared. She put a finger to Christine's lips to silence her.

"I mean it," Christine said. "I was a horrible bitch to you. But you never stopped searching for Emily. I blamed you so I wouldn't have to blame myself. I don't deserve your forgiveness, but I'm asking for it."

Brandy glanced at her dad, then down at Emily. "She's my sister. And I love her," she whispered.

Emily's eyes were closed. The ER staff had cut off her clothing and she wore a tiny hospital gown printed with puppies. Her breathing was quiet and regular. A plastic bag of fluid hung from a metal pole, and a clear tube ran from the bag to Emily's right hand.

Christine returned to the chair beside Emily's bed. "Why doesn't she wake up?"

Her dad placed his hand on Christine's shoulder. "She will."

Christine seemed to shrink away from his touch. Her gaze shot up to his face and hardened a little. "Why didn't you tell me Rose was mentally ill?"

Her dad stared straight ahead, his shoulders jerking as if he were cold. Incongruously, he made a sound like steam escaping.

"Because I didn't want it to be true."

Brandy thought about the way a person's life could change in an instant. She thought about her mother as she'd stood helplessly by while the escalator mangled her daughter's face. And then her father when he learned his beloved Rose was mentally ill. She thought about the split-second decision she'd made to park Emily's stroller in front of the bathroom stall. And what might have happened if Radhauser hadn't phoned for an ambulance and shown up when he did.

Emily's eyelids quivered and her left hand, lying outside the sheet, reached for a handful of air. Brandy moved closer to the bed.

Emily's eyes opened. "Band-Aid. I yost you."

Brandy hugged Emily to her chest and whispered in her ear, "That was some game of hide-and-go seek, Em."

CHAPTER THIRTY

In the visitor lounge outside Pediatric Intensive Care, Brandy sat on a blue plaid sofa. On a metal rack bolted to the wall in front of her, a television droned. She leaned her head back against the cushion and closed her eyes.

Someone called out her name.

In the instant it took for her to recognize his voice, Radhauser knelt in front of her. He held a shopping bag filled with an entire new Pooh bear family. "I tried to save the original ones. But the fire was too hot. The whole precinct pitched in to buy them. Mr. Pivorotto gave us a discount, even though his bowtie shook the whole time he rang them up." Radhauser grinned and set the bag on the floor beside Brandy's feet. "How is she?"

"Well," Brandy said. "It looks like you won't be needing another tattoo."

He swallowed, then smiled and took off his Stetson. "So how does it feel to be a hero?"

Brandy couldn't connect. "What's going to happen to her?"

Detective Radhauser cupped the fingers of both hands, palms up, in front of him as if holding a crystal ball and stared into them. "Let me see. Ah, there it is. Emily grows up to be the world's most brilliant and beautiful brain surgeon."

"I meant my…I meant Althea. Will she go to prison?"

Radhauser stood and pulled a chair closer to the sofa so he was face to face with her. "They'll be an arraignment to determine competency to stand trial. I suspect she'll go back to the hospital."

"Forever?"

Radhauser spun his Stetson in his hands and said nothing.

"I know it's crazy, but my mother thought she was protecting Emily." Brandy told him what her mother had said about Emily going to heaven while she was still perfect. "I think time was all messed up for her, and she believed Emily was me and she could save me from the escalator accident."

Something sad passed between them, some new kind of understanding. "Don't worry," Radhauser said. "We'll get her the help she needs."

Ever since the doctor arrived and asked Brandy to leave Emily's room while he examined her, Brandy had been reviewing the events at the cabin. And she'd come to a place where she needed to hear the thoughts take shape and travel toward someone else—someone who'd understand.

"It's like I've slipped through some crack in the world and I'm floating outside of logic or time. I know I should hate her for what she did to Emily. But…I feel…" When tears rose, she looked down at her hands. "I guess I feel sorry for her."

"No one who hasn't experienced it can understand. But this is what I've pieced together so far. Your mother met a patient at Bayview Hospital named Althea Wineheart. And when your mother was discharged, she was either given or stole Althea's identification. That's how she got an Oregon driver's license. What I don't understand yet is where she got the finances to support herself and buy that piece of property."

"My grandparents in Italy probably set up a trust." Brandy's tears flowed freely now.

Radhauser lowered his gaze. He didn't leave and he didn't watch her cry. He just stayed there, with his head lowered, as if offering her privacy and yet giving his support at the same time.

Finally, he pulled a clean white handkerchief from his pocket and handed it to her. "Tell your dad to call me tomorrow."

"Thanks," Brandy said.

"What are you thanking me for?" He stood and turned to go. "You did all the work."

Brandy shook her head to stop him. "You trusted my instincts. If you hadn't—" She couldn't make herself say the words.

After he left, Brandy stretched out on the sofa and within minutes was fast asleep.

When she woke, her dad sat in the chair across from her. There were dark circles under his eyes. "Let's go home. They're going to keep Emily overnight for observation. Christine will stay with her."

Brandy handed him the bag of Emily's stuffed animals, and told him about Radhauser's visit.

He clamped his hand on her shoulder and squeezed. "Detective Radhauser was there for you when I wasn't." He took the Pooh bear from the bag. "I'll be right back."

When he returned, she wrapped her arm around his waist. They walked to the car that way, as if consoling each other for everything that neither of them could change.

In the trees at the edge of the hospital parking lot, the wind made the sound of an oboe. Brandy turned toward it, but saw only the slow sweep of a solitary cloud, as if all the suffering and hope in the world had spiraled down into one white cloud that swept across the horizon in Ashland, Oregon.

CHAPTER THIRTY-ONE

In the dressing room, Brandy tucked the rose-colored pullover into the elastic waistband of the long, flowered skirt, then ran her fingers through her hair, taming the wild dark curls and capturing them with a barrette at the back of her neck. She'd used the makeover certificate Doctor Sorenson had given her and when she checked the mirror, her skin looked almost flawless. She couldn't help but smile.

The stage was set for the opening scene. A neonatal intensive care unit. Stone waited with the other actors behind the backdrop.

As the last ticket holders filed into Mountain Avenue Theater and surveyed the auditorium for empty seats, Brandy stood backstage and scanned the rows for Christine and Kathleen.

The lights were still bright, and she spotted one of the reporters from the *Tribune* who'd covered the candlelight vigil. He stood on the sidelines, clamping his camera onto a tripod.

Again, she searched. She found her father in the third row, an empty seat beside him, but no sign of Christine. Kathleen sat three rows behind him.

Just when Brandy was about to give up, she spotted Christine hurrying down the aisle. Her father stood and waved until she spotted him.

Brandy smiled. Her stepmother had kept her promise.

When Mr. Pritchard beckoned her from the opposite wing, Brandy hurried across the stage. "Carla came down with the flu. She's puking her guts out. Isabella and Jenny are never on stage at the same time. Can you play Carla's part, too?"

Brandy opened her mouth, but no words came out.

"You're about the same size," he said. "So, I suspect her costume will fit. You know her lines. And if you forget something, just ad lib."

Jenny was the teenage bimbo who'd given birth to baby Isaac. She wore tight leather pants, a halter-top, and constantly chewed gum. She had some of the funniest lines in the play. "I…I guess so. Sure," Brandy said, realizing she did know the lines. "It may not be perfect. But I can do it."

The lights dimmed. One minute until show time.

Brandy headed for the prop table in the wings.

In a moment that didn't register as real time, she closed her eyes and concentrated. She knew what Isabella wanted and just how far that character was willing to go in order to get it. And she understood, better than ever now, that actors must believe they are the characters they play. Everything she needed to become Isabella was contained in two memories. The day Emily disappeared and the night of her escalator accident—the sound of her mother's scream.

When the stage lights came on and the curtain lifted, Brandy grabbed a crib mobile, then burst onto center stage as a frantic Isabella, determined to make Isaac's hospital room look like the nursery she'd planned for him.

A rubber doll, the baby that Isabella and her husband, Walter, had arranged to adopt before its birth, lay hidden inside a plastic isolette attached to monitoring devices. Isabella was about to see the severely deformed and hydrocephalic infant for the first time. She felt a surge of grief as she approached the isolette. With tears brimming, she said, "I can't believe how much I already love him."

Her chin quivered and the air seemed to tighten around her. She stood profile left, at the edge of the bassinet. All self-awareness drained from her body as she leaned forward into Isabella's first look at the baby's swollen head. "Hello, little pumpkin," she said. "Hello, baby Isaac."

In the moving pictures inside her head, the infant stared up with a steady gaze, eyes shining for one improbable moment before they closed, claimed by sleep.

Jolted by a strange combination of hope, horror, and love, she remained shaken, but on guard beside him. She was Isaac's mother.

She was Isabella.

A mother afraid for her child.

A mother.

Once again, Brandy heard the low animal sound that had simmered for an instant, that boiled up and over until every gaze in the emergency room was glued to her mother's open mouth. And she plunged deeper into the memory of her mother staggering toward the hospital gurney where Brandy lay, her left cheek mangled.

Deep inside the memory, Brandy felt the stab of a suture needle as it dove into her toddler flesh and resurfaced. Transparent thread tied in a hundred separate knots. Powdered, antiseptic smell of gloved hands. The blood as it spread along cotton strands, staining the starched white fabric of her dress.

A voice inside Brandy's head kept her in control.

Breathe.

You are Isaac's mother.

You are Isabella.

She turned toward the nurse. "Do you think he hears me? Does he know how I…"

Somehow it all fell into place, the pace and rhythm, the way the actors projected their voices, the subtle moments where silence was more convincing than speech. Brandy released her hair and changed into the leather jeans and halter top, grabbed a piece of bubble gum when she played Carla's part. Her switches between Isabella and Jenny were seamless.

In her final scene, Brandy, as Isabella, said goodbye to her dead baby. "I will send prayers into the night sky with your name on them, Isaac. Each time a child takes his first step, you'll walk beside him, the grass peeking up between your bare toes. And in the morning, when the day awakens, it will be my son's face that shines above me."

Then, without warning, Brandy thoughts lingered on her

mother. And in Brandy's mind, the final words she uttered to baby Isaac belonged to Sophia Rose Michaelson. "You mustn't ever think our time together, though short, didn't matter. I learned everything I will ever need to know about love from you." Her voice wobbled, on the edge of tears.

At precisely the right moment, Stone—who'd wanted to back out of the adoption and had refused to see the baby—appeared, carrying a stuffed puppy meant for their son. Their eyes met and lingered. A single tear dripped down Brandy's cheek. Stone moved toward her. When the lights dimmed, Brandy picked up her guitar and sang the song she'd written for her mother.

At curtain call, Brandy was last to run onto the stage. She stood next to Stone, still shaken by the final dialogue, the song about her mother. When he grabbed her hand and lifted it, the entire audience rose, applauding until the curtain finally closed.

As she stepped into the wings, the reporter tapped her on the shoulder. "I'm Quinton from the *Medford Tribune*. I heard you sing at the candlelight vigil for your sister. You were amazing."

She turned and smiled. "Thanks, Quinton."

"And now I see you can act, too. You were damn good up there. You brought the house down." He told her he wanted to do a feature story and would need some photographs.

"Let me just say hello to a couple people and I'll be right back," she said, heading towards Christine and her dad.

Doctor Sorenson waved.

Brandy waved back.

Before she got through the crowd to her dad, she ran into Detective Radhauser and Gracie.

Radhauser wrapped her in a bear hug. "I'm speechless. And to think I was going to suggest you become a detective."

Gracie hugged Brandy, too. "Don't pay any attention to him. You were fabulous. The look on your face was so believable my eyes filled with tears. Go for the Oscar, Brandy. I hope we're both around to cheer you on."

Christine hugged Brandy from behind and unclipped the barrette holding her hair. She lifted the thick mound of dark curls and let them tumble, unrestrained. "There you go," she said. "A regular Julia Roberts."

When Brandy turned, Christine opened her arms. Brandy stepped into them. And they stood like that, their breathing the only sound Brandy heard in the noisy auditorium. She felt a new softness toward her stepmother, as if they were survivors in the same life raft.

"Where's Emily?"

"My mother is babysitting. Can you believe it? She had Emily in her lap reading a story when I left."

* * *

After the final performance and the cast party on Saturday night, Brandy said goodnight to Stone, eased the front door open, then stepped inside and closed it softly. It was after midnight and she assumed her father and stepmother would be asleep. She tiptoed through the entryway and into a thin stream of cherry-smelling smoke.

Her father sat alone in the darkened living room, his pipe in his hand. He flipped on the light. "I want you to know how proud I am of you. The way you stepped in when Carla got sick and played her role, too. What a talent." He reached into his stack of Saturday's edition of the *Medford Tribune* and flipped to the article. "Did you see this?"

Only about a hundred times. Every person she knew had clipped it out for her. She nodded and hoped he'd drop the paper back into his stack.

Ignoring her nod, he read Quinton's opening paragraph out loud.

When Ashland High School's Brandy Michaelson steps into a role, the audience feels that piercing physical reaction that comes from witnessing the extraordinary—the raw material from which stars are made. On stage, it is as if she is transformed, no longer made up of flesh and bones, but points of brilliant light. Like a sparkler on the Fourth of July, you can't take your gaze away—this young woman is simply irresistible. She flipped between the leading roles of Isabella and Jenny so skillfully most of the audience didn't realize she played both parts…

CHAPTER THIRTY-TWO

Two weeks later, Brandy slipped into Emily's room and stood beside her bed, watching her sleep and trying to decide how to approach her dad and Christine.

From the soft murmur of voices and the clink of glasses, she knew they were sitting in the living room, sharing a bottle of wine. The sound of their voices was the sound of home.

Fear for Emily had reconnected the three of them—given them a new appreciation for the value and comfort of family. They understood what mattered most was who you were to someone else. Christine would never be a mother figure to Brandy, but she could be a friend or a big sister.

A tree branch brushed against the window with a soft, scraping sound. Brandy looked out at the backyard. The upper sky was dark, but the lower sky was still streaked with pale light. She thought about her mother, the way Brandy had made a legend out of the woman who'd been in a mental hospital most of her adult life.

Brandy sighed, then tucked the blanket over Emily and stepped back into the hallway. As she moved closer to the living room, she heard her father offer to hire a nanny so Christine could finish her degree.

"Somehow it doesn't matter to me now," Christine said. "Everything I used to want or complain about feels so trivial. When you lose your child, all the meaning goes out of your life."

"Emily's back now," her dad said. "And it's important you finish your education."

"I'll have plenty of time once Emily is in school." Her

stepmother's voice held a private peace. Brandy didn't know how Christine had gotten to that place, only that she was there.

But for Brandy, something was still missing.

Again, she hesitated. The time to tell them would never be right or easy. Brandy collected herself, coaxed her feet to move, then sat on the living room step.

She cleared her throat.

Both her dad and stepmother looked at her.

"Do you remember what you told me about life being a circle?" Brandy asked her father.

He nodded, took another sip of his wine.

"I've been thinking a lot about that. And I hope this won't upset either of you too much, but I want to visit my mother." She held her breath. Waited for her stepmother's reaction to Brandy's wanting to see the woman who'd tried to kill Emily.

In the quiet that followed, her dad stared at her for a long moment.

"I wondered if I could borrow one of your cars."

He glanced quickly at Christine, then swallowed. "When?"

"Tomorrow. Salem is not quite a four-hour drive. Please. I'll go up and come back the same day. It's really important to me."

The room grew so quiet she could hear each tick of the grandfather clock in the entryway. Brandy had counted five of them when Christine reached across the sofa and laid her hand on Dad's knee. "Go with her. Brandy shouldn't have to do this alone."

* * *

With her guitar case in hand, Brandy stood beside her father, looking out the French doors at the courtyard of the Madrone Psychiatric Institute. On the grassy yard, beneath a big-leaf maple, her mother rocked on a wooden glider. Spots of lichen furred the soft gray wood. She was dressed in a pale blue smock, like the ones children wear over their clothes when they paint. She cradled her right arm, palm up, in her left one like a baby.

Brandy opened the doors.

Her dad took her hand as they stepped onto the brick patio. His face was a mask of sadness.

She thought about the wedding album and his life with her mother. He'd kept almost nothing except his memories—and maybe they were the heaviest baggage of all.

"Do you want me to go with you?"

"I need to do this alone." Brandy squeezed his hand, then let go and moved toward the glider.

Her mother's hair was clean, pulled back from her face and fastened at the nape of her neck in the same way Brandy had clamped hers for the play.

She had a moment when she wanted to go back inside, wondered if her actions were selfish, or if this visit might trigger other things in her mother she didn't want to see.

Breathe. This woman was her mother. And in spite of Brandy's jumbled feelings about everything that had happened, she longed to find a way to connect them. She thought about the many roles she'd played in an attempt to become someone else. Making herself up from bits and pieces of other people.

Though keenly aware of her mother's limitations, Brandy was rooted in this woman and she wanted to be a daughter now. But how would a daughter, even one devoted to her mentally ill mother, act at a time like this?

In the garden beside the patio, a fat bumblebee crawled up a coneflower, lifted into the drowsy air and sailed west where the sun hung, gold and pink, as if it would be there forever. Brandy watched the bumblebee fly, then stepped across the grassy yard.

Her mother kept rocking, tapped a slow beat on her cradled arm with her index finger and didn't appear to notice Brandy as she took out her guitar. "I wrote a song for you." She pulled a chair close to the glider and strummed a few chords.

A child is born and she learns to sing.
She sets her heart on elusive things.
But fate steps in and dreams come crashing down.

Her illusions gone, a truth reclaimed,
Nothing ever stays the same.

And all the while, the world spins round.
A child is lost and a mother found.

But what it takes, to change the tide,
Is just one single, just one single,
Slender slice of time.

When Brandy finished the song, she put her guitar back into its case. She glanced toward the patio where her father sat, wiping his face with a handkerchief. When her chest tightened, Brandy looked away. She couldn't imagine what this must feel like for him.

"The escalator accident wasn't your fault, Mom. You always told me to be careful. You loved me so much."

As the trees swished softly above them, Rose lifted her hand and touched Brandy's cheek.

The unexpected touch released a confusing wave of tenderness inside Brandy. She tried to maintain her mother's gaze. It seemed impossible, staring directly into this woman's eyes—this woman who'd tried to kill Emily—it was a burden Brandy couldn't carry for more than a few seconds without looking away.

But as the sun flattened and hovered for an instant before it dropped into the horizon, Brandy realized all she had to do was finally meet her mother, and it grew easy.

When her mother smiled, Brandy saw something of the young woman turning a cartwheel in the wedding album.

Brandy smiled back.

And then she saw the opening, a stirring deep in her mother's eyes, a place wide enough for a daughter to slip through. In that moment of understanding, Brandy was aware of the incredible elasticity of life, how each night we wait for the sunlight, the rising up of what once seemed lost.

She sat beside her mother, reached for her hands and held them.

Her mother's skin felt so cold that Brandy's own seemed hot in comparison. As some of her heat transferred, she understood how much this woman needed her. That in this moment, Brandy could be helpful by lending her mother the warmth inside her hands. And for the first time in her life, Brandy felt beautiful.

This was their beginning.

ABOUT SUSAN CLAYTON-GOLDNER

Susan Clayton-Goldner was born in New Castle, Delaware and grew up with four brothers along the banks of the Delaware River. She is a graduate of the University of Arizona's Creative Writing Program and has been writing most of her life. Her novels have been finalists for The Hemingway Award, the Heeken Foundation Fellowship, the Writers Foundation and the Publishing On-line Contest. Susan won the National Writers' Association Novel Award twice for unpublished novels and her poetry was nominated for a Pushcart Prize.

Her work has appeared in numerous literary journals and anthologies, including Animals as Teachers and Healers, published by Ballantine Books, Our Mothers/Ourselves, by the Greenwood Publishing Group, The Hawaii Pacific Review-Best of a Decade, and New Millennium Writings. A collection of her poems, A Question of Mortality was released in 2014 by Wellstone Press. Prior to writing full time, Susan worked as the Director of Corporate Relations for University Medical Center in Tucson, Arizona.

Susan shares a life in Grants Pass, Oregon with her husband, Andreas, her fictional characters, and more books than one person could count.

FIND SUSAN ONLINE

Website
www.susanclaytongoldner.com

Facebook
www.facebook.com/susan.claytongoldner

Twitter
twitter.com/SusanCGoldner

Blog
susanclaytongoldner.com/my-blog---writing-the-life.html

Tirgearr Publishing
www.tirgearrpublishing.com/authors/ClaytonGoldner_Susan

BOOKS BY SUSAN CLAYTON-GOLDNER

WINSTON RADHAUSER SERIES

REDEMPTION LAKE, #1
Released: May 2017
ISBN: 9781370712939

Tucson, Arizona–Detective Winston Radhauser knows eighteen-year-old Matt Garrison is hiding something. When his best friend's mother, Crystal, is murdered, the investigation focuses on Matt's father, but Matt knows he's innocent. Devastated and bent on self-destruction, Matt heads for the lake where his cousin died—the only place he believes can truly free him. Are some secrets better left buried?

-also-

A BEND IN THE WILLOW
Released: January 2017
ISBN: 9781370816842

In 1965, Robin Lee Carter sets a fire that kills her rapist, then disappears, reinventing herself as Catherine Henry. In 1985, when her 5-year-old son, Michael, is diagnosed with a chemotherapy-resistant leukemia, she must return to Willowood and seek out the now 19-year-old son she gave up for adoption. Is she willing to risk everything, including her life, to save her dying son?

Manufactured by Amazon.ca
Bolton, ON